MW01157065

A Clash of Civilizations

An Alternative History Novel

Hugh Auchincloss Brown

First Edition

PAGE PUBLISHING, INC.
Conneaut Lake, PA

First originally published by Page Publishing 2021

ISBN 978-1-6624-5049-5 (hc)
ISBN 978-1-6624-5048-8 (digital)

Printed in the United States of America

Dedication

First and foremost, I want to thank my wife and love of my life, Jane Riley Brown, who has encouraged me for more than a decade to write and publish a book. There are many, many more people who also supported me along the way, too many to mention. But I want to thank my mother, the friends who liked the book and/or made suggestions to improve it, Harry Turtledove and John Birmingham, Joel Naoum who provided an invaluable positive critical editing, Edward Dee who did a final reread of what I thought was a finished manuscript, the publishers who rejected my manuscript forcing me to rethink and rewrite, and the publishing staff who printed my book.

Chapter 1

There appeared to be a full platoon of infantry on the trail behind them. Lieutenant Taylor could see the green of their uniforms blending in and out of the new foliage of the deciduous trees growing along the trail, as well as periodic flashes of light caused by the sun glistening off the soldiers' belt buckles and muskets. The Italians were advancing on the double, a little close for comfort, but still almost a mile away. There was plenty of time to reach the bridge, cross it, and disappear into the thick woods beyond.

He collapsed his small telescope and slid it into the inside lining of his vest. The English officer was not in uniform but wore the same peasant's garb as the five men who stood behind him on the crest of the small hill. They were all dressed in loose shirts tucked into close-fitting pants, a vest, and sturdy boots that reached their knees.

To their right, rising into clouds, were the craggy mountains and glaciers that made up the Long Hohe Tauem Ridge. Snow glistened on their rugged peaks. The April sun shone brightly on these massive vestiges of an ancient ice age while all around birds sang and insects buzzed by oblivious to the men and their possible peril. It was spring in the year of our Lord 1811. Thousands upon thousands of colorful mountain flowers filled the lush meadows and blanketed the ground to either side of the dirt path they were traveling. They were surrounded by a profusion of colors: the bright blue of the stemless gentian, the red of the rusty-leaved Alpen rose, and the yellow and white of glacier buttercups.

The Englishman's companions carried muskets, haversacks, and cartridge boxes that had been picked off the bodies of dead Italians. Taylor's only weapon was his sword, a good English blade. He had been warned not to carry anything that might identify him when he joined the Austrian rebels, but the sword had been a gift from his commander when he left the Second West India Regiment stationed in the coastal lowlands of Southwest India. He could not bear to part with it even though the memories of that campaign were now distant.

All around them stretched the mountainous terrain of the Tyrol Region of the Austrian Alps. The trail they traveled crossed fairly open, though rather undulating, country that allowed them to make good speed as they wended their way down to the river from higher ground. This would have been nearly impossible without the footpath as the dense mountain flowers, with their thick vines, impeded and slowed down a man walking off the track. A little over a half mile from where they stood was the Salzach River and the timber bridge that would lead them to safety. On the other side of the turbulent river was a thickly wooded forest, and deep within those trees were the camps and hiding places of the Tyrolese resistance. Once they reached the forest, they would be safe.

"Taylor?" inquired a large red-faced man who stood a full head taller than his compatriots. "Is that son of a bitch Paparelli with the damn dagos?"

Andreas Hofer was the leader of the rebels. He spoke excellent English but with a hard German accent that betrayed his origin. That was good for Taylor. Although the British lieutenant spoke French and had a smattering of Italian, he only knew half a dozen words in German.

"That he is, Andreas," Taylor answered. "Near the middle of the ranks where he is well-protected, the same as usual."

To Taylor's way of thinking, Colonel Bruno Paparelli was a ruthless and cowardly knave. Placed in command of the Italian forces occupying the Tyrol Region of the former Holy Roman Empire, Paparelli was known throughout the countryside for his cruel treatment of those he governed, as well as his immense sexual appetite. The colonel abducted and raped any young woman he fancied, a practice that resulted in the local villagers keeping their daughters and wives hidden in the cellars of their homes when Paparelli was in the vicinity.

Another signature trademark of the colonel was his standing policy that ten villagers were to be executed for every one of his soldiers killed by the rebels. For this reason, and this reason alone, the Tyrolese rebels had withdrawn into the forests and ceased ambushing Italian patrols. They routinely sent individuals or small parties into the villages to scavenge for food and information but restrained themselves from harming any of the occupiers so long as the Italians stayed out of their forest.

"The bridge is not far, my friend," Hofer said, drawing in a deep breath. "Still, let us make haste. As much as I would like to stay and put a bullet in that butcher's head, the Italians outnumber us five to one. Four to one and I would take them on right here, but as your great English bard Marlowe wrote, 'The better part of valor is discretion'."

The six men set off down the hill. Taylor's scabbard banged against his side as he jogged along the path. The other men carried their muskets easily in the crook of their elbows. Cutting through a narrow ravine, then angling left around a large rock outcropping that blocked their view back up the hill, they passed through several hundred yards of boulders that had been strewn from the mountainside before emerging into the open. There they stumbled to a stop.

Two hundred yards distant was the bridge. It was a broad uncovered overpass with sturdy planks that could support a number of wagons. The river here was not wide, nor deep, but the spring runoff was fast, and a man could not wade through it without being swept away. A squad of Italian soldiers stood at the near end of the bridge. They seemed as shocked to see the rebels as Taylor and the Tyrolese were to see them.

The Italians were dressed in their standard green jackets over immaculate white pants tucked into black boots. The emblem of an eagle adorned each of their high-pitched hats. The soldiers seemed to be flustered, but their officer quickly formed them in two ranks facing the rebels, one kneeling and the second standing directly over the first rank, muskets raised toward their enemy.

"Damn!" cursed Taylor under his breath.

"We will need to split up," Hofer ventured. "We can climb into the mountains, taking our chances individually and making our own ways back to the camps."

"No!" Taylor's voice was not loud, but it was firm. The other men looked in his direction. "Some of us may get away, but if we split up the troops converging on us from behind will surely capture and kill a number of us. No, we need to be bold and assault the bridge."

"There are nine of them," Hofer noted. Then his lips took the form of a forced smile. "Of course, those are nine dagos against five Tyrolese. I pity the poor bastards. Fix bayonets."

The five rebels unhesitatingly inserted their bayonets onto the end of their muskets and then spread across the pathway with grim and determined faces. At Hofer's soft command, they began trotting toward the bridge. Taylor drew his sword and moved forward with the rest.

Muskets were not accurate weapons at any range over thirty yards, being best employed in mass as armies squared off against one another at a close range. The bayonet was another matter. Few men cared to face an enemy brandishing the long-sharpened knife at the end of a musket. A musket ball struck you if you were unlucky enough to be in its way, a piece of metal that either killed or wounded you in one sharp, stinging moment. A bayonet, on the other hand, slashed into your flesh and could be ripped up through your stomach and entrails, producing an often slow and painful death. Few men relished facing bayonets, and Taylor held on to the hope that the Italians facing them were inexperienced occupation soldiers and not hardened campaign troops and thus would be horrified by a bayonet charge.

A hundred yards from the bridge, as if one, the five rebels and the Englishman screamed out their own personal battle cries and broke into a full-out dash. Three of the Italians fired high well before the Tyrolese came within effective range, then all the green-clad soldiers broke, rushing for the safety of the woods immediately behind their position. Their officer turned and shouted after his men before, following a quick glance over his shoulder, he, too, dashed across the bridge and into the forest.

Taylor and his comrades did not attempt pursuit but continued running at a dead sprint over the wooden planks of the bridge and, for a good half-mile, down the path cutting through the woods. Only then did they slow down as Andreas Hofer led his party off the trail and into the safety of the forest that he and his men knew so well.

Chapter 2

Anne slept on the grand mattress of her four-posted bed situated near the fireplace. The hearth had been constructed into the wall on the far side of the room away from the drafty windows and their accompanying balconies; enormous stone verandas that looked over the expansive castle grounds from the advantage of the second floor. The walls about her were constructed of chiseled stone, cold to the touch and covered by a myriad of colorful tapestries that attempted to brighten the otherwise dismal surroundings during the daytime.

The great English chamber was nearly dark, save for the faint shimmering light of the full moon that provided a faint illumination, much like the opaque issue of an enormous candle. Outside the gray walls of the massive citadel that housed the chamber the bright sphere could readily be distinguished behind scores of frothy clouds. They were the sort of clouds that tend to fill a night sky like sheer fabric, distorting, but not quite blocking, the luminescence from the heavens. The light still managed to slip through the two large open-arched windows built into the immense walls, and it bathed the room in a pallid, eerie glow.

It was an unseasonably warm spring, and there had been no need for a fire, nor did Anne care for lit torches in her bedchamber while she slept. Still, had she been awake, there was just enough light reflecting off the uncovered pieces of stone in the great room that she would have been able to see the shadowy figure stealthily creeping toward her bed.

Anne was dreaming, and in her dream, she was not her nation's ruler but a six-year-old girl with no other responsibilities than to run barefoot on the lawns, to prance about in beautiful dresses to the delight of her father, the king, while playing with the other children of the court. It was a blissful fantasy, only to be abruptly shattered when a hand clamped down upon her mouth.

She awoke with a muffled gasp, her eyes wide with terror. The dark form of a slender man was standing over her, just to the side of her bed. Held in his free hand was the unmistakable silhouette of a knife. Anne's mind raced as she quickly took in her situation, but she remained perfectly still, her arms unmoving and outstretched over her head as they had been in her sleep. Her pounding heartbeat slowed as she locked her eyes on those of the terrifying apparition that had materialized out of the night. Her attacker stared back down at the young female.

*****

Francisco was momentarily disconcerted by his victim's inaction. He had expected to find an older woman, perhaps a fat older woman, who would struggle and attempt to cry out just before he slit her throat. It would be quick, her lifeblood rapidly spewing from her body, staining the bed sheets crimson and leaving her limp and lifeless. This woman was neither old nor fat, however. She was shapely, her firm breasts beneath her sleeping gown rising and falling with each strenuous breath as she fought to take in air through his rough, calloused fingers. Her reddish-brown hair was strewn out onto her pillows, and her extended arms magnified the heaving of her chest.

*****

Anne willed her trembling body to still itself and forced herself to remain almost perfectly still, save for her steady breathing. She had been initially frozen with terror, and that may have saved her life, yet her mind was active as she evaluated her situation and sought an escape. She realized if she attempted any quick movement or a single shout, this man would plunge his knife into her, ending her life.

Keeping her eyes fixed on the face of this unknown assailant, she ever so slowly eased her right hand further beneath the pillows cushioning her head, her fingers searching for the stiletto resting under the cushions. As her eyes adjusted to the dim light, she could now make out his features: jet-black hair, swarthy complexion, a thin mustache above equally thin lips, perhaps twenty-five, no more than twenty-nine years of age. His initially cold dark eyes now seemed questioning.

*****

The young assassin was torn between completing his task and a sudden desire for this woman. Why was she not fighting him? Perhaps, just perhaps, she wanted him as much as he now wanted her. He tried to shake off these thoughts, to get on with his assignment, but now he could almost feel the heat of his own blood as it coursed through his body and into his now fully rigid penis.

Slowly, keeping his eyes fixed on his victim's face, Francisco placed his knife on the mattress, close to his reach, next to her body. Keeping his left hand steadfastly over her mouth, he moved his right over the swell of her bosom. The woman's eyes now followed the movement of this hand, but still, she offered no resistance. Emboldened, the young man gently grasped her left breast, feeling the shape of her nipple beneath the cotton gown.

Anne let out a slight groan, which Francisco took to be a sound of pleasure, just before her right hand broke from under her pillow and drove the razor-sharp steel of the stiletto into the jugular vein of his neck.

His surprise at the quickness of this unexpected strike was far more startling than the pain. Francisco stumbled back a step, his left hand reaching for the thin knife protruding from his neck, his right groping blindly for his own weapon. Blood spurted from his throat as Anne scrambled to the far side of her bed and shouted for her guards.

The wooden doors to her chamber were immediately thrown open and two burly men, armed with pikes, rushed into the room just as Francisco dropped to his knees. His head felt light and dizzy. Staring straight ahead through eyes that were slowly misting over, he could just make out the bed to his front, now covered in a spreading thick red liquid.

That was quite stupid of me was his last thought just before he collapsed to the floor.

*****

Later that week, Queen Anne sat in her throne room, surrounded by her maids of honor. Her privy councilor and vice chamberlain stood to her side. She looked particularly regal this afternoon, dressed in a flounced white dress decorated with laces and ribbons. A string of large pearls adorned her slender neck. Her manner was composed. Anne's friends and advisers marveled at how serene she appeared, unaware of the fear she experienced each night or the dark dreams that continually invaded her sleep ever since "the incident." Despite her nightmares and the constant requests of her maids of honor, she had refused to allow any of these young women to spend the night with her in her chambers.

"We must not show any sign of alarm," she had told Sir James Townsend, her privy councilor. "We must demonstrate strength to our subjects and enemy alike, whoever this enemy may be."

The entire court was in turmoil as a result of the failed assassination attempt. Five days had passed, and there were no more answers than there had been that night. A two-mile radius of the surrounding area had been thoroughly searched without yielding a single clue as to the identity, or the entry point, of the young man. Word of the attack had quickly spread around the castle and now embellished versions of the story, as well as imaginative explanations as to the identity of the assassin, were making their way throughout London. The body of the would-be murderer was being preserved in a cask of rum in one of the castle's many cellars in the hope that someone might step forward to provide his identity.

*****

It was during a lull in the court proceedings that Madalyn Cook, the Queen's first lady of the bedchamber, entered the throne room and rushed over to Anne, falling to her knees at the Queen's feet. Tears streamed down her beautiful cheeks. Her usually bright green eyes were swollen and red.

"My lady, I came as soon as I heard," she sobbed. "I should never have gone to visit my parents. Are you…?"

"We are fine, Maddie," Anne replied, turning to the woman who supervised her immediate female staff. Her eyes glistened with affection for her best friend in the court. "You need to dry your tears and apply some makeup. Crying mars your beauty."

The first lady looked up and tried to smile. "I must be a mess," she stammered as she rose to her feet. Taking a deep breath, Madalyn composed herself as she moved to her station just behind the throne, at which point the captain of the Queen's home guards was announced. The senior officer strode across the room, approached the throne, and dropped to one knee.

The Queen inspected the older man. He was in his late fifties and dressed in the red jacket and black pants that made up the dress of the Yeoman of the Guards. Henry VII had created this special force in 1485 for the sole purpose of protecting the king. Their uniforms had changed little in the more than three centuries since their founding. There was no question as to this man's loyalty as he had been in her family's service for thirty years. But Anne considered, as she looked into his worried eyes, that it might be time to find a more efficient younger replacement.

"He came in through one of the windows, Your Majesty," the captain of the guards explained once again. "On my life, I have no idea how he got over the wall and past the men stationed on the grounds."

"And have we found out anything at all about this ill-fated individual?" she asked.

"Nothing, my lady," the captain answered. "He had no papers, nothing to identify him. His clothing was English but could have been bought in any part of the city. He could have been a deranged lunatic or hired by the reformers, the Irish, or some group who covet the throne. Perhaps even the Italians. I am afraid, my queen, that his lifeless body will never reveal that secret."

Chapter 3

Striding along one of the many wide streets that segmented the capital city, Mextli found himself once again conjuring up endless reasons as to why he had been summoned. His nostrils drew in the unfamiliar reek of the open sewer system running throughout the urban sprawl. His eyes took in the packed earth lanes branching off from the main thoroughfare between rows upon row of two-story adobe buildings. Merchants shouted all about him, plying their wares: crockery, textiles, feather work, tobacco, building materials, blankets, medicines, and all manner of foods. Crowds of buyers roamed the streets, haggling over the prices of the goods.

Traders from all four corners of the Empire converged on this city to sell the products of their particular territory or domain. There were flowers from Xochimilco, lobsters from the Northeast Territories, and stone cuttings from Tenajocan. Busy stalls lined the main streets, selling paintings by the renowned artists of Tezcoco, gold bracelets and medallions from Azcapotxalco, splendid jewelry from Cholula, and bear meat from the northern territories. Each street was set aside for a particular skill or product while many back streets were piled high with additional merchandise: bales of cotton, baskets of potatoes, tapestries, and more. They passed one street filled with the chairs of the hair cutters; on another were tanned hides, leather products, and a collection of raw hides covered by swarms of flies.

It had been several years since Mextli last visited the capital city of Tenochtitlan, and he found the outer municipal area both claustrophobic and repugnant. *Living on the sea will do that to you,* he thought to himself. *I am no longer comfortable in the midst of crowds of people, let alone hundreds of thousands.*

The buildings seemed to have no end. They stretched endlessly toward all points of the compass, broken only by the straight dirt roads and the higher profile of his destination, the inner city. He could now see the top of the great pyramid. It had been built nearly five hundred seasons ago, a season being the time it took for the sun to travel from north to south across the daytime skies and then return.

Mextli was dressed in a brightly colored cotton cape, appropriately decorated to denote his rank. He had chosen to omit the golden jewelry and decorative feathers worn by the majority of the nobility. Only the markings on his cape, and the short skirt that covered his loincloth, identified him as a member of the upper class.

To his left walked Tecocol, his most trusted friend and a captain in the fleet of the Eastern Sea. Behind them were four brawny sailors from his personal bodyguard—each dressed in their close vests of quilted cotton upon which were emblazoned the colors of the fleet. The guards were a traditional formality as they were certainly not required for safety in the capital city. Several of the men were breathing quite heavily, unused to the city's altitude. Tenochtitlan had been built more than seven thousand feet above sea level.

"For what purpose does the emperor summon you, Admiral?" Tecocol asked, breaking into the older man's thoughts.

Shaken from his musing, Mextli replied, "I know not, but I will be far happier when we leave these crowds and return to the sea, I assure you."

The admiral of the Empire's navies stood a shade less than five feet ten, tall for his people. A red tie string, enhancing the strong features of his hardened face, pulled his long black hair back from his face. His golden skin, tanned brown by years in the sun, was weathered by the sea and made him appear older than his fifty seasons, but his body was still solid and muscled, and aside from his skin, he could have passed for a man in his late thirties.

As they walked along the main thoroughfare, Mextli noted the masses of macehualles, or commoners, who made up the thriving city of more than a million people. The men were dressed in loincloths; all that was needed for modesty in the hot sun. Capes of cotton, or maguey fiber and even rabbit fur, could be donned if the evening or early morning breeze brought a chill to the air. The women wore long skirts descending to their calves and tied at their waists by an embroidered belt. An ample dyed cotton blouse was worn over the skirt, falling from the women's shoulders to just below their waists. The variety of colors of these blouses brightened the market stalls. Here and there, a slave, dressed in a loincloth or a feathered mantle, with a jewel of ownership pierced into his cheek, carried goods for his master.

The outer city was made up of many distinct districts and in each district lived a calpullis, or clan, of macehualles. The calpullis owned, and were responsible for, their own section of the city. They made up the backbone of the Empire. There were over 150 clans in the capital alone.

Nearing the lake region of the city, the buildings were set further apart while in between them grew vast gardens of maize or potatoes. Quickly passing through this agricultural area, the six men left the adobe buildings behind and crossed over one of the three great causeways that spanned Lake Texcoco. Guards armed with swords and lances looked them over but let them pass.

The causeway was built of great stone blocks that connected the mainland with the older inner city. Along the causeway ran aqueducts carrying fresh water to the public fountains and man-made pools bordering the larger buildings further ahead. On either side of the causeway, they could see, and smell, hundreds of chinampa plots. Dirt and human fertilizer covered these floating gardens. They were made of reeds and anchored firmly to the lake bottom. Whatever was planted in these plots was not yet apparent, as it was early in the growing time.

In the inner city, all the streets, except the main road on which they now traveled, were replaced by an abundance of canals that crisscrossed the entire island around which Tenochtitlan was constructed. The public traveled across these canals on a series of wooden bridges. The canals were filled with small boats and canoes carrying merchants and goods this way and that. Even here, away from the Eastern and Western Seas, water was the fastest and most efficient means of transportation. Deposited on the sides of the main road next to the canals were piles of heavy building material, stone and lumber, waiting to be transported from the waterways to construction areas.

As they walked on, the buildings became larger and were not only surrounded by canals but by huge gardens. The sprouts of the new spring growth were just beginning to show in the muddy soil of these sites. These gardens were constructed in long rectangular plots, side by side, often bordered by a canal on one side and tall, thin willow trees on the other. The plots were irrigated by a sophisticated system of gates, dams, and drains. Planted in these gardens were, among other crops, maize, beans, amaranth, sage, peppers, and tomatoes. The rich soil supplied from the lake bottom provided the city with up to seven harvests each season.

Mextli's group now turned toward the paved and whitewashed central plaza, called the Zocalo, which lay before the massive pyramid in the middle of the island. In point of fact, the great temple was a double pyramid, two pyramids set flush together side by side. The structure towered above the other large buildings. Its white limestone walls were polished and gleamed in the sunlight. Two sets of 114 steep stairs, also side by side, reached heavenward toward the twin temples at their tops.

All around the city's centerpiece were equally splendid government buildings and the palaces of the city's nobility with their flat terraced roofs. The plaza was clean and tended to by hundreds of slaves who constantly swept and scrubbed the polished stone. There was a time when the canal water had been brackish, but now a greater number of aqueducts brought fresh water into the city from Chapoltepec and other mountain areas, each aqueduct transporting the water through two earthen pipes set side by side. These pipes fed the reservoirs that in turn fed the fountains and baths in the homes of the nobility, the overflow of which drained into the canals. Openings had also been made in the pipes so that when they crossed the canals, additional water could spill into these essential modes of transportation. Tenders constantly inspected the pipes for leakage and repair, for this water was the lifeblood of Tenochtitlan.

Near the pyramid was the fabled Wall of Skulls, a remnant from the past. This was the sacred precinct—open only to the Empire's elite who lived there, the commoners who worked the gardens, and the rival priests who worked in the service of Tlaloc, the god of rain, or Huitzilopotchli, the god of war. And, of course, those like Mextli who had been invited, or more accurately "commanded," by the emperor to come to the inner city.

Stopping before the majestic royal palace, Mextli took in the splendor of his surroundings. Completed only forty seasons ago, the palace dwarfed the nearby public buildings. Only the ancient Templo Mayor, the great pyramid, stood higher. The palace was fashioned of polished white stone with a multitude of great towers and balcony gardens.

The admiral noted that the building's guards were armed with thundersticks, as well as the weapons intended for close combat. Their leader advanced to meet Mextli, and once he recognized him, he saluted the admiral by slapping the palm of his right hand above his heart. He then indicated that the party could proceed onto the grounds. Mextli turned to his bodyguards and instructed them to remain where they were. He then took in a deep breath and nodded to Tecocol. The two men entered the palace to meet the emperor.

Chapter 4

James Madison hurried along the busy London thoroughfare, dodging the short-stage coaches and hackney carriages. Unlike the potholed and muddy lanes amid the crumbling tenements making up the heart of the city, Parliament Street was a short side road, but it was paved. It was also relatively unsoiled as the animal dung deposited during the day by the hundreds of horses that pulled the various assortments of carriages and wagons was constantly swept up at night. A cart full of radishes and cabbages rumbled by, drawn by an aging gray nag that appeared ready for the glue factory.

Madison was perspiring, his heart racing. He was as concerned by the reports he had heard from the European continent as he was about how his colleagues in the English government would react to these reports.

All about him, the local populace hustled and bustled, the men dressed fashionably in tight trousers, vests, and jackets with wide lapels cut short at the waist to expose colorful cummerbunds. They also wore gloves, top hats, and the majority carried walking sticks that could also be used to ward off dogs and pickpockets. The few women in sight sported both long and short-sleeve dresses that billowed out below their waists and covered their feet. The necklines of the dresses were cut quite low, but not low enough to expose their femininity. They, too, wore gloves, as well as colorful shawls and large bonnets to protect them from the sun. A short jacket draped their shoulders. These were the middle and upper class of the city.

The bonnets and parasols were not really necessary as the morning fog, coupled with the soot in the air from thousands of coal-burning stoves, sullied the sun, leaving only the vague shape of a shimmering ball tucked behind the clouds. Still, it was a fine morning and unseasonably warm for London.

He was a small man, just five foot four inches in his stocking feet. To others, he seemed thin and withered with age, a physical appearance that concealed the robust energy flowing through his limbs. That energy was evident in the sparkle of his deep blue eyes, which were set under full eyebrows above a sharp nose. As he made his way around the obstacles in the street, his breath came in short bursts, not so much caused by the spring mist blanketing the city but more a sign of his age. At fifty-three, he no longer had the stamina of his youth, and his government position did not allow him any time for exercise.

Deep in thought, he rounded the corner of the Palace of Westminster and literally ran straight into the constable stationed there, knocking both individuals backward and off their feet.

"Blimey, Lord Madison," the officer exclaimed, standing up, brushing himself off, and replacing his stovetop hat. "Must be big 'appenings going on for you to be in such a rush." He reached down and helped the older gentleman to his feet.

Embarrassed by his folly, Madison straightened his wig. "I am truly sorry, constable. I am afraid I am late for a meeting with the first minister."

"Ah, I understand, Your Lordship. Has this anything to do with the bloody Italian?"

"I'm sorry, constable. I'm not at liberty to say," replied Madison. Then turning his head slightly just before he rushed off again, he loudly whispered with a wink, "But that was a damn fine guess."

*****

Spencer Perceval paced back and forth across the marble floor of the House of Commons, his hands clasped behind his back. Curious faces watched his movement from the benches on either side of the room as the low murmur of voices filled the hall. The first minister was not a man to be feared. In fact, his tall thin frame, balding forehead, and the quick anxious movements of his head as he snuck a peek to his left and right, mirrored his stressed and timid personality. The Whig party, his chief rivals, referred to him as the game hen. Perceval was not one to make strong decisions or to stand by his own pronouncements. He was, however, a professional lawyer, an avid and loyal Tory, and the leader of his political party. He was also, at least for the time, the elected head of the English government.

The voices quieted at the sound of the man-at-arms tapping his staff upon the floor. Perceval and the ministers looked up as Lord Madison was announced into the assembly. He strode into the chamber, taking in the expressions of the gathering. For the most part, they were sullen and worried. Something was brewing on the continent all right.

*****

Taking the seat of the opposition leader, across from the first minister's chair, Madison continued to look about the room, noting the faces of the men he knew so well, nodding to a few. These were the men who shaped England's political, economic, and military policy. The people living in the various political districts of the country elected them, but only entitled landowners were eligible to run for office.

These are good men, thought Madison to himself, *but they have been elected from a handful out of every hundred. There are other good men out there who would gladly and efficiently serve the government. If we Whigs have a say, someday they will get their chance.*

"Hear ye! Hear ye! Hear ye!" The deep voice of the man-at-arms resounded throughout the hall. "This meeting will come to order on this fifteenth day of April 1811. God save the Queen!"

"God save the Queen," echoed Madison and the assembled congregation.

"Gentlemen," Perceval began, "it seems that Italian brigand has been causing even more trouble..."

Chapter 5

The lieutenant reread the letter he had recently received by courier, a dispatch signed by none other than Arthur Wellesley himself.

Zachary Taylor was twenty-seven years old, five feet eight inches tall, with a compact, muscular build. His chiseled jaw, which appeared to need shaving just hours after he had used a razor, gave him a tough and determined look. Despite his young years, Zachary's hairline was beginning to recede above his temples, a detail he countered by growing the frontal locks of his hair long so that it hung over his forehead. The lieutenant was dressed in worn, stained, and rumpled peasant garb. Acknowledged by the army units in which he had previously served as a rough customer who was always ready for a fight, he was also easily recognized by his slovenly dress.

Zachary's father was a wealthy merchant in Carlisle, England, who had served as an officer prior to retirement. In 1802, he had purchased his oldest son a commission. Young Taylor excelled in his military training, and in 1805, he had shipped overseas to join the Second West India Regiment. In fact, the very ship bringing him to the Asian continent was to pick up General Arthur Wellesley and return the illustrious commander to England.

It was in India that Zachary distinguished himself. When his company was ambushed by insurgents led by Velu Thampi Dalawa at the start of the Travancore rebellion, his commanding officer, Colonel Macaulay, had been killed. Taylor organized what was left of the English forces, fought his way out of the trap, and led the surviving 126 men back to their regimental headquarters. It had been a monumental feat praised in all the English papers. Over one thousand soldiers had entered that ambush and most had been annihilated in the Aralvaimozhi pass.

Taylor served in India for four long years. He loved the life of a soldier, his men respected him, and his superiors recognized his leadership potential. Zachary found he actually enjoyed facing the enemy. He was calm under fire and quite good at devising a strategy to defeat his adversaries. In 1809, with the rebellion suppressed and talk of an inevitable clash between England and the Kingdom of Italy, the young lieutenant was sent home.

He quickly grew impatient with the lack of action, and the next year, he volunteered to serve as an unofficial liaison between the English and the Tyrolese rebels in the Austrian Alps. England was not at war with the Kingdom of Italy, but its government was supportive of any resistance to the Italian expansion plans, especially following the defeat of the Holy Roman Empire and Italy's occupation of that country's former southern regions.

Now nearly three months after joining the rebels, Taylor had received specific orders to seek out and kill one of the most ruthless and hated of the occupiers, the dastardly Colonel Paparelli.

*****

A week passed before Lieutenant Taylor slipped into the town of Mittersill at the base of the Alps. With him was the leader of the rebels, Andreas Hofer, and six of his men. This village was the site of Colonel Paparelli's current headquarters.

The town was fair-sized with a tavern and the Church of St. Nicolas east of the village and an Italian military encampment a little more than a mile to the west. Looking down from a rocky mount high above Mittersill were thick broken walls of stone, the remains of a castle that had been destroyed by a fire in the early sixteenth century and never rebuilt.

From this vantage point, Taylor and his companions spent several nights watching the home of the town's mayor. The building had been expropriated by the Italian colonel to be used as his personal residence. The rebels meticulously observed the number and positioning of the guards, noting when, and how often, they changed.

Taylor even obtained a description of the inside of the house from one of the mayor's former maids.

Each night, they watched helplessly as Paparelli sent soldiers to bring the younger and prettier girls of the village to his command center. One dark-haired lass strode into the mayor's former home defiantly, glaring at the guards, but most were dragged into the house, weeping and sobbing by their armed escorts. On the fifth evening, they witnessed the mayor fall to his knees in front of his own home, tears streaming down his face as he begged the colonel not to take his own fifteen-year-old daughter to bed. The mayor was stripped to his waist and lashed for this protest before Paparelli ushered the young girl into the house to have his way with her.

Taylor could stomach no more. Despite the guards surrounding the house and the company of regulars stationed on the far side of the village, the next evening, he would put an end to these abominations. He spoke quietly to Hofer laying out his plan.

*****

The night was dark with only the splinter of a waxing moon casting a faint light on the mayor's home. The house was a large rectangular building made of stone and containing a great many rooms on the first floor and a considerably smaller second floor. An open courtyard to the front of the structure faced the main street. Across this cobblestoned avenue, a number of shops overlooked the courtyard. Other shops and homes encompassed the remaining three sides of the mayor's house, though none were within thirty yards of the building. Narrow unlit alleys ran between groupings of these homes.

Taylor's plan called for the small rebel force to create a diversion to draw off the majority of the guards while he and Hofer worked their way past the remaining Italians and into the house. There they would confront Colonel Paparelli and dispatch him to the bowels of hell where he belonged. That was the plan, but Taylor had enough combat experience to know that no plan went flawlessly once the fighting began. The guards might not leave their posts despite the diversion. There could be more guards than anticipated in the house.

The colonel might have eyes in the back of his head and a dozen pistols at his side.

The English officer vigorously shook his head to clear it of such thoughts. He simply needed to keep his wits sharp, follow the well-thought-out plan as best he could, and deal with the unforeseen as he encountered those obstacles. Despite his concerns, and a quickened heartbeat, Lieutenant Taylor was resourceful and confident. He had gotten out of many a tight scrape both in India and in the surrounding Austrian mountains through quick thinking, strength of will, and sheer guts. He harbored no doubt he would survive this night, but could he succeed in bringing down the inhuman Paparelli? And could he, as a result of killing this fiendish brute, save the lives of many innocent villagers? That remained to be seen.

Taylor and Hofer, their faces caked black with mud to better blend into the darkness, slowly worked their way through a narrow alley until they were a mere thirty yards from the back of the mayor's home, a position giving them an unobstructed view of two sides of the building. To their left was the back door that served as an entrance into the kitchen. Patrolling the two faces of the house visible to them were two armed sentries. They each walked the length of one side of the building and then turned back again. Zachary was aware there was another pair of guards walking each of the walls on the far side of the house. If their observations during the past few days were correct, there were another four Italian soldiers stationed inside the home, two in the front entry and two in the kitchen.

The colonel's office and bedroom were upstairs, and they had seen him enter the building just a half hour earlier with a woman in her early thirties, the wife of the local tavern owner. She had not been manhandled into the home by his soldiers, as were most of his conquests. Perhaps, being older, she had accepted her fate and was resigned to endure whatever was in store for her this evening. Taylor hoped he might be in time to rescue the woman from Paparelli's lust.

Zachary was prepared for the sound of the explosion at the front of the house, but it still made him jump slightly. The detonation of the small bomb was closely followed by the sounds of musket fire. The half dozen rebels were pressing their diversionary assault.

Shouting to his companion to remain at the rear door, one of the visible outside sentries dashed toward the sound of the shooting. Zachary could now also hear return fire coming from the front of the home.

Taking careful aim from the alley's shadows, hoping the sound of his shot would be masked by the disturbance at the front of the building, Taylor squeezed his trigger. The musket went off with a loud bang, the stock thudding into his shoulder. He quickly dropped the weapon and, along with Hofer, raced through the resulting white cloud of smoke while drawing his knife. The remaining guard lay in a contorted heap by the rear steps. A thin trickle of blood flowed from the left side of his forehead, the musket ball having struck him square in the temple.

Andreas was three steps ahead of Zachary. The rebel leader threw open the back door without hesitation and dived headfirst into the kitchen, colliding with a heavy table and knocking the wind out of his lungs. A stunned young man in a green Italian uniform spun around from where he had been gawking at the action in the front of the house and, raising the business end of his musket toward the intruder, took two steps toward the sprawled figure. His eyes went wide a half second later when Taylor barged through the open doorway and slammed into him, shoving the young man against the wall. One hand went over the soldier's mouth as Taylor drove his knife up under the youth's rib cage and into his heart. The soldier collapsed into Zachary's arms and was lowered quickly to the floor.

Peering around the now-vacated doorway into the house's interior, Taylor saw the large dining room that made up the center of the home. A wide portal to the left of this elongated chamber led to a parlor. Through the doorway on the right side of the room, he could see stairs leading to the second floor. On the other side of the dining area was a third doorway that led into another large room. In this vicinity, Taylor could hear, and occasionally glimpse, Italian soldiers as they cursed and ducked after discharging their weapons at their assailants in the buildings across the main street.

Signaling Hofer to remain in the kitchen to cover his retreat, Taylor crept through the dining room and toward the stairs. Two burley green-clad soldiers were at the window in the next room, but they were concentrating on the enemy to their front and their backs were to the Englishman. Zachary inched his way to the stairs and began his ascent, never taking his eyes off the two Italians until he reached the second floor. Miraculously, there were no soldiers on this level.

The door to Colonel Paparelli's study was open, and the room was vacant. Taylor moved soundlessly down the hall to the door of the colonel's bedroom. His hand upon the door handle, he could hear a bed creaking, the hoarse gasping of a man, and what seemed to be the sharp gasps of a woman.

The bastard, Taylor thought as he turned the handle and slowly inched the door open. *His men are fighting below, and this shithead continues to satisfy his depraved lust.* Paparelli was stark naked on a midsize bed, his back to Zachary. He was hammering it home to the innkeeper's wife whose legs were locked around the colonel's considerable waist. The shooting continued both downstairs and outside the building, but the two of them were either oblivious to the sound or not paying it the slightest heed. On a small table at the end of the bed by a pitcher of water were the colonel's saber and pistol.

Zachary walked quietly to the table and picked up the pistol just as the innkeeper's wife opened her eyes and gasped in alarm. The colonel spun off her body with amazing agility for a man with such a large belly, only to be face-to-face with the barrel of his own weapon.

"Thank god, sir!" the woman screeched after a second's hesitation. "This beast, *this beast...!*"

Turning toward the colonel, her breasts still flush from where his chest had been pounding upon them, she struck Paparelli across his face as hard as she could and then scrambled off the bed to stand a little behind and to the left of Taylor.

"Let me kill the swine!" she screamed. "Let me do it! He has dishonored me. He has defiled me."

Zachary had killed many men, but they had all been in battle. He had never shot an unarmed man before, but Paparelli was not a man he reasoned. He was a savage animal who raped women and children and murdered innocent villagers. The colonel sat at the edge of his bed, sweat covering his body and fear contorting his face. His lower lip was trembling, and his eyes watered.

Taylor, his pistol still pointing at Paparelli, hesitated for a few more seconds, but he was a soldier, and he obeyed his orders. He slowly began to squeeze the trigger.

The crash of the water pitcher exploding against the back of his skull just preceded the discharge of the pistol. Taylor's right arm jerked up as his legs gave out from under him, sending his shot into the ceiling.

Down on all fours, Zachary shook his head to clear away the cobwebs and tried to regain his feet, only to be pushed back to the floor by Colonel Paparelli who now stood over him naked but with his drawn saber. In the courtyard below, the shouts of newly arrived Italian infantry replaced the sounds of musketry. Men in green were entering the house while others fanned out into the village in search of the retreating rebels.

Colonel Paparelli, his face red and veins popping as rage coursed through its features, bellowed for his guards.

*****

Held tightly upright by two soldiers, Zachary Taylor hung at the edge of consciousness. His hands were bound securely behind him—one eye was swollen shut, and blood clotted his mouth and nose from the beatings he had endured from both Paparelli and his guards.

The colonel's face was no longer flushed. In fact, he looked both exhausted and resigned.

"The rebel will not speak, sir," the villager who had been acting as an interpreter said once again.

"Obviously, you imbecile," Colonel Paparelli shot back. "Either that or he has no tongue."

Taylor was in a quandary. He could not answer the colonel's questions. He understood little German but understood enough Italian to know what he was being asked: "Where are your camps?" "Who are your leaders?"

Even if he wanted to talk, he could not. His English accent would betray him. He was a soldier of the Queen dressed as a Tyrolese rebel, and as such, he would be hung as a spy. His only hope was that his tormentors would tire of their sport, throw him in a cell, and his comrades might be able to come to his rescue.

More likely, he thought, *they will take me outside, put me against a wall, and shoot me.*

The colonel was now dressed in full uniform and brandishing his saber. As he stood looking thoughtfully at Taylor, the tavern owner's wife, clad in a simple woolen dress, walked into the room.

"Ah, Marie," exclaimed Paparelli. "Are you off to your husband? I am sorry we were interrupted, but I will make up for this disturbance next Tuesday."

The innkeeper's wife pecked the colonel on his cheek and smiled.

"My husband is an oaf and most likely dead drunk by now, Bruno," she purred. "No matter. You, however, must not forget that I saved your life. I am expecting much more in the way of lavish gifts than in the past."

The sly smile never left her lips as the woman turned her back on Taylor and walked from the room and out of the house.

"A remarkable woman for an Austrian," Colonel Paparelli mused to himself. "I like variety and enjoy slapping down the young resistant ones, but Marie is knowledgeable in the ways of lovemaking. She is also more than willing to leave her husband once a week to dally with me in exchange for good food and a few jewels, which I take from wealthy villagers of course. Yes, it is good to have reciprocal sex every now and again."

With a sharp laugh, Paparelli walked over to Taylor and put the point of his saber at the young man's throat. Zachary's hard blue eyes stared back into the cold gray eyes of his abuser.

"I don't suppose you ever will talk, will you?" the colonel said more to himself than to his prisoner. "No, I suppose not."

Without a trace of emotion, Paparelli stepped to the side of the young English lieutenant and drew his saber across and deep into the young man's throat. Taylor felt the cold razor edge of the sword cut into his flesh and his warm blood gushing from the wound. He gasped for breath, convulsed, and was engulfed by eternal blackness.

Chapter 6

The streets outside Windsor Castle were filled with a great many gentlemen and ladies; all on self-concocted missions so that they might, just perhaps, run into a member of the royal family. The Queen was going to be in attendance at her court, and anything was possible. The men were dressed in their finery. They wore top hats and long coats that fell to the back of their knees but were open in the front to expose their colorful vests lined with two rows of buttons. Some wore trousers, but most were in britches that tucked into high boots. Almost all the men sported popular thick sideburns. The women wore dresses that were either cinched at the waist with a belt or sown tightly just below their bosoms. These garments billowed and ballooned all the way to their ankles, allowing great freedom of movement. Although the dresses were cut low, scarves, or fur-lined long-sleeve vests, covered the upper portion of their chests. Many women wore hats, but most had bonnets that could be tied down under their chin by a scarf should there be gusts of wind.

Beggars were on nearly every corner of the streets, working the crowds and keeping an eye on their competition so they did not infringe into their own self-proclaimed territory. Most were male, and none were extremely old. They lived on the leftovers of society and, in most cases, would suffer an early demise from starvation, illness, or drink. One was a middle-aged female clad in a blue woolen dress and a black silk hat, supported by two wooden crutches. While the gentle folks hurried past the men, many would stop to give a few coins to this quiet woman.

Windsor Castle was a monstrous edifice, its huge chapel and rounded residence buildings surrounded by great thick stone walls and high turrets. The castle had been built more than 750 years before at a location chosen by William the Conqueror. He had wanted it positioned high above the Thames River on the edge of a Saxon hunting preserve but still within a day's walk of present-day London. Much of the outer walls had been constructed in the 1070s. Today, there were private apartments built into the massive Round Tower and the Upper Ward facing the north side of the quadrangle within the castle. King Edward IV had added the massive St. George Chapel between 1461 and 1483. Outside the castle were huge gardens filled with paths and mazes shaped by high hedges.

Anne II, Queen of England, sat in the Crimson Drawing Room surrounded by various members of her court. Huge murals of past coronations filled ornate hand-carved wooden walls. Red upholstered sofas and chairs were spread about on thick rich carpets. Huge undraped windows along the far side of the room filled the space with sunlight, leaving no need for the massive glass chandeliers to be lit.

The large room was filled with people coming and going, but for the moment, Anne had positioned herself in a well-lit corner with her first lady of the bedchamber, having requested that others not approach her for the next half hour. Should her instructions not be heeded, she would remove herself to her privy chamber next to the throne room where she could be assured of her privacy. Sir James Townsend, the Queen's privy councilor and vice-chamberlain, stood at the main entrance talking to a number of individuals who sought an audience with Anne. Her six attending maids of honor, all attractive young teenage girls from noble families, sat in the far corner, playing cards. Their only responsibility was to provide companionship for the Queen when she wished company. The sergeant-at-arms entered the room, checked the positioning of the royal guards, and left. Stewards and servants scurried about, following the orders of the lord chamberlain who was responsible for administering the household duties. A number of musicians and poets talked together in the opposite corner from the Queen.

These individuals, along with the cooks, gardeners, stable personnel, ladies of the bedchamber, additional guards and servants and maids, and many more, made up the nearly one-thousand-person staff that attended the Queen of England. They were now with her at Windsor Castle, but in a few weeks' time, the entire court, including the Queen, would move on to another of her residences, perhaps at Greenwich or Whitehall or the Buckingham House. With so many people crammed into even so large a space, palaces tended to become filthy from overuse. When this happened, the entire court would move on to another location along the River Thames while an equally huge staff of laborers would move into the vacated palace and begin cleaning it up for its next visit.

The Queen's first lady of the bedchamber sat on a small footstool just to the left of Anne. She was in her midtwenties, the Queen's closest friend, and was charged with supervising the maids of honor. Anne leaned toward her confident and whispered, "Oh, Madalyn, can you not stop asking about that dreadful night? It all happened so fast. No one has discovered the assailant's identity, and it is not something I wish to remember."

The first lady blushed deeply. She was a slim, beautiful girl about ten years younger than Anne. She dropped her head so that her long brunette hair partially fell across her face to mask the blush.

"I am so sorry, Your Majesty. I do not wish to pry. It is just that I am so concerned for your safety and—"

"Your Majesty?" Anne whispered with a trace of amusement. "You know that it is Anne in private. We have known each other since you were fourteen years old, Maddie. Your Majesty indeed!"

Composing herself, Madalyn attempted to change the subject. "Will you be speaking to any of your suitors today, my lady Anne?" A faint smile danced across her lips and was gone.

"Hang my suitors!" the Queen murmured under her breath. "A bunch of old geezers! I do not have time for suitors."

"I have heard there are two of your more frequent pursuers here today," Madalyn continued softly. "The rich one from Wylam and the earl from Northumbrian."

The rich one was John Molson, a forty-eight-year-old aristocrat who was now a prominent industrialist. He had close-cut light-brown hair, a sharp face, and a small mouth. Molson had opened a brewery in Wylam at a young age and expanded it into one of the principal distilleries in southern England. The steam engine had automated the brewing industry in the late 1700s, and Molson had been one of its leading advocates. At the turn of the century, his fascination with steam had led him to build a railway from Wylam to London, as well as other cities, further expanding the distribution of his ale. Just this year, he had partnered with Christopher Blackett to introduce the first twin-cylinder steam locomotive. John Molson was also a patron of the royal theater and very, very rich.

Charles Grey was the earl from Northumbrian. He was a year younger than Molson, with a baldhead surrounded by great tufts of hair and bushy sideburns. His eyebrows too were bushy, and his eyes, set above a long nose, seemed to take in everything about him. Educated at Eton and then Cambridge and the son of a knighted general, Grey had taken an immediate interest in politics and was elected to the Parliament at the age of twenty-two. He was an active member of the Whig Party who, it was said, was destined to be a first minister.

"No," whispered Anne, "I do not believe I will have time to speak to these gentlemen today."

"Perhaps you fancy someone younger?" Madalyn suggested with a quick glance at the Queen.

Anne laughed aloud. "Yes, perhaps I'll marry some twenty-year-old prince from one of those beastly German principalities. Is that what you want, Madalyn?"

The first lady looked up into Anne's eyes and smiled a beautiful smile. "You know I only want what will make you happy… Anne."

Chapter 7

Mextli and Tecocol were ushered into a large garden built into the center of an immense courtyard. There they were told to wait. Flowers bloomed everywhere in an excess of gorgeous colors, filling the air with their sweet fragrances. The most colorful was the amazing variety of orchids from the realm of the Inca—bright yellow, violet, and orange. Rivaling these were the red, pink, and white rose shrubs from the lands to the north. Mextli had never seen so many different kinds of plants in a single location. The flowers had been brought here from throughout the Empire, and the scent from the thousands of blossoms was delicious and almost overpowering.

The lack of a roof allowed the sun and rain free access to the plants. One side of the courtyard had been left open to provide a panoramic view of the teeming capital city across the lake from the island upon which the imperial inner city had been built. It was not the admiral's first time to the royal palace, nor would it probably be his last, unless he had somehow found disfavor with his emperor, but he never ceased to be astonished by its beauty and its riches.

*****

Mextli had been brought up on the sea. Born of Totonacas blood, his father had been a lesser noble in the port town of Chalchihueyecan southeast of the city of Xalapa. Chalchihueyecan was the Empire's main port on the Inland Sea and flourished in both trade and tribute.

Despite his noble birth, young Mextli played with both the children of the pilli, or nobility, and the commoners, called macehualles, although never together. His father was known as eccentric and disapproved of the strict societal standards of the Aztec Empire. His peers did not share this view.

The Empire, as were its nobles, was wealthy because of the tribute brought in from the lands that had been conquered and placed under its governors. These included the peaceful domains, making up the greater part of the Empire proper and the territories that were under military rule at the extent of the Empire's borders. It was the middle class, however, and not the nobles who integrated this tribute into the Aztec society. Unlike the majority of his counterparts, Mextli's father realized that without the merchants and the craftsmen, there would be no supporting base for the nobility. He also respected the commoners, for without them there would be no Empire. It was the middle-aged and older common men who farmed, raising the maize and potatoes and vegetables that were the staple of the Aztec population, and it was the young sons of these men who made up the well-disciplined and powerful military. The upper class, with its control of the tribute riches, provided the Empire's bureaucrats, military leaders, and priests, as well as its teachers, musicians, and poets.

It could not be said the macehualles and the pilli were inequitably divided by fate for all their lives although that tended to be true in most cases. It was possible for a commoner to rise to the rank of nobility by demonstrating great bravery and leadership during warfare. All the macehualle male children, regardless of rank, attended a telpuchcalli, or school, where they learned the art of war and how to fight, as well as the trade or craft that was the specialty of their district. This school also ingrained upon them the obligations of being an Aztec citizen. Hope of advancing to the ranks of the nobility drove the macehualles to excel in their military training, greatly improving the prowess of the army in which they were required to serve from the ages of seventeen seasons until twenty-five.

Mextli had also attended both this first school and, as he advanced in age, a second telpuchcalli required of just the pilli. At this school, the males of the nobility refined their fighting skills and learned to use all the weapons of war. Here, too, they were also taught the mysteries of the priesthood, military strategy, the intricacies of the government, and the principles of leadership. The upper class was not required to serve in the military, but at the age of seventeen, a male noble had to choose to either enter the priesthood, take a position in the government, or serve as a junior officer in the army or navy. All these positions, except the priesthood, were closed to women. Noblewomen had two options: to serve as priestesses or marry and raise a family.

When he reached his seventeenth season, Mextli elected to join the naval units protecting the merchant fleets trading along the coasts of the Empire. This enabled him to travel to the furthest reaches of the Empire's holdings at that time: to the Great Peninsula in the north and the River of All Rivers in the south.

At the age of twenty, he was promoted to serve as a lieutenant on a warship where he distinguished himself by fighting gallantly in a battle against the last of the Inland Sea pirates, thus ridding the Empire of that irritation. His success resulted in his being elevated in rank, and Mextli made the decision, much to the anguish of his parents, to dedicate the rest of his life to the military. By the time he was twenty-five, he was captaining his own ship.

While Mextli was undergoing his schooling and eventually working his way toward earning his commission as a naval captain, the Empire was encountering new peoples as its ships explored the eastern coast of the lands north of the Great Peninsula. One of these societies was the Iroquois nation who resided further up the coast in the northern lands bordering the Eastern Sea. More a confederation of tribes than a group of people united by a common government, the Iroquois-speaking people prospered through their system of councils and the peace resulting from both this alliance and the strength of their numbers. Although not a seafaring people, they had constructed huge canoes to travel the coasts of the Northeast Lands.

When the Aztecs arrived on their shores, the Iroquois initially welcomed the newcomers and did not hinder them as the strangers began building settlements and protective forts on the Northeast Islands. The two groups traded, the Iroquois exchanging crops and fresh meat with the Aztecs for blankets and trinkets, and locals helped the men and women of the Empire survive their first winter of unbelievable coldness.

When the Aztecs began moving inland and demanding tribute, the Iroquois nation resisted. As a consequence, the Empire's territorial governor issued an order to his soldiers to burn a random village and take its population into slavery. This was to serve as both a warning and a demonstration of the Aztec's power. The Iroquois were not intimidated and fought back.

It was an unequal battle. The native canoes were no match for the much larger Aztec ships, which now mounted big blasters on their decks. Fighting as individual tribes with their bows and arrows against the well-armed and regimented Aztecs and their thundersticks, the clash was short and decisive. The tribes of the Iroquois nation withdrew into the interior of their lands, protected by their dense forests.

The Empire continued to expand, building more settlements protected by massive forts on the rivers that could easily be navigated. Most of the Aztec colonies were built along the southern coast just above the Great Peninsula where the weather was more temperate and there was less resistance from the natives. But the settlement constructed on one of the islands off the northeast coast, in a protected harbor at the base of a large river, continued to prosper. It brought in a great amount of both tribute and trade. The food grown during the warm season was greatly needed by the growing heartland of the Empire, and the Aztec nobles prized the beaver and bearskins from that region. Despite the inhospitable winter weather, the island's settlement continued to grow as it became the focal point for expansion inland to the west.

Mextli saw action at the conclusion of the conflict with the Iroquois nation and worked hard to restore peace with the local natives who continued to live near the Empire's borders. It was through his leadership that the Northeast Islands, made up of the smaller settlement island and a great island to its immediate east whose length took more than three days to walk, were again made safe and began to prosper. It was shortly thereafter that he was raised to the rank of admiral of all the fleets. This included the Western Sea merchant fleet that traveled between the Inca Empire in the south and the Empire's settlements as far north as the Great Bay.

*****

And now, so many years later, the admiral was being conducted through the emperor's palace to see the great Ahuitzotl VI.

Summoned from the garden, Mextli and Tecocol were first taken through a great hall, lined with obsidian carvings. This included both high and low relief art carved in stone basalt and covered in a polished and painted plaster, and the newer "realistic" paintings that had been the rage during the last hundred seasons. Entering the interior of the palace, they walked through the huge archway of a great chamber that was illuminated by a series of skylights in the ceiling. Both men dropped to their knees upon entering this room and bowed their heads to the floor.

The emperor rose from a magnificent gold-plated throne that was encrusted in precious jewels. In actuality, Ahuitzotl VI was not an imposing man, thin and several inches shorter than Mextli, but his demeanor and his dress made him appear much larger. The emperor wore the traditional mantle of white and blue called a tlimatli. It was folded over his shoulders and held in place by a chalchivitl, or bejeweled clasp. Jewelry made of gold and precious stones hung from his neck and his arms. His tall headdress, made of bright feathers, added to his stature.

Behind him stood two priests, one dressed in a robe of blue and the other clothed in a mantle of red. All about him were lean youthful serving men, wearing only white loincloths, and beautiful young serving women dressed in bright multicolored dresses with cotton scarves binding their long flowing hair.

"Ah, Admiral." The emperor smiled, looking directly at Mextli. "I have been looking forward to this meeting. I believe I have an assignment that may interest you."

Chapter 8

Cacimar was a loner, a strange young man barely twenty seasons of age. His people had never really understood the youth. It was not that he was lazy or rejected the values of his village. He was obedient to a fault, and when he was about, he did twice the work of a normal man. After his father and mother had died during a violent storm when he was just ten seasons old, he had pretty much lived on his own. Despite this, as the seasons passed, Cacimar continued to provide for his village and to treat his elders with the customary respect that was their due. Yet his thoughts were always somewhere else. He would spend hours watching the sea and often disappeared for weeks at a time, something no other villager would dream of doing. Perhaps strangest of all, he would not take a wife.

A giant among his people, Cacimar stood a full thumb over six feet with powerful leg and arm muscles that fairly rippled when he moved in his smooth effortless manner. His hair was jet black and worn long to his broad shoulders. While not having a handsome face, it was pleasing, nevertheless, with its high cheekbones, smooth tanned skin, and sparkling brown eyes. The wistful look he wore when alone, which was most of the time, would be quickly replaced by a bright white smile whenever another villager approached. The women of the village found this smile irresistible and the young man's sexual reputation when in the company of an unmarried woman was renowned. No one had ever seen a look of anger cross his features, and Cacimar was generally accepted as a loner.

The young man's greatest pride was the canoe he had constructed from a hollowed-out cottonwood tree. Unlike the village's mighty hunting canoe, which was made from the cedar tree and could hold up to forty adults, his vessel had room for just two. In every case, this meant Cacimar and his supplies. When just thirteen seasons old, he had felled a cottonwood tree standing near the sacred place in the interior of the island and then dragged it a great distance to the beach. Setting the tree trimmed of its branches horizontally in the sand, he set fires along the top of its trunk, and every few hours scraped out the resulting charcoal with conch shells until he had a deep, but sturdy, interior. He then spent days carving the bow and stern and ornamenting the entire craft.

It was this canoe that Cacimar used when he first set out to explore the island world in which he lived. At first, he would leave for several moons, causing great concern among his people. His travels took him around his home island and then out to sea in different directions from that landmass, but he always returned to his village on the island of Ayti. He felt himself drawn back, as if some fate awaited him at this place, although he knew not the nature of that destiny.

In two weeks, the turtles would begin swimming in the current off his native island, and the villages on its northern coast would gather in their great canoes to hunt these animals. The villagers would fasten lines to remora, or hunting fish, which swam under the canoes. The remora was a long slender fish with a sucker-like organ at the top of its head. It used its sucker to attach itself to the sides of larger fish and turtles, thus utilizing them for transportation and feeding off parasites and small bits of food missed by its host. The "leashed" hunting fish would attach itself to its quarry, at which time the villagers would haul the catch into the canoe and detach it from the remora. Turtles weighing as much as a hundred pounds could be captured in this manner.

On this day, however, Cacimar had crossed the straight to the great island of Cubanacan so that he could be alone in thought. As his mind drifted, he trolled the warm waters of the tranquil green-blue sea for small fish for dinner. He was an enigma even to himself. While perfectly at home in his world, he felt out of place as if he were destined for something else. Yet many, many moons had passed with seldom any change apart from the great tropical storms that hit the islands every two or three seasons. When these storms came, the populations of all the villages would flee to the low mountains, making up the interior of the island, hauling their few possessions and their great canoes with them. Sometimes the storm would pass. Other times, it would attack the island with a fury that only the gods could create, and when the people returned to the site of their villages several days later, there would be nothing left of their huts. There would be no crying or gnashing of teeth, however, unless someone had been taken by the storm, for this was just a part of their lives. Everyone would busy themselves with rebuilding the villages' cane thatched huts and replanting the gardens that grew corn and potatoes and cotton and peanuts.

Sometimes the villages would trade amongst themselves and, less frequently, with the men of another island, or with the friendly Ciboney people. There was not a great need for such an exchange as the lives of the villagers on all the islands were the same, and food and housing materials were plentiful. Sometimes a young man would fall in love with a woman from another village or even another island, and this was encouraged unless that woman was already married. The islands provided more than enough to meet the needs of all the villages.

Cacimar was looking east, trying to imagine what lay beyond his vision. He had once paddled for three days toward the waters where the sun rose. He found himself in the middle of vast nothingness with only an occasional humpback whale for company. That had been the one time he could remember that he could feel fear in the pit of his stomach when there was nothing to really cause that fear.

His thoughts were abruptly extinguished when his fishing line went taut with a fierce sudden jerk. His small canoe was rocked violently, almost capsizing just before the line snapped. Cacimar grabbed at the sides of the craft to steady himself, but all was still once more. The sea was flat and calm, except…

Except for a slight wake first moving away from his canoe and now circling to return—a wake caused by the dorsal fin of a great white shark. Cacimar reached forward into his vessel and took hold of his sharp-pointed spear. Sharks rarely attacked a canoe, but then his was small, not the huge canoe used by his village.

The great white glided by Cacimar's craft. Rising slightly out of the water, its beady left eye was black as night and seemed to take in the vessel's human occupant. The shark's body length was easily the same as the canoe. Then, in an instant, it disappeared beneath the water.

With his right hand on his spear and watching the sea, Cacimar felt with his left for his paddle. As he was deciding how he could both propel his vessel and defend himself, the shark struck the canoe from its underside with such force that the paddle went flying into the air, landing in the water several feet away. His legs tense, Cacimar cautiously stood and scanned the clear waters surrounding his craft. From this higher vantage point, he could make out the form of the great white as it swung back toward the canoe. Was it making another pass or preparing to ram him again?

Setting his feet squarely on either side of his craft, he gripped his spear with both massive hands and waited. At the last minute, the shark veered and passed along the canoe's side. With all his might, Cacimar drove the spear into a precise spot on the upper neck of the great white. The shark shuddered and began to thrash and turn. Putting all his weight on the shaft, Cacimar drove the point deeper, probing for the creature's small brain. The canoe was rocked back and forth by the waves created by the thrashing brute as the young warrior held on for all he was worth, stabbing the spear within the shark's neck, ramming it into the space just behind the creature's terrifying black eyes. The minutes passed, and still, the battle raged. His arms were tight, tired, and stinging when the great fish gave one last violent lurch and then began to slowly roll over. Cacimar yanked the spear from the creature and, panting heavily and covered with sweat, knelt back in the canoe. There was no time to rest for the monster might have a mate and its blood would surely draw other sharks.

Using his cupped hands to propel his canoe, he brought it alongside the paddle floating a little way away, picked it up, and started to move away from the corpse now floating motionless, belly up, in the water. Shark meat, sliced and roasted, was delicious, but he would leave this fine fellow for the predators of the sea. His arms aching and weary, Cacimar began paddling back toward his village.

Chapter 9

They chose to meet in a private club on St. James' Street. James Madison enjoyed the seclusion afforded by the building but was not looking forward to the walk home. Perhaps he would invest in a carriage this evening. London was not a safe city at night, filled as it was by thieves and thugs and prostitutes who ventured out of the old rookeries of Seven Dials and Petticoat Lane to earn their livelihood when it grew dark. There were just not enough parish constables or night watchmen to patrol the streets outside the wealthier districts.

The city had a population of over half a million people with more coming in every day from the surrounding rural areas in search of employment in the factories springing up all about London. The countryside was still primarily pasture land, filled with sheep and cattle, as well as market gardens, but the manufacturing districts were spreading and now encompassed the entire east side of the city. Smoking kilns blackened the sky in Paddington and Kensington. London was expanding so fast that it was outstripping its street lighting.

Downstream along the Thames River, in Blackhall and Rotherhitle, were foul-smelling factories that boiled soap and made glue and tallow candles. Between them and the city, just below the Tower of London, were shipbuilding and import docks. Vessels were unloading their cargoes of tea, porcelain, silks, pepper, spices, mahogany, and teak. From these docks, cotton cloth from Lancashire, coal from Newcastle, and woolens from Yorkshire were loaded onto barges that would transport them up the river past the London Bridge. The Thames was full of barges and ferries, coming and going.

The main rooms on the first floor of White's Gentleman's Club boasted huge brand-new bay windows that looked out upon the street and provided ample light during the day. Large fireplaces were set in each meeting room. The rooms were quite grandiose with rich rugs covering their floors and hand-carved wall and ceiling panels. Each room had a large conference table and a number of comfortable chairs. Boarding rooms took up most of the second floor. Banned to women, this particular club had been built in 1736 to serve as both a retreat for men and as a gambling house.

Safely cloistered in a private room of the club, James Madison stirred the coals in the fireplace before turning toward his company. There was a chill in the air that filled the chamber except for the immediate vicinity of the freshly lit fire. Madison looked into the grim faces of the three men seated at the conference table.

"It is time that Perceval and the Tories were removed from power," said a rotund man with a red, ruddy face. William Corbett looked like a prosperous merchant, but he was not. The owner and publisher of an influential newspaper in London, Corbett, along with Madison, was a leading spokesman for Parliamentary reform. For years, he had urged the Whigs to fight for an increased voice in Parliament for all Englishmen, not just those with commercial and landed interests.

"The first minister has no direction." Corbett continued. "He fails to act, and in so doing, he supports the interests of our nation's enemies. It is time for a change."

"Hear, hear!" This came from a middle-aged man with a large nose and an extremely light complexion. Robert Owen was also a reformer, but his efforts were directed at the increasing number of industrial complexes. The advent of the industrial age had helped to bring England to its current world status, but industrialization also threatened the lives of the very workers who populated the multitude of factories springing up throughout the country. Their wages were minimal and their working conditions often deplorable. Few owners bothered themselves with such trivial issues as "safety." "Profit" was the centerpiece for industry.

"This government looks out solely for the wealthy," intoned Owen. "It gives not a farthing for the workers. It is time for change."

"I am in agreement, gentlemen, but not for all the same reasons you have repeatedly voiced although you know that I side with you on most of these issues," answered Madison. "Perceval has done nothing to better our country, but more importantly, he has done nothing to strengthen our nation. With the calamity that has befallen the Holy Roman Empire, will we not eventually find ourselves more severely tested? It is crucial that we move to strengthen the defenses of England and Brittany."

All four men sat in thought before Madison spoke again. "But who shall we endorse? Who can best lead the Whigs to power?"

"It is not the time to falter, James. Nor for modesty. As the leader of the opposition, you are that man."

Corbett, Owen, and Madison all turned toward the new speaker. He was a tall elderly individual with a freckled face and thin sandy hair, dressed in a slightly outdated suit. While never thought of as a good public speaker, his eloquent correspondence and ability to communicate on an individual basis had elevated him to leadership in the Whig Party. He was a former first minister and had the trust of all those who knew him.

"You are the one person who is not only respected by the Whigs," the older man continued, "but has the complete support of the military as well as the admiration of many in the Tory Party."

"But, Tom—" Madison started.

"He's right!" jumped in Owen. "You are the only man for the job. You best represent all the factions of our party. It is time that we raise the question as to whether or not our present military strength is adequate to defend the nation. You are the man best suited to present that question so that it is heard."

"But what of the Queen?" Madison asked.

"The Queen will continue to support the party that controls Parliament," responded Corbett. "She neither favors the Whigs nor the Tories. Queen Anne is a just leader, and she listens to her subjects."

James Madison peered into the fire. "Will you serve as my adviser, Tom?" he asked the older gentleman without looking up.

"I am sixty-eight years old and do not have your energy, James," answered the former first minister. "I would be pleased to be consulted now and again, but this is a new age. You are the future of our country."

With that statement, Thomas Jefferson rose and made his way out of the room.

Chapter 10

"Do you wish to rest, Your Majesty?"

The question abruptly jolted Anne back from her daydreaming. She gazed down from her slightly elevated throne at the individual who had spoken with the loud rasping voice and found herself once again in her court and looking at the personage of Spencer Perceval, the first minister of England.

How long has this man been droning on about the need to send troops to subdue the industrial unrest in Scotland? she thought to herself. *Has he no empathy at all for the factory workers? He certainly has no talent in persuasive speaking.*

*****

Thirty-five-year-old Queen Anne II had ruled England for the past decade following the death of her father, King James V. The House of Stuart's reign over the island kingdom was more than three hundred years old. In truth, the power of the crown had eroded somewhat over the past several centuries while, at the same time, the strength of the Parliament had grown, but the crown still wielded some power, even if that power was now more advisory than mandate. It had been Anne's namesake, her great-great-grandmother Queen Anne I, who had been the last monarch to veto an act of Parliament, and that had been back in 1712. Still, Parliament and the crown worked together to administer the country and its holdings.

The first Anne had married the fourth son of a minor German king and produced one male heir: Robert IV who ruled England from 1714 until his death in 1754. Robert proved instrumental in helping to ease the tension between the throne and the country's landowners. It had been his acts of reform that had led to the creation of a constitutional limited monarchy, wherein elected representatives of the Parliament carried out the nation's day-to-day affairs. Under the rule of Robert IV's son, Robert V, and his grandson, James V, the Parliament continued to become both the creator and implementer of national policy. The monarchy still had a say in all the major governmental issues and maintained its right of veto although this right had not been utilized for almost a century.

Over the past one hundred years, the owners of industry had become the individuals who held the real power in England. These were a substantial group of ambitious men who often squabbled amongst themselves even as they worked diligently to influence the military. Yet the military remained absolutely loyal to the government and the throne.

The English populace was forced to accept the industrial leaders, for they now controlled most of the nation's purse strings, but the common people's absolute loyalty and support were to the Queen. Realizing this, Parliament made every effort to work in tandem with the monarchy in running the government. Once each week, Queen Anne met with the first minister to be briefed, and consulted, about the affairs of the nation. She also met regularly with the leader of the opposition, her military commanders, and the bishop of the Roman Catholic Church of England. As were France, Spain, and Italy, England was a Catholic nation, and despite the weakening of the Vatican's power over the last decade, the pope was still given cursory acknowledgement.

As to her own government, Anne tried her stately best to side neither with the Tories nor the Whigs, both who strove to dominate Parliament. Over the past few years, however, her current first minister, the Tory Spencer Perceval, had worn her thin. Representing the owners of the countless factories and great estates that now spread across the land, the Tories were primarily responsible for raising England to its status as the greatest industrial nation on earth, but at what cost? The huge agricultural holdings were bankrupting the small farmers and throwing them off their land one by one, thus creating ever-increasing numbers of unemployed and angry drifters.

In the Midlands, there were reports of sabotaged textile production as the mechanization of the mills reduced the need for skilled workmen, thus adding to the ranks of the jobless. All the while, the Whigs cried for industrial reform.

Even more disturbing was Perceval's, and many of the Tory's, apparent disregard for what was happening in southern Europe.

*****

"Should I continue, Your Majesty?" the first minister again intoned, once again bringing the Queen back from her own thoughts.

"Yes"—Anne sighed—"but please move on to the disturbing news from London. Is it true that corpses are being sold?"

First Minister Perceval emitted an involuntary chortle before quickly composing himself.

"There appears that a number of businesses are springing up that deal in corpses, yes, Your Majesty," he replied while looking at his own feet. "Cadavers are being dug up from the cemeteries around London and sold to medical schools for anatomical exploration and practice in surgery. The reports indicate an adult corpse can be sold for as much as seven pounds while dead children are sold by the foot."

"How utterly shocking," gasped Anne while making the sign of the cross.

"Quite so, Your Majesty," deadpanned Perceval. "They say dentists are using the teeth of the deceased to make dentures for the rich. Of course, business is business, and I doubt the dead have much use for their teeth now, do they?"

Queen Anne shuddered.

Chapter 11

"You are familiar with the legends of the white god?"

The emperor's words were more of a statement than a question. All the citizens of the Aztec Empire were well versed in the religion and mythology intertwined with their history. That religion had evolved over the five hundred seasons since the founding of the city of Tenochtitlan—the city-state that had then expanded to create the Empire.

The legends proclaimed that a god named Quetzalcoatl came from the water to help guide the Aztecs when they were nomadic people, long before the founding of Tenochtitlan. It was this god who discovered maize, created fire, domesticated animals, taught the Aztecs music and dance, sired the royal lineages, and established the priesthoods while teaching them the art of "curandero," a diagnostic medical practice still in use. Quetzalcoatl had been distinguished from other gods by the whiteness of his skin.

When the Aztecs first entered their sacred valley, they had been a nomadic tribe that worshipped hundreds of gods. They settled down, raised crops, and built a capital city that was completed twenty-one seasons before the first fire ceremony, a season being calculated as the time it took for twelve full cycles of the moon to pass. The priests lit the eternal fires at the first fire ceremony to enable the gods to see the chosen people and watch over them. Ever since, history was recorded in terms of these observances, which occurred every fifty-two seasons. The priests approved the first emperor to govern the Aztec people thirty seasons after the first fire ceremony. After two fire ceremonies and forty-two seasons, Montezuma I came to power and began to carve out what was to become the Aztec Empire.

During the first several hundred seasons following the founding of Tenochtitlan, religion dominated the daily lives of the people. It was commonly accepted that the gods controlled human fate and therefore the destiny of the Empire. The priests who served these gods were their mouthpieces and thus held great power, second only to the emperor himself, who it was decreed descended directly from the gods.

As the decades passed, two gods gained greater prestige and stronger following than the others, and as the lesser gods lost favor and power, their priesthoods dwindled away and then disappeared. This came about as a result of two factors. First, as the Empire expanded its borders, taking in more and more land and people, the business of governing the Empire took more and more time away from the religious ceremonies demanded by the gods. Second, the sacrifices demanded by the myriad of gods resulted in the deaths of thousands of victims captured in war or paid in tribute. This practice was both abhorred and feared by the Aztecs' enemies. This dread stiffened their resistance and led to uprisings throughout the captured territories.

Six fire ceremonies and forty seasons after the founding of the Empire, Xolotl I came to power. A strong and wise emperor who was backed by both the nobility and the military, Xolotl reformed the Aztec religion and the political structure of the Empire.

The emperor acknowledged two gods as being all-powerful: Huitzilopochtli, the god of both war and the sun, and Tlaloc, the god of rain and fertility. He proclaimed these two deities to be the lords of all the gods. The priests who served the next two strongest gods (Chalchihuitlicue, the god of growth, and Xipc, the god of spring) were ordered to join the priesthood of Tlaloc. They dressed in blue, to symbolize the sky. The remaining priests, who had served Coyolxauhqui the moon goddess and the other lesser gods and goddesses, became members of Huitzilopochtli's priesthood. They dressed in red, the color of blood.

Xolotl then issued three major decrees that were to definitively strengthen the Aztec Empire. His first command called for a truce, ending the war with the Inca Empire that had raged for fifty seasons.

The emperor conceded all the lands to the southwest of the Aztec Empire to the Incas so that he could focus the energy of his military to the northwest and northeast.

Xolotl then eliminated all human sacrifice, except in time of great crisis or during the fire ceremony, which still occurred every fifty-two seasons. On these occasions, only great and honored chiefs from the newly conquered lands were to have their hearts cut from their still living, but drugged bodies, and offered to the two powerful gods.

The emperor's third decree brought great stability to the Aztec Empire. Xolotl divided the conquered lands into dominions, each governed by an appointed representative from the Aztec Empire working with a council of nobility selected from the people of those lands. Following a twenty-season period of tranquility, the inhabitants of dominion could petition for citizenship in the Empire with all its rights and privileges, and, upon acceptance, the annual tribute they paid to the Empire was cut in half.

With these reforms, resistance to the Empire decreased and eventually ended. The populations of the ever-increasing dominions grew to think of themselves as Aztecs, serving in the military and working with Tenochtitlan to support not only their domains but also the entire Empire.

*****

Mextli was a student of Aztec history and had read about Quetzalcoatl, the white god, of whom the emperor spoke.

"I am aware of the legends, O Great Ahuitzotl," Mextli replied. "Although I think of them as merely that…legends…myths…"

Behind the throne stood two priests, and at these words, they both scowled at the admiral.

"I, too, have my doubts." The emperor nodded. The two priests exchanged glances but held their peace. "As you are aware, I have continued to follow the practices established by Xolotl and carried out by those who have followed him. The Empire has never been as strong as it is today, and this can be directly linked to the elimination of the worship of the lesser gods and their accompanying nonessential sacrifices. I believe that two gods are enough, but I have recently received reports that have made me stop and think. They have also aroused my curiosity."

"Admiral," the emperor continued, "over the past two or three moon cycles, an intriguing story has come to my attention. Several of our merchants have heard the same tale while on their travels. The rumor is that white gods were seen on the outer islands of the Inland Sea hundreds of seasons ago. They say many different people living on a number of islands tell the same story. I want you to investigate these tales."

"Your wish is but my command, my emperor," replied Mextli. Then, lowering his voice, he added, "But I do not believe in these white gods."

Apparently, his voice had not been low enough, for one of the priests, dressed in the red coloring of the god of war, angrily stepped forward.

"You are a military man, Admiral," he exclaimed in a stern voice. "You best not offend the gods who protect you, especially the mighty Huitzilopotchli! You may find your head rolling in the dust."

Was that a threat on behalf of the god or a threat made by the priest? Mextli cared little. At one time, the priests dominated Aztec politics and exercised control over the emperor himself. Those days were now in the past. Influence? Yes, the priests still exercised some influence, especially over the superstitious commoners. But power? No, the priests no longer exercised power in the Empire.

Mextli simply smiled at the priest, a wicked half smile that turned the priest's face scarlet with rage. However, before any more words could be exchanged, the emperor spoke again.

"Let us continue our discussion by the ball court, Admiral. This is not an official matter for the imperial court but simply an interest of mine."

With that said, Ahuitzotl VI took Mextli's arm, and the two men walked through the back passages of the palace and away from the priests.

The ball court was built just outside and behind the palace. As they approached it, they could hear the shouts and cheers and hisses made by the game's spectators. Called a tlatchli, the court was made of stone. This one was 30 feet wide and 120 feet long, about mid-size in comparison to other courts. A ball game could be played in a smaller area by as few as two players or on a much larger surface by a great many individuals. High walls decorated by stone sculptures of jaguars and tropical birds ran along both sides of the court. Seated above the walls were hundreds of noblemen interspersed by food vendors and bet takers. At the center of each sidewall, or midcourt, was a large metal ring.

On the court were two teams of four players. They were dressed in thick leather yokes that wrapped around their waists, and each wore quilted cotton pads on their knees and elbows. A quilted cotton helmet completed their uniforms. These were dyed green or yellow, depending upon the team. They were professional players.

Using manoplas, or leather hand paddles, as well as their feet, knees, elbows, and hips, the players directed a hard rubber ball at one of the rings or their opponents' end zone. The ball was solid and weighed six pounds, and a direct impact on a player's vital parts could result in a serious injury and even death. Three points were awarded when a ball struck the wall in the center of one of the metal rings, and one point was earned when the ball got by the opposing team and rolled into their end zone.

In the early days of the Empire, the captains of the losing team would be decapitated. Myth had it that sometimes these heads would be used in place of the rubber balls, but no one was sure if this was true. Professional teams now played games before nobles and commoners alike, and gambling enhanced the sport's entertainment value.

During a lull in the game they were watching, the emperor turned to Mextli and said, "I really am fascinated by the reports from the islands. I want you to take time from your expedition to the Northeast Territories to stop there to determine if there is any truth to these stories."

Mextli smiled. "I do not think we will find anything, my emperor, but it honors me to carry out your request."

Chapter 12

The lush tropical forest was still, save for the buzzing of insects and an occasional birdcall. The broad green leaves were thick overhead, the palms forming a canopy that blotted out much of the light from the sky. Ferns filled the forest floor. Cacimar sat in a grove of cedar trees near the sacred place. Since his encounter with the great white shark, he had spent that last three days reflecting on his life. His life held little excitement. Cacimar now realized he could no longer continue to live the simple existence of an island villager. The calling in his heart was too strong, the urge to see what lay beyond his world too overpowering.

The sacred place sat in a large flattened hollow carved into the slope of the lower foothills of the mountains that rose in the center of the island that was his home. Further up the mountainside, it became cooler and dryer as the tropical forest gave way to pines. Much of the time, the higher peaks were shrouded in mist. The sacred place was where the inhabitants of the nearby villages fled when the great winds roared and the storms ravaged the island. This was also the place to which the elders came when they felt the need to meditate. Climbing into the mountains, one felt closer to the gods.

The storytellers said this particular sacred place had been the sanctuary of the islanders when the "white ones" had come to the island, bringing death and destruction. That was so long ago; no one was sure whether there was any truth to the tales. The sacred place had also been a refuge from the Caribs, but those fierce people had not been a menace to the villages for more than four generations now.

During the past several moons, Cacimar had spent more and more hours in conversation with Inez, the oldest and wisest person in his village. She was the official keeper of the village's history and was now in the process of passing the stories of her people on to her daughter who, in turn, was even now beginning to teach them to Inez's granddaughter. When Cacimar was a youth, he had spoken to other villagers about his yearning to leave the island and his belief there was something more beyond their homes. The villagers could not understand his feelings and whispered and laughed amongst themselves about his thoughts, so he stopped sharing them with everyone except Inez. She never laughed at Cacimar but urged him to have patience until the gods revealed their plans for his future.

Cacimar felt certain he could no longer wait. When gazing across the open waters at the empty horizon, he often felt tightness in his chest. This sensation was now intensifying, spreading throughout his entire body. He thought he would explode if he were forced to remain in such a small world much longer.

That afternoon, he had made a major decision. He would leave the islands after the next cycle of storms had passed less than a season away to see what lay beyond. This decision lightened his heart and his conviction filled him with joy.

Leaving the sacred place, he began the walk back toward his village. The trees seemed greener and the birdcalls merrier. He was in such a good mood; he decided to stop at a secluded pool to bathe. It would refresh him. The pool was small and seldom used by any of the villages unless a hunting party passed nearby. Continually fed by a mountain stream, its waters were clean and clear. Its runoff fed a larger stream further down the mountain.

Nearing the bathing pool, he heard the faint sounds of splashing water. As he rounded the large rock shaping one edge of the pool, his gaze fell upon a young woman. She was Mora, a beautiful youth of eighteen seasons from the next closest village on the island. Cacimar knew her father, a great fisherman. He had been trying to marry off his daughter for three seasons, but she had resisted the advances of all her suitors.

Mora was standing in the pool, the water up to her waist and her back turned to him, but she could sense his presence. Without showing any sign of fear, she slowly turned her head toward Cacimar.

A slight smile played upon her lips when she saw who stood there, and without hesitation, she turned her entire body toward the young man.

Cacimar took in a deep breath. She was dazzling. Her brown eyes sparkled brightly and her teeth were as white as the milky chamber of a junonia shell. Her breasts were rounded and full with brown nipples taut from the cold water of the pool. Her stomach was still the flat midriff of a young maiden.

Cacimar could feel his passion growing, and looking down, Mora could see the same. She began walking slowly toward him, moving gracefully out of the water, revealing the darkness of her pubic hairs and her long, slender, well-proportioned legs. Her smile broadened as he stood there in shock, taking in her beauty.

No words were spoken as she took the cloak from his broad shoulders and ran her hands over his muscular chest. After what seemed like an eternity, Mora stood on her tiptoes and gently kissed Cacimar's neck. A flood of warmth took hold of him as he reached out and brought her body into his, ardently returning her kiss.

The kiss lasted just a few seconds before she pushed herself away from him and looked into his puzzled eyes. Then, still smiling, she gently took hold of his arms and drew him back to her.

"I have yet to take a husband as I have forever dreamed of this day," she said softly, all the while guiding Cacimar to a large patch of soft moss by the side of the pool. "Tomorrow I will accept a suitor, but today, I belong only to you."

Chapter 13

The meeting room in the large house on Downing Street was packed. Seated at the oval table to Madison's left was Sir Arthur Wellesley, general of the armies and the commander of the English land forces. Wellesley was a stern taskmaster, a fact that did not make him beloved by his own troops, but he was respected and, more importantly, trusted. Brave and reliable, his men swore "his long nose could smell out the enemy well before they encountered them."

The first minister, Spencer Perceval, sat across the dark oak table. To either side of him sat Frederick Robinson, the Lord of the Admiralty, and William Wilberforce, a prominent Tory in the House of Commons. To Madison's right was George Spencer, also known as Lord Athorp, and an equally prominent member of the Whig Party in the House of Commons.

Also seated at the immense table was Mayer Amschel Rothschild, the financial genius who, in Madison's mind, was as responsible as the navy and army for maintaining England's power. To the right of Spencer sat George Clinton, a Whig and supporter of Madison. Filling the chairs positioned all along the wall behind these men were representatives from the courts of Frederick William III of Prussia and Alexander I of Russia, England's chief allies at the moment.

Arthur Wellesley pounded his fist upon the map of Europe laying on the table to his front. "Confound it, man! Can't you see France will be the next to fall if we sit here and do nothing?"

First Minister Perceval sat back in his chair and blinked. "Surely the Italians will be thrown back from any attempt to annex France. The Prussians have indicated they will send an army…"

"The Prussians! Damn the Prussians!" roared Wellesley. "King Louis will no more allow the Prussians into his country than we would. No, France will face the Kingdom of Italy alone, and alone they will fall."

"But, but…," stuttered the first minister.

"I think we need to look at the Italian's history, sir," injected James Madison looking at Perceval. Faint cries of "Hear, hear" echoed from the other politicians and military men assembled in 10 Downing Street. The house had been the former resident of William Pitt, the younger. The cabinet room, in which they now met, had been created at the turn of the century by knocking out a wall and inserting columns to extend a large dining room.

Madison continued, "You are well aware, sir, that this self-proclaimed Italian Caesar has designs as delusional as his military genius will allow. God knows how an individual from middle Corsican-Italian gentry came by this ability, but he certainly has demonstrated his prowess on the battlefield."

"His father was Carlo Buonaparte," explained George Spencer. "He was a minor nobleman. When the Republic of Genoa sold Corsica to France in 1768, he assisted Pasquale Paoli in driving out the French soldiers who tried to occupy the island. It is said his son wanted to be a soldier from birth. With Paoli's influence, Carlo got Napoleone admitted to the Military Academy in Piedmont. He was a scrapper who relished a good fight, and he eventually rose to the rank of lieutenant colonel in the Piedmont regular army. During those years, he was notorious for trying to convince all who would listen that Italy had the potential to return to the glory days of the Roman Empire. 'The peninsula is a mass of undisciplined splintered nations,' he would shout with both enthusiasm and zeal to anyone who would listen, and this fragmentation is preventing Italian destiny.' Of course, no one took him seriously at the time."

"If only the bastard had been killed during that farce of a revolution in France." First Minister Percival sighed. "I hear he was a friend of Robespierre's younger brother and led the Piedmont troops who revolted on the French-Italian border. When King Louis's armies defeated the revolutionaries, he melted back into Italy, but he had gained a peculiar loyalty from those who served under him. Even the senior Piedmont generals recognized what they termed his demonic genius.

"I can understand how he came to power," Perceval continued after a few seconds pause. "The Italian states were a hodgepodge of small kingdoms, each ruled by petty feudalistic lords. The northern states were under the thumb of the Holy Roman Empire. When this self-proclaimed unifier of the new Roman Empire came along, the people swarmed to his banner."

"He was a smart one, this Napoleone Buonaparte was," said Madison. "He went after the small states first, and as his successes grew, so did his army. He first unified the south and then marched north. The Hapsburgs did not recognize this threat until after the grand duchy of Tuscany fell. Lombardy went over to Buonaparte without a fight. The people rose and drove the Austrians out themselves. By 1798, all Italy was under his control."

"If that had only been the end of it," interjected the First Minister. "We warned the Hapsburgs. We warned Francis II that his so-called Holy Roman Empire was nothing more than a collection of weak German states, no more powerful than Italy had been and that he needed to consolidate and mobilize. But he wouldn't listen."

"But is there really a threat now? There has been peace in Europe for the last four years," William Wilberforce said half-heartedly. "Isn't this Napoleone now focusing on internal affairs?"

"That is a dangerous line of thought, Mr. Wilberforce," Wellesley said in a booming voice. "The Italians have been making threatening overtures toward both France and Spain. Louis XVI and Charles IV are trying to placate Buonaparte with favorable trade deals, but that will not keep the tyrant at bay for long. Our informants have told us the Italians have a large army training under General Severoli. My guess is France is next on his list of probable conquests. We must not underestimate him!"

"And there is worse news," Frederick Robinson announced. "Italy's naval forces have begun to attack shipping, including our own! Buonaparte claims these are attacks by privateers and not the Italian navy, but they are attacks nevertheless."

"First Minister…gentlemen," Madison said, looking around the room. "It is no longer the time to simply discuss these matters. It is time to act."

Chapter 14

The island was exceptionally large, a sweltering tropical paradise filled with bright flowers and a wide variety of brilliantly colored birds. It was situated to the immediate east of an even larger island that the natives called Cubanacan. Still further east was many smaller islands stretching away from the Inland Sea into the great unending Eastern Sea.

The island's shore was covered with a myriad of thick lush plants and towering trees. Forested mountains made up its interior. Green vines and brush seemed to cover everything that had not been cleared by the local villagers who lived in their straw huts just off the beach of a medium-sized cove. The natives' lives were relaxed and uncomplicated as there were fish and small game as well as abundant fruit in ample supply.

This was the fourth such village Mextli and his crew had visited, and there were many more spread along the coasts of this island and the other islands they had visited. In each settlement, the admiral had met with the village chiefs, and the wise men and storytellers of the hamlets, as he tried to track down the legend of the white god. Traveling in a southeast direction, tales of this "white god" became stories of the "white gods," and now, on this island, the "white ones." With each new lead, Mextli's curiosity quickened. He was now beginning to believe that he was close to discovering something unusual but something of substance. There seemed to be some truth to the legends of the "white gods," but that truth was still a mystery.

*****

The villagers in their current locale had greeted the arrival of Mextli's flagship in awe. The Aztecs had found this to be true at each of their previous stops on the islands. Their vessel was now beached nearby. The natives in this village had heard stories about the clumsy large merchant ships of the "tall ones" who had last visited their island generations ago, but no one now living had ever seen such an immense man-made structure. Its hull dwarfed the village's great canoe.

Fashioned of thick wooden planks secured by mortise and tenon joints, the warship was propelled by two levels of twenty oars each arranged in rows on either side of the craft. Eighty sailors powered these oars, one per oar. There were another forty sailors on board, as well as five officers and fifty soldiers. The soldiers were armed with devices made of wood and metal called thundersticks. Larger versions of these weapons stood on the front and rear deck of the ship.

A large wooden post, called a catch holder, stood in the center of the vessel and a smaller one jutted out from its front at a forty-five-degree angle. Toward the rear of the deck was a cabin for the officers. A tiller attached to an elevated platform behind this cabin was connected to a pair of steering blades. Two huge logs, called outriggers, ran parallel to the hull on either side of the ship just beyond the range of the oars. These were connected to the front and rear of the hull by perpendicular poles. These logs prevented the craft from capsizing in a rough sea or an extremely strong wind when under sail.

The soldiers and crew slept below deck to the front and rear of the ship. The center of the vessel could hold upwards of two hundred tons of cargo. Merchant ships could hold up to four hundred tons and were used to transport troops, or colonists, and to carry tribute back to the homeland from the far-flung reaches of the Empire.

The Aztec sailors and soldiers had set up camp around the beached ship and were enjoying the fresh food of the island. The villagers brought them cassava bread made from cooking the yucca plant over an open fire. They also provided clay plates filled with the meat of geese and turtles, as well as the flesh of boiled iguana. Fruits of all kinds topped off the feast: papaya, guava, and piña. Their guests were also provided with a mildly alcoholic beverage, fashioned from the juice of the yucca.

*****

Mextli, Tecocol, and the other officers sat in the center of the village, with the chief and elders, enjoying these delicious offerings. They were in the community's plaza surrounded by clean dwellings made of wooden frames, straw, and cane thatch. The chief's hut was large and rectangular. It was called a bohios. The remainder of the population lived in smaller round huts. The huts were sparsely furnished with earthen floors and sleeping hammocks made of cotton cloth.

This village was constructed a hundred paces into the jungle away from the beach. A wide straight path, similar to a road back in the Empire, led from the beach area to the dwellings. Beautiful gardens surrounded the village, and to the south were orchards of citron and orange trees.

Mextli's guide was an elderly woman. With her, acting as an interpreter, was a young man of massive proportions, broad of shoulder, and wearing a cloak of brightly colored cotton. Old and shriveled, the woman was named Inez. She told Mextli a story that had been handed down to her from her mother and her mother's mother. Inez was the village storyteller, the keeper of the history of her people, and her people, who called themselves the Taino, could not remember ever having lived anywhere but on the islands at the edge of the Inland Sea.

According to Inez, life and time remained relatively unchanged for the Taino, except for three major events in their history. The initial event had occurred many, many generations ago when the tall ones first arrived on their shores. Mextli knew of this incident from his own Aztec history. It had occurred approximately three hundred seasons in the past when his people had first explored the islands on the Inland Sea.

Inez described the tall ones as much like themselves, but massive and warlike. Fortunately, there was nothing of worth for them to take and they soon left. Every now and then, they would reappear, usually when a storm drove their merchant ships to seek the safety of a harbor or when a ship was wrecked and its crew cast ashore, but these happenings were extremely rare and had not occurred on this island for quite some time. These sporadic episodes had significance in the Taino's history as the assimilation of these castaways, for however brief a period, led to the birth of stronger children and a temporary break from the villagers' routine existence.

Once or twice a tall one had chosen to stay on the island and take a mate. Nodding at the young man who was translating her words, Inez indicated that her interpreter was the descendent of one such man who had been shipwrecked four generations before. A minor leader of the tall ones, the newcomer had been celebrated for his strength and his intelligence, and he often talked about his former life and the great empire that lay to the west of the Inland Sea. Although adopting the Taino language and their ways, he had passed his own native language down to his son and his grandson. Mextli was mildly interested by these stories, but they were not of real consequence to his quest.

The tales fascinated Cacimar who was acting as the interpreter. This was the first time he had ever heard Inez speak of lands to the west. His heart had not stopped racing since he had first seen the gigantic ship and the tall men who called themselves Aztecs.

Inez paused and drank a cup of water before continuing. She said the second important event occurred under the leadership of the shipwrecked man from the west, who the old woman called Cacama. Apparently, a warlike and cannibalistic people called the Caribs inhabited the chain of islands to the east of Ayti, the island on which this village was built. The Taino were a peaceful people and fled before the raids of the Caribs, but these raids had been increasing for many generations. Cacama united all the villages of the Taino, as well as those of the neighboring Cibaney, trained the men in the art of war, and led them against the Caribs. They took the cannibals by surprise and systematically killed all the men and boys while driving the women from the islands.

It was a terrible time for the Taino and Cibaney as these people abhorred killing. Yet this was the only way they knew to eliminate the threat to their own existence. When the Caribs were finally vanquished, the Taino burned their bloodied weapons and returned to their villages, vowing to their gods never to kill again. That vow had yet to be broken by the villages.

These tales were fascinating, but it was the storyteller's third major event that transfixed the admiral. According to Inez, more than half the time again from when the tall ones first came to Ayti, the white ones had visited the island. They were as large as the tall ones but fiercer and armed with powerful weapons. And they smelled like death itself.

According to her tale, the white ones did not last long. They arrived on the island from the sea and cleared a patch of forest a half day's walk from Inez's village. They built huts of wood from planking similar to that used to fashion the Aztec warship, then they surrounded those huts with a wall of stakes and brush. Once this fortification was completed, the white ones attacked the village and forcibly took young men and women to be their slaves.

The elders cursed the white ones and called upon their gods to wreak vengeance upon these foul beings, and the gods complied. The white ones grew sick, and most died. The Taino who had been taken captive turned on the few survivors, who were far too sick to defend themselves, and killed those who remained. Fearful of the illness that destroyed these powerful invaders, the elders gathered their lifeless bodies, and they were burned. The fences were torn down, the huts too were set afire, and the entire area was marked off as a place infested by evil spirits to be avoided at all costs.

The village chief then reluctantly assembled the young people who had suffered at the hands of the white ones. He decreed that these youths had lived in the midst of the white one's evil and it now permeated their beings. They had also broken the Taino's vow and killed. The young people were given a large canoe and tearfully told they must leave their home forever. When they left, a small animal was sacrificed to the gods to prevent more evil ones from coming to the islands. This must have worked as the white ones were never seen again.

"These white ones do not sound like gods to me," Tecocol told Mextli when they were back in the privacy of their own ship. "They do not sound like the legend of Quetzalcoatl."

"I do not know what to make of this," answered the admiral, "but tomorrow, the old one will take us to the site where the white ones were said to have their dwellings. The Taino will not go near the place and have not for hundreds of seasons, but I intend to give the entire area a good going over."

*****

The next morning, Inez and her interpreter led Mextli and a dozen soldiers along a faint, overgrown path that wandered inland through the jungle, parallel to the northern coast. It was apparent the trail had not been used for a long, long time, and equally obvious was the fact that Inez was growing increasingly edgy as the group proceeded. In many places, the trees and vegetation shut out the sun, and the resulting darkness made the path hard to follow, but the older woman never faltered and continued to lead the way. The trail traversed over several large hills and then began to descend toward a location west of the village but still on the northern side of the island. Parrots squawked and white-faced monkeys scampered overhead.

The trail had long ago become seemingly nonexistent to Mextli's eyes when he began to hear the sound of waves washing against the offshore coral-coated rocks. Inez was following a faint opening in the tropical leaves. The Aztec could not see the opening. It appeared to the admiral that she was simply moving through the areas of least resistance. As the sounds of the sea increased, Inez's pace slowed until she stopped altogether.

"This is as far as I go," she said turning to Mextli. "From here to the beach is forbidden land. Evil lurks there. No one has come to this place since the last of the white ones died. I do not think you should go either."

"I thank you for your words and your willingness to take us this far," the admiral replied through Cacimar. "Our gods will watch over us. We have no fear." Glancing at his men, Mextli was not so sure this was true. Many of the soldiers were clutching amulets worn to protect them from evil.

"Let us see what this myth is all about," he said to his men, trying to keep bravado in his voice. "I will wager you a keg of chicha we will find no more than this thick green forest that surrounds us and perhaps a few white-faced monkeys. At least, by the sound of things, we can get out of this accursed vegetation and onto the white sands of the beach." With these words, Mextli left Inez and her interpreter and led his crew in the direction of the waves.

*****

Tecocol was the first to find anything. After spending half of the afternoon stomping through the thick plants and underbrush that grew to the very edge of the beach that formed a secluded cove, he tripped over what he thought to be a large branch. Cursing the object and attempting to lift it so he could break it into pieces, Tecocol noticed that smaller branches had been chopped off the limb. With the aid of one of the soldiers, he pulled the object from the dense foliage in which it was entrapped to discover it was five feet long and had once been sharpened at the far end. This set off cries for Mextli and the rest of the party.

Clearing away the thick leaves and brush where this stake had been found, the partial remains of a fence were revealed. Only bits and pieces were still intact, but it appeared a stockade might have once existed here long, long ago. Most of the branches that would have made up the wall were long since decayed, but a few sections of the fence had been buried in compost and dirt and remained fairly recognizable.

Mextli then had his men investigate the area in the approximate center of this enclosure. Most of whatever had once been there had returned to the forest, but they were excited to find the remains of several wooden planks buried beneath the dirt and leaves of the jungle. After another quarter of a day spent pulling away vines and other growth, just as the setting sun was nearing the horizon, they made two startling finds.

The first was a metal pot, worn away by rain and rust, but with definite markings carved into it. The second was a length of hollow metal tubing attached to trigger housing. The wooden stock no longer existed, and the tube was rusted, but it was apparent that it had once been a thunderstick, not so dissimilar in design to those presently in use by the Aztec military. Yet it appeared this device had been buried on this remote island for an extremely long time.

Chapter 15

It was a lavish affair, a grand ball held in what had become referred to as the Queen's house, otherwise known in London as the Buckingham House. The three-story building was originally the Duke of Buckingham's townhouse, but it had been given to Anne's predecessor in the latter part of the eighteenth century. The house was a huge rectangular block connected by colonnades. There were plans to begin the construction of three wings around a central courtyard, but the recent activities in Europe had deviated much of the funding that had been earmarked for this enterprise. Still, great expense had been put into remodeling the building's interior.

The main rooms of the Buckingham House were a profusion of gilt and color. The ballroom featured brightly colored stucco columns that resembled marble, a technique that had been developed in Italy and had been popular well before Napoleone had come into power. Pink and blue lapis, a semiprecious stone from the northeast of India, sparkled in the ceiling. Red carpet covered the floor.

Despite all this gaiety, the ceilings in most of the rooms of the great house were blackened and often smelled of smoke. This was because the chimneys did not provide the ventilation they should have, causing a fair amount of their emissions to remain in the rooms. As a result, the staff used the fireplaces as seldom as possible, and the entire house was usually quite chilly in the winter. The ballroom was an exception, partially because it was so large, partially because it had been submitted to an intense scrubbing, and primarily because there was no need for the fireplaces to be lit this evening. It was late July, and the room was packed with hundreds of men and women.

As the noblemen and ladies entered the chamber, they presented their invitations to an impeccably dressed footman. The men were dukes, earls, and counts, all dressed in stunning uniforms or dark fine suits. The women wore loose colorful dresses that, although they dropped to their ankles, would allow them freedom of movement as they danced across the floor. Candlelight sparkled off their pearl, gold, diamond, and ruby necklaces.

The room was filling up, and it smelled of perfume and powder and perspiration. The windows had all been opened to allow a faint breeze to gently move the thickening air. The guests made every effort to look pleasant in the summer heat as they politely greeted one another and made small talk. There were seats all along the walls of the chamber and a refreshment table not far from the orchestra. The musicians sat on an elevated stage at the far end of the great room away from the huge arch of the main doorway. There was a buzz in the air as tonight a new dance would be introduced, a dance called the waltz. The older nobles had resisted the introduction of the waltz to English gatherings as they claimed it, quite unlike the minuet, was both immoral and lascivious. This added to the excitement of the evening.

Queen Anne II sat on a chair to the far end of the refreshment table. With her sat Madalyn, Sir James Townsend, her privy counselor, and Count William of Hesse-Kassel. William was a blond giant of a man, six feet three inches tall, young, and extremely handsome. He was dressed in a gorgeous silver-and-black uniform. The Queen's strikingly attractive maids of honor stood all around her, acting as a buffer between her and the growing crowd. Anne was dressed in a pale dress of delicate blue. As was the case with the rest of the women in the room, her neckline was cut low to expose her neck, shoulders, and well-formed cleavage. In her hand, she held a scepter. Her reddish-brown hair was piled on top of her head, accentuating her strong facial features and natural beauty, but Anne's face was flushed with irritation.

"We are tired of your prattling, Sir James," the Queen said to her privy counselor and vice-chamberlain, looking him directly in his eyes. "We are aware of your impatient with us, but we grow tired of your nagging."

Sir James Townsend looked concerned. "You know I only think of England, Your Majesty. I realize we have talked about this pressing matter many times in the past, but your line and your nation are in need of sons, of an heir. Parliament keeps asking me if you have plans for marriage and there are a number of impressive…"

"I support Her Majesty's request," interrupted the young man with a smile. He spoke excellent English with just a trace of a German guttural accent. "Queen Anne knows that I am one of her greatest admirers and worship her as a woman, but a ball is a place for dancing and merriment, not politicking."

"You are right, Count William," the privy counselor acknowledged with a sigh of frustration, "but our current situation is unprecedented. It is unheard of that England should not have a king to rule by the Queen's side."

"Perhaps the Queen does not wish to share her power," the first lady of the bedchamber interjected, her face looking as upset as Anne's.

"This is not your affair, Madalyn," Anne said with a faint smile. Turning back to her privy counselor, she continued, "Your concern touches us, Sir James, and we understand that you are under as much pressure as we, but William is right. This is neither the time nor place to have this discussion. Let us begin the ball."

"I readily agree, Your Grace," the count proclaimed with enthusiasm, and then with a quick wink, he added, "But who knows, my queen, perhaps our futures may intertwine elsewhere than on the dance floor."

The Queen now gave William her full radiant smile before turning to join her maids of honor and making her way toward the center of the room. Her first lady of the bedchamber glowered at the count's audacity and then followed. Moments later, Sir James Townsend took a step closer to the German noble.

"She confounds me," the privy counselor said softly. "Does not she recognize the nation's need to have a man help guide her rule? And has she no physical needs of her own, no passion? She is the Queen, but she is also human."

Count William only smiled.

Chapter 16

When the Aztecs and Inez parted company, Cacimar waited until Mextli and his men were out of sight before turning to the old woman. His heart was heavy, but he now knew where his destiny lay.

"I must go," he told Inez. He had not really realized until now how much she meant to him. She had been his confidant, his teacher, and his protector. He would miss her friendship and her wisdom.

With moist eyes, the old woman reached up and caressed the young man's face, gazing upward into his eyes as if she were trying to see something beneath their surface. Then, without a word, Inez turned and slipped away into the forest. Cacimar watched her disappear before turning to follow the Aztecs.

He crept forward cautiously, staying slightly off the trail and following the sounds made by Mextli and his soldiers as they worked their way clumsily through the heavy foliage. Finally reaching the beach at the end of the trail, they spread out and began a systematic search of the area. Some of the Aztecs walked along the water's edge while others backtracked as far as 150 paces into the jungle. They tramped down the brush, and every now and then, one would stop to dig under the dense plant growth. On a number of occasions, someone would shout excitedly and Mextli would run over to look at a branch or a stick. Cacimar could not imagine why these objects would cause such excitement or what they were searching for under the canopied forest. As the daylight began to fade, they all became particularly exhilarated when one of them discovered what appeared to be pieces of metal buried in the jungle.

Cacimar had no idea what they were doing, but he felt vibrant and thrilled. And extraordinarily, he had followed the Aztecs into this sacred ground without a hint of fear. As the night began to fall, he made a decision.

*****

The next morning, as Mextli led his party back along the forest path, Cacimar ran swiftly ahead. Skirting the village, he waited near the beach for the Aztecs to return. Just as he had expected, when they arrived the sailors and soldiers who had camped by their ship left their stations to gather around their leader to learn what he had found. There was a great commotion as the admiral displayed the objects discovered in the forest.

No one noticed Cacimar as he slipped silently into the warm sea, inhaled, and dived beneath its waters. He swam unerringly to the rear of the large Aztec warship that had been partially beached on the white sand, his head breaking the water just behind its wooden rudder. Climbing nimbly up the backside of the great ship, he cautiously looked over the rear railing. There was no one on board. Further up the beach, he could see the Aztecs crowded around Mextli.

Stealthily, lest there be someone left on board to guard the craft, Cacimar made his way around the cabin structure and down into the hold of the ship. He passed by a set of upper and lower rowing benches. Each bench had oars stowed under them and were built securely by an open port that could be closed by a wooden shutter. From here, he climbed down a ladder into the darkened interior of the vessel. All about him were large barrels full of maize and potatoes and other vegetables he had never seen before. Strange four-legged animals squawked or bleated from cages. There were also barrels of foodstuffs he recognized from the islands. Great skins had been sewn together and hung from overhead beams. These were filled with drinking water.

Quietly, Cacimar slipped behind the largest collection of barrels in the darkest recesses of the hold and made himself as comfortable as possible. He planned to remain there for quite some time.

Chapter 17

The Madison's home was a three-story terraced building constructed in the Georgian style just off Oxford Street by Hanover Square. Not as fancy as the huge elegant residential homes found in the nearby West End, it was never the less quite comfortable and well-furnished. Similar houses, sharing a common brick wall, stood to either side of the Madison's. A great many glass windows filled the front and back walls, with those facing the main street also looking out upon a communal garden in the center of a square. To the northwest was the recently finished Regent's Park, a beautiful place for afternoon strolls, or picnics of chicken or beef washed down by wine.

Comfortably seated in the drawing room of their home, Rebecca Madison politely asked her husband's two guests if they would care for some tea. Thomas Jefferson nodded in the affirmative as she knew he would. The elderly Jefferson was known for his sweet tooth and usually put as many as two or three lumps of sugar into a single cup of the hot beverage.

"I will decline, Mrs. Madison," replied the second guest. "I lost my taste for tea while in India."

George Canning, despite his baldness, possessed an elongated and youthful face. Canning had been appointed secretary of state for foreign affairs by William Pitt at the young age of twenty-six. In this capacity, he toured India. Now having returned to London, he was a strong supporter of both Madison and strengthening the English military.

"Perhaps some warm milk then," asked Mrs. Madison. Rebecca was ten years younger than her husband. She was a lively woman with curly red tresses, a spring to her step, and an extremely curious nature.

"Perhaps a gin and tonic," said Thomas Jefferson. "I believe that is George's acquired taste."

"It is a taste acquired as the result of a slight bout with malaria," Canning replied as he nodded in approval. Rebecca Madison rose, mixed the drink, and served it before retaking her seat next to the fireplace to knit.

"I appreciate the two of you coming to my home," Madison began. "I intend to press Parliament on our plans for the expansion of the army and the navy, but I am first keen to learn your insights as to what is happening in the rest of the world. General Wellesley has kept me up to date with daily reports on the activities of Buonaparte. It appears he is expanding his naval forces, but as of yet, he seems content to wage his 'unproclaimed' war on the shipping lanes. I believe that Wellesley's fears of Italian aggression are valid, however. There is no doubt in my mind that Napoleone has designs in Europe. France will be next, and there is no doubt that his eyes feast on England like those of a Frenchman watching the dancers at the Folies Bergeres.

"Tell me, George," Madison continued after taking a sip of his tea, "What is the news out of India?"

"The East India Trading Company is doing quite well," replied Canning. "The company just celebrated its two hundredth anniversary since the granting of its charter. As a result of our victory over the Maratha Confederacy six years ago, the country has been peaceful, and our imports have risen sharply."

"That is good and reassuring." Madison sighed. "I would like to see us also expand into China, but the continual civil wars in that region make a total hash of that country. No, Napoleone must be dealt with before we think of any further trade centers. What of our allies, Thomas?"

Thomas Jefferson settled back in his chair and, as was his nature, reflected upon this question before answering.

"Sweden is staying neutral at the moment," Jefferson replied after half a minute's pause. "I believe they feel unthreatened and thus uncommitted at this time. Frederick William is building a large army in Prussia. He will put his forces in the field to support France against Buonaparte if Louis requests his aid. Alexander is also mobilizing, but he is reluctant to send assistance. Speaking of Alexander, there is a fascinating story from our embassy in Russia."

Jefferson hesitated before continuing, looking pleased as the others in the room leaned forward slightly in expectation.

"Our ambassador sent a sealed report providing details of a Russian expedition led by an Alexander Baranov that crossed the Bering Sea and entered Alaska in search of furs. After passing through some very uninviting territory, this party turned south and ventured several hundred miles along the coast of that land. They reported Pacific currents that warmed the air even in the winter months, and they discovered native people living by the sea who told them stories of a vast empire still further south. Eventually, they returned without having encountered anyone from this so-called empire, but they also returned rich with pelts."

"Good god, man," Canning exclaimed, "the Russians sent an expedition across the Bering Strait? You have read, of course, that the noted geographer James Rennell theorizes that the land they claim in Alaska may be connected in some way to the Colombo Islands. What of the plague? Are they mad?"

The mystery and horror of the Colombo Islands still generated fear in the hearts of all Europeans even though it had been well over 300 years since that ill-fated venture and more than 450 years since the Black Death had swept the continent.

"Please forgive me," intoned the small but inquisitive voice of Rebecca Madison. "I am aware of the plagues, but I am quite illiterate when it comes to history. What are the Colombo Islands?"

All three men made the sign of the cross when Rebecca uttered the word "plagues," then Madison and Canning turned to Jefferson, who was an avid historian.

"You are well aware that the Black Death, brought to Europe by Italian merchant ships sailing from China in 1347, was devastating," Jefferson began. "The disease struck down and killed people with terrible speed. In Venice alone, 60 percent of the city's citizens died over an eighteen-month period. The bodies of the dead, covered with black spots, were burned as fast as they possibly could be, but only the winter months seemed to slow down the sickness. The Black

Death killed one-third of the inhabitants of Europe, reducing its population from seventy-five million to fifty million. By the end of the following century, however, the outbreaks of this plague became limited to smaller, isolated cases, and Europe's population had grown back to sixty million."

"Little did they know the Black Death would just be the start," muttered Canning.

"Yes," continued Jefferson. "It paled in comparison to the Colombo Plague."

After a moment of silence, Jefferson continued, "The year 1492 was a dark one for all Europe. It was the year that set back civilization and shrank the world. Just as Napoleone threatens us now, it was again an Italian who brought Europe to its knees. His name was Cristoforo Colombo, and he was an adventurer. He persuaded the queen of Spain to furnish him with three ships to sail to the west in search of China. We are now fairly certain many islands lay between the two coasts of Europe and Africa and the lands of the East, but in those days, it was thought that nothing but a great ocean stretched between the three continents.

"Colombo left with three ships, the *Santa Maria*, *Nina*, and *Pinta*. He believed that if he sailed far enough west, he would reach India. Six months later, two of the ships returned. They reported that the *Santa Maria* sank off the coast of a tropical island containing great riches. As a result, thirty-nine men had been left on the island that Colombo named Espanola. He had believed he was off the coast of Asia. The islanders had not been oriental, however, but dark-skinned like Arabs.

"Not long after the two ships returned, their crews fell ill. They grew feverish, and a rash appeared on their faces and then spread to cover the rest of their bodies. The rash developed into painful blisters on their skin. As the fever intensified, the sailors suffered from delirium and lost consciousness. All but eighteen, including Colombo himself, died cruel deaths from this disease. The eighteen who survived were marked. Scars pitted their faces and bodies.

"Within a month, the Colombo Plague spread throughout Spain. During the next three months, it spread across Europe. The pope, Alexander VI, issued a decree quarantining the Colombo Islands as he lay on his deathbed, his face covered by the rash that characterized the illness. The decree proclaimed that anyone seeking to sail west beyond the sight of land was to be excommunicated and then burned at the stake. The warning was too late to stop the Colombo Plague, however. As it spread, it deformed, and it killed. When the disease had run its course, half of Europe that had survived the Black Death lay dead."

"How horrible!" gasped Rebecca Monroe.

"Interestingly," continued Jefferson, "no nobility died as a result of the Black Death. This was not true with the Colombo Plague. In England, King Henry VII died in 1494 along with his two-year-old son and heir Henry VIII. It was the end of the line of the Lancastrians and the Yorkists. England, as was the rest of Europe, was thrown back into the dark ages. Panic and turmoil grasped the hearts of the stoutest of men. On the continent, law and order vanished. The masses rioted, thinking it was doomsday. Feudal lords emerged, each trying with little avail to seal off their own lands from the plague. It took nearly half a century to restore a degree of stability on the European mainland.

"England experienced the same panic. Bands of brigands roamed the countryside looting and pillaging. The small numbers of populace who retained their faith gathered together in communities around the larger churches, but others forsook the Lord God and fell upon the righteous.

"In 1497, twenty-four-year-old James IV of Scotland, a land of isolated villages that did not suffer as severely as the rest of the isle from the plague, marched an army south and took control of England. James put down the bandits and began to rejuvenate the country. He was welcomed by the English people and strongly supported by those who had tried to maintain a semblance of government. James closed the ports and sent armed men to protect the farming communities. The country rallied to their new king."

"And he enforced the pope's decree," interjected Madison. "In 1497, John Cabot was captured when he tried to sail west and burned at the stake."

"That is true," said Jefferson. "God knows what Cabot may or may not have brought back from those western islands.

"With law and order, England grew strong while the rest of Europe fought amongst itself. As the years passed and no new reports of the Colombo Plague surfaced, we English grew bolder. In 1513, we sent troops into Brittany. In 1532, we began to colonize the coast of Europe, thus our present-day settlements in Portugal and the English Netherlands. Governments began to reform and take control in Sweden, Austria, Prussia, Russia, and later, in France. Germany and Italy remained broken into many states although the Austrian Hapsburgs began exercising more and more control over the loosely formed Germanic and northern Italian states."

"Until Napoleone," exclaimed Canning.

"Again yes, until Buonaparte united the Italian states and defeated the Hapsburgs," replied Jefferson before returning to his discourse. "As you know, London now has a sizable population of five hundred thousand. Imagine what its population, and that of England and Europe, would be if there had not been the Black Death and the Colombo Plague. I would wager that European nations would rule the world."

"What most people do not know, however, is that a second expedition, after Colombo, returned from the deadly western lands," said Madison.

"What!" gasped Canning. "You must be mad? I have not read this. When? Where?"

"In 1637, an explorer named Peter Minuit was secretly commissioned by the king of Sweden to explore the islands north of the Colombo Islands," answered Jefferson. "Sweden only lost a third of its population to the Colombo Plague and its kingdom included parts of Norway, Finland, and several states in Germany. King Gustavus Adolphus believed the threat of the plague was over, that it had run its course a century before, and he was convinced there were riches to be taken on the Colombo Islands. As a Protestant, he was not bothered by the papal mandate, forbidding him to sail west, but he did not want to risk the wrath of the other European rulers, so he kept his intentions to himself and a few trusted Swedish leaders. He ordered Minuit to sail to these new lands and then remain there for six months. If the Colombo Plague infected his crew, he was not to return to Sweden.

"According to the little we now know, Minuit found a land rich in forests and game but devoid of gold or silver. He and his crew did contract the Colombo Plague, unfortunately. Only it did not affect them as severely as those poor Italian sailors 150 years before. Although half of his crew grew sick, only three died. Minuit was stricken by the disease but survived. He waited in the new territory, living off the land for over a year, and then risked returning to Sweden. Gustav was overjoyed when he learned of the explorer's return, but when he was told that Peter had been exposed to the disease and that his face had been pitted as a result of it, he had Minuit and his crew quarantined in an isolated mountain village. The Colombo Plague infected the people in that village, but once again, only half grew sick and only a few died.

"Still, the return of the Colombo Plague caused great fear among the Protestant leaders in Sweden. The church urged Gustav Adolphus to kill Peter Minuit, as well as all the remaining villagers, and burn the town to the ground. Gustav reluctantly followed his church's prodding and had the village and its inhabitants destroyed, but he remained loyal to Minuit. Peter and his crew were provided with all they would need to live a comfortable life, but they were condemned to remain within a large stockade far from civilization for the rest of those lives. Minuit spent the rest of his days writing of his explorations and never left his prison. He reported a land settled by gentle friendly savages. By his estimate, it was a huge island that seemed to stretch endlessly westward, and its temperatures were similar to that of Sweden."

"Fascinating," exhaled Rebecca Madison.

"Do you suppose," asked James Madison, "that Europeans could have gained some sort of resistance to the Colombo Plague in the century and a half following Colombo's first contact with the illness? If that is so, could it be possible that we would now be even more unaffected by that disease?"

"I would not want to chance ever having to find out," said Canning.

"We could have developed a resistance to the illness. That would also explain why the Black Death has never reappeared," speculated Jefferson, "but there are those who think the colder temperatures of both Sweden, and Minuit's northern Colombo Island, kept the plague to a minimum. We know that in Europe both the Colombo Plague and the Black Death were less prevalent in the winter than in the summer, and fewer died in the northern countries than in the southern nations."

"Whatever the reason," said Rebecca Madison, crossing herself, "I pray we never see the likes of either malady again."

Chapter 18

The two priests handled the artifacts with great reverence. These were the objects that Admiral Mextli had sent back to the emperor from the island in the Inland Sea. Laid out before them were two strange pots made of metal, three long metal tubes—one with trigger housing—the broken scabbard of a long knife, and a rounded rock into which had been engraved symbols that were worn by age. The admiral had continued on north to lead the war effort in the Northeast Territories, but he had sent one of his smaller ships back to deliver these items to the ruler of the Aztecs.

Ahuitzotl VI paced around the table containing the objects. They appeared both commonplace and mystical at the same time. The priests had been given two full weeks to study these artifacts and had taken every bit of that time, but now the emperor wanted answers.

"What are they?" he demanded. "Were they made by the gods?"

The high priest of Huitzilopotchli, the god of war, answered first. His name was Tizoc, and he was a thin man with a hawked nose. His dark eyes, set deep into his shaved skull, gave him the frightening appearance of one who could peer into a person's very soul.

"O Great One, these are truly very old items. I do not believe they are as old as some of the religious items dating back to the founding of our capital, but they are ancient. Matching the wear on the pots and rock with similar wear to objects of which we are familiar, I would estimate they are about three hundred seasons old."

"I would agree," concurred Itzcoatl, the high priest of Tlaloc, who was the god of rain and fertility. He was a well-fed rotund man, but his eyes reflected the same intensity as Tizoc's. "The pots are obviously made for cooking, no doubt for some sort of religious ceremony. Tizoc thinks the tubes are from thundersticks. I do not know how this could possibly be, as we have only discovered the secrets of thunder powder and the thunderstick in the last hundred seasons."

"Could they be the tools of the white god Quetzalcoatl?" asked Ahuitzotl.

"No!" both priests answered simultaneously.

"These are definitely man-made," answered Itzcoatl. "If they had been forged by the gods, they would not have weathered and rotted."

"I agree," said Tizoc, holding a metal pot in his hand, "but that fact worries me."

"How so?" asked the emperor, looking puzzled.

"This is not a cooking pot," responded the high priest of war. "I believe it is some sort of helmet made of metal to protect a man's head. Look how it has been fashioned. Although worn and faded, there are intricate carvings in the metal, and it appears there was a metal brim that ran around the outside edge of the head covering. It also looks as if there was some sort of raised ridge on its top. That alone would eliminate its use as a cooking device.

"And in this one," Tizoc continued as he picked up the other pot, "there is the remnant of a buckle that may have been used to fasten the helmet securely on a person's head. Everything we have found, the metal hats, the broken long knife, and the thundersticks, indicate the owners of these objects were warriors. And…"

"And?" responded Ahuitzotl.

"And," answered Tizoc as he stared at the helmet in his hand, "if these men had thundersticks hundreds of seasons ago, what sort of warriors were they, from where did they come, and where are they now?"

The emperor's eyes opened wider, but he did not speak.

"They may all be dead men," the high priest of Huitzilopotchli reflected after some thought. "According to the natives' stories, the white ones who invaded the island and inhabited the stockade all died. Why has no one seen these people since the season of the legend? They may have had modern weapons, but they were surely weak men. Our gods must have killed them to prevent them from reaching the Empire."

"May the gods preserve us," intoned the emperor. "If they had continued to the Empire with their thundersticks three hundred seasons ago, our ancestors would have been no match for their might. Our power was not yet solidified. We held total control only in Oaxaca, the land surrounding our original homeland. The other peoples who have now been citizens of the Empire for hundreds of seasons were at odds with us in those times and may have rallied to the white ones to spite us. Our warriors fought with wooden clubs edged with sharp pieces of obsidian. We had just invented the atlatl to increase the range of our spears, but our bows and arrows could have not prevailed against thundersticks."

"We are fortunate our gods protected us," the high priest of Tlaloc affirmed.

"I think we have been given a sign," interjected the high priest of Huitzilopotchli. "I believe the men who came to visit the island of Ayti possessed great power but were spiritually weak. They tried to enslave the backward people of the Inland Sea and were destroyed. The Aztec Empire is now strong. We are the masters of our world. These artifacts are a sign that great wealth and power lie across the Eastern Sea, ripe for our taking."

"No, no!" shouted the priest of Tlaloc. "Death and destruction wait to the east. Even if we did not encounter powerful white warriors, our ships would sail off the face of the earth itself."

"Nonsense," answered the emperor. "The Mayans said the earth is a ball."

"And the east is the source of life, O Great One," added Tizoc with a rueful glance at the rival priest. "Does not the sun rise in the east? Is that not where Huitzilopotchli gains his power?"

"I am indeed curious," speculated the emperor. "Perhaps we should send an exploration fleet to determine just what lies to the east."

"Do not do so, O Great Lord," warned Itzcoatl. "Do you not remember what lies ahead in just three seasons' time?"

"And what is that?" asked Ahuitzotl, knowing full well the answer even as he spoke but failing to see the significance of it.

"In three seasons, we will have reached the end of another fifty-two-season cycle," replied the high priest of Tlaloc, pausing.

"Continue," ordered the emperor.

"As you know, Great Lord, we live in the world of the fifth sun. Four times in the past, the gods have destroyed the world and all the men who inhabit it. And you know that at the end of each fifty-two-season cycle, the gods judge us to determine whether or not they should again destroy all life. That is why we perform the fire ceremony."

The fire ceremony was performed every fifty-second season when the religious calendar of 260 days coincided with the solar calendar of 365 days. Five days before the end of this cycle, the fires in all the religious altars in the capital of Tenochtitlan were extinguished, and the Aztec people throughout the Empire went into mourning and prayed fervently that their two gods would judge them worthy enough for the world to continue.

On the fifth day of the ceremony, the high priests traveled to the Hill of the Star and waited for a cluster of stars known as Tianquiztli to appear. It was the appearance of this constellation that signified the world would continue for another fifty-two seasons. Human victims were sacrificed in jubilant celebration when the stars appeared, as they had after each of the previous fire ceremonies dating back to the founding of the capital city. This was the only time outside a major catastrophe, such as an earthquake, that human sacrifices were still allowed. The victims were held in high esteem and were chosen from only the worthiest of men, usually captured war chiefs and the leaders of vanquished nations. A new fire was started in the victims' chest cavities and runners carried this fire to each temple throughout the capital city to relight the altar fires and renew life.

"The first recorded fire ceremony was held three seasons short of ten fire ceremonies ago, twenty-one seasons after our capital was built," continued Iztcoatl. "Since that time, the gods have favored us. Ten is a magical number, my lord. Should we count our fingers or our toes, there are no more digits after ten. I greatly fear that sending ships to the east, to the source of the sun and life itself could anger the gods and bring about the end of the age of the fifth sun."

"Absurd!" scoffed Tizoc. "You have misinterpreted the will of the gods. They have given us a sign. I believe it is their will that we continue to expand the Empire, and they will be angry if we fail to sail east. There has been little wealth gained in our wars with the Iroquois and the Shawnee. Those people live in wooden huts. They have no gold. The natives of the northwest fare no better.

"We have had no great conquest since we made peace with the Incas two hundred seasons ago. That had been a great war against a strong adversary, and it resulted in many honors, incredible riches, and thousands of slaves. But now the Incas go their own way, controlling the west coast of the southern lands. Our armies have been victorious in the north, but there are little gold or precious stones to be found in those regions. I believe Huitzilopotchli is tired of waging war against impoverished native peoples. The great god of war yearns for a worthy opponent who has great riches, riches that will be ours for the taking. There are no people in the world that can stand against the might of the Aztec Empire!"

"Enough!" said the emperor in the voice he used for command. Both priests dropped to their knees. "I will consider all you have said, but my curiosity is truly aroused. At this time, I am not advocating an invasion fleet into the unknown, but if we had not explored beyond our own borders, we would never have discovered the riches of the Incas nor the unlimited quantity of animals and furs to the north, wondrous furs from the beaver, the elk, and the moose. Perhaps it is appropriate that we first send a small expedition to see what lies to the east before we risk launching a full-scale invasion fleet."

Chapter 19

Two sailors found Cacimar hiding in the ship's hold just a few cycles of the sun out from the island, and they immediately took him to Mextli. By this time, the young man was happy to be discovered. He was not hungry or thirsty, having had his fill of both food and water at night, but he was filthy and had soiled himself. His spirits were lifted when he climbed out of the hold and onto the deck. Ignoring the strange looks he received from the crew at their oars, he felt the invigorating warmth of the sun on his skin. Taking in a deep breath of fresh maritime air, it felt good to be alive and once more out in the open. The sky was cloudless. The sea was calm, and he noted that it was the familiar green-blue of the island waters.

Not more than a minute after he emerged on deck, a moderate southwest breeze reached the ship. One of the Aztecs shouted out orders, and Cacimar watched in fascination as sailors scurried up the tall pole in the center of the boat and unfurled a huge sheet of some unknown cloth. The wind caught the sheet, and suddenly, the ship was miraculously being propelled through the waters without rowers. While all this took place, the men on both sides of the craft pulled in their oars and fastened them down below their rowing benches. A spirited and jovial mood seemed to spread throughout the vessel.

When he was brought before the admiral, he was surprised that Mextli was not angry but laughed at Cacimar's appearance before ordering him to wash himself. This was accomplished by carefully walking out on one of the beams that attached the outrigger logs to the ship and scrubbing himself down with sea water. Fifteen minutes later, refreshed and dressed in a clean loincloth, the youth was taken back to Mextli.

Cacimar was quite a bit taller than the so-called tall ones who made up the ship's company. He was even taller than the admiral. His skin was also a shade or two darker than the Aztecs. Mextli was as muscular as the young man, however, and his confidence and demeanor added to his stature.

"You are the young interpreter," the admiral began, "and you have chosen to hide away on my ship. Why have you done this, and why should I not cast you ashore at the next island we pass?"

"This is my destiny, O Great Lord," Cacimar replied, unafraid and smiling. "Whether I am to continue with you and your ship, or begin my adventures on another island, I do not know. But I do know that my life is just beginning. I was not fated to remain on the island of Ayti for all my seasons."

"The crew believes you are a good omen, my young friend," Mextli replied. "The moment you came on deck, the wind appeared. The crew is not fond of rowing, and we have been becalmed for almost three cycles. How come you to learn the words of the Aztec? I never did ask."

"It seems my great-grandfather was a tall one," answered Cacimar. "Inez said he was shipwrecked on Ayti. He taught his son his language, and that son passed it to his son. My father taught me before he died although he never told me from where it had originated. He said I picked up the language quickly. I seemed to have a gift for it."

"Well, Cacimar," exclaimed the admiral, "it appears the gods shine upon you. As long as they do and as long as you work hard and obey the officers on this ship, you may remain aboard."

"Thank you, my lord," replied Cacimar with a huge grin. "Where are we going? Will you tell me about the world? Will you teach me the ways of the Aztec? Can you—"

"One question at a time," interrupted Mextli. "We are heading north, to the far reaches of the Empire, to a place called the Northeast Islands. There we will join a fleet of merchant ships transporting one of our army units. After we refit and resupply, we will travel still further north and take a river to the Great Lakes. There the Empire is building its newest and northernmost settlement. I hope to find and defeat a war chief who is trying to unite the northern lake tribes against us. He has killed many of our people."

"He must be found and either killed or captured," interjected Tecocol, the admiral's second-in-command. "It needs to be made clear to the natives that no one can stand up against the will of the Empire!"

"This leader is a brave warrior and a clever adversary," Mextli mused. "He would make an excellent sacrifice to the gods at the next Fire Ceremony. In the meantime, Cacimar, you are to go with Tecocol. He will teach you the ways of the ship and see to your instruction in hand-to-hand combat. If you are to remain with us, you will need to become an Aztec."

*****

Over the next few days, Cacimar was instructed in the ways of the ship. He climbed the tall catch holder and learned to unfurl the catchers, which was short for wind catchers. These were the great sheets of cloth that caught the wind to propel the vessel. He was taught the use of the various ropes and how to tie them to and unfasten them from the vessel.

He also began combat training with Atonal, the officer in command of the soldiers assigned to the ship. Atonal was short but massive. His head seemed to be attached directly to his shoulders, with no need of a neck, and his biceps were half again larger than Cacimar's. A dark scar ran from the right side of his forehead down to his jawbone. Despite his fearsome appearance, Atonal was a jovial man who loved to laugh. He took great delight in Cacimar's total lack of fighting skills and hooted with glee when he continually threw the far larger man to the deck as he taught him how to fight and wrestle. Atonal could see great potential in this gentle giant, so he also went to great lengths to encourage the young man, and the two quickly became fast friends.

*****

Four days following Cacimar's discovery in the hold, while traveling up the coast of the Northeast Territories, dark clouds filled the sky, and the wind suddenly strengthened. Common practice was to run for shore, find a bay or inlet, and ground the ship until such a storm passed. But Mextli was behind schedule and wanted to reach the Great Lakes by midsummer, so he pressed forward staying well in sight of the land.

As the hours passed, the sky darkened, and the storm intensified. Lightning flashed in the distance, and the waves grew larger. Both the water and the wind, which drove sheets of rain onto the craft, buffeted the ship in the choppy seas. Men clung to ropes or the railing for stability while many an experienced sailor emptied his stomach overboard or on the deck.

With visibility rapidly decreasing, Mextli grew alarmed and directed the ship to work its way closer to shore, all the while scanning the rocky coast for an inlet or a beach. Cacimar stood on the steering platform with Tecocol, next to a pair of sailors who were straining to hold the tiller that was connected to the twin steering oars in place. He gripped the rail with both hands as the ship rose on one great wave and then plummeted into the trough between that wave and the next. While riding the crest of a wave, he could see the distant shore lined with trees. When down in the trough, it was as though a wall of water surrounded them.

All the catchers had long ago been hauled in and tied down. The sailors were now rowing with all their might. They were keeping just far enough from the shore to avoid possible rocks or sandbars, moving first in and then away from the land so as to avoid being hit broadside by the waves. Standing on the cabin's roof, Mextli thought he could see the faint outline of a bay a little farther north, and he gave orders to head the ship into its relative safety.

Just as the vessel was making its last turn to begin a run straight into what was indeed a large bay, a huge wave caught the ship from its rear and washed over the steering platform. Everyone on board grabbed hold of whatever was close and held on for dear life as the salty water stung their eyes, entering their mouths and noses, and threatening to carry them off.

Tecocol was intently watching the entrance of the bay for signs of rocks and was not prepared for the wave. He was swept to his left, lost his balance, and hit his head on the platform railing before being washed overboard.

Cacimar, clinging to the railing, saw Tecocol's limp body fall over the side of the ship. Without a second's thought, he ran to the rail and dived into the angry sea. In an instant, the ship was past him and out of sight.

Spitting water from his mouth as his head surfaced, Cacimar looked frantically about. As he was lifted on the next wave, he could see Tecocol's inert form floating face down not fifty paces away. In three strong strokes of his arms, he reached the Aztec and turned him over in the water. Not knowing if Tecocol were still alive or dead, he held on to the body with one hand and used his other to keep them both afloat as the waves brought them toward the shore.

*****

Quite sometime later, the storm was in the process of abating. The size of the waves had greatly decreased, and random beams of sunlight slipped through small holes between the clouds.

Mextli sat in the sand next to his ship, which had been successfully beached in the protected bay. Most of his crew had built fires just off the beach and were drying out their clothes. Others were in the hold of the vessel, salvaging what they could and repairing the damage done to the food containers and water barrels. The admiral had sent soldiers south along the coast to try to locate the bodies of his best friend and the island youth.

Intent on guiding the ship to safety, the admiral had not seen Tecocol washed overboard. It was only when he turned to issue an order to the rudder men that he knew something was wrong. His concern for the safety of the ship's 170-man compliment superseded his grief, and he continued to guide the vessel into the bay.

It was only after the ship was beached in those protected waters that one of the sailors had who manned the rudder told Mextli he had seen Tecocol's head smash against the railing and his body wash overboard and how Cacimar had dived over the side in an ill-fated attempt to rescue the ship's captain. The Aztecs were not sea people by nature. Few knew how to swim. There was no doubt that both men were lost.

Mextli sat weeping for his lost companion and friend.

The hours passed, and it was growing dark when the soldiers returned from their search. There were shouts, and suddenly, everyone was rushing to surround these men. When the admiral made his way through the laughing and exuberant crew, he saw two individuals standing in their midst—a huge well-muscled youth with a sparkling grin and Tecocol, his head wrapped in a bloodstained cloth, his arms around the shoulders of two soldiers for support, and a dazed smile upon his lips.

Chapter 20

"Order, gentlemen! Order!" James Madison's voice filled the hall. Slowly, the men in attendance seated themselves on the red benches of the Royal Chapel of St. Stephen, situated within the Palace of Westminster. The newly sanctioned first minister sat on a high chair in the midst of more than six hundred MPs, or members of Parliament. A huge chandelier hung from the ceiling above him and the three scribes who recorded the proceedings. Fixtures with candles protruded from high on the walls. To his immediate right were his Whig supporters while to his left his opposition, the Tories, spoke softly to one another. The senior representatives of both parties sat on the front benches.

The last month had proved hectic for Madison. The Whigs had taken over the majority of the House of Commons as a result of the popular support for their stance, urging the strengthening of the military, and a new first minister had been named. It had now been thirty-four days since the Queen had removed Spencer Perceval from office and asked Madison to assume the duties of the head of the Parliament and the English government. This request had been precipitated by two major events.

The first was the alarming report that Napoleone Buonaparte's recently reconstructed Italian fleet was now expanding its influence throughout the Mediterranean Sea. Napoleone's naval power had not been a factor since Admiral Lord Horacio Nelson had destroyed half the Italian ships at Gibraltar in the infamous three-week war of 1808. England was now painfully aware that the Kingdom of Italy had built two new fleets to replace the ships lost three years earlier.

An English squadron under Commodore Oliver Hazard Perry had been dispatched to the Mediterranean to protect English shipping. Thus far, Napoleone's fleet did not openly interfere with English trade, but Italian ships flying skulls and crossbones had been attacking isolated English craft. Perry had been ordered to the south coast of France to intercept and destroy such a group of these so-called pirates.

Despite the Italian naval activity, Spencer Perceval had urged restraint and continued negotiations with the Kingdom of Italy. Only with great reluctance, under the constant haranguing of Arthur Wellesley, Madison, and other members of the Whig Party, did Perceval agree to consider strengthening England's army and navy.

A second event caused the realignment of Parliament. In September, Napoleone marched toward Nice with the announced intention that he planned to strengthen his forces on the Italian border facing France. King Louis XVI had sent General Joachim Murat to deal with Buonaparte and Murat had been soundly beaten in a short decisive battle. Fearing an invasion of France, an election had been quickly called, and the voters had thrown out Perceval. Queen Anne had then endorsed James Madison as the first minister. Since that victory, however, the Italians had not advanced and seemed content to spend the winter consolidating their gains, but the frightened French monarch still appealed to England and Prussia to come to his aid.

Madison's first acts were to begin efforts to greatly strengthen the English army, to start the construction of new ships, and to fortify English holdings in Brittany. Under discussion was the possibility of sending an army, under General Wellesley, to Europe.

"Gentlemen, please," Madison began again. "Napoleone has given us time to react to his latest transgression. The French army has pulled back to Paris. Our allies in Sweden, Prussia, and Russia are mobilizing, as are we. Buonaparte is no fool. He is now faced with adversaries to his west and his north. As soon as our fleet is strengthened, he will find his kingdom is in fact penned in."

"Not if his fleet is stronger than ours!" shouted Frederick Robinson, a staunch Tory and former lord of the admiralty under Perceval. Robinson was a constant thorn in the side of the Whigs, a fact that had earned him the nickname the Blubberer.

"And why would his fleet be stronger than ours?" shouted back the Lord Althorp George Spencer, a former Tory, but now a staunch Whig. "Because you did nothing to strengthen it, and now it is second rate to those bloody Italian bastards!"

Shouts went back and forth. Madison was again forced to pound his gavel to gain a semblance of order.

"We are all well aware of our military situation, gentlemen," continued Madison, "but that is no longer the issue. The question now before us is what are we going to do to strengthen our position? England must stand united in the face of this threat. I fear Napoleone Buonaparte has the ambitions of his Roman ancestry. He sees himself as another Caius Marius or Julius Caesar. But we must not forget that England is protected by the sea."

Cheers and hand clapping came from both the Whigs and a number of the Tories.

"We need to build our defenses and fortify the island!" shouted out Robinson. "We need to bring back our forces from Brittany and the English Netherlands."

"No!" responded Madison in a loud stern voice. "We will not flee from our enemy. We will not desert our ally in France. We will not turn our backs on those who need us! It will take time to strengthen our forces, but when we are ready, we shall show this Napoleone the stuff that Englishmen are made!"

Parliament erupted in cheers and backslapping as a message page made his way through the crowded assembly and handed a note to the first minister.

"Gentlemen!" Madison again shouted. This time, having seen the note being passed to the first minister, the members of Parliament swiftly quieted. "I have word from Commodore Perry."

There was absolute silence in the building.

Madison looked around the assembly and continued, "His squadron encountered the Italian pirates off the coast of Marseilles. Commodore Perry writes but a hand full of words. He says, 'We have met the enemy, and they are ours!'"

Parliament erupted in a new wave of cheers.

Chapter 21

It had been a grand banquet, held in the great hall of the Whitehall Palace upriver from Westminster and the center of the English government. Externally, Whitehall was one of the least attractive of the Queen's palaces. It had been added over the centuries so that its many buildings, as well as the nearly two thousand rooms within them, varied in architectural style with no central artistic theme. Anne thought the structures themselves, spread out on twenty-three acres, to be quite plain and dismal. King Street ran through the center of the grounds, splitting the palace in half. The buildings were connected by a series of passageways.

The interior of Whitehall was something else again: lavish and luxurious, the rooms were filled with color and light. The banqueting hall alone was 332 feet around with 292 windows. Its interior walls had been covered with canvas painted to look like stone. Just below the lofty ceiling was also canvas, supported by thirty wooden pillars, each forty feet high. It was painted to portray branches of ivy and holly as well as exotic flowers and a myriad of fruits: oranges, carrots, pomegranates, grapes, and cucumbers.

The court and its guests were seated at tables all along the sides of the hall, the backs of their chairs against these walls. This allowed the servants to dole out and clear away the plates and cups from the near side of the tables that faced the center of the hall. Ninety sheep, a dozen oxen, eighteen calves, and an assortment of venison, poultry, rabbits, and wild boar had been prepared for this one meal alone.

It had been a splendid evening, but Anne felt exhausted by the festivities. Further taxing her had been the suitors who had continually approached her prior to the dinner. Their number included Charles Earl Gray and Count William of Hesse-Kassel. She had marveled at how young and dashing the count appeared in contrast to the middle-aged Gray. She had mentioned this to Madalyn only to get a sullen look in return. Maddie did not care for the flirtatious German or his blond good looks.

At about ten o'clock, Anne informed Madalyn and her maids of honor that she did not wish to stay up to play games or gossip this evening. She spent a half hour moving about the room, excusing herself from her other guests, and then returned to her own quarters. Her bedroom was in one of the private apartments in a separate building. Two guards stood outside its door in the hallway along which were scores of additional rooms that housed members of her personal staff. A library had been built just off her bedroom and also a bathroom, with an ornate bathtub and a portable toilet that was upholstered in satin and velvet. The floor was covered with woven carpets and the walls decorated with brocades of silks and velvets. The Queen's bed was made of walnut with carvings of mythological animals on its posts. The mattress was thick and quite comfortable, and the quilts were made of silk velvet with gold and silver embroidery.

Attended by her ladies of the bedchamber (four women between the ages of thirty and seventy who saw to her private needs), Anne took a long bath, letting the hot water soothe her tired body. Both the bathwater and drinking water came into the room through lead pipes. She then excused the ladies, saying she wanted to read and then go to sleep. Instead, she brushed her hair, loosened the top strings of her nightgown, applied a trace of perfume above her breasts, and checked her face in a mirror. She then walked to a secret entrance concealed just inside the left side of the lone fireplace in the room. Pulling a chain beside that hidden door, she moved aside as it swung in, and her lover entered the room.

Anne stepped forward into a strong embrace. She could feel smooth warm flesh through her lover's thin nightshirt. She was trembling. Her loins ached with desire. These were the moments she lived for—when she was no longer a monarch but a woman.

"I do not know what I would do without you, without these moments alone with you," Anne whispered. "I can hardly wait to touch you, to kiss you. I long for these moments."

Her lover stepped back slightly and undid the strings of the Queen's nightgown, letting it fall to the floor at Anne's ankles. Soft hands caressed her neck, her shoulders, and then roamed gently, fondling her aroused breasts. Warm lips took hold of one of her nipples and gently played with it, a tongue flicking at its tip.

As the passion filled her entire body, Anne could only gasp. "Take me. Possess me! Oh, how I love you, Maddie!"

Chapter 22

The Aztec Empire had established numerous isolated colonies in the Northeast Territories. These settlements could now be found on the Great Peninsula that separated the Eastern and Inland Seas, on several of the multitude of islands bordering the Lands of Marshes and Mountains, and even on the two islands in the cold north. Those islands were called the Northeast Islands. One was extremely lengthy with only a few farms any more than a half day's walk from its western edge. It was called Long Island. A substantial colony had been built on the smaller island as it could be more easily defended. Large rivers ran to its east and west and only the sea provided access from the south.

The Aztecs who lived in this northernmost settlement hated their island home. Only military personnel and the "unwanted" from the Aztec homeland populated this place. The unwanted were the exiles sent to the settlements by the Aztec courts.

A Supreme Judicial Council sitting in the capital city of Tenochtitlan, and a number of lesser courts spread throughout the Empire, made up the Aztec justice system. Appeals from the lesser courts were given a maximum of eighty cycles of the sun to be evaluated by the council. Their judgment would then be run by the emperor for final approval. As the Empire had grown, it had become so increasingly difficult to make an appeal to the Supreme Council that now, almost ten fire ceremonies since the founding of the Aztec nation, only the wealthier of the nobles were able to get their pleas reviewed by this body.

The unwanted were minor felons and their families who appeared before the lesser courts for repeated offenses. Murderers and rapists were sentenced to capital punishment and died by public strangulation, beating, or stoning. First offenses for less serious crimes resulted in a public humiliation, followed by lengthy public lectures and a warning. A repeated crime—such as theft, the intentional infliction of serious injury, or major fraud—resulted in the confiscation of the convicted individual's property and exile to one of the Empire's settlements. The unwanted were shipped off as slaves, but they could eventually free themselves when they had worked off their purchase price.

These unwanted, as well as a strong military garrison, made up the population of the Northeast Islands. Crops grew well during the warm period on the islands, but a portion of the harvest had to be stored away for the harsh cold periods. The trees on the smaller island, as well as the nearby vicinity of the longer island, had almost all been cut down as large quantities of timber were gathered each season. This wood was not only used to build houses and ships, but it was burned during the cold period—a necessity to stay alive when the white frozen rain fell and covered the ground, often many feet deep. The first blankets of cold whiteness were a horrifying experience for any Aztec stationed in the north. This phenomenon was not unknown, as it was commonplace in the mountain regions of the Inca and occasionally in the high elevations around Tenochtitlan itself, but this frozen rain amazingly occurred at sea level, and once it fell, it stayed for such a long period. The hunting was plentiful, however. There was so much game in the Northeast Territories, and the animals were so large!

Like their counterparts on the western coast of the lands to the north, the native tribes in the east initially welcomed the Aztecs. Unlike the docile western tribes, once the Aztec soldiers had expanded out from their settlements and made it clear they were there to take what they wanted and to enslave the natives, the locals went to war to protect their lands. One entire settlement in a southern region of the Northeast Territories had been destroyed and its inhabitants killed before a large military force arrived to punish the insurgents.

An organized group of natives, calling themselves the Iroquois Nation, opposed the Aztecs when they first moved inland from the Northeast Islands. The weapons of the Iroquois had proved no match for the Aztecs' thundersticks and big blasters. After ten seasons of fighting, the Iroquois nation was defeated, and its people faded away to the north and west. The Aztecs began again to spread inland, interbreeding with the native people and learning their ways.

The unwanted, once they earned their freedom, relished the chance to establish new homes west of the Northeast Islands. They learned to fashion furs into warm coats and pants, clothing that was unneeded in the heart of the Aztec Empire, and they also learned to trap as well as to hunt. Their children, and their children's children, remained citizens of the Empire but adapted to this new land. Some intermarried with the native peoples who readily accepted individuals who wished to adopt the ways of their tribes.

These Wild Aztecs, as they became referred to in the homeland, also learned to cut ice from the frozen lakes and to use this ice, as well as salt, to preserve animal meat. Furs for couches and bedding, as well as meat, were sold to the settlements. The settlements, in turn, salted or packed the meat in ice and shipped it, with the furs, south to the homeland. This became profitable for all concerned: the Wild Aztecs, the settlements, and the merchants in the heart of the Empire. Along with these products were sent slaves captured from the tribes who lived even further west.

Additional explorations were sent north of the Northeast Islands. After first being forced eastward around a cape, the ships found the coastline turned north again, but the weather became even colder. A large river was discovered flowing out of the west, but it could only be sailed upon during the half of the season when it was warm, for it froze solid during the cold portion of the season.

The eastern coast in the north was so different from the western coast. The Northwest Territories, bordering the Western Sea, were much warmer. The northernmost settlement on the west coast lay in what was known as the Great Bay. Although it was as far north as the Northeast Islands, this northwest bay was a desirable location. It was temperate, and crops grew abundantly. Although there was often a chill in the air, it never experienced the frozen rain. The Empire easily conquered the tribes on the western coast, and its settlements expanded inland with little opposition.

The Empire operated on a tribute system crucial to the thriving Aztec economy. Tribute in the form of precious stones, such as gold, jade, and other jewels, supported the emperor, the nobles, the military, and the religious institutions. Tribute in the form of food and materials supported the growing homeland populace. These materials included textiles, feathers, building materials, tobacco (which was produced in great and fine quantities in the warmer settlements to the northeast of the Empire), chocolate, and coffee (from the southeast settlements). Tribute in the form of slaves supported the urban society and the settlements.

Slavery was neither racial nor permanent. Both slaves captured in the northern or southern territories, or individuals sold into slavery for their crimes, could earn their freedom through their work and then become an accepted, productive members of the Aztec society. Only great chiefs, captured in battle, were not released from their bondage. These individuals continued to be treated as royalty and were provided with everything they desired until they died a natural death or were sacrificed to appease an angry god or to celebrate the successful conclusion of a fire ceremony.

*****

Admiral Mextli was far from the Eastern Sea and the security of the Aztec coastal settlements. It was now the warm period in the Northeastern Territories and the admiral led a large military expedition that had been brought west in ships along the "River of the Great Falls" to the far end of the first of the Great Lakes. The massive falls that gave the river its name actually lay between this first huge lake and four larger lakes even farther west. The Aztecs had built a fort at this location and were in the process of establishing a settlement, but the locals had been putting up fierce resistance. Mextli's orders were to land his troops at the fort to the north of the natives who opposed the Empire. He would then march southwest into a land populated by many tribes of these people and defeat a great leader who was trying to unite all these smaller groups in a war against the Aztecs. This powerful man was the chief of the Shawnees and had been traveling the countryside gathering together a force made up of clans called the Sauks, Foxes, Miamis, Potawarmies, Ojibwes, Mingos, Senecas, Kickapoos, and Wyandots. Even the reluctant Chikasaws and Choctaws, as well as a few surviving Creeks—a tribe that had been massacred by the Aztecs—sent braves to fight under the leadership of this renowned warrior. The chief's name was Tecumseh.

*****

"I do not like having to leave our ships," Tecocol told the admiral as the Aztec forces moved inland and away from the protection of the fleet. "There is great security with the big blasters. The savages are frightened by the mere sound of them, let alone the damage the blaster balls create."

"It is too bad the big blasters are not easily transported," Mextli thought out loud. "Imagine warfare if such weapons could be moved about easily to back up a mobile land army. Imagine what they would do to ranks of armed warriors."

Both men shuddered. Big blasters were larger versions of the thundersticks and used thunder powder to send large metal balls into other ships, or sometimes into the wooden walls of a stockade village built too close to the sea. The great weapons were also mounted on the walls of the Aztec settlements, making them nearly impregnable. The weapons were far too heavy to be moved any distance manually.

"We still have the advantage of our thundersticks," observed Mextli.

"It is true these savages fight in close with hatchets, knives, and clubs," replied Tecocol, "but they are also exceptionally skilled with their bows and arrows, and a few have learned how to use thundersticks from the Wild Aztecs. Fortunately, they have not captured many of our weapons."

"Then it is important that we crush this resistance now," responded the Admiral. "We need to capture this Tecumseh and send him to Tenochtitlan to appease the gods before he has gathered too great a force."

*****

Tecumseh was a tall man among the Shawnee. At forty-three years of age, his body was lean and well-muscled. He walked with pride, his back straight and his eyes taking in everything about him. His black hair was worn long, hanging to his shoulders, unlike many of his braves who shaved their heads bare for warfare or wore a single scalp lock. Today he wore a breechcloth and fringed deerskin leggings. His moccasins were beaded, and his body and face were painted red for war. An eagle plume was braided into his hair.

Tecumseh sat in a war council with Roundhead, a war chief of the Wyandot, and Walk in the Water, of the Huron. At his side was his younger brother Tenskwatawa, known to the Shawnee as the prophet. All about him were the fires of men who had left their tribes to join his war party, now numbering nearly nine hundred braves.

For decades, the Aztecs had been slowly moving inland from the great ocean, sticking primarily to the rivers where their ships, armed with the mighty big blasters, could protect their new settlements. The tribes south of the Great Lakes had initially been little concerned and made room for the eastern peoples who were driven from their homes and forced to relocate westward by the Aztec.

The many tribes who inhabited the lands of the Great Lakes were primarily hunter-gatherers because of the short growing season and the poor soil. They harvested wild rice and grew corn during the summer. Game was plentiful, and the men of these groups were skillful hunters and trappers. The more northern tribes were also excellent fishermen.

These tribal communities lived in birchbark lodges in small villages scattered across the land. The hides of the animals they killed were tanned and used for clothing. Birchbark was also used for utensils, storage containers, and canoes. There were disputes between the different tribes and many small skirmishes. Warfare and hunting were equally accepted ways to obtain manhood, but all in all, they lived in relative peace with one another in a great and bountiful land that teemed with game.

Then the Aztecs discovered their way into the Great Lakes. They built a fort on the southern bluffs overlooking the Great Falls and began enslaving the natives living in that region. Many of the local tribes simply moved away, but others had chosen to stay to contest, or live with, the invaders.

"We have had conflicts with one another for as long as the people have lived on the earth," Chief Hole in the Day of the Ojibwe said. "The Aztecs are but another people who inhabit the earth. There is room for all."

Many of the older chiefs agreed with Hole in the Day but not so Tecumseh. He saw the Aztecs as more aggressive and more organized than the scattered tribes. He realized they were better armed, and he saw them as people who wished to enslave rather than coexist. For several years, Tecumseh traveled, talking to any chiefs who would listen, urging a uniting of the tribes to drive the Aztecs from their lands.

Many listened. Young men from dozens of different tribes joined him, for a time. Tecumseh did not want to face the Aztecs until his forces were strong enough to fight on an equal footing, but the young men did not want to wait to go to battle, and when they failed to immediately attack the Aztecs, many drifted back to their own lands. Others left when it came time to plant. Still, others disappeared when it became necessary to hunt to provide meat for the cold winter. As a result, the Shawnee chief fielded a continually shifting force of braves that came and went, never numbering more than a thousand men.

Exchanging tobacco with the other chiefs, Tecumseh passed on the message he received earlier in the day from one of his scouts: "The Aztecs have reached the Scioto River."

"They are a thousand strong, led by a warrior who calls himself Mex-te-lee," he continued. "They are systematically burning the villages they encounter, harvesting the crops for their own use, and then burning the fields. They do not take scalps but kill all the wounded."

"The Aztecs usually take many slaves," said the prophet. "They are not taking any slaves with this war party. I believe this Mex-lee is searching for you, my brother. He wants to force you to go and meet him. If you do not, he will continue to burn and kill."

Tecumseh sat in thought. Although his forces roughly equaled those of the Aztecs, he did not feel they were ready to fight. Could he unify the tribes and gather more warriors, or would they simply continue to drift in and out of his camp? In the meantime, the Aztecs were destroying their homes and taking corn and other crops needed for the winter. Just last week, twenty Sioux braves had joined him, but they were already restless.

With a deep sigh, the Shawnee chief came to his decision.

"It is time we go to war," he declared. "If we do not, we are condemning our children to a life of servitude, and we will see our lands continue to shrink until we have nothing."

"But what of their thundersticks?" asked Hole in the Day.

"I am not fearful of these Aztec devices," replied Tecumseh, his voice full of scorn. "I have no use for their thundersticks. They make a loud noise and are useless weapons in the woods. We can defeat these invaders with our own weapons, our scalping knives, bows, and war clubs. It is time we paint our faces for battle and drive these Aztecs from our lands. We will kill as many as we can and drive off the rest. That will send a message to their leaders that the tribes of the Great Lakes are no longer to be troubled. It is time for war!"

"I will pray to the Great Spirit tonight," the prophet vowed. "I will ask him to shield our warriors from harm so that none of them will be killed in battle. The Great Spirit will give us victory!"

"It is time then," said Tecumseh. "Listen to my plan of battle."

*****

The Aztec infantry was divided into groups of one hundred men called calpullis. In point of fact, each unit came from the same district in one of the Aztec cities and had trained together since they were boys. Each calpullis was led by a senior officer and a number of lower-ranking officers who directed the men using voice commands and, during combat, through a series of signals made by blowing whistles. The pitch of the whistles for each calpullis varied enough that the men of their respective units could identify them. A series of short or long blasts on a whistle directed the calpullis to change direction, fan out in a predetermined formation, attack, or retreat. Years of drill made the Aztecs a formidable foe against untrained enemies.

Each calpullis contained a group of thirty men armed with thundersticks. The thundersticks were long hollow tubes made of metal and mounted on a wooden frame. At one end, there was a firing mechanism, or trigger, and a wooden stock that fitted into the shoulder of the individual firing the weapon. Prior to going into battle, the weapon's owner would ram a course powder, called thunder powder, down a hole at the front of the tube of the thunderstick. A metal ball followed the powder. During combat, the weapon was propped up on a support stand and held in place with one hand while its owner put a finer ground thunder powder on a plate set just above the coarse powder. The soldier then lit a slow-burning match. Upon command, the match was touched to a slow-burning piece of vegetable fiber mounted on a moveable arm. Upon another command, the soldier pulled the trigger, bringing the lit fiber onto the plate to ignite the powder. The resulting explosion projected the ball toward its target.

Thundersticks were cumbersome, but they had two advantages over a bow. They drove their metal balls with a force unmatched by an arrow—a force so great that it could penetrate a metal plate at close range. They also provided the Aztecs with a huge intimidation factor when facing an adversary who had never encountered the noise and power created by such a weapon. It also helped if the opposition was unaware of the considerable time needed to reload these weapons.

When facing a large adversary, the thundersticks would be lined in a row and fired simultaneously when the enemy came within range. They could also be set up on walls or the perimeter of an encampment as defensive weapons.

In each calpullis, there were also ten exceedingly large men, each of whom carried a mascuahuitl, a huge wooden club edged with sharp pieces of obsidian. These were swung with two hands and could open holes in the enemy's ranks. These men were treated with great honor, not only because of their sheer size but because they normally led an attack.

Another ten men carried short bows that could send arrows over defensive screens, such as a fallen tree or a wall. The arrows could also be coated in pine pitch and lit to set enemy strongholds on fire. The final fifty men of a calpullis carried spears and round convex shields made of leather and painted with the picture of a fierce animal symbolic of their particular unit. They also carried short obsidian knives. All the men wore close vests of quilted cotton that covered their bodies, as well as helmets of wood and leather. The vests were surprisingly light, yet nearly impenetrable by a spear or arrow although a metal ball fired by a thunderstick would go through them with little trouble.

The officers carried wide long metal knives that had replaced the shorter obsidian blades more than fifty seasons ago. They also carried metal shields that could deflect a metal ball fired from a great distance and wore metal plates tied to the front and back of their quilted vests. These were relatively new creations. There were not enough metal plates to cover the common soldiers as there was not enough metal mined to produce thundersticks, knives, and protective plates for the entire army.

The tactics used by the Aztecs worked exceptionally well as the Empire defeated its enemies in its homeland and battled the powerful Incas to a draw. Sheer numbers, not tactics, had overwhelmed the natives along the western coast of the northern lands. The native tribes in the heart of the Northeast Territories were another matter, however. They had learned not to mass together when fighting the Aztecs and preferred striking from ambush or picking off stragglers. They would hit the rear or flank of a unit and then disappear into the woods. Their bows were longer in length than those of the calpullis and capable of sending an arrow a greater distance. Their arrows could also penetrate the vests of a soldier at close range.

Worse of all was the fact that these natives were as ruthless as the Aztecs themselves or perhaps even more bloodthirsty for they took the scalps of the enemy they killed.

*****

As Mextli marched south, Tecumseh's forces melted into the dense woods, only venturing forth to strike when the Aztecs least expected. Hoping to force the natives to meet him in a decisive battle, the admiral had begun burning all the villages through which he passed. These were small communities, with lodges made of dry bark, and could easily be rebuilt. Mextli also raided the gardens around the villages, taking most of the crops and setting the rest on fire. Without the corn and other produce the plots provided, the native tribes would go hungry come the cold period.

This tactic forced Tecumseh's hand. The Shawnee chief gathered his men and prepared for his assault.

Chapter 23

Mextli situated his camp in a clearing at a bend on one of the floodplains of the Scioto River in a wide valley cut by the waterway. The river was deep and wide enough at this point to provide an element of protection. Military procedure dictated that all brush and trees be cleared within fifty paces of an encampment, but weeks of marching without ever encountering the enemy had resulted in a considerable degree of slackness on the part of a number of the culpallis. The men were fatigued. They had given up any hope for a full-out confrontation with an enemy that seemed content with occasional raids or picking off a straggler now and again. As a result, a significant amount of low brush remained on the eastern side of the camp—high grass grew in clumps that approached to within twenty paces of the perimeter.

The thundersticks were set up in a square, facing away from the Aztec position. Every third weapon was manned throughout the night by a rotation of soldiers. Mextli also posted a number of his men to the east and the north of the camp at the edge of the woods, fifty paces in front of the thundersticks. These were his advance sentries. It was not necessary to have as many sentries to the west and south of this particular encampment as the river provided ample security to those flanks.

The troops were just settling down for the night, exhausted from another cycle—from just before sunup to almost sundown—of continual marching, followed by setting up the camp, clearing away the brush, and establishing their defensive positions.

"I wonder if we will ever face this Tecumseh. He seems to have no wish for a battle," Tecocol worried.

"It is his decision," replied Mextli. "If he fails to show himself and fight us, I will burn all the villages and crops between here and the river they refer to as Wabash. Tecumseh will be forced to take his people and move all the way west to the great river they call Missi or they will starve. If this is what he chooses to do, I will then recommend a larger force repeat our expedition next year and that we begin establishing forts along the rivers we have encountered. It may take us many seasons, but we will eventually control all these lands."

*****

Tecumseh climbed a tall spruce tree on a small hill not far north of the Aztec camp that had been erected the previous evening. In the faint early morning light emanating from a sun that had not yet crested over the forest line, he could see the Aztec fires and their defensive positions. To his left, east of the camp, seven hundred of his braves were slipping silently through the woods, moving in a slow but steady crouch. To his right, on the river above the enemy encampment, he could just make out the shapes of a dozen canoes. These crafts would create a diversion, allowing his main force to strike the invaders.

*****

The Aztec guard pulled his blanket closer around his shoulders to fend off the morning chill. He was grumbling to himself. Why had he been so unlucky? Why could he not have drawn sentry duty watching out over the river? The river afforded an open panorama across its waters to the far shore with little chance of anyone sneaking up on him. No, he had not been assigned to the river—he had been placed, alone, at the edge of dark and frightening woods. He had never imagined that there could be so many trees! Ever since they had left their ships, they had marched through thousands and thousands of trees. They were tall and foreboding, especially in the dark, offering many places to hide. He hated them with a passion. There was nothing like these forests back in the heart of the Empire.

A twig snapped close to his station. What was that? Was it the sound of the enemy or some small forest creature? He had been hearing noises and seeing silhouettes that faded away into the darkness when he stared at them all through his shift. It would not be long until the sun would fully show itself and drive away the night, then he would be able to see again and breathe more easily. Still, there had been the sound of a snapping twig, and this Aztec was a veteran of a number of campaigns. His experience and training would not allow him to let down his guard. Grasping his shield with his left hand, and his spear with his right, he peered out from behind the large pine tree that had been his hiding place. The sound had come from his front left, so he carefully peeked out to the left using the trunk as partial cover. This would hamper him if he needed to use his spear, but what good was that weapon in the middle of the woods anyways? A spear had a huge advantage over a tomahawk in the open, but it restricted his movement and could only be used for thrusting in the confining forest.

There was something moving through the low shrubs further to his left, he was sure of it, but was it a deer or a man? The guard stepped out from behind the trunk while still debating whether or not to shout for support. He never saw the man who had been pressed against the far side of the tree nor felt the club that caved in his skull.

*****

Running Bear saw the Aztec sentry go down. Off to his right, Walks a Lot made a hand signal that indicated another guard had been dispatched. Running Bear motioned for his war party to continue to move forward to the very edge of the woods. Fifty paces away were the loud and devastating weapons of the enemy, and they were pointing directly at him and his fellow braves. Only a few soldiers stood anywhere near these devices, however. Perhaps the stealth of his warriors had achieved the intended surprise and the Aztecs were not prepared for a battle?

Dropping the flat of his right hand toward the ground and moving it forward and back, he gave the signal for the men in his party to begin crawling ahead through the low foliage that had not been cleared between the woods and the camp.

*****

As was his habit, Mextli rose early and began walking along the banks of the river. He liked to check the sentry posts first thing in the morning. Thus far, all the men on duty were wide awake and alert, scanning the woods that grew on the far banks of the river to the west of camp. It would be suicide for anyone to try to swim through those waters toward his position, he thought to himself. He should have begun his inspection on the two sides of the camp that faced the forest.

At that precise moment, the early morning calm was broken by the piercing cries of hundreds of warriors. All about the admiral his soldiers jumped to their feet and rushed to man the thundersticks or grabbed their clubs and spears lying near their sleeping blankets.

The enemy had silently drifted in from the north using birch-bark crafts they called canoes, hugging the inner bank of the river in the faint morning light so that they could slip to the shore just above the open ground cleared by the Aztecs. As warriors leaped from three canoes that had been grounded just above the camp, other canoes appeared in the water from around the river's bend and headed straight for the western flank of the campsite. The occupants of these crafts ceased paddling and began to fill the air with arrows.

Despite the surprise attack, there was plenty of time for the disciplined Aztecs to prepare themselves. Shields were raised to protect the soldiers stationed at the thundersticks. Mextli watched as an officer gave the command to light matches, followed by the order to take aim. The command to fire followed as the canoes and dismounted natives closed on the camp, furiously shrieking their war cries. Matches touched powder, which in turn ignited the weapons, causing a thunderous boom. Acrid smoke billowed from the thundersticks, and rain of metal balls was propelled from the tubes into the attackers. A number of men in the canoes screamed as the projectiles smacked into their bodies. They fell into the water, and two of the vessels capsized, but still, the tribal warriors came on.

Shrill whistles filled the air and the Aztec infantry, armed with shields and spears, stepped forward to meet the advancing warriors.

Despite the whoops of the attacking natives, Mextli could hear the whistles and shouts of the Aztec commanders as they strove to wake the sleeping soldiers on the far side of his encampment. As those men began moving to their stations, the roar of the thundersticks along the river further shattered the stillness. Despite their training, many of the Aztec troops facing the forest stopped to try to see what was happening to the northwest. It was at this instant that the Shawnee, and their brethren, sprang from the brush not twenty paces from the camp and, with their blood-curdling screams filling the air, fell upon the invaders.

Only three or four thundersticks could be discharged before the enemy was within the Aztec's perimeter.

*****

Running Bear was beside himself with joy. The ruse had worked, and they were past the dreaded weapons that shot metal that tore through men's bodies. The Aztecs were not ready for this initial onslaught. Arrows ripped into their ranks, and soldiers cried out in pain. One man dropped like a stone with a wooden feather-tipped shaft protruding from his eye. Another ripped an arrow from his shoulder only to have two more sink their metalheads into his abdomen. The Aztecs were easy targets to pick off as they were silhouetted against the glow of their own campfires. Painted warriors raced through the individual soldiers, clubbing them down or knifing them. Many paused long enough to take a scalp.

The Aztecs stationed deeper in the camp began to form ranks. At a command shouted by one of their officers, these men dropped their spears and drew short knives while raising their shields into an interlocking defensive pattern. The shields slowed the attacking wave, but the sheer numbers of the warriors began to drive the Aztecs back toward the center of their encampment.

Looking around, Running Bear saw the rugged form of Tecumseh race past him and toward the Aztec leader, Mex-te-lee. A dozen warriors followed the Shawnee chief.

*****

Mextli was aware of the sounds of the attack on the east side of the camp, and from its increasing din, he immediately realized the river attack was a feint. Leaving Tecocol to deal with that threat, he called for two culpallis from his northern and southern ranks to join together and then led them at a jog toward the battle.

*****

Tecumseh felt the wind in his hair as he inhaled the smells of warfare. The reek of death was all about him, the familiar odor of fresh-spilled blood and the stench of emptying bladders. It was strange that in battle, with men dying all about him, he should feel so alive. He was proud of his warriors. They were fighting with inspired fearlessness against the better-armed foreigners.

Darting in and out of isolated pockets of invaders, the Shawnee leader searched for his opposite number. If the Aztec leader could be killed, he was sure the invading forces would lose direction and could be driven off. A short stocky soldier leaped at him, brandishing a knife, only to stagger and fall as two arrows suddenly appeared protruding from his chest.

The morning air continued to be filled with screams and shouts. Then a new sound was added, the resonance of high-pitched whistles.

*****

The eastern culpallis were barely holding off the howling natives, their ranks thinning with each onslaught from the superior numbers. So engrossed were the tribes in killing these enemies, they were taken by surprise when Mextli led his reserves into their flank.

Jogging in closed order with their spears held rigidly to their front, the Aztecs impaled dozens of warriors before the hostiles recognized the danger of the flanking attack. Quietly and efficiently, the culpallis advanced, thrusting their spears into the natives, retracting, and thrusting again. The men of the tribes tried to rally, but their clubs and tomahawks could not reach the soldiers behind their long spears, and their arrows were proving ineffective against the Aztec shields.

*****

A spear thrust caught Running Bear just under his left rib cage. He felt a sudden pain and the sensation of a warm liquid spilling down his side before he doubled over and collapsed to the ground.

*****

Tecumseh and his men had raced around the left side of the initial battle, arriving just after the Aztec reinforcements. As a result, the Shawnee chief found himself behind the massed rows of the invaders who were now slaughtering his men. Mex-te-lee was standing behind the ranks of his spearmen directing their offensive. He was more or less in the open with only a small number of bodyguards by his side. Tecumseh rushed forward to kill the Aztec leader, followed by the six braves who still remained with the Shawnee chief.

*****

Mextli did not see the tall, lean warrior with his red-painted face and an eagle feather in his hair until the native was a step away. Tecumseh swung his tomahawk, and it was about to come down straight into the admiral's skull when a huge man with dark skin drove his shoulder into the Shawnee, knocking him backward. It was Cacimar. Standing behind Mextli, he had just enough time to see the attack coming. It was too late for him to draw his long knife, but his automatic reaction to the danger saved the admiral's life.

As Tecumseh leaped back to his feet, Mextli's bodyguard closed around their commander. Realizing his advantage of surprise was gone, the Shawnee chief cried out in frustration. With another shout to his men, he turned and, followed by those warriors still on their feet, raced for the protection of the woods. The exhausted Aztecs did not offer pursuit.

*****

The battle had been a stalemate with many dead on both sides. Tecumseh's bold attack had checked the Aztecs' advance, and in doing so, he had protected the villages south and west of the Scioto, but the Shawnee leader had also lost many braves. His failure to defeat the invaders would result in a harbinger of fear in the minds of a number of the tribes who supported Tecumsuh. The Aztecs had proved once again to be ferocious fighters. If they were to return in the future with even greater numbers, many of the tribal chiefs would believe they were certainly strong enough to defeat the people of the forest.

The Aztecs now too had cause to worry. The natives who had attacked them had been armed with inferior weapons, but they had demonstrated an understanding of strategy, and their surprise assault had come close to a resounding victory against well-trained troops. As a result of this battle, Mextli did not want to venture any further into hostile territory and began preparing his men to return to their ships, a journey that would be all the more arduous as they would be carrying their wounded.

"Do not fret over this setback," Tecocol said as he attempted to pacify the Admiral's anger after the army had begun its slow trek back to the north. "We have little use for this land. Let the Wild Aztecs settle it and let the Empire continue to profit from our trade with them. This land is huge. Both the natives and our people can exist on it."

"No, my friend," Mextli answered solemnly. "The natives are a brave people, but they will not prevail in holding this territory for their own. There are more of us, and we will slowly take over their land and eventually make Aztecs of their children's children. It will take many, many seasons, but it will come to pass."

Chapter 24

Orderlies rushed in and out of the magnificent house built in the western reaches of Mondovi in Northern Italy. The day grew hotter as birds sang majestically in the trees outside the building. The thick heat that characterized the end of the summer was enveloping the Italian countryside.

The house had been built in the late eighteenth century, designed to emulate the Renaissance—the bygone era of wealth and opulence, as well as cultural revival, that had lifted Europe out the middle ages before the Colombo Plague had almost plunged the continent back into those troubled times. Each room in the huge house featured Milanese plaster with an abundance of turquoise, gold, red, and jade brightening its interior.

Inside the mansion, Napoleone Buonaparte stood studying a map of France. To his left stood Antonio Severoli, general of the Northern Army of the Kingdom of Italy. Behind them were Napoleone's personal staff and Severoli's military aids headed by Bruno Paparelli. The colonel had recently returned from commanding the occupation forces in the Tyrol region of Austria.

Buonaparte wore a flamboyant military uniform, one of several dozens in his closets. No one could remember seeing the Italian head of state dressed in anything other than military attire. Rumors had spread throughout his staff that the emperor even wore a light modified version of a uniform when he lay with his wife at night. Today he was dressed in the green and gold tunic of the emperiorial general, a rank he himself had created after the defeat of the Hapsburgs.

He was not a tall man, his five-foot-six-inch frame about average height for the early nineteenth century, but Napoleone was an imposing figure. The paleness of his skin, along with his small hands and feet, was offset by a short stocky neck and broad chest. His face, while nearly angelic when he smiled, turned dark and demonic when he was angry. His eyes were clear and penetrating, and his sharp nose, which he referred to as Roman, gave him a hawkish look when he grew somber. Napoleone Buonaparte radiated power, and by now, all Europe knew this was not a man with whom to trifle.

At the age of twenty-four, Napoleone had taken command of a Piedmont regiment and, against the express written orders of his king, marched them into France to assist the revolutionaries. Fed and housed by the jubilant French villagers, he had won a few minor skirmishes against disorganized Loyalist troops. All went well for the insurgents and their Piedmont supporters for several weeks until King Louis XVI escaped the mob that had come to execute him at his palace at Versailles. Louis had made his way to the safety of his Royalist army and then marched back into Paris. He defeated the revolutionaries and sent Robespierre and his other conspirators to the guillotine.

The French Royalists, assisted by military detachments supplied by other European monarchs who feared the spread of the revolution, then marched south and defeated the remaining rebels. By this time, the men who had led these radicals had scattered, and those insurgents who continued to resist were nothing short of a rabble. They were swept away by the blue-jacketed Loyalist soldiers. The one exception was Napoleone's small army that had grown in size as it took in several thousand now leaderless French soldiers who had joined the revolutionaries. Through a series of deft military actions, Buonaparte was able to defeat the vanguard of the Royalist forces and make his way back into the Kingdom of Piedmont in Northern Italy. He was not pursued. His reputation as an exceptional military leader had been established, and because of his popularity among both the populace and his troops, he was chastised by his Piedmont superiors but not relieved of his command.

Little thought was given to this rogue Corsican by the major European powers. Most of the nobility in Spain, Sweden, Russia, and the other European monarchies felt a great relief with the crushing defeat of the French Revolution. This episode was only the start for

Buonaparte, however. His soldiers adored him. News of his success against the well-trained French army spread throughout Italy and men rallied to his side.

Italy was not a country at that time but a collection of small states and independent cities that had not experienced glory since Venice and Genoa controlled the trade to the East. To the south, the mountainous southern states were sparsely settled, and the Bourbons ruled Sicily. The northern and middle sections of Italy contained rich farmland owned by a great number of dukes and barons.

For more than a century, the peninsula, inappropriately referred to as Italy, had been under the thumb of outside powers. Spaniards fleeing the Colombo Plague had settled the Grand Duchy of Tuscany north of Rome during the early years of its devastation. They still controlled much of that region, including the so-called Republic of Genoa. Now dependent upon trade with Spain, even as weak as their homeland was militarily, the nobles in Genoa were heavily influenced by Charles IV of Spain.

The Austrian Hapsburgs had invaded Lombardy and taken over that territory and the shattered remains of the Republic of Venice. So powerful were the Hapsburgs, and their Holy Roman Empire, that in 1720, they placed Duke Amadeus II of Sicily at the head of the Kingdom of Piedmont. It was the Austrian wealth that also supported the Papal States in Central Italy. As a result, the pope, the Kingdom of Piedmont, and the small duchies that existed between these states and Lombardy were all subjects of the Hapsburgs.

With the populace cheering Napoleone and men flocking to his banner, the king of Piedmont felt he could not discipline the young commander. In fact, he promoted Buonaparte to the rank of lieutenant general. Having failed to make any gains in France, Napoleone saw the disunity of Italy, as well as Northern Italy's indignation at Austrian subjugation, as a great opportunity. He spent months reorganizing the Piedmont army and then marched it south to conduct training in the sparsely populated southern region of the Italian Peninsula. The king objected in private, but he was a weak man and did not interfere. The Hapsburg's were unconcerned and joked that the little general could fashion an Italian Empire in the heel of the Italian boot.

All the while, the ranks of the army of Piedmont, which Napoleone now began referring to as his Italian army, swelled. After two years of intense training and ignoring his king's urging to return to the Kingdom of Piedmont, Buonaparte marched on the city of Napoli, several days travel south of Rome, and within four months, he had defeated King Ferdinando IV and taken that harbor town. A month later, he crossed over the mountains to the eastern side of the peninsula and began a series of campaigns to unite the smaller states and duchies along the Adriatic Sea. As he successfully marched north, word of his fame grew and more and more Italians flocked to his colors.

The stronger states in the north of Italy, bolstered by their ties to the Holy Roman Empire, did not show a great deal of concern about the happenings to their south. The European nations looked at Buonaparte as a brigand. Pope Pius VII sent out envoys to Napoleone, sometimes threatening him and sometimes begging him to stop his warfare. Buonaparte viewed the pope and the Papal States as the puppets of the Hapsburgs and would not respond to the messages from His Holiness.

In 1797, Buonaparte recrossed Italy to the north of Rome and was confronted by his first real opposition, an army from Tuscany supported by a contingent of the Spanish military. In a brilliant campaign, Napoleone flanked this larger force outside Firenze and defeated it in its entirety. Following his victory, he offered the defeated Tuscanian soldiers the choice of returning to their homes or joining his forces. The majority elected to enlist with his army. The captured Spanish military units, along with any aristocracy with ties to Spain, were exiled back to their home country. Italians once again governed Tuscany.

Napoleone's victory at Firenze thrilled the Italian population. Troops began deserting in the northern regions and made their way to join his ever-swelling ranks. Among them were veteran officers, including General Antonio Severoli, formerly in the service of the Kingdom of Piedmont and trained in the Holy Roman Empire.

At the age of twenty-nine, Napoleone Buonaparte, at the head of an army of seventy-five thousand men, marched to the plains outside Rome where he, at last, responded to the Vatican. Napoleone petitioned Pope Pius VII, along with the Papal States, to recognize a united Italy. Surrounded by a huge army, and realizing that the Italian people were in total support of Buonaparte, the pope had no choice but to agree. In 1798, the Kingdom of Italy was founded. Shortly thereafter, Genoa joined the kingdom of its own accord.

Napoleone spent three years reorganizing the states that made up the middle and south of Italy into a true country. He stimulated agriculture and began projects to modernize Rome with a system of sewers, wide paved streets, and street lamps. He financed a full-time fire department and created the Bank of Italy. He also made peace with Pope Pius VII and the Vatican.

His greatest nonmilitary feat, in the eyes of his people, was the creation of a civil code based on the concepts of liberty and equality, the key words of the French revolutionaries. In so doing, he set standardized and regulated civil laws, established administrative procedures that replaced the feudal jurisdiction in the south of Italy, and guaranteed a separation of church and state, freedom to choose one's own occupation, and the right to get a divorce. He also guaranteed Italians that they could aspire to any trade or profession regardless of their birth, thus partially eliminating hereditary privileges. The people loved him, and the prominent Italian journalist, Gian Domenico Romagnosi, wrote in support of these reforms.

Napoleone also spent this time training a larger and more modern army while proclaiming the rebirth of the Roman Empire. In 1802, Buonaparte called upon the Kingdom of Piedmont to voluntarily join with his new Italy, fully expecting that country to comply. Under extreme pressure from the Austrian Hapsburgs, their king resisted his people's cries to annex with the Kingdom of Italy and refused the request. This resulted in the Piedmont military taking matters into its own hands as its general staff overthrew the government in a bloodless coup and exiled their former monarch.

When Napoleone, at last, marched north toward Lombardy, the people in that state revolted against their Hapsburg masters. Lacking any support from the locals, and with his administrators in a total panic, Francis II chose to pull his Austrian forces out of the northern Italian states and recognized Napoleone as the legitimate leader of the new Kingdom of Italy. With the addition of Lombardy, Italy was now wholly united for the first time since the old Roman Empire had fallen fourteen hundred years earlier.

With the ensuing peace, the Hapsburgs turned their thoughts from Italy and concentrated their efforts on their control of the Germanic states. The danger from Italy was over, or so was their perception. The Holy Roman Empire, and all Europe, was shocked when Napoleone regrouped his forces and resumed his march northward two years later.

Francis II quickly sent a large army to meet this threat at the border of their two countries. He may have been able to defeat the Italians, or at least hold them at bay, had not Andreas Hofer sided with Buonaparte. The Tyrolese ambush and total defeat of the Austrian army in 1804 opened the Alps to Napoleone and allowed him free access into the Holy Roman Empire. Francis II called for help, but France, Spain, and England had no military forces in a position to respond while Sweden, Prussia, and Russia saw this as an opportunity to strengthen their own ambitious control within the German states.

In a campaign lasting just over three years, Napoleone Buonaparte defeated three separate Austrian armies of the Holy Roman Empire. In 1807, with the death of Francis II by his own hand, the Hapsburg Family—one of the oldest and most prominent dynasties in Europe dating back to the fifteenth century—ceased to exist as a power. The treaty of Campo Formio ushered in a new age in Europe, and when Buonaparte was crowned emperor of the Kingdom of Italy by Pope Pius VII in the fall of 1807, the remaining European powers were now faced with an extremely dangerous foe.

Unfortunately for Andreas Hofer and the Tyrolese, the Kingdom of Italy turned on its former ally and sent a strong occupation force into the southern regions of the Holy Roman Empire. Hofer found himself fighting the Italians.

Napoleone now redirected his efforts toward strengthening his kingdom and its borders. Over the next five years, he created thousands of new jobs by establishing factories throughout the northern states. Italy entered the industrial age. He spent millions of liras on public works projects, such as building a highway system on which to move both products and his army. He built canals and harbors and began to build a navy that could challenge England's.

The Kingdom of Italy had entered the nineteenth century with a vengeance.

*****

Turning from his map, Napoleone addressed his staff.

"France is ripe," he observed. "I think it is time we pluck her and join her to the Kingdom of Italy. These modern-day Gauls are unhappy with their lot. The French people resent their king, living as he does in squalor, and they will welcome us as liberators. The French army has proved to be weak. Murat is as good a general as they have, but he is no match for the Italian army!"

"That is true, my emperor," Santorre Santarosa, one of Napoleone's aides, ventured. "But our intelligence indicates the French will not stand alone. The English are sending men to reinforce their troops already stationed in Brittany, and their new first minister, James Madison, is calling on the Swedes, Prussians, and Russians to join in a coalition against us."

"Damn England!" cursed Napoleone as he slammed his hands down on the table before him. "They have their empire in the Netherlands, Brittany, Africa, and India. Why should they care for the plight of France, their age-old enemy?"

Pacing the floor with his right hand thrust into the front of his tunic, Buonaparte spoke aloud as he thought. "The Russians are scattered. The Czar has no organized military of any real capability. The Swedes are concerned with Denmark. The Prussians...yes, the Prussians could cause a problem if they are allowed to join forces with the English."

"And we must not neglect the English navy," added General Severoli. "Our fleets are building in strength, but England still controls the seas."

"That will not be for long," countered Napoleone. "But for now, we will concentrate on France. The English navy will not be a factor in our war with the frogs, and they do not have time to mobilize in support of the French. No, now is the time to move while the English are still arming, and a coalition is only in the minds of men. General Severoli, prepare the army to march."

Chapter 25

Mextli was enjoying the evening. He was not only sitting in an enormous room in the midst of the lavish confines of the royal palace, but he was surrounded by all manner of entertainment and fine food. Best of all, he was warm. When he had left the Northeast Islands, the sun had been moving to the south and the leaves were turning red and gold as they began to drop from the trees. It was beautiful; the breathtaking colors unmatched in the heartland of the Empire. It was also the gods' warning that the white frozen rain would soon follow. He shivered just thinking about the chilling winds and the cold that would have by now enveloped those lands.

The admiral was seated on a stool in front of a low table covered by a white cloth. Hundreds of burning torches lit the immense hall. Mextli, as were the other guests, was adorned with wreaths of flowers. To his left sat his trusted friend, Tecocol. To his right was Cacimar, his good luck charm. The hall was filled with scores of similar tables, all piled high with food, around which had gathered all the wealthiest and most powerful nobles of the Empire. The emperor had summoned them, and they were restless to learn why. The nobles had not been brought together since the last emperor died. Something out of the ordinary was happening, and they did not know what it could be, but they were eager to learn.

The tables were laden with all manner of cooked poultry: turkey, pheasant, duck, quail, pigeon, goose, and partridge. Next to these fowl were plates filled with rabbit, venison, and wild boar. There was even buffalo meat, a rare treat, imported from the north. The platters were set on earthenware braziers to prevent them from becoming cold. Beans, maize, squash, and yams grown in the homeland, and potatoes from the land of the Inca, were in countless bowls next to the meat—each especially prepared with sauces of tomatoes, chilies, herbs, mushrooms, wild greens, and toasted seeds. The delicious aromas filled the hall.

"If I eat much more, I am afraid my stomach will explode." Tecocol laughed, holding a cake made of maize that had been kneaded with eggs. "But such a feast! I want to try everything."

Mextli smiled and bit into a tamale filled with venison, cooked with maize, and spiced with yellow chili. This he washed down with an alcoholic beverage made from the fermented and watered-down sap of the maguey cactus plant.

Ahuitzotl VI sat alone at his private table on a slightly elevated platform. A hundred seasons ago, he would have been shielded from the other eaters by a wooden screen, but this was no longer the practice of the emperors. Four beautiful young women served him his meal on brightly colored ceramic plates. One of these women was outfitted in a yellow dress embroidered with the likenesses of flowers, and she kept glancing at Mextli's table.

The emperor concluded his meal. He slowly washed his hands in a bowl held by one of the young women to remove the grease from the meat he had consumed. Ahuitzotl was thoroughly enjoying himself and looking forward to making his announcement. Although he never met their eyes, he was well aware of the furtive looks he drew from his nobles. He was taking great pleasure in their mounting anxiety. Several plates of fruit, and a large gold cup full of hot steaming chocolate, were placed before the ruler of all the Aztecs.

The center of the hall was filled with dancers and acrobats and musicians. Mextli had never seen so many entertainers in one location. The musicians played a great variety of instruments: snail shells with clay mouthpieces, single and double drums fashioned of hollow wood, pan pipes, flutes made from reed grass and bone, and metal bells.

All this activity came to an abrupt stop when a large club was struck against a metal gong, the resulting sound reverberating throughout the great room. The musicians and entertainers scurried out of the hall. The nobles immediately stopped talking and looked up toward the raised platform. Everyone was silent as the emperor slowly rose to his feet and surveyed the room. Behind him, the Empire's two highest priests—Tizoc and Itzcoatl—appeared.

Ahuitzotl addressed his nobles in a loud, yet serene, voice. His words seemed to echo through the still hall.

"There are a few epochal times that make up the history of our great Empire," he began without a lengthy prelude. "The founding of the capital city, the defeat of the Tepanecs, the riches taken from the Incas, and the reforms made by Xolotl I are examples. I believe we are now about to enter another time of great significance for our people."

The nobles looked at one another, but no one spoke a word.

"Last year, I sent Mextli, the admiral of our great fleets, on a secret mission to the eastern islands of the Inland Sea. He returned with an amazing discovery."

With these words, the two priests stepped forward, Tizoc holding the metal tube found on the island while Itzcoatl held aloft a metal pot. Every person in the room turned their eyes toward these objects and the hall remained absolutely quiet.

"These artifacts are the remains of a metal helmet and a thunderstick," Ahuitzotl continued. "They were found buried in a place where a stockade once stood on one of the eastern islands."

The nobles found nothing remarkable in this pronouncement.

"My priests have taken a long time to examine them." The emperor went on with a smile, "And they have concluded, without a doubt, that these objects are over three hundred seasons old!"

Upon hearing this statement, the normally reverent nobles could not contain themselves. A startled gasp came from their collective throats, and their shocked whisperings filled the hall. The emperor beamed and waited for the nobles to regain their composure.

When the vast room had quieted once again, he went on, "I, too, had trouble believing such a thing. A metal thunderstick that old! The Aztec Empire did not possess such knowledge so long ago, nor did the primitive tribes surrounding our lands. How could this be? I will tell you…

"Over three hundred seasons ago, a ship full of white men landed on the island of Ayti on the edge of the Inland Sea. They were large and ambitious men who were armed with thundersticks two hundred seasons before we discovered such powers. They tried to enslave the local people, but despite their weapons, they proved to be weak. They grew sick, and within half a season, most of them had died. The natives killed those who had not fallen ill.

"Itzcoatl and Tizoc have been praying to the great gods Tlaloc and Huitzilopotchli for many cycles," the emperor continued. "Our investigations conclude these white ones came from across the Eastern Sea, and our priests believe their islands to contain great riches. The Empire has not added significant treasure to its coffers since we warred with the Inca. The gods have responded to our prayers and now urge us to go and take these riches. The gods also want us to capture one of their leaders to be sacrificed at the next fire ceremony.

"We know that these white people who live across the great Eastern Sea are weak. We also know that no outsiders can stand up to the might of the Aztecs. I have decided to be cautious however and have ordered ships of exploration, rather than an invasion fleet, to sail to the east. We have no idea how far it may be to these new islands or how long it will take to reach them."

The emperor looked around the room, and now there were nods and smiles on the faces of his nobles. New lands to conquer! Everyone would become wealthier.

"I am sending Admiral Mextli, with five ships, to explore the east," the emperor concluded. "We do not know for certain if these white ones are still alive. Perhaps they have all died and their wealth is just lying there waiting for us to scoop it up. If they live, they may recognize our strength and choose to become an Aztec dominion. We need to know what we will find on the far side of the Eastern Sea. The admiral will leave when the days begin to grow longer and the sea calmer."

The nobility was now excited and slapped the flats of their palms on their tables to show support of the emperor's decision. Ahuitzotl VI raised his hands above his head and made two fists. "For the Empire!" he bellowed at the top of his lungs.

Everyone in the great hall jumped to their feet and shouted, "For the Empire!"

Chapter 26

The banquet was over. A servant carrying a lit torch led Cacimar through the palace to the sleeping chambers. There he parted company with Mextli and Tecocol and entered a small room filled with the soft furs of large animals. The flickering flame from a single burning torch on one wall partially illuminated the chamber. A large open window looked out across the lake to the darkness that was now Tenochtitlan. All was quiet.

Cacimar stripped naked, put out the torch, and nestled down into the furs. They were comfortable and welcomed as a slight chilly breeze wafted through the room.

He was not sure how much time had passed or what awakened him, but he was suddenly aware that he was no longer alone in the chamber. A form was slowly approaching him, the dim figure ever so slightly outlined by the pale light entering through the open window. Cacimar reached warily for his obsidian knife before he remembered he had not brought it into the palace.

As he tightened the muscles in his arms and legs in preparation to spring at this intruder, the form stepped into a patch of starlight. It was one of the serving women who had attended the emperor, the beautiful maiden who had been clad in the yellow-flowered dress. Only now she was fully naked.

Cacimar gaped in astonishment as the woman hesitated and then began searching for him with her hands in the dark. Her well-developed breasts rose and fell gracefully with each breath. Her skin was a light brown, and she was slim and supple. Hearing the sound of his breathing, the young woman stepped onto the furs and lowered herself until she was next to him, close enough that they could see one another in the faint light that kept total darkness at bay.

"My name is Coatlicue," she said softly. "I have never seen another like you. You are dark and beautiful. I have come to pleasure you and to be pleasured."

Cacimar reached out and stroked the side of her left breast, running his hand gently around the natural curve of her bosom and then gently fingering her nipple. She shuddered and let out a soft moan. As Cacimar leaned forward to kiss her, Coatlicue ran her hand down his muscled chest, across his firm belly, and cupped his erect penis. Then she bent over and took him in her mouth.

"What are you doing?" the young man gasped in a startled voice.

Coatlicue raised her head slightly. "Do you not know the ways of oral pleasuring where you come from?"

"I do not," Cacimar answered honestly.

"Then you have much to learn tonight," Coatlicue said as she lowered her head again, her moist lips parting, and began to send Cacimar's body to ecstatic heights he had never before imagined.

Chapter 27

The emissary from the Italian emperor was a dandy. Queen Anne II hated to admit it, but the man was extremely good-looking and possessed a melodic voice. His seemingly perpetual smile displayed the whitest teeth she had ever seen, and these pearl-like dentures were further set off by his smooth olive complexion. His hair was jet black, and he wore the pencil-thin mustache that was now the rage in the French, Italian, and Spanish courts. Dressed in the finest fashion of the European retinues, the ambassador cut a splendid figure. He spoke English with just the slightest trace of an Italian accent while compliments and exaltations flowed from his lips with the effortlessness of turds in a Paris sewer.

"Once again, Your Gracious and Esteemed Majesty," Giuseppe DiCaprio was saying, "it is my duty and my pleasure to assure you, and your nation, that the Kingdom of Italy wishes nothing more than lasting peace with its longtime friend and benefactor, the magnificent and powerful English Empire. The Emperor Napoleone desires to extend our trade relations with your nation and to quell the disturbances that have jeopardized the relationship between our two countries. He has dispatched his navy to subdue the pirates who have threatened your shipping in the Mediterranean, a tragedy that has resulted in tension between our great nations."

The Italian ambassador paused and looked at Queen Anne II with an expectant smile on his lips. Anne stared back at the man without expression, her eyes locked on his, trying to read his true intentions. Why had Napoleone sent him to England?

DiCaprio was unfazed by the Queen's stare and continued. "Our two nations are truly the greatest in Europe. England controls the seas and has developed favorable trade relations at the expense of

India and several African states. Italy wishes to trade alongside her friends, the English, returning to the era when Venice and Genoa brought the riches of the Far East to the European markets. There are those who would disrupt this friendship, however. There are those who would try to pit our two great countries against one another."

Here it comes, thought Anne, her expression still unchanging. To her right, James Madison stood with a slight smile. Glancing at him from the corner of her eye, she could tell the first minister was also aware that the Italians were seeking something more than trade relations.

"First, it was the pirates," continued Giuseppe, his smile receding. "Barbarians who preyed upon hapless shipping and then disappeared into the ports of Nice and Marseilles before our Italian navy could react. Thank God for your victory over those terrible buccaneers."

Anne now turned and looked at Madison with a furrowed brow. He returned her gaze with a slight nod. It was now clear to both of them where this oration was headed.

"Then our peaceful villages along the Piedmont border began coming under attack. Armed forces, forces that we have now learned were under the direct orders of Louis XVI, raided our farmlands, killing poor unarmed Italian farmers and taking their crops. The emperor has sent countless emissaries to the French court begging for a cessation to these hostilities but to no avail."

The ambassador paused for effect before continuing. "I am afraid we will be forced to strengthen our border defenses with France. To do so, we are sending a small army into Piedmont to deter the French raiders. Emperor Napoleone wishes to inform you of this relocation of forces and to assure you that our only objective is to prevent French aggression."

Anne raised her right hand, and the ambassador abruptly stopped speaking.

"We wish it to be perfectly clear that England will not tolerate an Italian advance into France." Her words were direct and forceful. "The emperor must understand that an attack upon France will be considered an attack upon England itself."

"That is not the emperor's intent, Your Majesty," the ambassador hastily replied. "The Kingdom of Italy has no desire to secure French soil or to anger the English.

"Although," he continued after a second's pause, "the French are no friends of the English, are they? Your nations have waged countless wars, the French still resent your occupation of Brittany, and the unrest caused by France's ill-fated peasant uprising resulted in tremors throughout all the European monarchies, even so liberated a monarchy as yours."

The ambassador had regained his full smile. Madison had half expected DiCaprio to follow this last probe with a wink.

Queen Anne rose from her throne as the thirty or so individuals who made up her court stood looking at her in anticipation.

"You are dismissed, Ambassador DiCaprio," she said, "but before you go, hear my words and take them back to your emperor. England is in alliance with France and will not stand by should Italy cross the French borders. Is that clear?"

The Italian ambassador bowed deeply before turning and leaving the meeting chamber. Anne gathered her dress and exited to a small room behind the throne, trailed by James Madison.

*****

"What are your thoughts, James?" Anne asked as she sipped a cup of tea.

"I do not trust Napoleone, Your Majesty," the first minister responded. "He has his eye on France, England, and the remainder of Europe. I fear he only wishes to delay us in sending new forces to Brittany."

"It is an odd situation," Ann mused aloud. "If there were no Napoleone and Italy had remained a land of fragmented states, it might be France that was now concerning us. I am no supporter of Louis XVI and his corrupt government. He has bled the French people dry with his taxes to support his copious lifestyle and those of his court. It is no wonder the French people rose in revolt. I wonder what would have happened had they succeeded."

"I am afraid there would have been anarchy on the continent, Your Majesty," Madison conjectured. "Tyrants would have battled for power in France, the country would have been divided under the rule of different petty robber barons, and the seeds of revolution might have spread to other countries. I, too, have no love of Louis, but he brings order to France. Louis is a fat harmless king. Napoleone, on the other hand, is a serpent and must be watched."

Chapter 28

Angelo Conti sat alongside a number of his comrades in front of a small fire made up of sticks and branches. They were somewhere in Central France, and the succulent smell of a pilfered chicken slowly roasting over the flames of their campfire filled the air. The men wore their gray greatcoats, trimmed in green, over their uniforms to warm them against the chill of the autumn night. After leaving its staging area in Torino the Italian army had endured cold harsh weather while crossing over the Col du Frejus, the mountain pass through the Cottian Alps. This hardship, and the weeks of continual marching, had been rewarded when they had reached the plains beyond and been greeted by unseasonably warm sunny days. Now they all hoped to be barracked in comfortable Parisian homes before the first snows of the winter fell.

Angelo, as were the other men of his company, was a veteran. He had been raised in the town of Pesaro in the Marche Region of the Italian Adriatic Coast, the son of a small-time merchant. Pesaro had once been a dominant trading center ruled by the Sforza family until Giovan Galeazzo Sforza had died from the plague in 1494 along with 60 percent of the city. For the next three hundred years, the town had struggled to survive under a system of feudal lords until the liberating armies of Napoleone Buonaparte had swept them aside and incorporated the entire region into the growing Kingdom of Italy. That had been in the year 1796, and the twenty-two-year-old Angelo had left his job working in a warehouse and readily joined that army.

He had been surprised when instead of immediately marching off to glorious victories, he, and the other fresh volunteers from throughout the Italian peninsula, had been sent to San Marino to train. San Marino was isolated in the Apennine Mountains, and it was here that the new recruits learned to be soldiers. At first, they were not even issued uniforms. They were drilled, day in and day out, learning how to march, instructed how to form columns and lines, and taught how to rapidly shift in and out of these formations without getting in one another's way.

It was not until the second month of training that they were each given a new smoothbore muzzle-loading firearm, copied after the French Charleville musket, but manufactured in Rome. The new troops were instructed in how to clean and load these pieces: how to keep the barrel of the musket free of spent powder, how to replace the brass frizzen, how to tear a cartridge with their teeth, how to insert the powder and the ball, and how to aim and fire the weapon. They were told their musket was their best friend and they were to care for it and protect it with their lives.

The marching continued, but now they also learned how to mount their bayonets and then how to use those frightfully deadly weapons against straw dummies and then one another. Those who were slow to learn often suffered accidental cuts and/or the lash of their officers. Every day, they spent hours at the firing range. They drilled and drilled and drilled, learning to move as a single unit and to hit targets consistently up to 100 paces. Their massed fire was relatively effective at over 150 paces.

Another two months went by as they became even more proficient at marching and musketry. They now functioned as units and not individuals. After ninety days, they were issued uniforms: a dark green woolen coat with white lapels and gold embroidery on the collar and cuffs, white trousers, a black cartridge box with an outside flap made of linen, black boots, a backpack, and a tall green shako with a visor over which was mounted the badge of the Roman eagle. Standing in rank, indistinguishable from one another, they now felt like part of an army.

Angelo had marched on Papal Rome and fought in the battles that finally united all the Italian states. He was a member of the Eighty-Eighth Fusiliers. The Italian army was organized into battalions of 840 men that formed line and light regiments. The heart of these battalions was the infantry, and the heart of the infantry was the fusilier. Battalions were generally made up of four companies of fusiliers, one company of skirmishers, and the Melograno—a company of elite assault infantry, the strongest and bravest and most experienced men of the battalion. During the victorious campaign against the Holy Roman Empire between 1804 and 1807, he had learned to stand in line against the withering fire of a determined enemy and return that fire. His fighting skills had been sharpened, and he had become a professional soldier. He was now a thirty-seven-year-old veteran, and he, as well as everyone else in the army of the Kingdom of Italy, was confident in the fact that there was no force on earth that could stand against the emperor.

"I hear the French will turn and run," Corporal De Luca told the men seated around the fire. "They say their army has been spiritless ever since the peasant revolt was crushed and frogs have no love of their king."

"That fat turd of a king who lives in Versailles," responded Sergeant Rossi, "is not loved by his people, but the French army is still a force to be reckoned with. They are well-trained and well-led and probably, along with the Prussians, the best fighting forces in Europe."

"Outside the Italian army," Conti interjected, then continued to ask, "where does the English army rate?"

"The English!" scoffed De Luca. "They may match the Italian navy at sea, but they cannot field an army that would be of any threat to us."

"Fuck the English," swore Private Bianchi. "Tomorrow we fight the French, and tonight I am cold and starving and thirsty. I'm off to find food and wine. Who's with me?"

After gulping down a small portion of the roasted chicken, Conti and De Luca joined Bianchi and set out through the adjoining fields. Sergeant Rossi elected to stay and tend the fire.

The Eighty-Eighth was positioned on the army's left flank in one of several groves of trees that grew in the midst of the French countryside. All about these scattered woods stretched miles of empty fields that had long since been harvested and their crops carted off to Paris. The sky was cloudless, and the half-moon provided just enough light to cause faint shadows. It was the kind of night that was made for lovers.

The three men walked a couple of miles, splashing across a small stream and passing by a deserted farmhouse. They talked quietly, mostly about women they had known or past friends. There was no talk of the upcoming battle. Angelo had been a soldier for fifteen years and never married. Fulvio Bianchi was also single, but he was just a youngster of twenty-six years. Gabriele De Luca was another fifteen-year veteran. He had a wife and three boys who lived in Fano, just south of Conti's hometown.

Passing through a fairly dense strand of foliage, mostly oaks with a few chestnut trees growing in their center, De Luca raised his left hand, and the others stopped and stood listening intently for whatever had drawn the corporal's attention. In the summer, the woods would have been pitch black as a result of the dense leaves on the trees. This vegetation had long since fallen from these woods, however, and the bare branches let the moonlight filter through to the ground. The partially decomposed remains of the leaves padded the ground on which they now walked. The soft bleat of a goat broke the stillness.

"Meat and milk and perhaps more," whispered De Luca, and the three men began to move stealthily toward that sound.

Coming out of the trees, the Italians found themselves at the edge of an empty garden. Thirty paces away was a shed, and through the broken walls of that shed, they could just make out the gray shape of a goat moving restlessly about. Not far from the shed was a small one-room house made of wood and thatch, and there was a light shining through the one window that was covered by semitranslucent linen to keep out the night chill.

Although the three men all carried their muskets, they were well away from their own encampments and had no idea how close they were to the French positions. They did not want to cause any kind of major disturbance that might draw attention to their presence. Furthermore, the emperor was interested in bringing France into the boundaries of the Kingdom of Italy and did not want to alienate the peasants who he hoped would desert their pompous king and rally to his banner. To accomplish this, he had put out a directive outlawing theft from the locals. This was largely ignored by the army, but Conti was aware that some of the more pious officers would occasionally make an example of one of the men, publicly flogging a man for thievery and even hanging one for rape.

With Rossi and Bianchi acting as lookouts, Angelo worked his way cautiously across the garden while keeping the shed between him and the farmhouse. Safely reaching the small structure, he saw the front of the edifice was open, and the goat was tied to a stake near its entrance. He could also now hear two muffled voices coming from the house, that of a man and a woman.

Sliding out his bayonet, Conti quickly cut the rope that held the animal to the stake and picked up the goat. It began to kick and let out loud frightened bleats. The voices in the house stopped. Angelo tried to run back toward the woods, but he found it awkward to move very fast while holding both his musket and the struggling goat. He was halfway across the garden when the door to the farmhouse flew open and a large mustached man, armed with an ancient blunderbuss, stepped out.

"Hé! Qu'est-ce qui arrive ici?" he shouted, then spying Conti's dark shape he began to give chase.

Angelo stumbled into the woods just as the farmer fired into the trees. He could hear the ball smack into a tree trunk not ten feet away from his head. The younger Bianchi hurriedly handed him his weapon, grabbed the goat, and bounded away through the woods. Laughing hysterically, Conti and De Luca were right on his heels. The last thing they heard from the farm was a loud "Merde! Merde, merde, merde!"

Chapter 29

One month to the day following Ambassador Guiseppe DiCaprio's return to Italy from Queen Anne's court, Napoleone Buonaparte brought his army unopposed into France, crossing the border and marching due west. They made their way through the mountains to Lyons before turning northwest to follow the Loire River to Orleans, the legendary birthplace of Jehanne d'Arc. Napoleone expected opposition in the mountain passes, and again at the bridges in Orleans, but it had not materialized. The French army had withdrawn all the way to Paris, and so the Italians had continued to advance to meet their advisory.

*****

An English major general sat on his horse, a large brown stallion, on a small hill to the rear of the French battlefield positions. He was there at the request of his government to observe the anticipated battle. Mounted to his left was Andre Dupuis, an aid of General Murat. Louis XVI, the fifty-eight-year-old king of France, sat to his right in a gilded carriage gaudily decorated by ornate cherubs and angels. His wide girth took up most of the carriage's rear seat, and he was noisily eating from a basket stuffed full of chicken breasts, grapes, and various cheeses.

The Army of Northern Italy spread out before the French forces were made up of eighty thousand men, including fourteen thousand cavalries, and two hundred and fifty artillery pieces. The left-wing was under the command of General Severoli, the right-wing under General Lorenzo Mariani. It was a tightly disciplined and well-trained force made up of veterans who had fought with Napoleone to unify Italy and defeat the Holy Roman Empire. To a man, they loved their little general.

The Italians marched as if on parade, looking splendid in their battle dress: green jackets crossed by the white bands that both fastened their ruck packs to their backs and held their bayonet scabbards. The remainder of their uniforms consisted of white trousers and high-pitched green hats with the emblem of a Roman eagle on the front. The men were armed with smooth bored, muzzle-loading muskets, each with an attached bayonet holder. They had a range of two hundred yards and his best infantry—the elite of the Melograno—could get off a round a minute.

Opposing them, drawn up in positions on the flat plain southeast of Versailles, was a French army of fifty-five thousand men under the leadership of General Joachim Murat. Murat knew he was presently outnumbered, but he had been counting on receiving support from the twenty-five-thousand-man English force stationed in Brittany under Major General Rowland Hill and perhaps even the massive Prussian army under Marshal Gebhard von Blucher. He had withdrawn his French forces toward Paris to give these reinforcements time to arrive, but that support had yet to come.

The French left was under the command of General Drouet, the right under General Bertrand. A formidable ten-thousand-man cavalry was held in reserve under Marshal Ney. The French were formed in two ranks, interspersed by artillery, spread across the plain. Their blue uniforms were no less impressive than the Italians.

The battlefield Murat had selected for his defensive position was a flat limestone plain with the Seine River protecting his left flank and forest to his right. The plain was covered by a soil of loosely compacted, wind-blown sediment—yellowish gray in color—that was used extensively for farming. These fields now lay bare, having been harvested earlier in the fall.

*****

The English general was well-aware of the disparity in the numbers of the two armies facing one another, and he was concerned.

"Is there no hope that reinforcements will soon arrive, Monsieur Jackson?" asked the French aid by his side.

The Englishman turned in his saddle, his tall, slim frame ramrod straight. He wore the fine red uniform of an officer and had thick locks of premature graying hair that covered his large, but narrow, head. His brow was deeply furrowed.

"No bloody hope," responded Andrew Jackson in a calm voice. "Our forces are scrambling to set up their own defensive positions in Brittany. The Prussians have not yet marched. This is your battle and your battle alone."

"We hold strong positions," observed the aid, turning again to face the plain. "A man on defense is worth two or three on the offensive. We will hold."

Jackson only grunted.

*****

The lead elements of the Italian army advanced in a formation four hundred men wide and twenty-four ranks deep. Closing to within five thousand yards of the French, they deployed into smaller massed columns preceded by skirmishers and spread across the plain to the front of the enemy.

The French artillery, made up of twelve pounders, had a range of three thousand five hundred yards although they were ineffective much over two thousand. These guns would send time-fused shells at the Italians, followed by iron balls as the range closed. Grapeshot—a mass of loosely packed metal slugs, rocks, and even shards of glass—would be fired during the final assault. The French infantry was formed in two ranks between these cannons with additional columns immediately behind them in reserve. When the Italians drew within range, the front rank would kneel while the rear rank remained standing. As one rank fired, the other would reload. The result would be a withering fusillade that only the most disciplined of troops, with great superiority in numbers, could overcome.

It was just before noon and the sun beat down on the two magnificently clad armies facing one another. Napoleone did not continue his advance into the range of the French artillery. Instead, he sent the six thousand horsemen of the Italian heavy cavalry, under the command of Colonel Mancini, around his left flank. They were clearly visible to the French. Stealthily advancing a little way behind this force, undetected on a dirt trail running through the woods, were a number of light artillery pieces and the eight thousand horses of the light cavalry.

Buonaparte had secretly rearmed his heavy cavalry. They still carried their traditional sabers, but in place of lances, they had been issued short carbines. These weapons, coupled with months of intense training, had effectively created a unit of mounted infantry.

Napoleone's military genius was again reflected in another aspect of his army. His artillery regiments operated independently under their own officers, unlike other European artillery units that were attached to the infantry. This made them more mobile and better able to quickly respond to the changing scenarios of a pitched battle. He had also perfected lighter six-pound cannon that were far easier to maneuver and more accurate in a high wind than the larger guns. There were fifty of these lighter horse-drawn field pieces on the move with his hidden light cavalry.

As the Italian heavy cavalry moved to its left in full view of its enemy, France's Marshal Ney advanced to his right with his entire ten thousand horse cavalry to counteract their threat. Forty-four-year-old Michel Ney was a fearless and brave commander. His military reputation had not been made by tactical acumen, however, but by his ferocious personal courage. General Murat had ordered the marshal to face down the Italian cavalry wherever it should appear, but not to seek engagement. Yet as the two forces neared one another, Ney was cognizant that his forces outnumbered the Italians by almost two to one. In the eyes of the marshal, this was too much of an opportunity to be lost. Visualizing a sweeping charge that would rout the enemy's horse and turn the Italians' left flank, and the resulting glory that would come with this victory, he ordered an advance.

The French cavalry spread out in an assault formation, their lines spaced forty yards apart, and came on at a trot. Surprisingly, the Italians stopped where they were and dismounted, forming two closely packed lines close to the forest on their left. They appeared isolated from the support of their own infantry positions several hundred yards to their right. This made little sense to Ney, but he was not about to pass up an attack on dismounted cavalry. He ordered his men into a canter, and they responded with a cheer as they dropped their long lances into a forward striking position.

As the French horse closed on the Italians, Ney heard the crisp clear clap of light artillery pieces being fired and then was aware of shells arching toward his forces—gray traces of smoke trailing from their fuses. The Italian six-pound gun crews had emerged from the woods undetected behind the heavy cavalry and swung their artillery pieces about to fire over their dismounted troops at the unwary French. These projectiles exploded above and among Ney's horsemen, causing startled cries from his men and high-pitched whinnying from the frightened mounts. Screams came from both the troopers and horses as they were pummeled by the hot jagged metal of the exploding shot. The marshal's forces were veterans, however, and as fast as men and horses went down, the remaining cavalry closed ranks.

Furious at this Italian duplicity, Ney signaled for the final assault. Horses broke into a gallop as the shouting French charged. Engrossed in the battle and shielded by the heavy cavalry standing to their front, Ney could not see the Italian artillery pieces, nor the light cavalry that was now moving out of the woods and forming ranks immediately behind these guns.

Thundering toward their enemy, who was now little more than a hundred yards away, the French were met with still another surprise. Marshal Ney could not hear the sound because of the pounding of thousands of hooves all about him, but the flashes of exploding powder mixed with clouds of white smoke to his front revealed that the enemy horsemen were armed with muskets or carbines. A wall of metal balls fired in a concentrated volley by the Italian heavy cavalry smacked into the lead rank of French, toppling horses and riders alike. The second line of charging horses could not avoid the carnage to their front and stumbled over their fallen comrades only to be, in turn, hit by another volley of mini balls. Men and animals tumbled in blood-spattered anguish. The grass was turning red as falling horses crushed those beasts and riders who had already fallen. Legs and arms and spines were snapped. As quick as it had started, the attack came to a complete stall as the ranks piled into one another. Officers shouted and tried to reform the lines but to little avail. Marshal Ney was waving his sword and urging his men forward when a bullet entered the right side of his head, toppling him from his saddle and killing him instantly.

With a continued volley pouring into their position, the French cavalry began to pull away from their enemy. In a state of disarray, they did not take notice when the artillery barrage halted. Minutes later, the rumbling hooves and victorious shouts of the Italian light cavalry filled the air as it charged around the right flank of the remounting heavy units and drove into the retreating French with their long lances. In absolute terror, the Royalist forces to the rear spun their mounts about and raced for the safety of the infantry, many tossing away their cumbersome weapons to gain speed. The rout had begun.

*****

From his hilltop vantage point, Andrew Jackson watched the retreating French cavalry. He could see the entire battle as if it were being drawn up on a map. Napoleone's army had held its position for a short while before beginning again to march forward. Approaching the French infantry in massed columns, they drew its full attention. The pursuing Italian light cavalry was now closely following the retreating horsemen on the French right while Italian artillery pieces, protected by their heavy cavalry, were now deploying to fire on that same unsuspecting right flank.

"Monsieur Dupuis," warned Jackson, "you had better inform General Murat that his right might be turned. They need reinforcements in that direction."

"I have already sent word," replied the alert Dupuis.

King Louis XVI had ceased eating and now stared at the battle with a look of stricken horror. His bulbous frame was trembling, and sweat poured from his forehead and down his neck onto his fine rich clothing.

*****

In full flight, the remaining French cavalry galloped between the right flank of the French army and the woods. Because of the close proximity of the pursuing Italian light cavalry, the French infantry could only get off a single volley before they were struck by the full weight of the horsemen. With sabers and lances flashing among the French host, the Italian cavalrymen created a bloodbath. Those infantries that remained composed behind the wall of their extended bayonets remained safe, but many others panicked and turned to run, only to be hacked down from behind by the Italians. The noise of cannon fire now erupted from behind this attack, and shells began to fall on the Royalist infantry ranks, holding their lines further toward the middle of the French formation.

The French infantry in the center was now cognizant of three factors: there were masses of Italian infantry advancing toward them with their bayonets flashing in the afternoon sun; artillery shells were now bursting in the midst of their ranks; and the enemy cavalry had infiltrated their right flank. An exploding shell sent metal fragments into shrieking men. A cannonball hit the ground between the French ranks and bounced into three men, smashing bodies, taking off a head, splattering blood and killing them all. With men screaming and dying from the cannon fire and the Italians closing to within musket range, the Royalists in the center were filled with terror. Men began breaking from the ranks and started running from their lines in a state of panic, ignoring their superiors' shouts and threats.

The Italian infantry closed on the remaining French, who fired a scattered and ineffective volley. The Italians returned their own volley and then charged. As if one, the entire Royalist center collapsed and began to run, an act that now exposed their comrades on their left. The French left, under General Drouet, tried to reform to face the enemy as the Italian center wheeled and drove into Drouet's right flank. A Frenchman parried a bayonet thrust and shot an Italian in the face. He then doubled over in pain as an officer stabbed his sword into his abdomen. Men grappled and cursed and bled in hundreds of individual life and death encounters. The fierce hand-to-hand fighting lasted for about twenty minutes before the increasing Italian numbers began to overwhelm the surviving French. Drouet was forced to surrender or be annihilated. Soon after, General Murat raised the white flag.

The battle for Paris was over. The city lay at the feet of Napoleone Buonaparte.

*****

Louis XVI watched as the soldiers in green swept his forces from the plain below his hilltop sanctuary. He had escaped the mob that had been intent upon his death just over twenty years before, but now his country was vanquished, and his fate again in jeopardy. He would be forced to surrender France to this Corsican misfit and then abdicate his throne, but would he survive? And if he did, who would take him in? Who would feed him? Tears ran down Louis's cheeks.

Two men, an English officer and General Murat's aide, watched him from their horses.

"The king cries for France," Captain Dupuis observed.

"I doubt it," answered Andrew Jackson, and with that, the lieutenant general turned and spurred his horse in the direction of Brittany, the last bit of land that stood between Napoleone and England.

Chapter 30

Despite a favorable breeze that continued to fill their wind catchers, it had been seventy cycles of the sun since they had last stood on dry land. Mextli could see apprehension steadily creeping into the eyes of more than one member of his crew. Only the firm discipline ingrained into the Aztecs as youths, and their trust in the admiral, kept outright fear from their hearts. Were there actually islands this far from the mainland? Was the earth round, or was there an edge over which they would plummet? The officers attempted to ease this latter thought through logic, telling the sailors that if there were an edge to the world, the sea would pour over its side until no water remained. They reasoned that as there was water all about them, it had to be contained by landmasses even if the world were level and not round as the Mayans had argued.

The five exploratory ships, and their crews, had been fortunate in that the sea had remained calm and the winds had continued to come steadily out of the west since they had departed the Empire. There had been no need to man the oars at any time. The fishing was quite good, but the fresh water and food supplies they had stored in their hulls were more than half gone. Mextli was contemplating just how much farther he could risk sailing and be able to return on half rations should they fail to make shore when a shout came from the lookout at the top of the catch holder of his vessel.

"Birds! Birds!" The sailor was pointing off to the northeast.

Everyone rushed to the deck. Far off in the distance, but just visible to the naked eye, were dozens of seabirds, some bobbing in the water and others in flight.

Slapping Tecocol on his back, the admiral turned toward Cacimar, whose face reflected his puzzlement. "If there are birds, then land is near. I should never have doubted that we would find the islands as long as you, our good luck charm, were on board. Signal the other ships, Tecocol. Let us all rejoice! We will soon step again on solid earth."

*****

Captain Isaac Hull was a heavyset man with rosy cheeks. He was barely thirty-nine years of age. Leaving his home to venture off to sea at the age of fourteen, he had joined the Royal Navy. A steady and competent officer, he had slowly worked his way up the ranks. His diligence had recently been rewarded when he was promoted to the command of the thirty-eight-gun frigate HMS *Guerriere*.

With the *Guerriere* were two other frigates, the 36-gun *Blanche*, under Zachary Mudge, and the 38-gun *Lively*, commanded by Lord Probus. The squadron was completed by the 74-gun *Defiance*, a third-rate ship of the line under the command of Captain Durham, and the 104-gun *Victory*, a first-rate ship of the line and the squadron's flagship.

Hull's frigate was constructed to sail faster than the ships of the line. His vessel had recently had its copper hull scraped clean of barnacles and its displacement lessened to further increase its speed. With a good wind, the *Guerriere* could make thirteen knots. His ship, with its single deck of eighteen-pound cannon, would have a hard time standing up to the firepower of a ship of the line, however. Those larger crafts boasted two or three decks of cannon, depending upon their size and the number of their guns. This disparity in armament gave emphasis to the frigate's need for speed and maneuverability.

On this fine cloudless day, Hull's ship was the lead vessel of a squadron that had been sent in search of Italian warships. An Italian squadron of three ships had been spotted passing through the Straights of Gibraltar a week earlier, and just three days ago, an English merchant ship reported seeing them sailing north. The sighting had been from quite a distance away, but they had been the same three ships. English intelligence believed Napoleone was strengthening his naval forces at his newly acquired port stronghold in Calais. The continent was now seen as a far more dangerous threat since Buonaparte had added France to his domains, an action that had resulted in both England and Prussia declaring formal war on the Kingdom of Italy.

"It appears the admiral is intent on doing battle with the Italians, sir," the first mate speculated to Hull. "He has had us systematically searching for their sails for five days now. I would not like to be in that bloody wop squadron. When the admiral has his mind set on accomplishing something, he is usually successful. The Italians had better beware."

Captain Hull nodded and raised his spyglass to his eye as he continued to scan the horizon.

*****

"Sail ho!" shouted the lookout high on the mizzenmast. He was pointing due west.

"Quite odd," mused Captain Garibaldi raising his glass to his eye. "The English should be looking for us to make a run up the coast of France. They should not be looking for us this far from land, nor should they be to the west of us. This is quite strange."

The three Italian warships, two frigates and a seventy-four-gun man of war, were making their way west off the southern coast of England. They planned to sweep around Ireland and enter the safe harbor of Calais from the northeast, thus bypassing a possible interception by the Royal Navy. It was not that the ships of the Kingdom of Italy were inferior to those of the English. On the contrary, the Italian ships were new and formidable. English seamanship was second to none, however, and that nation had ruled the waves for the last two centuries. It was best to have an advantage in numbers when taking on the English navy.

"It appears there are only five small craft, my captain," observed Lieutenant Colosimo, the ship's second-in-command. "Perhaps they are merchants. We are still too far away to make out their lines, but their build seems strange. For one thing, they only have a single mast."

The lieutenant had also chosen to use the word strange, Garibaldi thought to himself. *How odd?*

*****

Without the aid of spyglasses, the Aztecs did not detect the ships bearing down upon them until those vessels' catchers began to fill the horizon. As the ships drew closer to their position, Mextli was amazed by their incredible size. The lead vessels had three monstrous catch holders and sported what seemed to be dozens of wind catchers above their huge hulls. These ships were approaching his at an astounding speed.

"Bring down our catch holders," the admiral ordered to his crew. Then, turning to Tecocol, he said softly, "Bring all the men on deck without their weapons. I do not want to provoke a fight, but have the men keep their thundersticks within quick reach. We better also load the forward big blaster, just in case."

*****

Closing to within a thousand yards of the five smaller craft, Captain Garibaldi could make out the forms of a hundred or so men standing on the deck of the lead ship. The Italians were at a loss. None of them had seen ships or people like this before. Most were clad simply in loincloths, but there were two men standing on the roof of a small cabin dressed in brightly colored robes with feathers in their hair. The men on these boats were lighter in skin coloring than the Africans he had encountered; more the color of the people of India of whom the captain had heard of but never seen in person. These unusual people had furled their single sail and stood waving and smiling at the larger vessels.

"Good god, sir," exclaimed Colosimo. "Who are they? I have never seen such boats. They seem to have banks of oars, like the early Greek or Roman ships. And their skin coloring, could they be Greek?"

"They look more Arabic," mused the captain.

"What are they doing out here?" the second officer continued. "They appear to be coming out of the west!"

In one brief moment, Garibaldi glimpsed the truth. "The Colombo Plague!" he gasped.

Colosimo looked at his captain without understanding.

"They are coming out of the west," Garibaldi said, wiping the sweat from his suddenly pale face. "They are the savages from the Colombo Islands, the ones who Cristoforo Colombo discovered over three hundred years ago. They must have built ships, and now they have come east…to Europe. And they have brought the Colombo Plague with them!

"Man the guns!" the captain bellowed without hesitation. "Battle stations! These vermin must not be allowed to reach the mainland!"

*****

Cacimar was aware that something was wrong. Despite the crew's waving and shouting, the three huge ships had not stopped but passed by at full sail. They were now in the process of swinging about, and as they turned in the sea, he could see small doors opening all along the sides of the ships and the front ends of enormous big blasters emerging.

"Set up the thundersticks!" shouted Mextli. "Load the rear big blaster! We are no match for these monsters, but we will not go down without a fight."

As the first of the three gigantic ships began to pass broadside of the five smaller vessels, eighteen guns exploded in a devastating roar. This deafening noise was followed moments later by the total disintegration of one of the Aztec craft. Six cannonballs smashed into its hull, splintering the ship and sending bodies flying in all directions. Within half a minute, the Aztec warship had been broken in two and began sinking. The surviving crew floundered about in the water before slipping under its surface. Only a few were left, clinging desperately to the wreckage.

*****

“That was the sound of a broadside,” Lieutenant Adams exclaimed as he pointed his glass to the southwest.

Captain Hull did likewise as he heard a second dull roar of thunder come from that direction. It was followed by a third, even greater in volume.

“The latter was fired by a ship of the line,” Hull judged. A thin wisp of dark smoke began rising from the horizon.

“Full sail!” shouted the captain. “Press on for that smoke at full speed. Battle stations!”

The 260-man compliment of the *Guerriere* came alive, scrambling up the rigging or rushing to their posts. The other four ships of the English squadron were also unfurling additional sails and turning toward the sound of battle.

*****

Realizing there was no real danger to their own vessels, the unknown enemy was now toying with the one remaining Aztec craft. The largest of the ships had taken down its catchers and was sitting still in the water, while behind it, the two other vessels were completing their turns to begin yet another deadly pass. The Aztecs had fired their big blasters at the huge ships—only to have their blaster balls fall short, not even carrying the distance to the enemy.

Mextli stood on the steering platform of his craft in a combination of anger and disbelief. He had traveled for seventy cycles only to have his ships destroyed and his people blown apart or drowned by some unacknowledged foe. Worst of all, there was nothing he could do to stop the massacre. All about him, awash in the sea, were the dead bodies of his men floating in water murky from their blood. Perhaps three-dozen more were clinging to pieces of wood in the midst of the resulting carnage. Three of their craft no longer existed. A fourth was halfway down in the salt water and on fire. Thick black smoke drifted up into the sky.

The admiral’s ship had taken eight hits, killing a number of the crew but miraculously not causing any major damage. Mextli and Tecocol stood grim-faced with their hands clenched in rage, waiting for death to take them as the two smaller enemy craft began their fourth run. Standing at their side, Cacimar pointed behind the enemy ships.

"It seems more vultures are coming for the carrion," he said quietly. "Perhaps they will get here in time to fire their big blasters into us, perhaps not."

Behind the three enemy ships were five more huge vessels with their dozens of wind catchers, and they, too, were bearing down on the lone Aztec vessel.

*****

The two Italian frigates made their final run, but this time, they furled their sails as they approached their pitiful target, slowing and then coming to a standstill about seventy yards from the remnants of the five-small craft. Behind them, the man of war also sat dead in the water. The lead ship then unleashed a broadside that not only shattered the lone remaining western boat but also sent its remains quickly beneath the sea.

On board all three of the Italian ships, the eyes of the sailors were fastened on the wreckage in the water. No one was exactly sure what he had seen or was seeing. Forty minutes ago, there had been five strange boats filled with dark smiling men. Now bodies, both alive and dead, floated on the surface of the sea amid small clusters of wood.

Captain Garibaldi let out a deep breath. He was not pleased with having to destroy people who obviously meant no harm, but he was well aware of the possible consequences should these diseased savages reach the French or Spanish coast.

"Should I signal the frigates to lower their boats and pick up the survivors, sir?" asked Lieutenant Colosimo.

Garibaldi turned weary eyes toward his second-in-command. "No, Lieutenant," he said. "Signal the musketeers to fire into their midst. I do not want to leave one of them alive."

*****

"By god, sir!" exclaimed Lieutenant Adams. "The bloody Italians are firing into the survivors!"

The *Guerriere* was at the lead of the three frigates that were just closing within firing range of the Italian man of war becalmed in the water. The Italians were apparently so intent on their prey they had failed to send sailors up their masts to look elsewhere. Or perhaps the gruesome killing to the port side of their ships had mesmerized the lookouts.

"Prepare for action!" Isaac Hull shouted.

Men unshipped the bulkheads while others opened the magazine to run out powder for the cannon. The passages were wet down with buckets of water to minimize the chance of fire, and sand was poured on the decks to prevent men from slipping on the blood of the wounded. Shot, grape, and wads were piled up by the guns, tubs were filled with fresh water for the men to drink, the pumps were rigged, and the matches that would be used to ignite the cannon were lit. Marines took their positions along the rail or in the rigging. The well-disciplined crew of an English warship could clear for action in fifteen minutes. The *Guerriere* had been preparing for combat ever since the Italian flag had been identified flying over the enemy ships, and these final actions took just minutes to complete.

*****

Cacimar could hear the white men on board the huge ships laughing as they shot at the few Aztecs who were left clinging to the wreckage floating in the water. He was a strong swimmer, and Mextli had moderate swimming skills, so the two men had developed a strategy of diving as far beneath the sea as they could, surfacing only to draw a deep breath before going under again. The men shooting at them seemed to find the two men's life-or-death struggle to be not only sporting but also incredibly amusing. A number of them were now holding their fire while they tried to guess where Cacimar and the admiral would reappear. Wagers were being made on who would make these kills.

Cacimar could stay underwater for more than two minutes at a time. When he came up to catch a breath of fresh air, he would try to surface where there were pieces of wreckage between him and the enemy ship. The few Aztecs who were still alive and could not swim also tried to use pieces of wood as cover, but they were being systematically picked off one by one.

During one surfacing, Cacimar glimpsed Tecocol holding on to the remains of a catch holder with both hands while ducking his head under the sea. The metal balls shot from the white men's thundersticks made splashes in the water all about him. The next time Cacimar poked his face above the surface, the sea was red around the Aztec second-in-command, but he was still holding on to the piece of wood.

Preparing to dive once again, Cacimar was suddenly cognizant of the fact that there were no splashes in the sea around him, nor were the sounds of little thunders any longer coming from the enemy ship. Risking the possibility that this was a trick to keep him from going back under, Cacimar tread water and looked in the direction of the closer of the white one's vessels. The men on it were now running about frantically. Several were pointing and looking to the rear of their craft. In that direction, no more than five ship lengths away, was another huge vessel, its catchers full of wind, rushing toward and overtaking the two motionless ships at an unthinkable speed.

*****

Isaac Hull made his decision. He passed by the Italian man of war at no more than three hundred yards and made straight for the two frigates. They both became aware of his presence as he emerged from behind the larger ship. He could see the soldiers on the closest Italian craft racing to the railing with their muskets to face their attacker as the crew dashed for the gun deck or began unfurling the sails. He would pass two hundred yards from the hull of the first Italian frigate, opposite the wreckage of whoever had been their victims, and there was no way in hell the enemy gunners would be ready to return his fire.

Behind him, *Lively* and then *Blanche* fired broadsides at point-blank range into the Italian man of war as they passed by.

Less than a minute later, *Guerriere* opened up on the first enemy frigate. Cannonballs smashed into the ship just at the waterline, creating ragged openings into which the sea rapidly began to pour. Captain Hull's nostrils took in the sharp smell of powder smoke, and he could hear the sounds of his ship's cannon as they were pulled back along the gun tracks to be reloaded.

Tongues of red and orange flames could be seen through the open gunports as the Italian frigate began to list in the direction of the passing *Guerriere*. The enemy ship was then rocked by a series of explosions as the powder magazines by each gun ignited and detonated. Lifeboats were already being lowered into the water.

By this time, the second Italian frigate had raised the majority of its sails and was picking up speed, heading south at full speed away from the attacking English ships.

*****

Captain Garibaldi stared in shock as the first English frigate swiftly passed to his starboard side.

"What in blazes were our lookouts doing?" he shouted at Lieutenant Colosimo. "Sound battle stations!"

His crew, who minutes before were enjoying the spectacle to the front of their ship, were running for their stations when there was the deafening roar of a cannonade. Garibaldi's man of war was rocked by the impact of shot that burst into its hull, ripped through its sails, and took down two of its tall masts. Cries of anguish and pain filled the ship as men were impaled by wooden splinters or crushed by cannonballs.

A second broadside, just minutes later, took down the remaining mast and opened gaping holes above the waterline while killing scores of sailors. The ship's rudder was blown away and she was now crippled in the water. Captain Garibaldi, who had been knocked to the deck by the concussion from the second shelling, regained his feet only to see two English ships of the line, still just out of firing range, bearing down upon his position.

With an angry curse from a rasping voice, he ordered Lieutenant Colosimo to raise the white flag in surrender. Lieutenant Colosimo was unable to respond, however, his head having been taken off by a cannonball.

*****

Cacimar was not aware of who had come to their rescue or why. Nor did he care. As he looked about him, he realized that only he, Mextli, and Tecocol remained with their heads above water. All the other Aztecs, over eight hundred and fifty men, had been killed by the big blasters or the thundersticks of the white ones or drowned when their ships went under. Eight hundred and fifty men!

Exhausted by his constant diving and panting for breath, he slowly swam over to the wooden beam to which Tecocol still clung and grabbed onto it for support just as Mextli reached the same wreckage.

Tecocol looked at the admiral with a faint uneven grin. A metal ball had crazed Mextli's forehead. The cut had stopped bleeding, and the blood washed off by the salt water, which left an elongated open wound with a little bone showing just above his right eye. Cacimar was miraculously unscathed.

"You look a mess." Tecocol laughed, raising his left hand to point at the admiral. Then his eyes glazed over, and he began to sink slowly beneath the surface.

Cacimar swiftly reached down and grabbed Mextli's friend under the arm, pulling his head and shoulders back above the water. Two shots from the enemy's thundersticks had struck Tecocol, one in his right shoulder and another in the right side of his chest, glancing off his ribs. His body was lifeless. He had bled to death while holding on to the catch holder.

Tears came to Cacimar's eyes. Mextli's suddenly pale face showed no emotion.

*****

Forty-five minutes later, *Lively* and *Blanche* were in pursuit of the lone surviving Italian frigate. Several lifeboats from the *Guerriere* searched the wreckage for survivors. They picked up a number of the Italian sailors but found only two of the dark-skinned men who had been originally attacked. They had placed these two in one of the longboats and transported them to the English squadron's flagship.

Even as the two stunned natives were climbing aboard *Victory*, escorted by Lieutenant Adams and two armed Marines, *Defiance* was taking aboard Captain Garibaldi and the surviving members of his crew from the slowing sinking Italian man of war.

Wrapped in blankets, Mextli and Cacimar were led to a thin yet distinguished-looking man dressed in a long blue coat—its white front decorated by two rows of gold beads. He appeared to be in his midfifties, and great locks of light curly hair covered his head. He appraised the two men from under a pair of thick eyebrows.

Snapping off a salute, Lieutenant Adams reported, "These are the only two survivors from the wop's attack, sir. And odd ones they are. Neither speaks any language that I have ever heard. They both look like natives of India or Egypt, but they appear to be stockier. The younger one…the big one…tried to talk to us in his gibberish. The older one has not said a word and carries himself like a noble."

"You have done well, Lieutenant," replied Admiral Lord Nelson, commander of the English fleets. "I want them taken below deck and fed. Something unusual has happened out here, and I want to find out what it was. From the looks of things, the Italians sank a number of boats and killed hundreds of men. Bring the captain from that captured man of war on board *Victory*. I want to question him."

Turning to the two natives, Lieutenant Adams pointed toward a cabin door and made the motions of eating with his hands.

The larger of the two survivors gave a slight smile and bowed. The older one continued to stare at him defiantly.

*****

It was close to midnight. After having returned from dinner aboard *Victory* with Admiral Nelson and Captain Garibaldi, Isaac

Hull stood on the forward deck of the *Guerriere* in conversation with his second-in-command.

"Everything the bloody Italians said is so hard to comprehend." Lieutenant Adams sighed. "Five ships sailing out of the west…from the Columbo Islands. That in itself is frightening. What does it mean for us and for the two men we fished out of the sea?"

"That is for the admiralty and the government to determine," answered Hull. "I keep thinking about those poor blighters in the water being shot like clay pigeons. And can you imagine their thoughts when they first saw our, and the Italian, frigates? Compared to theirs, our ships are immense. From what the Italian captain said, the shot from their miniature cannon would have bounced harmlessly off the side of our hull."

"Perhaps they would have thought they were fighting a ship with iron sides," Lieutenant Adams half chuckled.

Captain Hull was forced to smile. "'Old Ironsides,' that's what they would have called the *Guerriere* had they tried to fire on us."

Chapter 31

The white ones who had come to their rescue and fished them from the sea initially welcomed Mextli and Cacimar. They were fed and gawked at by a number of smiling sailors who were dressed in strange striped shirts and clothing that covered their legs all the way down to their footwear. The two Aztecs had also been issued a set of clothing, including the strange woolen coverings that one of the strangers called trousers.

Several hours passed before two soldiers with stern faces made their appearance. When the men in the red uniforms spoke to the sailors, the seamen stopped smiling and backed away from the two castaways. The soldiers pointed their thundersticks at the two Aztecs and motioned them to leave the cabin. Something had drastically changed the dispositions of their hosts. They crossed the deck of the huge ship and climbed down into the hold where they were directed to enter a large cage, the size of a small room. It was fashioned of crisscrossed strips of thick metal that created a series of open symmetrical squares approximately two hands wide and two hands high. The door to the cage was closed and locked once they were inside. The two men were quite conscious of the harsh stares they received from everyone on the ship as they were escorted to their new location. The strange-looking white ones were definitely no longer friendly. Instead, they kept their distance while talking excitedly amongst themselves. Many made a crossing sign, their hands quickly dabbing across their foreheads and chests, as if protecting themselves from an evil spirit. There was no question about it; everyone now seemed to be frightened of the two Aztecs.

Close up, the white ones did not appear that much different from Mextli and Cacimar, except for their pale complexions and their hair. The sailors wore their hair in pigtails, but that was not the most surprising thing about their locks. The white one's hair came in so many colors: black, brown, yellow, gray, white, and even red! And many of these men wore great tufts of hair under their noses while others had masses of the stuff growing on their cheeks and chins.

Even more startling was their smell. Their leaders emitted a slightly foul odor while the crew and soldiers positively reeked.

*****

Confined in the midst of the great warship, the cycles of the sun passed undifferentiated from one another. They were never released from their cage, having to relieve themselves in a metal bucket that was taken on deck to be emptied every two or three days. The hold was dark, except for a strand of daylight that came from an open hatch twenty paces away. There was always a soldier sitting across their prison, watching them with more than a trace of anger and loathing on his face. Their guards, dressed in uncomfortable-looking jackets of bright red that were lined with two vertical rows of identical decorative beads, were changed several times each day.

The Aztecs were not treated poorly and received the same meals as the crew three times each sun cycle. This repast rotated and was varied but usually consisted of some combination of molasses, cheese, raisins, rice, hardtack, salted sardines, anchovies, dry salt cod, pickled or salted beef and pork, fresh fish, as well as dried vegetables, such as chickpeas, lentils, and beans. The two meats, as were several of the other items, were unrecognizable to the captives as they did not exist in the Empire. Only the meal in the middle of the day was served hot. It consisted of fish or meat and was usually prepared in a stew with peas and other legumes or rice and served with hardtack biscuits. These biscuits had to be soaked in the soup to be eaten without chipping a tooth. Water, or a strange brew called beer, was also included, both served mixed with lemon juice.

From observing the sky through the open hatch, the two captives could count how many cycles of the sun had passed since the sinking of their ships. They could also tell when the craft was in motion and when it was still, but they could not see what lay outside the walls of the hold. Once or twice, the vessel's leaders had come down below deck to look at them. When they did, they maintained a distance of several paces from the cage and would talk amongst themselves. On these occasions, both Mextli and Cacimar would get to their feet and stand tall, looking back at the men in their blue-and-white coats and trousers. The nobility who commanded this huge vessel seemed to delight in wearing as many articles of clothing as possible. Perhaps this was a sign of wealth or prestige among these people?

The Aztecs' only reprieve from total boredom came when they stretched and worked their muscles, which they did twice a day much to the amusement of their guards or when they were fed. They had been unsuccessful in using hand signs to try to request seawater in which to bath, but judging from the rank stink of their captors, bathing was not a common practice among the whites.

A yellow-haired youth of about fifteen seasons brought them their meals, and as the cycles of the sun continued to pass by, his curiosity seemed to overcome his fear. He began to sit at the side of the cage while the two men ate, and after a long time just spent watching them, he began trying to speak to them. At first, his words were just an unusual jumble of sounds, but by pointing at objects and repeating the same sounds, Cacimar and Mextli began to associate these words with objects and actions. Cacimar was far quicker than the admiral in picking up the strange language, but the progress made by both men delighted the youth.

After three full cycles of the moon, which the golden-haired youth called months, the young boy began to spend considerably more time with the two Aztecs, usually the entire period between their first and second meal. By now, the two men could no longer detect the once recognizable smell of the white ones. One cycle, which was referred to as a day in the new language, the youth brought an object with him that he called a book. It was full of thin white sheets made of some type of plant, and on each sheet were small forms, not at all resembling the logographic, or pictogram, forms used in Aztec writing. These were squiggles and lines all printed uniformly in black. There were many images of recognizable objects as well. Both men spent the next two months studying these pictures as the youth, whose name was David, would sound out the pronunciation of the objects in the pictures. In this way, the islander, and to a lesser extent the admiral, were able to learn many words, such as day, which was one sun cycle, and year, which was the equivalent of an Aztec season made up of twelve moon cycles or months.

So it was that time slowly passed until it was October in the year of 1812, as measured by the men who called themselves English.

*****

It was afternoon, and the great ship was at anchor. Cacimar and Mextli stopped their conversation when two Marines descended into the hold, opened the door of their prison, and motioned for them to come out. The soldiers held thundersticks, but they were pointed at the floor and not at the two men.

The Aztecs were taken topside and across the deck to the main cabin in which they had been given a meal when they were first brought aboard the ship more than five months previously. Looking about, they were quick to notice that the crew no longer seemed afraid of them and were even smirking or openly smiling in their direction.

Cacimar pointed out items to Mextli that David had explained to them about the ship. There were three huge catch holders, which the English called masts. Each mast held four massive wind catchers that were called sails. Ropes, called rigging, ran up to the tops of the masts and out onto yards. The sailors could climb this rigging almost as quickly as monkeys navigated the trees back home.

This vessel could cross the sea to our homeland in far less time than it took us to arrive here, regardless of the direction of the winds, Mextli thought to himself.

A figurehead was carved into the front of the ship, or bow, depicting two young boys—David had called them cupids—holding a shield. A huge balcony encompassed the entire stern set above a massive steering oar called a rudder. Rows and rows of gunports stretched along the side of the craft. David had explained there were more than a hundred cannons called thirty-two, twenty-four, and twelve pounders, depending upon their size and the size of their shot. The larger guns could reach a range of one thousand five hundred yards. Using the English form of measurement, Mextli calculated that the Aztecs' big blasters were less than eight pounders.

Even more incredible was the fact that this ship of the line could not only carry forty-eight thousand gallons of fresh water but had a device on board that could turn salt water into drinking water. It was called a distillation apparatus. Such a ship could go anywhere and would not have to rely on islands or rainstorms for water replenishment.

The English had the odd habit of giving names to their ships. This one was called *Victory*. It was 226 feet long, with a mainmast 205 feet tall. This could be compared to the 100-foot length and 25-ton weight of the slimmer, two-deck warships built by the Aztecs. *Victory* was made of oak and carried a full complement of 820 sailors, as well as 146 Marines, more men than had filled all five ships of Mextli's expeditionary fleet.

The English ship of the line was currently anchored in a large river. Further out on its waters, they could see dozens of smaller craft moving both up and downstream, loaded with all manner of goods. Other large ships were either anchored along the northern shore or tied up to large docks made of wooden beams and planks. There were so many ships; their numerous masts appeared to form a man-made forest along the shore. Buildings made of wood spread along both banks as far as the eye could see.

Conducted into the cabin, the two Aztecs faced three men seated at a large table. They had already met the man who sat in the middle when they had been rescued and later when they were being held captive. He commanded the ship, and David had said his name was Admiral Lord Nelson. They had never before seen the two men sitting at either side of this admiral. One was wearing a colorful red uniform vest with gold lapels over a white blouse. It was covered with what was called buttons and gold string—called epaulets—decorated each shoulder. The other was a small man with a cheerful smile, dressed in all manner of clothing: shirt, vest, dark coat, and gloves. The clothing of the three men looked so funny that Cacimar laughed. The smile on the face of the small man widened, and the corner of Lord Nelson's lips slightly turned up. The third man sat stone-faced.

Looking at Cacimar, Lord Nelson spoke, "I understand you have learned some English."

Cacimar nodded. "Not good, but David understand," he said.

"Excellent!" responded the little man to the admiral's right.

"Speak to me, Cacimar," Mextli sharply ordered his companion in Nahuatl, the Aztec tongue. "Tell me what they say before you answer any questions. I fear these white ones."

And so began a three-way conversation between the English, Mextli, and Cacimar with the young islander acting as an interpreter.

"Who is this man who speaks in your native tongue?" the uniformed man in red asked Cacimar.

After conferring with Mextli following each question, Cacimar would reply as the admiral directed. "He is captain of ship like *Victory* but much small."

"Where do you come from?" asked the small man.

Another exchange between the Aztecs, and then, under Mextli's stern glare, Cacimar responded, "We come from islands to west. Small islands. We come as friends to…to…explore.

"What names of you?" Cacimar then quickly inquired before they could ask another question.

"I am Horatio Nelson, commander of Her Majesty's navies," the blue-uniformed individual answered. Nodding at the man dressed in red to his left, he continued, "This is Lord Arthur Wellesley, general of the English armies." Turning then to his right, he went on, "And this is the first minister of England, James Madison. He is the leader of our people."

Both Mextli and Cacimar were shocked that a man of such an unimposing stature could be the emperor of such a powerful nation. James Madison must have seen this on their faces, for he stood and said, "In England, our chiefs are elected. This means our people decide who will be their leader. We also have a queen."

The two Aztecs exchanged baffled looks. The words elected and queen held no meaning, but they both bowed to the small man.

"Why we prisoners and live in cage?" Cacimar asked Madison. "What do you do to us now?"

Madison sank back into his chair and studied the two men before answering. "Three hundred years ago, three ships sailed west from Europe…the name we have given all our lands. Two returned from this voyage, bringing word of your islands, but they also brought back a great sickness that killed many, many people. Millions of people! We did not know whether or not you had brought this illness to our lands. We had to place you in quarantine. That means we had to keep you away from our people so they would not get sick. We only allowed four people to come near you, your three guards and David, Lord Nelson's cabin boy. David and the guards slept and ate in a small cabin away from the rest of the crew, so in a sense, they were in quarantine also. When five months passed and none of them had shown any signs of the Colombo Plague…the sickness…you were released."

"You think we have sickness?" asked Cacimar, the anguish sounding in his voice.

"Captain Garibaldi, the Italian who sank your ships, said you were sailing out of the west and he believed you came from the Colombo Islands, the lands from where the plague…the disease… first came," replied Lord Nelson. "We had to be sure that you were not carriers."

Upon hearing Cacimar's translation, Mextli spoke sharply in Aztec.

"We come from clean islands. We not sick or 'carriers'," Cacimar interpreted. "We come to explore."

"You will be free to roam the ship," said Lord Nelson. "In a few days, you will go ashore and then travel with Lord Madison to meet the Queen. You will have the chance to learn about us, and we want to learn about you. In the meantime, take a swim, clean yourselves, and we will provide you with new clothing. In the name of Her Majesty, we welcome you to England."

*****

When the two natives had been led away, James Madison spoke to the commanders of his armed forces in private.

"There is something of a mystery here," he proclaimed. "Captain Garibaldi said five ships, and over five hundred men came out of the west, and the ships carried small cannon and muskets. That does not sound like the craft and weaponry of peaceful islanders, especially if they are coming from small islands, as they claim. A civilization needs to be well-developed before it can conceive of gunpowder and construct cannon. No gentlemen, these men need to be watched, and we need to learn all we can about them."

"I am afraid, sir, that you are correct," replied General Wellesley. "We have far more pressing matters before us, however. We have received word that Napoleone is once again on the march."

Chapter 32

Walking down a gangplank and then across a large wooden platform that had been built out into the water so that ships could tie up along it, Mextli and Cacimar stepped onto dry land for the first time in over seven moon cycles or months as they were called in English.

"My legs feel wobbly," the young islander noted.

"It is a result of being at sea for so long," replied the former admiral of the Aztec navy. "Your legs will feel normal again in a day or two."

The platforms, called docks, were lined along what was referred to as the wharf front. Ships could pull along these docks, their hulls protected by a thick twisted rope that lined their sides, and unload their passengers and/or wares. The front was extremely busy as brawny men with pasty skin loaded and unloaded cargo from ships both large and small. Huge wooden warehouses, made of the same planking as the ships, stood in rows along the street opposite the docks. Bales of cloth and barrels of foodstuffs were being hauled from the vessels to land vehicles, or vice versa. There was a biting chill in the air, similar to that of the Northeast Territories. The two Aztecs were thankful for their new woolen shirts and coats. In truth, they had not grown used to the heavy trappings worn by the Englishmen, but they now understood why they were needed. The sun was weak overhead, which also explained the pale complexions of these people.

With a start, Cacimar jumped backward, almost knocking down both Mextli and Lieutenant Brewer, the commander of their escort. The lieutenant told them that he and his soldiers were there to keep the two men from harm. Mextli believed they were still under guard.

"What are you…?" Mextli started to harshly ask as he regained his balance. Then he looked in the direction the young man was pointing, and he, too, froze in astonishment.

A large animal, the size of a deer or a small moose, but broader in body, was pulling a platform mounted on round wooden objects that were somehow fastened to the underside of the platform. The platform was loaded with barrels and crates. A man sat on a bench to the front of this contraption holding ropes that extended to leather straps fastened around the beast's head.

Lieutenant Brewer found their reaction to be quite amusing. "Have you never seen a horse before?" he inquired.

"What is horse?" asked Cacimar. "Is it animal or platform?"

Brewer laughed out loud before, replying, "The horse is the animal pulling the cart, or the platform as you call it. Have you no horses on your island? I suppose not," he deduced by Cacimar's gaping mouth.

"What round things?" Cacimar asked. "How they work?"

"What? Oh, you mean wheels?" responded Brewer. "They are attached to an axle under the cart that allows them to rotate…to go around. They enable horses or oxen or other beasts to pull large loads of goods. How do you transport merchandise…goods…on your islands?"

"Boat or back of man," answered Cacimar, then he explained everything that was being said to Mextli.

"Horses and wheels," replied the older man in his native Aztec tongue, his face showing not a trace of the emotion he felt. "Think of the advantage of such things. These horses and…carz? They could not only carry great loads, but our armies could use them to transport big blasters. What an advantage that would be…"

His voice trailed off as they rounded a street corner and saw several more carts, some of a tremendous size being pulled by teams of four horses fastened together. There was also a beautiful walled cart, like a small hut with lavish engravings, in which sat a man and a woman. Even more amazing, standing in the middle of the street, was a half man-half horse. Only it turned out to be a man sitting on a leather device tied to a horse, his legs stretched out on either side of the animal. This horse was sleeker than those pulling the carts but about the same height.

The man shouted something at one of the drivers of a cart and then, turning his horse, started up the street. When he cleared the gangs of workmen and reached the open road above the warehouses, the man and beast tore up the thoroughfare at an astonishing speed, leaving behind a small cloud of dust.

"These horses are a marvel," Mextli observed. "They can pull large objects or one can sit on them and be carried a great speed. What else will we see and learn?"

*****

The two Aztecs were treated politely, but with great curiosity, wherever they went. As the days passed, their continual companions—Lieutenant Brewer and six-armed soldiers—began to accept Mextli and Cacimar, especially Cacimar, as the pleasant but docile natives of some remote island that they claimed to be.

Over the next week, the two men were wined and dined and met many prominent English people. They were also asked hundreds of questions about their homeland. Cacimar described the island where he was raised in great detail, omitting nothing, but under Mextli's strict orders he never mentioned the Aztec Empire. When pressed, he said they had been fishermen and did not know how his people had discovered thunder powder or built the boats that had brought them to the east. They had been recruited as simple sailors by the exploration fleet.

The two men traveled throughout London and the surrounding countryside and saw more than they could have ever imagined existed. They tasted foods they had never before encountered and, in turn, learned that the English had no maize or potatoes or tobacco. They saw massive buildings that rivaled those of the Aztec capital, factories that poured foul smoke into the sky while producing incredible arrays of goods, carriages pulled by teams of horses, streets that were lit at night by gas lamps, and thousands of chimney pots that spewed even more coal smoke into the air resulting in a layer of soot that covered almost everything. They had even been taken to a play called *Hamlet* written by a man named Christopher Marlowe.

Cacimar found it all overwhelming. He began to yearn for the simple life of the islands. "I set out to see the world," he told Mextli, "but the world is too overwhelming. I have seen more than I ever bargained for."

Mextli seemed to take the English civilization in stride, his facial features never changing. His guides were well aware of this fact and so began a quest by Lieutenant Brewer and his men to find something, anything, which would cause the older man to show any sort of emotion. The two Aztecs were taken to huge churches and houses of ill repute, to magnificent estates, and to the dungeons of the Tower of London. They were entertained at an elegant ball, peopled with gentlemen dressed in finery from head to toe and swirling ladies in gorgeous dresses decked out with all manner of jewelry and precious stones. And they drank ale in a pub situated in the squalor and filth of the heart of London amid staring workers in dirty clothing. Nothing fazed the older Aztec, nothing until one morning during their fourth week in London.

It was a Saturday and Lieutenant Brewer informed the two men that they were invited to attend a military review. Over the past few months, the English had been transporting a large army across the channel to their province in Brittany. Cacimar informed Mextli that there was talk of war with the Italians everywhere they traveled. These Italians were the same people who had destroyed the Aztec ships and killed their crews. The admiral had also heard some of this talk, as his understanding of English gradually improved, but he never let on to Cacimar or the white men that he understood their words.

They sat on wooden planks called bleachers. In a box to their right sat General Arthur Wellesley and members of his staff. To their front, on what was called a parade ground, stood row upon row of soldiers, dressed as finely as the dancers at the ball they had attended, in bright red uniforms with white pants and the now-familiar X of their white cross belts. Their boots and the buttons of their uniforms were polished and gleamed in the sunlight. The soldiers had marched onto the field in neat orderly ranks, stepping off in unison and coming to a halt as one man. They now stood ramrod straight, quite unlike Aztec soldiers, as if they were made of stone.

When their officers shouted orders, they snapped their thundersticks, or muskets, straight out in front of them as if they were a single entity. Upon another order, the weapons' wooden stocks struck the ground in a single thud as the men spread their feet in what Lieutenant Brewer said was called parade rest. It did not appear restful. Aztec soldiers were also disciplined and moved together as a unit but not in step or with such exactness. These English soldiers took the word unit to a new level.

The clatter of galloping hoofs came from their left. Onto the field raced a hundred horsemen, dressed in the same manner as the foot soldiers, but riding their mounts at an astounding speed. Each was armed with a long knife called a saber. The horses, arranged five across and twenty deep, moved with the same precision as the marching men.

These cavalrymen passed by the reviewing stand followed by twenty teams of horses, each pulling an eight-pound cannon mounted on wheels. These cannon carts were, in turn, attached to a wheeled carriage that Brewer explained carried powder and shot.

Mextli stared at the sight. With men and cannons that could move at a far greater speed than foot soldiers, this army would be invincible in a war with the Aztec Empire. Horses! Horses were the key. If only he could take some back to the Empire to breed. If only he could get back to the Empire!

When the cavalry and artillery had passed and the noise and dust subsided, Mextli spoke to Cacimar. The young man turned to Lieutenant Brewer and asked, "Can we walk to soldiers? Mextli like to see them close."

The troops were beginning to shoulder arms and march off the field when the lieutenant sent a runner to the command box. As the runner was making his way back, one of Wellesley's staff shouted out to the nearest group of soldiers. Twelve men, under the command of a sergeant, detached themselves from their company and marched smartly to stand at attention in front of the bleachers.

"Let us inspect these men," Lieutenant Brewer said to the Aztecs. "You may get as close to them as you wish."

Mextli climbed down from the bleachers, followed by Cacimar and the lieutenant. He walked up to one of the soldiers who remained rigid, staring straight ahead.

Cacimar interpreted the admiral's words as they were spoken. "Mextli would like to hold a…a musket."

Lieutenant Brewer nodded and barked a command. The soldier standing before the admiral snapped his left hand to the center of his weapon and then brought it forward with both hands. Mextli took it from him and examined it carefully. From a distance, it resembled a thunderstick, but up close, he could see it was far more refined. The weapon was much shorter and lighter than a thunderstick, yet it was sturdy. Mextli could see that its size would allow its handler to use it from a kneeling or a prone position, as well as standing. There were attachments on the wooden support below the firing tube to hold a ramrod and a short bayonet.

"This particular piece is actually not a musket," Lieutenant Brewer was saying. "It is called a Baker Rifle. The majority of our troops still use muskets, but a number of our elite units are slowly switching over to this weapon. It is simple enough to be mass-produced in our factories, but it is lighter than a musket. It takes a little longer to load, but it is far more accurate as it has rifled grooves in the barrel. The short carbines carried by the cavalry are a variation of this rifle. That's probably just a lot of gibberish to you, ain't it?"

Cacimar smiled in assent while the admiral looked closely at the weapon's firing mechanism. There was a piece of stone attached to the movable arm that came down on a surface set just over the pan. Mextli motioned at the stone with a curious expression.

"That is called flint," Brewer said proudly. "When it hits the striking surface, it creates a spark that detonates…er, lights…the powder in the pan. That fires the weapon."

As Cacimar translated, Mextli eyes briefly expressed shock, a fact that was not lost on the lieutenant. This rifle did not need to be ignited by a match.

"A trained soldier can get off several shots a minute," Brewer continued as Cacimar translated, noting that the older man was also briefly startled by that information.

Mextli raised the rifle to his shoulder and looked down its barrel, as Brewer explained the weapon's backsight, which was used for aiming. Lowering it again, he continued to stare at the rifle in his hands.

"Not just horses," he muttered to himself, "their big blasters and their thundersticks are far superior to ours. These people pose a great danger to the Empire."

As he passed the rifle back to the soldier, Lieutenant Brewer was aware that Mextli's hand was slightly trembling.

*****

The next evening, Mextli and Cacimar were provided robes, which Lieutenant Brewer explained were the clothing worn by a people called Arabs who lived further east. The robes were light and far more comfortable than the intricate English clothing and more closely resembled their traditional Aztec garb.

The two men were to meet the sovereign of all England. They had an audience with Queen Anne II in her residence at the Windsor Castle. Brewer said the royal court had been moved to Windsor in 1698 when a fire had destroyed a place called the Whitehall Palace.

"Imagine a woman emperor," Mextli said under his breath. "There is nothing about this land that surprises me anymore."

"Yet there are no women in other high places," whispered Cacimar. "I have been reading the books of thc English, and I have noted there are a number written by a female called Jane Austin, but as in our society, there are no women in leadership positions other than this Queen."

They were ushered down a richly carpeted staircase and into a great hall with high ceilings supported by gigantic pillars. The walls were covered with ornate carvings in relief or featured painted pictures of very serious men and women. There were large windows made from the marvelous substance the English called glass, a matter that was solid, yet one could clearly see through. Chandeliers made of a transparent stone called crystal held hundreds of candles that filled the room with a bright flickering light. At the far end of the room, sitting on a tall decorated throne, sat the ruler of England.

Queen Anne II was a short, slender woman, thirty-six years of age, and quite attractive. Her forehead was wrinkled, the only indication of the stress that she was under as head of the English nation, but her eyes flashed with youthfulness. Mextli and Cacimar approached her throne and, as they had been instructed, dropped to one knee and bowed their heads. Beside them knelt James Madison and General Wellesley.

"Rise," the Queen commanded in a throaty voice. "We would speak to you."

The four men rose to their feet.

"You have come a long way and are seemingly trapped in a strange and foreign land," the Queen began. "Perhaps someday we may be able to transport you home."

As Cacimar translated her words to Mextli, both General Wellesley and the first minister were aware of the great smile that came to the young man's face and the brief look of horror that flashed across the facade of the older one before it was quickly replaced by his normal expressionless stare.

"But for now, this will not be possible," continued the Queen, "We are about to go to war with an evil man who has designs to conquer all Europe. We must focus on this effort."

Queen Anne sighed and then resumed, "In the meantime, we would like to officially welcome you to England and do our best to make this, your temporary home, as hospitable as possible for you. Is there something that we may do for you toward this end?"

Cacimar translated this question for Mextli and the Admiral responded in Aztec.

"We wish to go with Well-es-ley," Cacimar told the Queen. "We wish to fight Italians."

"Oh dear," gasped Anne. "But why?"

"They kill all our people," Mextli replied through Cacimar. "They sink our ships and make war on Aztecs. We want to fight with English!"

The Queen looked uncertainly at the general of her armies.

"So be it," roared Wellesley. "With Her Majesty's permission, you will travel with me to face Napoleone and defeat this Italian warmonger. We will sail on two day's tide."

The Queen nodded her approval before beginning a string of questions about the homeland and experiences of the two men.

*****

Later that night, when they had returned to their lodging, Cacimar asked Mextli why he wanted to go with General Wellesley.

"I do want revenge on these Italians," answered the admiral, "but I also want to observe the whites at war. I want to know how they fight and what tactics they employ. Someday in the future, when we escape this land, this information will be crucial to the Empire."

*****

Lieutenant Brewer stood before General Wellesley, Lord Nelson, and the first minister.

"I have no doubt that Mextli has handled a rifle or a musket before," he added, concluding his report. "Despite claiming that he had never seen one in actual use, other than being carried on parade, he raised the weapon to his shoulder like a practiced marksman."

"This man says nothing but seems to observe everything with great interest," the general responded. "And the only time he has shown a trace of emotion was when he was watching our military or when he heard we might take him home. What is going on in that head of his? What does this all mean?"

"We must not forget one important fact," Lord Nelson interjected. "The Italians reported the islanders' ships were armed with cannon. This does not fit into the description Cacimar has given us about homeland."

"Not at all," Madison replied. "They contend they come from a backward island over two months' sail to the west, but this does not seem to match the facts at all. I think their islands are far more developed than they have let on. I also think that this Mextli is more than he pretends. But why do they hide this from us?"

"And what shall we do with them?" asked Nelson.

"For the time being, let us honor their request that was granted by Arthur and the Queen. We will allow them to travel to Brittany with General Wellesley," answered the First Minister. "Lieutenant Brewer, I want you to keep them both under close surveillance, but I would also like you to work diligently to become a close friend to Cacimar. Speak with him often when out of the presence of Mextli. Gain his confidence. We may be able to learn something more from the young man. He seems far more willing to trust us."

Wellesley rose to his feet and saluted. "With your permission, First Minister," he said. "I am off to join my army on the continent."

Chapter 33

Brittany was an English province situated to the west of France on a peninsula that jutted out into the Atlantic Ocean. To its south was the Bay of Biscay. To its north was the English Channel that furnished a direct shipping route to the mother country.

The craggy coast of Brittany was as frost-free as the French Riviera, allowing the rich farmlands of that vicinity to produce great quantities of grain, vegetables, and soft fruit. The region was also ideal for livestock breeding. These products, and the abundant supply of cod, oysters, lobsters, and tuna that were caught just off the province's shores, were shipped directly to London from the seaport at Brest to help feed the home island.

The ownership of Brittany had been in constant dispute between the English, the French, and the Bretons themselves. In 1488, a French army under Louis de La Tremoille invaded Brittany. Henry VII of England, and the Archduke Maximilian of Austria, threatened to send in troops to prevent the French from swallowing up the duchy, but those forces failed to materialize in any numbers. The Bretons put up a weak resistance, and when the ruling Duchess of Brittany, Anne, was besieged at Rennes in 1491, she was forced to marry King Charlcs XIII of Francc to savc thc city and bring about peace. The territory appeared destined to become absorbed by France. Just a year and a half later, fate intervened when Charles died from the Colombo Plague.

For the next twenty years, there was an uneasy peace as tens of thousands died, the plague's dead were buried, and the Bretons were left alone. The remnants of the governments of Europe were far more concerned with survival than politics. When a number of French feudal lords began to push into Brittany in 1513, however,

Anne appealed to England for military support. A garrison force was sent to occupy the duchy, and the French withdrew. The following year, Anne married Lord Edward Woodville, the commander of this force, which cemented the province's ties with England. During the next century, English culture gradually supplanted French until it was generally acknowledged that the peninsula was English.

Brittany's interior was a relatively unproductive and hazy plateau full of woods and small fields surrounded by hedgerows. The province's capital was Jamestown. That city had been formerly called Rennes but had been renamed to honor King James IV following Anne's marriage to Woodville. It was a municipality of broad streets and canals, located to the east of the province at the edge of an agricultural belt, just three hundred miles southwest of Paris.

It was along a line of woods that faced the great open fields to the east of Jamestown that Wellesley chose to position his army and make his stand against Napoleone.

*****

For a number of months, Napoleone Buonaparte had been aware that the English were sending troops to strengthen their forces in Brittany. He also knew the Prussian army, under Marshal Gebhard von Blucher and ninety thousand strong, was finally on the move and planned to link up with the English. Blucher was marching across the German states and would pass through the northwestern provinces of France, but informants indicated he was still several weeks distant.

Buonaparte was unaware that General Wellesley had replaced Major General Rowland Hill as the commander of an English army in Brittany and that these forces now numbered some seventy-five thousand men.

After delaying in France for almost a year to reorganize that country's government and disband its army following the capture of Paris, Napoleone put together his battle plan. Reinforcements had raised his fighting strength to eighty-five thousand troops. His veteran army began its march toward Brittany. He would defeat the English, who his general staff estimated at less than fifty thousand men, and then he would turn and deal with the Prussians. The Kingdom of Italy was expanding. Soon it would truly rival the glory of the Roman Empire.

*****

Mextli and Cacimar stood on a wooden deck built into the upper branches of a large oak. It was situated at the front edge of clump of trees that overlooked the battleground. With them were the ever-faithful Lieutenant Brewer and a Colonel Pettigew from Wellesley's staff. At the base of the tree were two of Brewer's men and runners mounted on horses who waited to take the colonel's messages to the unit commanders during the conflict.

The English had reformed their ranks at six o'clock in the morning, expecting an early assault from the Italians who had arrived on the battlefield the previous evening. It was now nearing nine o'clock, and although they could hear the sounds of an army far across the fields to their front, no attack had come. It was unseasonably warm, and a thick fog blanketed the open ground. This mist was gradually being eaten away by the sun so that, now and again, a single patch of blue appeared and then disappeared in the higher swirling haze.

The English infantry was drawn up in two long rows, interspersed with artillery. These lines spread out for thousands of yards on either side of a dirt road that emerged from the woods behind their lines to meander between the empty harvested fields. Included in their ranks were the Fourth Royal Veteran Battalion, the Ninety-Third Regiment of Sutherland Highlanders, the well battle-tested Forty-Ninth Regiment, the Welsh Forty-First Regiment, and the Royal North English Fusiliers, among other units. There had been a time when these ranks would have been dressed in a myriad of colors, uniforms designed by each unit independent from one another. That had resulted in considerable confusion in battle, with friendly forces sometimes firing upon one another. It had been an English general in India, an individual named George Washington, who had mandated in 1775 that all his forces be outfitted in a comparable uniform. The results had been so effective that this policy had been adopted by the entire English military. The armies of many of the other European nations followed suit. The men in the English lines who now stood in the fields of Brittany were all dressed in red uniforms that stood out sharply even in the mist. Patches on their collars distinguished each regiment.

The troops stood at ease, talking to one another in nervous anticipation, their muskets or rifles ready by their sides. They had placed their field packs and haversacks in orderly piles behind their lines and wore only their cartridge belts. Just behind them, hidden by the woods, was the third rank of infantry. Wellesley held two cavalry units, the Fourteenth and the Nineteenth Light Dragoons, in reserve.

Out in front of the infantry were the outposts; men hiding behind fence rails and hedges or laying in shallow ditches, listening for the advance of the enemy through the fog so they could fire warning shots to alert the main body.

*****

Napoleone allowed his men to have a leisurely breakfast before they began forming ranks for their assault. General Severoli was anxious to begin the attack, but Napoleone was in good spirits as he tried to calm Antonio's nervousness.

"An army travels on its stomach," he told the older general. "Well-fed, the men will fight all the harder. Besides, the Italian army is far superior to the English. It will be to our advantage to hold off our offensive until the fog lifts. We will then drive the English dogs back to their ships at Brest."

"So you plan a frontal assault, sir?" Severoli questioned.

"Exactly!" replied Buonaparte. "Facing the massed formations of our magnificent troops, they will collapse just like the French."

"Perhaps we should first send in the heavy cavalry to soften up one of their flanks," Severoli suggested.

"That will be unnecessary," answered Napoleone. "I want our cavalry ready should the English try to send their horse around our own flank. No, we will begin the assault with the planned artillery barrage as our men advance, and then we will smash them back through Jamestown. I want this field carried today so that we can begin to prepare for the Prussians."

As the fog continued to thin, glimpses of red uniforms could be seen across the field. Napoleone looked proudly at the forward ranks of his green-clad Italians, now ranged in battle order four deep to his front. They were nervous, but they were also eager and confident. The Army of Northern Italy had never tasted defeat—their little general would not allow it. His personal Imperial Guard stood behind him, held in reserve. Each man stood over six feet tall and had been selected to serve in this elite force from the cream of the crop of the tough Melograno units in each regiment. Each had repeatedly demonstrated his fighting ability and lack of fear in past battles. They wore eighteen-inch black bearskin headdresses to distinguish themselves from the regular troops, an accouterment that made them appear even larger in size.

At precisely nine o'clock, sixty massed Italian cannons erupted in a volcanic volley as they sent shells skyward toward the English lines. Wellesley's guns began to return fire, bugles sounded, and the Italian infantry began its advance across the thirteen hundred yards that separated the two opposing armies.

*****

The cannonade raised a huge ruckus and kicked up dirt and dust around the English lines, but remarkably, it inflicted few serious casualties. When the first shells began to land, Wellesley sent off his Nineteenth Light Dragoons on a feint well beyond his left flank in the hope of drawing off the Italian cavalry, which the maneuver succeeded in doing.

Cacimar and the admiral watched in fascination as the battle unfolded before their eyes. Never had Mextli seen such firepower. Despite the shelling, the soldiers in both armies displayed the same courage inherent in Aztec soldiers. Would his countrymen be able to hold their lines if faced with an adversary as formidable as the Italians or the English?

As the fog lifted and swirled away, the long green ranks of the Italians were fully revealed. Their lines were spread across the field as they advanced on the English positions like a wave curling in from the sea. Lit matches were thrust into touchholes, and the English cannon began firing into those ranks, thundering as they sent off their lethal discharges. Orange flames burst from their brass muzzles and blue-black smoke drifted heavenwards as the six, eighteen, and twenty-four pounders filled the air with projectiles just before they crashed back in their trails, disgorging dirt from under their jerking wheels. Dark streaks filled the sky and descended into the green-clad ranks, plowing channels through the columns and opening holes in the lines as bodies were tossed to and fro. As soon as these soldiers went down, however, men from the ranks behind filled the empty spaces.

As the Italian infantry drew closer, their artillery fire ceased. The English cannon continued, the guns lurching back after each discharge before being rolled back into position and reloaded for the next volley.

The two Aztecs were now aware of different sounds. There was music playing behind both armies. A marching band followed the Italian soldiers, their drummers beating out a cadence for the advance. This was countered by the throaty blare of English bagpipers.

A small crackle of rifle fire could be heard from the English ranks, and officers swore at the men who had discharged their muskets out of fear or nervousness, then shouted at the remaining troops to hold their fire until the enemy was well within range. Mextli and Cacimar could now make out individual faces in the advancing ranks. Officers on horseback rode in front of the Italians, brandishing sabers and encouraging their men. The soldiers in green were still moving in good order.

The English skirmishers were either down or racing back into the friendly lines of their comrades. As the Italians drew to 150 yards of their objective, the English muskets exploded up and down their line. A number of men in green were spun around or toppled over. Many grabbed at their stomachs or heads, screaming in disbelief and pain, but still, the remaining Italians advanced, their trailing ranks stepping over the bodies of the dead and wounded lying on the field.

A second volley raked the Italian front, and now that line stalled. Many men had been hit, but others simply stopped in place, their will to advance shattered by the English musketry. The Aztecs continued to watch in fascination, their eyes and noses stinging from the powder smoke of the battle that was drifting back and up to their position high in the tree. Some of the men in the Italian front rank began to turn back, stumbling into those behind them. A mounted colonel, with gold epaulets on his shoulders, shouted for the men to continue their advance. Lieutenants on foot, red-faced and angry, struck at the retreating men with their sabers.

The fog had totally dissipated, replaced by the smoke of battle that drifted above the lines. "How can men stand there and take such punishment," Cacimar whispered.

Regrouping despite a third volley by the English, the Italians pressed forward once again then halted one hundred yards from the English lines where they unleashed their own barrage of musket fire. Now Englishmen began to fall. A soldier directly in front of the platform doubled over, a stain of dark red growing on the backside of his uniform. Another man spun to his right, his hand pressed to the side of his head and blood flowing down into his collar. Wellesley was everywhere, highly visible on horseback and risking his life while entreating his men to repel the enemy. His presence and valor spurred on the English ranks.

The Italians were now firing, reloading, advancing ten yards, and firing again. Musket fire rippled along both lines in intermittent bursts. The green line stopped again just fifty yards from the soldiers in red. The concentrated volleys had ceased. Most of the men on both sides stood firing independently, but a few dropped to the ground in an effort to protect themselves using the downed bodies of their fellow dead.

For a minute or so, the two ranks emptied their weapons at one another. Men on both sides bit into cartridges, aimed, and fired. Their mouths were dry, and their lips cracked. Their faces were filthy from the smoke from their own discharged weapons, their fingers cut and bleeding from pulling back the flints on their muskets. Then the sound of bugles came from behind the Italian lines. Slowly, the men in green began a deliberate, organized withdrawal.

From the English ranks, there rose a ragged cheer.

*****

Word had come to the Italian headquarters that Blucher had initiated a forced march, and the Prussians were now less than two days away. Thus far, the battle at Jamestown had been a stalemate. Napoleone was worried that Prussian cavalry could be approaching his rear in advance of Blucher's infantry. He also did not want to risk a frontal bayonet charge into grapeshot without knowing for sure the English strength in the woods behind its front lines. He was now aware that he had greatly underestimated Wellesley's strength. He ordered a careful retreat.

The green-clad infantry moved back through the ranks of the imperial guard who were covering their withdrawal. There was no panic; their movement was precise and orderly. They left the bodies of their comrades, both dead and wounded, on the field behind them. Wellesley, having suffered substantial losses of his own and not knowing Blucher's whereabouts, chose not to counterattack.

*****

Exhausted men in red collapsed where they stood. Others began drinking water in great gulps from their canteens, their faces black from gunpowder. General Arthur Wellesley climbed to the decking that held the two Aztecs and looked out at the retreating Italians.

"It appears," he said to no one in particular, "that Brittany is safe for the moment and Napoleone has been checked. When the Prussians arrive, we will take this war to the Italians."

Cacimar watched the withdrawing enemy and was only now aware of the cries and moans coming from just behind the platform. Walking to the rear of this perch, he nearly gagged. Lying there, behind tables covered with blood, was a pile of unattached arms and legs. Frantically workings on men lying on these tables were surgeons with saws, their white aprons covered with bloody smears. Wounded soldiers littered the ground as the surgeon's mates moved among them, marking the dead with a tag and moving the less seriously wounded to nearby tents. The amputees were being carried to another tented area where they would wait out the next few days. Many of these men would die of the fever that so often took wounded men.

Mextli joined his friend. "These are incredibly brave soldiers," he said. "It is unbelievable how they could stand there killing one another from such a close range. And even when the enemy withdrew, it was methodical and without fear. Both armies are made of men equal to Aztec soldiers but better armed. I am extremely disturbed by their strength."

Chapter 34

Mextli and Cacimar sat on their beds in a small room of a large house in Jamestown. Outside the chamber were stationed two of Brewer's ever-present men. The lieutenant was an extremely friendly man who repeatedly assured the Aztecs that his soldiers were there for their own protection, but they still felt like prisoners in this strange and hostile land.

The Prussians had arrived, and Wellesley and Blucher were arguing about how they should move against Napoleone. Wellesley had only a few minutes to spend with Mextli and Cacimar, but the admiral could still hear his barely understandable words ringing in his ears.

"With our Prussian allies," the general had told them, "we now have the superior numbers. It is only a matter of time until we defeat this Italian upstart and drive him back across his border. Then, my friends, perhaps we can return you to your islands. You would like that, wouldn't you?"

Seeing Mextli's frown, Cacimar asked, "What is troubling you, Admiral?"

"The words of Well-es-ley," replied Mextli. "How does he plan to return us to our homes? I would venture that it will be with a fleet of his giant warships. I tell you again, I fear these white men and their weapons. When they see the riches of the Empire, they will want them for their own."

"Is that not what we intended when we set sail, to take the riches of the white ones?" asked Cacimar with a grim smile.

"That is true," answered Mextli. "But we owe it to the emperor, and our people, not to let this happen to us. The Empire must be warned of this threat. I do not know how we will do this, but we must find a way."

Chapter 35

The winter months passed slowly for Mextli. He grew increasingly agitated. The continual cold and dampness that permeated into every corner of London did not help his disposition. The two sentries who were constantly assigned to him "for his own protection" further increased his ire. Worst yet, he was losing Cacimar. The young islander had become fast friends with Lieutenant Brewer and seemed content to spend his days sleeping and his nights drinking and whoring.

At first, Mextli tried to gently dissuade Cacimar from his nightly reveling. The young man laughed and said it was just something to do to take his mind off the cold. When Mextli later grew angry and attempted to reprimand the youth, ordering him to stop these excursions, Cacimar scowled. He told the older man, in no uncertain words, that Mextli was no longer an admiral and, in these new lands, had no authority over the islander or his actions. The two parted with antagonistic words, as a result of which both were now uneasy in one another's company. As the months passed, the only occasions they spent any time together were during their regular evening meal.

As winter turned to spring, Mextli contented himself to prowling London during the day, accompanied by his two guardians. He spent a great deal of time by the docks, learning about the Thames River and even going on brief sails in the small riverboats. Although he understood English fairly well by now, he still communicated by sign language and kept his knowledge of the white men's language to himself. He circumspectly watched, and took note of, how the sails of the small craft were raised and lowered. Several of the boat owners, pleased by his interest in their vessels, allowed him to operate the rudders of their craft, or raise and lower the sails, and complimented him on his ability to read the wind, accurately judge the currents of the flowing river, and come about on the water.

Some days, Mextli visited the museums and shops spread throughout the city. He discovered the office of a cartographer not far from his boarding house and spent hours poring over maps of Southern England, paying particular attention to the outlet of the Thames. When questioned, he would sign that he was a seafaring man and was fascinated about everything to do with ships and water.

On those occasions when he and Cacimar were invited to the home of a politician or a military officer, Mextli would use Cacimar's skills as an interpreter to ask as many questions of his hosts as they would allow. In this manner, he learned a great deal of useful information about the English merchant fleets, the tides and currents of the ocean they called the Atlantic, and the dispositions of the continents of Africa and Asia. The world was truly huge, but the maps of the English still depicted the admiral's homeland as one of the dozens of mysterious islands lying between Europe and China. The white ones had no inkling of the large landmasses, making up the Northern and Southern Territories to either side of the great isthmus of the central Aztec Empire.

Unfortunately, the opportunities to gain information through interactions with the whites were becoming rare as the novelty of the Aztecs dissipated. Mextli began having more and more free time alone although he was never out of shouting distance from his two-man escort. He was no longer summoned by First Minister Madison, and there had been no more talk about returning the Aztecs to their island home, the single possibility that had kept a flicker of hope, and fear, alive in the admiral's otherwise dreary existence.

As the month of April replaced May in the year of 1813, the admiral's informational resources, as well as his former connections to those in authority in England, had dwindled to next to none. His only contact with the government was in the form of discussions with Lieutenant Brewer at their evening meal before the young officer left with the now usually quiet Cacimar to carouse away the night. Reluctantly, the island youth still acted as an interpreter for the admiral. Through the lieutenant, Mextli learned that the Italians, faced by the combined forces of the Prussians and England, had withdrawn back across their border. France had been liberated and their king reestablished to his throne in Paris. There was now an uneasy peace in Europe.

*****

The winter months passed slowly for Cacimar. He took a fancy to drinking ale and visiting the brothels of London with his new friend, Tom Brewer. Tom was a young unmarried gentleman of twenty-six who seemed to genuinely enjoy the islander's company. During the past few months, the lieutenant had stopped quizzing Cacimar about his homeland, and the two had become frequent visitors to Madame Renaud's and the Purple Parrot, two of the finer houses of ill repute in the English capital.

The massive islander, with his muscular physique and dark olive skin, was an instant sensation with the women of both establishments. The house's regular customers had also grown fond of this unassuming giant with his marvelous smile and friendly manner.

Cacimar was unhappy about his current relationship with Mextli and how it continued to deteriorate, but he found the older man to be sullen, gloomy, and unpleasant company. The past could not be changed, and he was now a captive in a strange but exotic land. But what a captive! Lieutenant Brewer—Tom—saw to all his needs. Cacimar had a room, three meals a day, clothing, and, in the evening, all the ale and women he could consume. He was young. Why should he not enjoy himself? What was the use of brooding? He was seeing a world that he could never have dreamed existed. No, Mextli could go ahead and waste away sulking; he would live his life and enjoy what came his way.

*****

The brothel had been full of laughter and singing earlier in the evening, but now it was late and its customers were emptying the premises. Dozens of candles reflected off the huge mirror behind the bar, allowing the patrons of the establishment a better opportunity to take in the richness of the purple velvet covering the walls and the upholstery on all the furniture. Paintings of naked women in seductive poses filled the main salon.

Not everyone was leaving, however. This evening, Cacimar and Tom Brewer were still playing dice with two gentlemen in the Purple Parrot. It was nearing midnight, and Cacimar had been drinking tankards of ale while enjoying a light conversation with the men in his company. His ability to consume great quantities of beer, while remaining relatively sober, was already legendary in a number of taverns, drinking clubs, and brothels.

Cacimar had already picked a girl named Polly for his bed, and the rosy-cheeked young woman with golden hair, and an ample bosom, stopped by the gaming table periodically to see how he was doing and bring him more ale. When he had first arrived in England, the young islander had yearned for his home and thought often and fondly of Coatlicue, the serving girl with whom he had spent several months before sailing east. These thoughts had left him morose, a condition that he felt could only be remedied by beer and prostitutes. Now he seldom thought of his past. Polly was pleasant and her pale alabaster skin, and the pink nipples of her large breasts, fascinated Cacimar. With enough to drink, he could ignore her plumpness and could lose himself within her before passing out for the night.

This evening, Cacimar had lost all the money Tom had given him, but he was not yet ready for bed.

"Tom, I feel luck coming. Please give me more pounds." He laughed. Usually, the lieutenant was quick to accommodate his wishes, but not this evening.

"I'm sorry, my friend," replied Lieutenant Brewer, "I have no more money."

"But I feel luck coming, Tom. I want to play more."

"I'll tell you what," answered one of the two gentlemen. "I will put up half the money I have won against your renowned drinking ability. If you win your dice roll, you get my money. If I win, you will be required to drink shots."

"Drink musket balls?" the astonished youth inquired.

"Not metal shots," Lieutenant Brewer chuckled. "Shots of Irish whiskey. A shot is a splash of liquid in a very small glass. Take the bet, Cacimar. You have nothing to lose."

"Whiskey?" The islander laughed. "Whiskey burns like fire and makes my head spin."

"You won't lose, and I will watch over you if, by some far stretch of the imagination, you do," replied Brewer as he stood up in front of Cacimar so as to block the islander's view of the gaming table and his fellow players. As he did so, one of the gentlemen pocketed the dice they were using and replaced them with another pair.

"I will try," the young man agreed. He hooted with a burst of laughter as he reached past the lieutenant and took the new dice.

The first shot burned all the way down his throat and into his stomach while bringing water to his eyes. He tried to get up from the table, but his friend—Tom—pushed him back down into his seat, steadfastly reassuring Cacimar that he would win the next roll. The dice remained cold. By the third shot, the burning was not as bad, and he was finding everything to be incredibly funny. Cacimar howled with hilarity at jokes he had heard before and still did not really understand. Following his fifth shot, the room was spinning, and he toppled from his chair, wheezing with glee.

Tom Brewer lifted his friend to his feet, while draping the youth's right arm over his own strong shoulders, and began walking him toward the door.

"We'll be taking a short stroll to sharpen up his wits," he told a concerned Polly. "Be back in half an hour."

Once outside, the two men walked up and down the narrow deserted street as Lieutenant Brewer talked softly to the inebriated islander.

"I guess you don't have whiskey back on the islands," he commented softly.

"No whiskey, pulque," sputtered Cacimar.

"Pull-kay?" laughed the Lieutenant. "Where do they make that?"

"I do not know," slurred the youth. "In the country, in the cities, I think everywhere. It does not burn like whiskey but makes you happy like ale."

Brewer instantly picked up on the word "cities." He kept talking in a calm soothing voice. "You must be homesick, Cacimar. Do you have a woman back in the city?"

"Coatlicue. I miss Coatlicue. I miss islands."

"Tell me about Coat-le-cue," continued Brewer, walking slowly as the Aztec stumbled along beside him, his arm still wrapped over the lieutenant's shoulders. "What does she do? Where does she live?"

"She is so beautiful, my Coatlicue. I miss her so much. She is serving girl in Emperor's palace. She is so good-looking, so nice to be with. She is smart and—"

"Did you live in the emperor's palace too?" questioned Brewer.

"No," answered Cacimar in his drunken stupor. "Mextli and I live in house in Tenoch… Tenochtitlan. Met Coatlicue at banquet in palace before we sail to east…to England."

"Tenoch… I cannot say that word. What is this place?"

"It is capital city," answered the young man.

"It is the capital of your island?" asked the puzzled Lieutenant.

"No," Cacimar laughed drunkenly. "Tenochtitlan bigger than all the villages on all the islands. It's bigger than many of the islands. Tenochtitlan is capital of Aztec Empire."

Over the next twenty minutes, Cacimar rambled on about the Empire, its territories, and the sights he had seen while traveling with Mextli in the Northeast Territories. Then his stomach did a flip-flop, and he vomited its contents all over the cobblestones before passing out.

Chapter 36

A flood of light streamed into the room through the large glass windows. The bright sunlight illuminated the antique stone sculptures that were aligned along the far wall, statues that had been chiseled centuries ago during the height of the Roman Empire. Paintings by celebrated Italian artists were hung between these statues while handcrafted mahogany cases displayed bronze figurines and fine china at either end of the room. The floor was polished wood, and the walls were faced with artificial marble.

Captain Alonzo Garibaldi sat in a chair facing Napoleone Buonaparte, the emperor of the Kingdom of Italy. Buonaparte was not in a good mood. A dark melancholy had enveloped him after he was compelled to withdraw his army east of the mountains—the Alps—that separated France and Italy. His forces had not been defeated, but they were overwhelmingly outnumbered by the English, Prussian, and now French coalition. The situation had gone from bad to worse when Sweden and Russian had announced their support, at least politically, of his enemies.

Napoleone listened intently to Captain Garibaldi's report, asking direct questions when the information was sketchy. As Garibaldi concluded, the emperor continued to stare at the man wearing the uniform of Italian naval command.

"So you took it upon yourself to sink five ships, killing hundreds of men?" the emperor asked without a trace of emotion.

Captain Garibaldi swallowed hard before answering. "Yes, my emperor. I feared they were carriers of the Colombo Plague. None of us had ever seen ships constructed in such a manner or such strange-looking people, and as I told you, they were coming directly out of the west—"

"Relax, Captain, relax," Buonaparte interrupted. "You did well. I find no fault in your logic, but why have you waited a full year to tell your story?"

"I have been held captive by the English," Garibaldi responded. "I was only released in March as part of an exchange of prisoners. I immediately filed a report with the naval office upon my return to Italy."

"Thank you, Captain," Napoleone said warmly. "Go get yourself something to eat, but stay close. I will have need of you later."

Garibaldi rose from his chair, saluted, and left the emperor and his staff.

Buonaparte glanced at General Severoli, and then he turned to one of his aides. "Santorre, bring in the scholar."

Santorre Santarosa left the room and returned minutes later with a small trembling man wearing wire-rimmed glasses that pinched his nose. Enzo DeLucia was the most prominent historian in Rome and had recently been summoned to the imperial mansion outside that city by Napoleone. He carried three large books and a box full of handwritten notes.

"Stop shaking," commanded the emperor, "and tell me about the Colombo Islands."

"The Colombo Islands were discovered in 1492 by…," the scholar began with a quaking voice.

"I know when the damn islands were discovered," thundered Napoleone. "I want to know what this Cristoforo Colombo found on the islands besides the plague."

DeLucia carefully placed the books he carried on a table and began going through his notes. "With your leave, Excellency," the scholar began again, "I had no time to prepare for your questions, so please allow me to speak aloud to myself as I gather the information you seek."

Napoleone frowned but nodded slightly. DeLucia shifted through a pile of loose papers.

"Colombo was detained by the Portuguese when he returned from his ill-fated adventure. I am not sure how long…ah-ha, here it is," Enzo continued as he picked out a specific crumbled sheet of paper. "On March 15, 1493, Colombo returned to Palos, the town from which he had initiated his journey thirty-two weeks earlier. He then journeyed to Barcelona where he appeared before King Ferdinand and Queen Isabella at their palace. The Queen noted that he seemed weak and his complexion was poor, but she attributed his appearance to his voyage. As a side comment, it is interesting that although King Ferdinand died of the new plague—"

"Get on with it!" bellowed Buonaparte. "What did Colombo say about the islands?"

Frightened but contentedly immersed in his own studies, Enzo hurried on with his findings. "Colombo reported islands with lush vegetation. He told stories of cannibals and mermaids. He also said the islands were rich in spices and gold."

"There, that is it!" shouted Napoleone. "That is what I heard. Did he bring any gold back with him?"

DeLucia thumbed through two more pages and then looked up with a smile on his face. "Yes, sire. Colombo brought back several natives and colorful birds called parrots. He also returned with gold encrusted in ornaments, such as crowns and masks, as well as nuggets and gold dust."

"Is there more?" asked the emperor.

"No, Your Excellency," the scholar replied. "There is nothing more reported, except the fact that Colombo died believing he had found lands of great riches."

"Great riches," Napoleone said softly. "Thank you. You are dismissed."

When the scholar left, Buonaparte sat down and beckoned General Severoli to join him.

"A land of great riches, Antonio," he said with a gleam of satisfaction in his eyes. "And these lands belong rightfully to Italy. Although he commanded Spanish ships, Colombo was an Italian!"

"I do not wish to trouble you," replied Severoli. The older soldier was one of the few men who could speak his mind without fear of consequences to the emperor. "But are you not forgetting the sickness? Colombo brought the plague back from those islands. The pope restricted all ships from sailing west—"

"That was a different Vatican. The current pope will do as he is told," countered Napoleone. "However, there is more to this story than you know, Antonio. A month ago, our spies in London brought word that two natives from those islands survived Garibaldi's attack. They were kept isolated for many months, exposed only to their immediate guards. When the guards did not contract the plague, they were released and have been living in England, under guard, for more than six months. No one in London has come down with the Colombo Plague. It is my belief that just as the Black Death burned its way across Europe and then was consumed, Europeans no longer need to fear the Colombo Plague. General, I want you to take a fleet, with an army of twenty-five thousand men, and find these islands. We will claim them for the Kingdom of Italy and use their riches to finance our military needs."

"And what if these natives in London came from a different island than the one on which Colombo landed?" asked Severoli. "What if the plague still exists on another island?"

"We will take our chances on that, General," the emperor replied. And then as an afterthought, he added, "And may God go with you."

Chapter 37

Upon awakening, Cacimar found he was in a small dark room, its plain undecorated walls made of solid stone. A single barred window let in a faint light. His head still throbbing from the previous night's drinking, he was lifted to his feet by two soldiers and seated on a stool facing four Englishmen who identified themselves as officers under the command of General Wellesley. At this point, the grilling began.

The youth quickly realized from their questions that he must have told Tom Brewer about the Empire while under the influence of the whiskey, but he could not remember what, or how much, he had said to the lieutenant. He felt betrayed and angry and would not answer any of their queries.

Several hours later, Mextli was roughly taken from his room and subjected to the same treatment as Cacimar. The admiral sat stone-faced, staring straight ahead. The officers assumed he could not understand what they were saying and sent for Cacimar to act as an interpreter. When the young man refused to translate their questions, they grew angry and placed the two Aztecs in a larger cell where they were deprived of food for twenty-four hours before being returned to again face their inquisitors.

It was during the days they spent in that cell that the bond between Cacimar and Mextli was restored. The islander broke down in tears and told the admiral what he thought had transpired during the previous night with Lieutenant Brewer. Instead of growing angry and shouting, the older man embraced him. He told the youth he had made a mistake in judgment, but he had not committed a wrong knowingly and should not be ashamed. A cunning people who pretended friendship had tricked him.

Mextli was confident that even if the English were now aware that the Aztec Empire existed, they had failed to learn much information that was of use to them or they would not be trying to gain further information. Cacimar had seen and heard many things on their travels together, but he did not have a detailed knowledge of the Empire and its inner workings. The two men resolved, even should they be tortured or starved, they would say nothing more.

The questioning continued day and night for several weeks.

*****

"There are ways to make them talk," the newly promoted Captain Brewer suggested.

"We are not a barbaric country, nor have the two Aztecs done anything to warrant such punishment," General Wellesley answered harshly. The captain took a step back.

"Let us once again review what you learned and then discuss why they are unwilling to share any additional information," suggested James Madison, getting up from his desk. The three men were gathered in the first minister's private office at 10 Downing Street. The room was small but comfortable. The floor was covered by a plush red carpet. The sparse furnishings included a single bookcase, a desk, and a portrait of the Queen hung on one wall facing a window looking out on the street.

"These men came from a large empire far off our west coast," Madison continued. "A land filled with cities and thousands of people, perhaps more, who are ruled by an emperor and, in turn, rule over extensive conquered lands to their north and south. This should lead us to deduct that there is a large continent between us and China, not just islands as we have been led to believe."

"This fits with the information brought back by the Russians in Alaska and the Swedes under Minuit, if their tales are true," conjectured Wellesley.

"They are true. Thomas Jefferson swears to both stories." The first minister paused. "We now know that Mextli was an admiral, so this empire has a navy although, from the Italians' description of their ships, it is not a significant force. We know Cacimar served in the Aztec army, and once again from what the Italians told Admiral Nelson and was later confirmed by Captain Brewer on the parade grounds last fall, this army is armed with some type of musket. We have to assume it is similar to ours."

"Admiral Nelson told us the Italians reported the Aztec ships were armed with small cannon, perhaps eight or ten pounders," Wellesley offered.

"This could mean they have not yet developed larger armament, or they did not feel a need to put larger weapons on their ships," mused Madison. "Both men claimed they were on an exploration voyage and not a military venture. No, until we have further information, we must accept the supposition that this Aztec Empire is as well-armed as ourselves. It is possible they have larger warships armed with bigger cannons. Where we exhibit military superiority seems to be in land transportation. We know neither man had ever seen a horse or a carriage prior to coming to England. Therefore, they lack cavalry. They probably use beasts such as oxen to move their artillery pieces."

"They could have camels," Brewer suggested hopefully.

"That is a possibility," replied Madison. "What else do we know for certain?"

"Their ruler lives in a palace in a large capital city. Cacimar has a woman friend in that city, and she is a servant to this emperor. And they are fighting a war with people in their northern territories," Captain Brewer ticked off confidently.

"And neither man will now say a word about their empire, and both hate your guts," added Wellesley, taking some of the blusters out of the captain.

"Why do you suppose that is?" queried Madison. "Why are they not willing to say anything more?"

"Suppose this Aztec empire does control all the lands between Europe and Asia, and as a result, it is a more than wealthy nation," answered the general. "And suppose their army and navy, and their weapons, are not up to our standards. If a people who appeared more powerful than yourself captured you, would you not want to keep the whereabouts of your nation a secret for fear these people may seek to exploit your country? The Aztecs have conquered all the lands around them, so would it not seem logical to them that we would want to do the same?"

"A sound deduction, General, especially in light of what they have seen of the Italians," Madison replied. "Or perhaps the simple fact that we have broken their trust has rendered them mute. I think if we are to learn any more about these Aztecs, we will need to change our tactics. We need to convince these men that we do not wish them, or their empire, any harm. Perhaps they will then talk to us over time. Captain Brewer, I am reassigning you to your old unit in Brittany. You have been a great help, but we must now rebuild the faith of these Aztecs."

Captain Brewer stood at attention and saluted.

"Arthur," the first minister continued, "I want you to explain to Mextli and Cacimar that we understand their concern for the safety of their empire, and we have no intention of doing anything more than establish trade relations with their emperor, should we ever rid ourselves of Napoleone and sail west. I also want their guards removed."

"Sir?" General Wellesley began to question.

"You may assign a plainclothesman to keep watch on their movements," Madison stated, "but from a distance. If we are to gain their trust, we must first at least appear to give them their freedom."

*****

The two Aztecs were returned to the building in which they had been living. The days passed uneventfully. Then early one morning, Mextli woke Cacimar from a sound sleep. He had been dreaming of his village back on Ayti, only Coatlicue was there with him in his warm sleeping furs.

"It is time for us to leave this place," Mextli said simply. From under his bed, he pulled out a number of folded sheets of paper and a large knapsack. "Take two blankets and bring your warm woolen coat."

Cacimar did not know where they were going, but he obeyed. For the past ten days, the English had given them the free run of the city. There had been no guards and no Lieutenant Brewer. General Wellesley explained why the English were doing this, but neither man trusted him or his countrymen.

"We will go out the back window," Mextli explained. "There is a man watching our front door, but I believe he is asleep."

"I have seen no one," Cacimar said.

"This one does not wear the red uniform of the guards," the admiral explained. "He tries to blend in with the other people in the streets, but he is always there. He, and another man, trade places and follow us everywhere. This is why I have split up from you when we visited the docks. He could not follow us both, and the times he chose to follow you, I made certain arrangements."

The two men slid out a back window into the alley running behind their London apartment house. It was one o'clock in the morning and no one was in the streets, save their dozing watchman tucked into a doorway across their building. They walked silently between the still houses, staying in the shadows, heading toward the docks on the Thames River.

*****

A little over forty-five minutes later, they reached the waterway and walked along it until they came upon what appeared to be a broken-down, abandoned boathouse. It turned out that it was not deserted. On the far side of the building, in the water, was a fifteen-foot sailboat with a single mast and a steering rudder. A tough-looking man, his straggly black beard hanging down to the front of his chest, stood by the boat. A knife was tucked into his belt.

"You took long enough," he said sharply. "Did you bring the money?"

Mextli opened the knapsack and pulled out several hundred pounds, the currency used by the English. Handing the banknotes to the bearded white man he said, "This more than agreed. You keep mouth shut after we go."

The man laughed, snatched the money out of the admiral's hand, and disappeared into the night. Cacimar was as startled by the admiral's command of English as he was at seeing the pound notes.

"Where did you get all that money?" he asked.

"You asked for money to drink ale and sleep with white women," Mextli replied. "I asked for money to visit museums and purchase rides on carriages and to eat fine food in fancy restaurants. I put away half of everything they gave to me and did not spend it."

Cacimar suddenly felt ashamed.

"It is just the way things are," Mextli said, seeing the young man's discomfort. "If it had not been for you, we would not have learned of the white one's dishonesty until it was too late."

The two men climbed into the small boat, and Mextli adeptly hoisted the sail, then steered the craft out from the dock and into the fog that was forming in the middle of the river, spreading toward the shores like a huge, gray thundercloud.

"What is your plan?" Cacimar asked the older man.

"We will make it to the mouth of the Thames by daybreak," Mextli answered while flashing the first smile the young islander had seen on the admiral's face since they had encountered the Italians more than a year ago. "We will wear our coats, and I have two fishermen's hats in my pack to put over our heads. I also have a little food, a map of the European coastline and its offshore currents, and lots of money. We will sail to a place called Africa and attempt to buy a larger boat. There we will hire a crew to help us get home. If that fails, we may have to take in provisions and try to sail this small craft back to the Empire ourselves. I do not know if we will succeed, but we will try."

*****

Wellesley stood before the first minister, his face still red with fury.

"Damn those Aztecs!" he hissed. "And damn that plainclothesman. I should have put a military man on them and not relied on Scotland Yard."

It was noon on a sweltering day toward the end of May. Drops of perspiration fell from the general's forehead. James Madison seemed unruffled.

"How far could they have gone in, say, twelve hours?" Madison asked.

"Not very far at all," responded Wellesley. "I have cavalry units out for fifty miles in every direction."

"And what if they went by sea, taking a boat down the Thames?" the first minister inquired.

"That is not damn likely," answered the general. "Pardon my language, sir. How would they get a boat? Could they sail it, and where would they go?"

"The latter is exactly my question," Madison said. "We know Mextli spent much of his free time pouring over maps and visiting the docks. He was an admiral and knows the sea. No, I would venture the river is their mode of escape. If this is so, I ask again, how far could they have gone?"

Wellesley thought before speaking. "They would now be out of the Thames and could be nearing Brittany or halfway to the Netherlands or Spain. Or they could be heading around the south coast of England and preparing to make for the open sea with the intent to sail back to their own lands."

"Brittany would be my guess." Madison sighed. "I want fast ships sent out looking for two men in a small craft, and I want them sent out in all directions. We cannot be sure where they are going. I want word sent to Brittany, and our provinces in the Netherlands and Portugal, to keep their eyes peeled. And I want word out on the streets of London that I will pay two hundred pounds for any information about the two Aztecs that leads to their recovery."

Chapter 38

Napoleone sat in an open carriage, watching the troop movements on the docks situated at the innermost recesses of the Bay of Napoli. Having recently arrived in the emerging industrial city, the Italian emperor had spent the preceding night attending a performance at the Teatro San Carlo on the Piazza del Plebiscito. The seventy-six-year-old opera house was the largest in Europe and the performance excellent.

Italian soldiers stood in orderly ranks with their weapons, bed-rolls, and large backpacks that were loaded to the brims with excess rations and a full change of clothing. As each company received its orders to move forward, they marched in a single file line to the gang-planks of their designated transport ship. Once on board, each man struggled to create a space for himself, and his equipment, below deck. The top deck was kept clear for the ship's crew to perform their duties and to store additional equipment although there was a small area designated for the various infantry units to exercise during the ocean crossing.

Several piers away horses were being loaded aboard other ships. The beasts were reluctant to climb the wooden planking to the boats, neighing and prancing despite the firm handling of their grooms. They were even more skittish when they were lowered into the dark recesses of the ships. Caissons and light artillery pieces would later be lashed in place on the top deck of these crafts.

"The horses have more sense than soldiers," remarked one sailor to his shipmate. "I would not want to spend God knows how long down below deck in the dark." He crossed himself and went back to work on the sail he was mending.

More than 130 brigs had been stripped of the majority of their guns and converted into transport ships to carry the artillery, supplies, horses, and twenty-five thousand men. Outside the harbor, a small fleet made up of men of war and frigates waited to escort the brigs.

Captain Garibaldi and General Severoli approached the emperor from two different directions, reaching him at the same time. They saluted before making their reports.

"The loading is going as scheduled, my emperor," Severoli stated. "We will have all the infantry on board by this evening. The cavalry units and supply trains will be in place by midafternoon. The holds of those ships have already been filled with hay for the mounts."

"All is going as planned. We will sail tonight as you have ordered, Your Excellency," Garibaldi added. "We will rendezvous with the battle fleet in the morning, and I will transfer to my flagship. In three nights, there will be no moon. I will do my best to slip past the English base overlooking the Straights of Gibraltar, staying close to the African coast. It will be difficult, given the size of our task force, but the straights are thirteen miles wide at their narrowest point, and that should provide me with the distance needed to get by undetected on a moonless night. My only concern is that noise from the fleet may alert their sentries."

"I would like you to set off without being seen," replied Napoleone, "but it is not imperative. The English have no force in the Atlantic that can challenge you and their spies here in Napoli will no doubt inform them as to my intentions within the week anyway. I am more curious as to how they will react. I am speculating they will, for the most part, be unconcerned. What do they care if we sail off to conquer islands far from Europe? I think Wellesley will be relieved that our attention has been diverted away from France and Brittany."

"If I may be so bold," Garibaldi ventured timidly, "but what should we expect to find to the west?"

"General Severoli has been fully briefed," responded Buonaparte. "Your orders are to protect the convoy ships at all costs, but I suppose you should be appraised as to our intentions."

The emperor paused and looked at Severoli, who nodded, before continuing. "We have every reason to believe the islands to the west are full of riches. We are certain there is much gold to be had and perhaps other precious metals. Colombo visited the islands with fewer than one hundred men and returned with a considerable amount of gold.

"We know Colombo met unsophisticated natives when he reached the islands over three hundred years ago. We also know, from your encounter, that this island civilization has evolved over the past three centuries. They now have ships and primitive cannons, but we, too, have evolved and we also know that our ships and our weapons far surpass those of the islanders. I expect you will encounter little opposition, Captain. If the islanders send ships against you, sink them. You are to land the army units at the discretion of General Severoli. He has absolute command over this expedition, and that includes authority over all the actions of the fleet once you have reached the islands."

Turning to Severoli, Napoleone asked, "You fully understand your orders, Antonio?"

"I am to locate the centers of their civilization and occupy those islands," Severoli answered. "If I can do so with only a show of force, so be it. If not, I am to defeat the natives, establish forts, and extract as much gold and other precious metals as I can find to transport home. These are to be shipped back to Italy under the protection of the captain's fleet."

"Precisely." Buonaparte nodded. "We will then claim the islands as New Italiana and see if there is anything else of worth we can extract from them. With the wealth of these new possessions, the Kingdom of Italy will become the greatest nation of earth. Our cities will be extraordinary centers filled with modern buildings and magnificent art. Our industry will surpass that of England. Our armies will be invincible. And then, and only then my friends, we will deal with the French and the Prussians and the damnable English!"

Chapter 39

Upon reaching the sea, Mextli initially steered his tiny vessel out into the Atlantic Ocean and away from land for two purposes. He felt the further out on this vast body of water they traveled, the less noticeable they would be, and he also wanted to learn how the small craft would handle the vastness of the ocean. If they had ample food and water, could they cross the Eastern Sea in this boat? Trying to obtain a larger boat and recruit a crew in Africa would be risky. How much would it take to induce a white man to sail west? They needed to consider all their options.

Four hours off the English coast, they saw the great sails of a ship far off on the horizon. Whether it was English or Italian, or that of some other country, they could not tell. Aware the white ones had glasses that magnified images at great distances, they dropped their sail and waited until the ship was out of sight before raising it again. The wind was slight and out of the southwest, but they were able to make some headway by tacking into the breeze.

On the third day following their escape, they turned back to the east and were making for the African coast when another set of sails appeared to the north. Once again, they furled their canvas, but this time, the unknown vessel continued toward their position in the water. It turned out to be an English cutter, a fast sloop with ten guns and a crew of thirty-four men. They did not resist when they were boarded and taken back into custody.

"Next time," whispered Mextli. "Next time we will steal a larger craft and take what we need in the way of food and water. We will make for home, and if we die trying to get there, so the gods will have decreed."

Cacimar nodded. He had had enough of England and Europe, as well as the ferocious and dishonest white people who lived in these cold villainous places. He would follow Mextli wherever he led.

*****

Barely six hours after picking the two men out of the sea, a storm forced the English ship into the port at Brest where the Aztecs remained under arrest for two days until the skies cleared. As a result, it was still another three days before the two men were delivered to London where they were taken to Downing Street.

The building was a hub of activity with men in uniform and politicians, dressed in dark suits and top hats, rushing in and out of the house. The two Aztecs had visited the first minister's office several times before, and it had always been quiet. In retrospect, as they were disembarking at the London docks, the two men had noted several large ships of the line and a great many frigates in the waters of the Thames River just below the city.

With two large Marines standing guard over them, they sat in a waiting room just outside the first minister's study for nearly an hour before being ushered into his office. The room was cluttered with maps and dispatches. James Madison sat behind his desk talking to Arthur Wellesley. The general stood to his left side facing the door. When the two Aztecs entered the room Wellesley glared at them, but the first minister's face brightened, and he actually smiled.

"Welcome, my friends," Madison said, rising to his feet. "You gave us a scare."

"Thought you might be in the hands of the bloody Italians," added Wellesley, his tight facial muscles relaxing somewhat. "That would not do. Not now."

Mextli spoke to Cacimar in the Aztec tongue.

"That ruse will not be necessary any longer, Admiral," Wellesley barked. "We know from Billy Higgins, the scoundrel who sold you his sailboat, that you speak English. I thought it all along."

Mextli looked at the two men, accessing his situation. They looked back at him in silence. Finally, he spoke in English. "Have the men from Italy attack France again?" he asked.

"No, my friends," answered Madison. "I fear they have gone to war against a far more unsuspecting people than the French."

Wellesley put a map on the desk and spread it out in front of Cacimar. "Do you recognize these?"

The paper was old, and although he was not proficient at reading English, the young man recognized that the writing symbols were not of that language. He was not sure what the pictures represented. There were two larger shapes, many smaller circles, and what appeared to be a marked path between the objects.

The long shape, looking like a fish with a tail, ran from the upper left of the page downward and to the right. Its head faced a second shape more rounded than the first with a spur running out to its left. To the right of this second shape were lots of tiny circles running right and down the depiction. All these objects were drawn in black ink. The path, or trail, was drawn in blue ink, marked with arrows to indicate direction. It ran right to left from the upper right-hand corner of the paper, across the page, and then down to the larger shape. There, it doubled back, running along the top of the first fishlike shape and then the second larger figure before rising back to disappear in the top right corner of the page.

Mextli, who had learned the science of mapmaking as a boy and who had spent many hours studying European maps while living in London, noted the crossed arrows in the corner of the paper, with a capital N above the top arrow. He knew exactly what was drawn on this paper.

"This is map," he told Cacimar in broken English. "This is map of Cubanacan and Ayti and smaller islands of the Inland Sea. The second object represents your home island."

With great concentration, the island youth stared at the picture, trying to envision mountains and beaches and water. When this failed to work, he looked at the relationship of the larger and smaller oblongs and then the smaller circles and grasped what he was seeing.

"Who draw this?" he asked, looking up in disbelief.

"This map is a copy of one drawn three hundred years ago by an Italian sailor who commanded three Spanish ships," answered Madison. "We just recently obtained a copy of it."

"He discovered these islands and returned to Spain to draw other maps like this one. One of his boats was wrecked, and its crew remained behind on this middle-sized island, which he called Espanola," he added, pointing at the island of Ayti. "Now we have some grave information to share with you, and we need your honest answers. I am aware this may be difficult for you, given your warranted lack of trust in us, but your answers may determine the fate of the Aztec Empire."

Both Mextli and Cacimar were startled by this last statement and looked intently at the first minister.

"Three days ago, our posts at Gibraltar reported a large naval force exiting the Mediterranean and heading due west," Wellesley said. "They could not count the number of ships in the dark, but it was a large force."

"This morning," Madison went on, "our agents in Italy appraised us…told us…that Napoleone has sent a fleet to the Colombo Islands. He is convinced the islands are filled with gold, and he plans to take that gold for the Kingdom of Italy."

"What we need to know, and this is important to both us and your people, Admiral," Wellesley continued, looking Mextli in the eye and addressing him by his rank, "is what he will find beyond these islands? What will he find when he reaches the lands of the Aztec Empire?"

"Will he find gold to plunder?" asked James Madison, "Will he find an Empire strong enough to defend its cities and its people, or will he find a land he can conquer and pillage?"

Cacimar looked at Mextli. "Men from Italy are evil men!" he pleaded. "They will kill my people. They will also kill Aztecs."

Mextli's face showed no emotion, but he was torn inside. It was true the Italians were evil and intent on conquering their neighbors. It was also true they were far more powerful than the Empire, but were the English telling the truth, or was this just another trick to determine whether or not the Aztecs had wealth that the English could take for themselves?

"Think, Mextli," said Cacimar. "Men from Italy killed Tecocol."

Pain flashed across the admiral's face. He had not thought about his second-in-command for almost a year, repressing the memory of the man's death. The Italians had sent cannonballs into his ships even as his men stood waving and smiling. They had shot the crew of his fleet in the ocean waters and killed his best friend. They had attacked France. The English had saved his life, and that of Cacimar, and gone to the aid of the French.

"I will tell you what you need to know," he replied.

*****

As Mextli explained the structure and expansiveness of the Aztec Empire over the next two hours, James Madison and Arthur Wellesley listened in rapt fascination. Ten minutes into the narration, the first minister called for his personal secretary to come into the room and transcribe the admiral's words.

It was apparent the Aztec Empire exceeded any European domains in size, including the far-flung English holdings. The Aztecs were a well-developed society made up of millions of people, with an organized military establishment, a navy, and a political system that vaguely reminded Madison of the old Roman Empire. It was now clear that Mextli was one of the leaders within this system and Cacimar was merely a citizen.

When the admiral finished, the first minister sat back in his chair and exhaled.

"I believe the people living in your coastal cities are in great danger, Mextli," Madison began. "The Italian fleet will raid those cities, destroy their defenses, and then take anything of value. They will then bring their ill-gotten gains back to Italy to enrich Napoleone's war chest. For the sake of your people, and England, we must not allow this to happen. I have already ordered Admiral Nelson to ready a fleet to pursue these…these villains. They will track down and destroy the Italian invasion force. We will try to protect the Aztec Empire and its people."

Reaching into his desk, the first minister produced a paper bound with a red ribbon. "You may not be able to read this, but it is a decree made by Her Majesty, Queen Anne. She has authorized Admiral Nelson and General Jackson to establish trade relations with your people, recognizing your Empire as a sovereign nation. This means England accepts the Aztec Empire as an equal to itself and any other country in Europe."

Madison handed the paper to Mextli who took it from his hand and slightly bowed his head.

"Will you and Cacimar travel home with the fleet," the First Minister continued, "to act as guides, interpreters, and to serve the role of an intermediary…a middle man…in establishing a good relationship between your emperor and the Queen?"

"We will," answered Mextli solemnly.

*****

When the two Aztecs left the room, Wellesley asked the first minister. "How many ships will you send west, James?"

"A fair-sized fleet, but not a huge one," answered Madison. "Our intelligence estimates the Italian battle fleet to be less than a dozen ships, not including transports. I will send two ships of the line and fourteen frigates. I dare not send more ships, as I fear a ruse by Napoleone. He has his eye on the English Isles, and we cannot leave our home islands undefended."

"That should be more than enough to defeat the bloody Italians," observed Wellesley. "At sea, they cannot match the Royal Navy. Nelson will sail circles about their ships. May I ask one question, however?"

"Proceed," answered the first minister.

"These trade relations with the Aztecs, sir," Wellesley said. "This is all good and proper, and I am in full agreement, but…"

"But?" asked Madison.

"But treating this heathen Empire as an equal?" the general continued. "After we establish a trading company and secure relationships with these Aztecs, surely we will want to establish a colony or two? Perhaps set up something similar to our arrangements in India?"

"Eventually," answered the first minister, "I would think something like that might evolve. Perhaps there will be a West Indies Trading Company."

"Jolly good, sir," Wellesley replied with a laugh.

"But first," James Madison concluded, "we must find that bloody Italian fleet and sink every one of their bloody ships!"

Chapter 40

The 153 ships making up the Italian invasion fleet were comprised of three men of war, ten frigates, and 135 brigantines. The five to seven hundred-ton brigs had been stripped of all but four of their normal compliments of twenty to twenty-six guns. This created additional space so that they could better transport troops, horses, and artillery pieces. Each brigantine was fitted with two masts, with square rigging on the forward poles and fore-and-aft mast rigging on the after masts. Each of these converted ships was capable of ferrying between 175 and 250 infantry. There was a tradeoff, however. Now that they had become troop transports, they were no longer functional as combat vessels.

A total of twenty-five thousand Italian regulars, the best troops Napoleon could spare, were crammed on board. Of these, three thousand were cavalry. The horses were secured below. The decks of these troopships maintained one small open space that could be used for exercise; otherwise, the remainder of the top side was piled high with supplies, caissons, and artillery pieces, or with stacks of small boats that would be used as landing craft.

The brigantines were small ships well suited for high speed when under full sail. Should they encounter an absolute dearth of wind, these ships could be rowed ever so slowly. Their size made them far more maneuverable than the accompanying frigates and men of war, and thus, they had been the chosen craft for both troop transport and reconnoitering once they reached their objective. For a number of years, Napoleone had been building a huge fleet of these vessels in preparation for his planned invasion of England, but he had now released them for another mission, and they were bound for the mysterious west.

The pride of the Italian fleet was the *Emperor*, a monstrous 136 gun, 2,500-ton man of war that was far larger than any English ship of the line. The *Emperor* had been built in secret and held back from combat, having never before put to sea other than for trial runs along the Italian coast. Now it had been joined the invasion fleet.

The Italians took eight weeks to cross the Atlantic to the Colombo Islands, following the aged writings of Christiforo, the seafarer and explorer who had recently been elevated to the ranks of past Italian heroes. They found the islands without much trouble, but there were no gold or precious stones on these tropical lands. The natives were backward, docile, and offered no threat to the Italians. Even under torture, they swore there were no riches on their island homes.

After long months at sea, General Severoli let his men loose in the various villages they encountered, paying little regard to their actions. His priests had assured him that the heathen natives were little better than animals and failed to possess souls. His men were in need of fresh food and entertainment.

*****

Antonio Severoli stood in the midst of what had once been a village. The thatched huts had been burned to the ground. The bodies of the few native men who tried to defend their homes lay sprawled about the ruins, their beaten and mutilated bodies covered by swarms of small flies. Two or three old crones remained on the outskirts of the village wailing in tormented grief.

Thc majority of thc villagers had fled into the interior of the large island when the pillaging began, but the Italian sailors and soldiers had captured a few unlucky younger females. These women and girls were raped repeatedly until the men tired of them or death mercifully released them from their fate.

The general had seen similar acts of barbarity on the other islands. He was aware that his chief aide, Colonel Bruno Paparelli, seemed to take cruel delight in ransacking these isles. Just a week ago, the colonel had led a company of men on this same island to raid and pillage a village ten miles or so further west of the decimated village in which he now stood. Paparelli had captured a beautiful native girl named Mora and then taken her on board the flagship, boasting of how he had run his blade through a young savage who tried to stop him from abducting the woman. After two days, the colonel had grown tired of Mora's aggressive nature. Rather than submitting to his lustful advances, she tried to rake out his eyes with her fingernails. Furious at her behavior, Paparelli turned her over to his soldiers. Five men had her before she was able to snatch a bayonet from one of them and run out on the deck. When she found herself surrounded by the crew and unable to escape overboard, she had plunged the knife into her own heart. They had thrown her lifeless body over the side of the ship.

It was not that his soldiers were beasts, the Italian commander reasoned; it was simply the fact that they were taking out their anger on the natives. They had been confined below decks for two long months during which time their spirits had been kept elevated by stories of great wealth. The officers had repeatedly told them there would be an enormous amount of riches to plunder and mountains of gold to be divided amongst them as spoils. Thus far, the invasion force had encountered nothing but dirt-poor villages. Once on shore, the soldiers drank heavily and then unleashed their frustration on the villagers. Their officers chose to look the other way. Drunken men could just as easily turn on their superiors. The soldiers would be brought under control far more easily after a night of inebriated sleep.

*****

Severoli was sipping a fruit drink while he surveyed the intense green foliage that surrounded the remnants of the destroyed village when a commotion at the edge of the jungle drew the general's attention. An old woman was walking toward him, carrying a bundle and ignoring the insults and jeers made by the soldiers who were sitting on the ground, eating their morning meal. As she came closer, Severoli saw that she was ancient. Her skin was wrinkled with age and her hair gray and thinning. Her eyes, however, stood out in her leathered face. They were bright and unafraid.

Stepping up to the general, who towered over her, she slapped her chest and said, "Inez." He recognized the gesture from those used in other villages. It indicated her name. Amused, he loudly slapped his hand on his chest and said, "General." The men around him burst into guffaws and raucous laughter.

The old woman stared up at Severoli for a few moments, and then she slowly placed her bundle at the general's feet. It was a blanket containing a number of items. She stooped over and carefully untied the blanket, opening it and spreading it out on the ground. Wrapped in its folds were three objects: a necklace and two engraved bracelets. They were all made out of solid gold. The soldiers stopped snickering and got to their feet to move closer to the old woman and their commander.

Inez smoothed out the dirt next to the blanket and then picked up a short stick lying on the ground. She drew a series of small circles and two larger oblongs. She then raised one of her hands and pointed at the morning sun, still low in the sky and just above the ocean waters to the east. At the same time, she lowered the stick in her other hand so that it pointed at the small circles closest to the sun. Next, she pointed to the largest oblong farthest drawn in the sand away from the small circles and then slowly raised the stick to point to the waters to the west. Finally, she pointed to the oblong in the center of her drawing, and then, dropping the stick, picked up dirt from within that figure and let it slide through her fingers back onto the oblong.

The flagship's navigator looked at General Severoli and spoke, "I think that's a map of these islands, sir," he said. "We passed the smaller islands coming into these waters. The larger one is that big body of land we encountered two weeks ago. I think the middle one is supposed to be this island."

Severoli pointed at the smaller of the two oblongs in the center of the drawing and then at the ground and trees all about him. He picked up a handful of dirt and placed it on the oblong. The old woman nodded in the affirmative, then patted the ground at her feet.

"Ayti," she said, patting the ground again and then pointing all about her with a gnarled finger.

The general pointed at the woman and said, "Inez." Then he pointed at the ground with both hands and said, "Ah-e-tee."

The old woman gave a tired half smile, revealing a few worn and yellowed teeth, and nodded. Turning, she picked up the stick and walked three strides to the west, ignoring the men standing there, where she drew a long line from north to south. Walking back to the blanket, she picked up the gold objects and carried them to that line, placing them on the ground behind it. She then walked over to a bucket of drinking water and reached into it. Several soldiers started to move to stop her but held their places at Severoli's sharp command. Inez's hands made a cup as she scooped up some of the water. Carrying it carefully back to her drawing in the dirt, she bent over and poured the water between the line and the largest oblong.

Standing up again, Inez pointed to the spilled water, now soaking into the dirt, and then at the ocean to the west. She then picked up a handful of dirt and one of the gold bracelets lying behind the line and then returned them purposefully to that same spot behind the stripe. Pointing at both the dirt and the objects, she said one word, "Aztecs."

That single utterance set off excited murmuring among the Italians. During their long voyage across the ocean, they had learned about the ships Captain Garibaldi had sunk over a year before and they had heard stories about the two survivors from the west, men who called themselves Aztecs.

Severoli stared at the old woman. "Aztecs," he repeated.

She nodded her head up and down, pointed to the west, and again said, "Aztecs." Then she picked up the gold objects and held them out to the general, once again saying the word Aztecs.

Severoli took one of the bracelets from the woman's wrinkled hands and looked at it closely. Clearly engraved on the object were images of men and women, dressed in robes and wearing jewelry. A broad smile spread across his face as he turned to his men.

"Enough of these islands, lads," he shouted. "It's the Aztecs who have the gold, and they are to be found further to the west. Back to the boats! We have land to conquer and riches to take!"

All about him, the soldiers and sailors erupted in cheers.

*****

Inez watched the cruel white ones as they loaded into their small boats to take them out to the huge craft that had brought them to her island. Her people would be safe again and could return to their village from the interior of the island. Their homes could be rebuilt, and life would continue. They had been after gold, not slaves. Perhaps the Aztecs would be able to defeat these cold-hearted men from the sea.

*****

Angelo Conti stood on the deck of one of the troopships. They had returned to the vessel the previous day and set sail in the early morning, just before sunrise, and now the tropical island they had recently visited was slowly receding to the stern of the great fleet. The top of the sun's rim was just peeking above the flat edge of the vast Atlantic Ocean, turning the few clouds in the sky a bright red. The color of the sky matched Angelo's anger.

Conti was not a compassionate man. He had seen his share of innocent men and women killed when warfare erupted in and around their homes in Europe. He had readily stolen food from villagers who did not have enough to feed their own families. He had burned houses when those dwellings might conceal, or serve as a defensive base for, his country's enemies. But Conti had always drawn the line at rape.

He was not much of a religious man, but he had been close to his younger sister, Maria, while he was growing up in Pesaro. He remembered fearing for her physical safety, and virtue, when the emperor's liberating army had annexed his city. The first time he had the chance to ravish a terrified young woman following a battle in Austria, he had been reminded of his sister's face. Instead of waiting his turn to rape the girl, Angelo had gone into an insane fury, attacking the two men who were holding her while they attempted to tear her clothes off her body. When the men tried to fight back, he had almost killed one of them. He then guarded the young woman until her parents were found. Word spread throughout the Eighty-Eighth Fusiliers about Conti's actions, and after that, no one attempted to take sexual advantage of a woman while he was in the vicinity.

Angelo understood men's lusts, especially when were confined for long periods in only the company of one another. He totally understood, and had even experienced, blood lust in the midst of, and following, a pitched battle. What other men did away from his presence was their business, but when he was around, even if the women were little more than native girls—nothing more than savages in the eyes of the Italian conquerors—they would not be subjected to this demeaning cruelty.

Corporal Gabrielle De Luca and Private Fulvio Bianchi joined Angelo by the railing of the ship.

"What are you thinking about on such a beautiful morning?" asked De Luca.

"I was thinking about Colonel Paparelli's behavior," Conti answered slowly. "The man is a pig. Sergeant Ricci said he raped a twelve-year-old girl in front of her parents and then slit the throats of both the girl and her father before turning the mother over to his men. If I had been there—"

"If you had been there," interrupted Bianchi, "no doubt you would not be here. Most likely, you would have tried to attack Colonel Paparelli and you would have been hung for that offense."

"Let's not think of that unpleasantness," said De Luca, seeking to change the subject and Conti's mood. "What do you think about the Aztecs and their gold?"

"I talked to a cavalryman who spoke to a soldier who said he was with Severoli when the general found the treasure house full of gold," Bianchi exclaimed. "The natives said the Aztecs have so much wealth that they toss away armfuls in exchange for fruit and meat on the islands. We are all going to return to Italy wealthy beyond our dream."

"Stories are embellished," Conti answered. "We'll see what riches we find when we come upon these Aztecs." With that statement, the veteran turned from the rail and walked away, but both of his friends were well aware that Angelo was now smiling.

Chapter 41

With their flags of red, white, and blue flapping off their sterns and all their sails hoisted and fully stretched out to catch the strong prevailing wind, the ships of the English fleet cruised effortlessly through the sea leaving a trail of white waves in their wake. The small armada was made up of two large ships of the line, *Victory* and *Intrepid*, and fourteen frigates. Battle-hardened sailors, the best in the Royal Navy, manned these vessels. There were no troopships to slow down the fleet, but the fourteen fighting ships carried 6,750 English infantry, and a number of mules, who were crammed into every spare square inch of the vessels. It was terribly uncomfortable, and the soldiers were forced to sleep in rotating shifts while others stood in designated sections on the deck.

By all educated guesses, the English had set sail from Plymouth Harbor a little more than a month after the Italian fleet had departed, but they had a major tactical advantage. Mextli and Cacimar were familiar with the waters of what they called the Inland Sea and could guide the ships directly to the ports of the Aztec Empire. The Italians were following Colombo's maps, and it was speculated that they would spend several months searching Cacimar's home islands before moving west. This would allow the English time to close on their enemy.

*****

Two frigates, along with 750 infantrymen, were lost in a tragic gale one week off the coast of England, but the remainder of the ships survived the great storm. After fifty-eight days at sea, they reached the outermost islands of the Inland Sea where they briefly took on fresh provisions before continuing southwest of these landmasses toward Chalchihueyecan, the primary Aztec port in that region.

A day and a half out from that seaport, the fleet had come across twelve Aztec warships. As soon as those ships sighted the huge English vessels, they veered away and tried to flee, but they were quickly run down. The Aztec sailors were manning their cannon when Mextli's voice, amplified by a device known as a megaphone, cut across the water.

"Do not fear! We are not your enemy. It is I, Admiral Mextli, who has returned from across the Eastern Sea, and I bring friends."

There was confusion for a few moments on the smaller ships, and then the Aztec sailors began shouting to one another in excitement. One of their boats inched alongside the massive ship of the line on which Mextli sailed, and an officer named Cenyatol boarded the English vessel.

Meeting with Mextli and Admiral Nelson, the Aztec officer informed them that his ships were all that was left of a larger fleet that had originally been made up of thirty vessels. A Captain Tlaloc had been the commander of this force. Seven days earlier, the fleet had encountered other giant ships, like Mextli's. Awed by the size of the strange craft, as well as their number, the Aztecs tried to communicate with the white men on board, but the huge ships had opened fire on the smaller boats and destroyed eighteen of them before the rest could sail out of range. The great ships seemed to have no interest in pursuit and were last seen heading for the beaches of Xoco. Captain Tlaloc had been killed in the conflict. Cenyatol assumed command and dispatched one of his boats to alert the Empire of this threat. That ship had just returned two days ago with word that a massive Aztec army was being assembled to repel the invaders.

*****

Three days later, the remaining six-thousand-man English expeditionary force landed at the harbor of Chalchihueyecan. Led by Admiral Mextli, and under the command of now Brigadier General Andrew Jackson, the infantry units, accompanied by eighty mules carrying boxes of ammunition and eight of the medium-sized cannons that had been stripped from the frigates, moved into the interior. Their destination was the Aztec capital of Tenochtitlan.

As Jackson and Mextli marched off, the English fleet—accompanied by a number of Aztec sailors—set off for the island of Cozumel, reportedly a five-day sail around a peninsula to the southeast. There they would refit and rendezvous with the remainder of the Aztec fleet.

Chapter 42

The battered Aztec warship that had been dispatched to warn the Empire of its impending danger reached the seaport of Chalchihueyecan three days before the English fleet made its startling appearance. They told a strange and frightening tale. Hundreds of giant ships, powered by massive wind catchers, had appeared out of the east. The larger ones, each armed with scores of massive big blasters mounted in rows along the sides of their hulls, had fired on the smaller Aztec vessels. Most of the fleet had been destroyed. These huge ships had not stopped, however, and were on a course that would take them a mere half day's walk above the beaches of Xoco, to the north of Chalchihueyecan. Lieutenant Cenyatol had sent this one ship to warn the dominion governor.

*****

General Ocelopan was a grizzled veteran of the Inca campaigns. At sixty-six seasons of age, he held the title of general of the Dominion of Totonaca, a vast coastal area that was seven days east of Tenochtitlan. The population of this particular dominion had been granted citizenship by Emperor Xolotl I hundreds of seasons ago and were fiercely loyal Aztecs.

He may have been old, but Ocelopan was experienced, energetic, and sharp of mind. Born and raised in a military family and possessing a decisive and firm style of leadership, he insisted on keeping the men under his command fit and trained even though there were no local enemies to fight. The general was known for his discipline and his ability to mold raw recruits into fighting men, and for this reason, new troops were constantly sent to him from all over the

Empire to learn the art of war under his watchful eye before being shipped back to their units.

After dispatching runners to Tenochtitlan, the general immediately mobilized all the military forces in his surrounding area, summoned troops from the neighboring dominions, and then moved them northward. Within a week, he had amassed a force of 115,000 men, more than enough to overpower any army that could be landed by the reported two hundred ships, which he doubted was an accurate number. Men suffering from fear tended to vastly overestimate their enemy, especially sailors who had recently suffered an embarrassing defeat.

This army was now massed along the beaches of Xoco, the only stretch of sand wide enough, and protected enough, to serve as a landing site for many a days' sail. Spread out on the calm waters of the Inland Sea to the front of this immense Aztec force were three gigantic warships, their masts towering several times higher than any vessel the navy of the Empire had ever built. These ships had arrived at Xoco just hours after the Aztecs but sat passively in the waters just outside an outcropping of sandbars for the remainder of the day. Ocelopan noted that the sides of these vessels were filled with neat rows of what appeared to be dozens of boarded windows. There were no big blasters mounted on their decks. Behind these huge ships were an endless number of smaller craft, each easily twice the size of the largest Aztec naval craft.

*****

A week earlier, the Italian invasion force had come into contact with the mainland just a four-hour sail north of the wide beach at Xoco. The fleet had opted to turn north however as they dropped the majority of its sails and slowly moved up the coast searching for possible landing sites. The ships had anchored each evening so that they would not miss locating such a beach during the night. Their diligence had not been rewarded as they encountered miles of steep cliffs. These obstacles were followed by a number of beaches that were protected by barrier reefs, making them unsuitable for landing troops and horses. Thick, impenetrable jungle grew to the very edges of most of the shoreline. When they stopped at the few stretches of sand that might have been utilized as landing sites, they discovered impassable marshes behind these beaches. Nowhere did they find a site suitable to accommodate twenty-five thousand men and horses. Even more discouraging, they had only come across a few isolated villages, and they were deserted. There had been nothing resembling a port or a city. General Severoli wondered if the old woman had created the story of the Aztecs just to rid her island of the Italians. But if this was true, how could one explain the three handcrafted objects made of gold?

At the end of the fifth day of creeping up the coast, having traveled a distance they could have covered in a single complete day under full sail, a discouraged Captain Garibaldi informed General Severoli that he believed they were headed in the wrong direction. He felt sure there was a seaport on the mainland, reasoning that the Aztec fleet they had encountered must have been operating from a base. He now felt that base was most likely to the south. The next morning, the entire fleet came about, raised additional sail, and retraced its path until they discovered the Xoco beaches, with its finely grained brownish sand that lay undisturbed and protected from the pounding surf by a series of sandbars. It was an ideal landing site, but the seven days that had been spent searching the coast to the north had provided the Aztecs with enough time to organize a reception committee. More than one hundred thousand soldiers stood in ranks just off the beach, waiting to repulse any landing attempt.

Given the huge numbers of their foe, the Italians spent a full day readying their forces in preparation for their assault.

*****

Sub-General Zeia, the second-in-command to Ocelopan, was alarmed by the size of the strange ships. There was no doubt in his mind that the Aztec navy was no match for such monsters. He expressed his concern to the general, only to be sharply rebuffed.

"The ships may be large," Ocelopan scolded him, "but they are not to be feared unless they have the ability to sail on land. The men on board them appear to be no larger than us. Let them try to land on our beaches, and we will sweep them back into the sea from which they come."

After an uneventful first day, the enemy's continued inaction further reinforced the general's belief that these newcomers were truly afraid of the size of his army and would probably move on. Nothing happened during the first few hours of the day following the fleet's arrival as the two opposing forces continued to watch one another. This inactivity was finally ended when the wooden windows on the sides of the three largest ships were raised. Large iron tubes poked their ugly heads from these spaces.

"They have giant big blasters!" gasped Zeia.

A detonation of flame and smoke bellowed simultaneously from the guns on one of the vessels. A thunderous roar that shattered the silence on the beach came on its heels a split second later. Twenty seconds after the detonation, large cannonballs crashed into the midst of the army massed on the shore, crushing men and knocking others into the air like leaves in the wind. And now the guns on the other two of the larger ships began firing the iron projectiles, adding to the devastation.

General Ocelopan was not a fool. He immediately recognized the danger facing his army given the size and range of the enemy's big blasters. He ordered his men to fall back on the double.

The Aztecs withdrew in an orderly fashion but took an incredible pounding as they did so. The general could not believe the range of the weapons on these ships. It was not until the army had moved back to a position twenty minutes from the sea that the shelling stopped. Hundreds of Aztec warriors had died during the withdrawal, and worse yet, the beach was left undefended.

*****

General Severoli watched the huge native army pull back under the barrage from his three men of war. "I would estimate there are over a hundred thousand men on that beach," he muttered to Colonel Paparelli.

"They are only armed with spears and clubs," scoffed the colonel. "We will make short work of these savages once we have landed our artillery."

"I do not think they are savages," observed Severoli. "They appear to be an organized and disciplined force. Untrained natives would not withdraw in such an orderly fashion while under heavy fire. They would have turned and run. These men have been well-trained."

"There is no sign of any cavalry," remarked Paparelli. "Do you suppose they are being held to the distant rear in reserve?"

"I had expected to see their cavalry behind their ranks when they were formed so close to shore," replied Severoli. "I cannot suppose where they are positioned. We will need to remain alert and wary."

Turning toward the colonel, the general continued, "As a result of our bombardment, we now have ample room to maneuver once we are on shore. If the Aztecs attempt to move toward the beach, I will cover your landing with the ships' cannon. Secure the beach, bring in your artillery with the second and third waves, and then land your horses with the final units. The animals are frightened enough by the water. I do not want their fear compounded by the sounds of battle."

Colonel Paparelli saluted and headed off to a smaller boat that would transport him to the closest troopship.

*****

Hundreds of small flatboats were lowered over the sides of the brigs that were anchored just beyond the three men of war. Eight to ten rowers manned each boat. Scrambling over the sides of the brigantines, the green-clad Italian infantry climbed down netting that hung from the ships' railings and extended to the water and small craft below. Between thirty and forty men filled each landing boat.

As the first wave of troops headed for shore, more small boats were lowered into the water. Many of the flatboats in the second grouping rode lower in the sea as they each carried a single heavy artillery piece. The first boats would return to the ships to pick up the third wave of the attack. Further back in the invasion armada, screened from the Aztecs by the more forward vessels, men began using slings to carefully transfer six to eight jittery horses, along with their riders, from the brigs to the landing craft that would make up the fifth and final wave

General Severoli was committing fifteen thousand men to his initial assault on the beach while holding ten thousand in reserve.

*****

As the flatboats glided through the water toward the tranquil surf washing gently onto the beach, General Ocelopan made the mistake of trying to advance warriors to counter the landing. The big blasters from the enemy's ships resumed fire, sending devastating shots into these unprotected troops, and he was once again forced to order a withdraw.

Powerless to stop the enemy from coming on shore, the Aztecs could only watch as the green-clad foreigners landed in four precise waves timed forty-five minutes apart. Men jumped from the small craft and splashed out of ankle-deep water to form ranks on the beach. Soldiers with stripes on their arms heeded the commands of their leaders and then shouted at the troops, getting them to form well-organized ranks. The first wave, dressed outlandishly in long white pants, tall green hats, and green coats with white belts crisscrossing their chests, moved a hundred paces inland and then knelt, facing the Aztec army.

General Ocelopan's recognized that these were well-trained professional soldiers, perhaps as proficient as his own warriors. While the Aztec troops joked about the strange dress of these men, the general was mentally calculating their strength and noting they all carried unusual wooden weapons appearing to be smaller and more manageable versions of a thunderstick.

As the second wave landed, Zeia commented, "They do not seem to be too formidable a force. Their weapons look puny. We should be able to defeat them soundly if they are foolish enough to try to advance inland and away from the protection of their ships."

"Perhaps that is not their intent," responded Ocelopan. "They may be content to establish a beachhead and then build a fort on our shore while they wait for reinforcements. It is what we have done in many foreign lands."

Zeia was silent.

*****

The second wave landed behind the first, men dragging small-wheeled three-pound artillery pieces through the sand from the boats to the infantry positioned inland. These boats were followed by the third and fourth waves of infantry who also advanced across the beach to form three long lines of green. Four hours after the initial landing, sometime in midafternoon, all the Italian ranks rose to their feet and began a slow advance toward the massed Aztec army.

*****

"It appears they have a little more than ten thousand men on the beach," Zeia estimated. "Are they insane to attack our force? We outnumber them ten to one."

General Ocelopan was not as smug. These enemy soldiers were well-disciplined and confident. More importantly, they seemed to have big blasters mounted on wooden circles that were moved along with the infantry. He did not like the looks of these new weapons.

Cautiously, he ordered his thundersticks posted well to the front of his army. His forward units were formed in interlocking calpullis of a hundred men each.

*****

When the first ranks of the Italians were three hundred yards from the leading elements of the enemy forces, they stopped and advanced their cannon through gaps created between the troops. Several minutes later, these artillery pieces opened fire on the forward

Aztecs manning the large musket like weapons mounted on supporting poles that were driven into the ground.

The Aztec soldiers and their officers reacted in shock. Many had seen such weapons mounted on ships or the walls of forts, but none had ever seen big blasters that could be moved with foot soldiers. It took only a matter of minutes before a third of the thundersticks were out of commission without having fired a shot in return. It was once again necessary for General Ocelopan to order the surviving Aztec advance forces to withdraw behind the ranks of the massed units. These calpullis were formed in extended interlocking lines, the spearmen to the front of the foot soldiers and the bowmen to their immediate rear.

The Italians continued to move forward until they were only 150 yards from the massed Aztecs. Their cannon remained behind, protected by the three ranks of infantry, but were rolled to within 200 yards of the enemy. To the Aztecs, these green men did not appear entirely human. They were exact duplicates of one another, each soldier dressed and armed exactly like the men to either side of him. There was a surreal quality to this foe, and it was slightly unnerving and somehow frightening.

The first rank of the Italians simultaneously dropped to one knee with the second rank standing in line directly behind the first. In one synchronous motion, all the men in green slapped their hands to their right side and then lifted bright glistening knives from their belts that they then fastened to the ends of their wooden weapons. The Aztecs could now clearly see these weapons had metal tubes and were, indeed, smaller versions of thundersticks.

After another few minutes, the Italian artillery once again commenced fire on the Aztec lines, sending their deadly projectiles over the heads of their own infantry. These cannonballs were different, however. They trailed smoking fuses as they flew through the air. These missiles exploded just above the massed army, driving deadly shrapnel into their ranks. Hundreds of warriors screamed and fell, their blood soaking the ground, but the disciplined ranks stood staunchly in place.

*****

General Ocelopan had only seconds to make the decision whether to further withdraw from his enemy to a position of safety or to strike a swift and overwhelming blow to destroy these invaders. He ordered a charge.

Whistles blew all along the ranks. Screaming their war cries, the forward units of the hundred-thousand-man army leaped into action, surging toward the strangers who dared to attack the Aztec Empire, who had the audacity to bring war to the land of the strongest people on earth.

Ninety yards from the men in green, the front rank of Italian infantry braced and fired. Smoke temporarily obscured their ranks as a wall of led smacked into the charging Aztecs, making dull thudding sounds as the balls hit flesh and dropping scores of men. As the front rank reloaded, the second green rank stepped through their kneeling comrades and fired. Twenty seconds later, the third rank emulated the move of the second, stepping through their fellow infantry to discharge yet another deadly volley. The sulfur stench of rotten eggs from the expended gunpowder filled the air.

Capable of delivering nine volleys a minute in this fashion, the Italians were killing and wounding thousands of their attackers. As the bodies began to pile up, the Aztecs stumbled to a stop, hesitant to advance against such devastating firepower.

General Ocelopan watched his warriors as they began to falter before he quickly pushed his way to the front of their ranks while waiving his maquahuitl and shouting, "We are many! We are Aztec! Death to the green men!" Turning, he rushed forward at the enemy, miraculously unscathed by the Italian's fire.

The Aztec warriors, spurred on by Ocelopan, let loose with a great cry and, consumed with hatred and vengeance, sprinted after their general. Many went down, but their front rank closed and then collided with the Italians in a shattering crash of shields and muskets. It was now a battle of bayonets versus spears and war clubs. These weapons were evenly matched, and the men wielding them on both sides were well-trained in their use. After a few minutes, the sheer weight of the Aztec numbers began to force the men in green back, but the Italians gave their ground grudgingly, taking down many a warrior with their long knives. It was apparent that the superior numbers of the Empire would very soon envelop the green men's flanks as the fighting progressed.

The two armies had only been engaged in hand-to-hand combat with one another for a few minutes when the din of the battle was broken by the piercing blare of a distant bugle. Moments later, despite the shouts and cries of battle, the Aztec left flank was aware of a growing rumble. This noise steadily escalated until it could be identified as the sound made by thundering hooves. General Ocelopan had heard such a reverberation once before when he had been a young officer. Stampeding buffalo had created that thunder. The warriors nearest this increasing clamor continued to yell, but now their cries of anger had turned to screams of terror. The men making up the Aztec left turned and tried to flee to the rear, many losing all discipline and dropping their weapons as they took flight. These Aztecs crashed into the warriors behind them who were straining their necks to see what had caused this fear, sending their ranks into disarray.

The center of the Aztec forces, hearing the commotion on their flank, came to a standstill and then backed off from their green-coated foe as they, too, tried to see what had inflicted such dread into their comrades. What they saw froze their insides. Rushing towards them from their left, at an unbelievable speed, were huge beasts. The upper halves of these creatures resembled the green men with whom they were now engaged in combat—a head, a trunk, and two arms, one of which held a long fearsome spear. It was the lower half of these beasts that brought bile to the mouths of even the bravest warriors. They were similar to the bodies of a moose or great elk, and these four-legged monstrosities were covering the ground between them at a murderous pace—far faster than any man could run, as fast as deer in flight before a grass fire.

More Aztecs started to run, but many stood in a state of disbelief as the Italian cavalry swept into their flank, pinning down multitudes with their lances and hacking down the foot soldiers with their swords. Given a reprieve from the fearsome Aztec onslaught, the Italian infantry reloaded and unleashed a final deadly barrage straight into their frozen enemy, and then they advanced with their deadly bayonets.

A few of the Aztecs regained enough composure to fight back, but they were quickly surrounded and chopped down by the experienced professionals of Napoleone's army. The majority turned and began to run for their lives, the unlucky warriors to the rear being bayoneted by the advancing green-clad soldiers or struck down by the huge half monster-half man creatures who were in pursuit of the fleeing army. Slashing away at the defenseless heads and backs of the men running in panic, killing and maiming thousands, the cavalry followed the routed Aztecs for nearly a mile before returning to their infantry. The victory was complete.

Over thirty thousand Aztecs were killed or wounded, their bodies covering the ground. Only fifty-eight Italians had died while another 172 received wounds. General Severoli had only read of such magnificent victories in books detailing ancient Roman history. It was clear that the native army, no matter how many men they could amass, was no match for the Italians.

*****

Angelo Conti sat stoically still while a surgeon put the last of twenty stitches in his cheek, closing a gash that had been inflicted by an Aztec war club that had fractured the bone below his right eye socket. Now that entire side of his face was dark purple and had swollen so much that he could not see out of that right eye. The doctor had informed him that nothing was broken, and once the swelling had gone down, he would be as good as new. He could not say the same about Angelo's best friend, Corporal Gabriele De Luca.

De Luca had been standing to Conti's right when the Aztecs had charged. He had no idea how many they had killed as they discharged their deadly volley into the screaming masses, but the warriors kept on coming. This was unlike the ordered battles in Europe in which he had fought, where rows of men stood apart and fired their muskets into one another until one side broke or retreated. He had been in occasional hand-to-hand combat in the past; fights that had been settled by bayonets, fists, and rifle butts. He had never before been attacked by thousands upon thousands of berserk men who seemed to have no regard at all for their losses.

The Italians had been hit like a tidal wave and almost washed back, but the discipline of the infantry, and the sharp knives mounted on their muskets, had held off the Aztecs until the cavalry arrived and routed their foe. Angelo had blocked a spear thrust and bayoneted the first warrior to reach him. Two more went down to his immediate front, and bodies were piling up when a huge man with a war club crushed De Luca's skull. The follow-through from that swing had hit Conti in the cheek, but he had had enough strength left to ram his own bayonet up under the rib cage of that warrior before he collapsed. It was at that moment that he had heard the sound of the cavalry bugle.

"Those sons of bitches," Private Bianchi swore. He had fought to Conti's immediate left and helped take the wounded veteran of the Eighty-Eighth Fusiliers to the doctor's tent. "They killed De Luca."

"And we made widows of thousands," Angelo grimly answered.

*****

Three days after the battle, the Italians had been reinforced by the additional ten thousand troops that had been left on the ships. They were now preparing to march inland and then south. General Severoli had dispatched one of the brigs back to Italy to report his victory to the emperor. In his communiqué, he wrote that there was the great promise of abundant amounts of gold and that the so-called Aztec Empire would be under his complete control in a matter of months. His army physicians treated their own soldiers and then saw to the needs of those enemy soldiers who still lived. Graves were dug for the Italians who had died in the conflict while the Aztec dead were buried together in a single great pit.

As best as the Italians could determine from the wounded, through hand gestures and drawings, there was a harbor several days' march to the south of their present location. And to the west of that port, just a little over a week's walk away, was the Aztec capital. When the wounded Aztecs had been shown the three gold objects from the island, and the Italians had pointed at the port and capital on a map they had created, the injured soldiers had all nodded in the affirmative. Severoli decided he would march on the harbor, establish it as the base for his fleet, rest and feed his army, and then turn toward the riches of the interior. Perhaps the native people would simply surrender before his might. If not, they would be brought under his thumb easily enough. They were fearsome warriors, but their weaponry was inferior and could not match the Europeans. It was also apparent, from the frightened babbling of the wounded, that not only did the Aztecs fail to have cavalry units; they had never before seen horses.

God had been kind to General Severoli, and one day, he was sure his name would go into the history books along with those of Caesar, Alexander the Great, and, perhaps, even Napoleone. On September 14, in the year 1813, the general planted a flag in the hallowed Aztec ground at Xoco and claimed all the new lands for the Kingdom of Italy.

Chapter 43

Ahuitzotl VI, emperor of all the Aztecs, sat on his golden throne cloaked in his traditional tilmatli, a mantle of blue and white held in place by a jewel-studded buckle. The bright gems and golden bracelets adorning his arms and neck glittered as they reflected the light of the torches impaled into the walls of his imperial chamber and surrounding his throne in his capital palace. On his head, he wore a bright headdress of colorful feathers.

In the great hall, all about the emperor were the nobles and servants of his court. The aristocracy had been jittery ever since word had come from the coast that giant warships had attacked their navy. Today, they were dressed in their finest garb, looking quite wealthy in their cotton tilmatli that was dyed in a myriad of colors and bordered with exquisite designs. A thick sash encompassed their loins and bejeweled ornaments adorned their mantles. A few wore fur that often replaced the cotton capes on chilly mornings or evenings. There were no women among the nobility, but there was an ample number of beautiful young serving girls, their lush, copious black hair swirling down past their smooth tanned shoulders. These women were dressed in skirts of differing lengths, each with jeweled borders.

Several days ago, the second group of runners had arrived with word that Admiral Mextli had returned in huge ships like the ones that had attacked the Inland Sea fleet, and that these vessels had also been filled with strange white men who wore bright red clothing. The runners reported that these strangers, and the admiral, were wending their way to the capital through the rugged mountains separating Tenochtitlan from the coast.

Mextli, and a small army outfitted all in red, arrived several days later. The white soldiers were provided with food and drink and settled into quarters outside the capital city. Their officers were allowed to wander about the palace, under the watchful eyes of several armed guards, while the admiral was summoned before the emperor. He arrived with Cacimar, the young man who had accompanied him during his war with Tecumseh in the Northeast Territories and again on his exploratory voyage to the east.

The admiral and his friend were not the same two men who had set out over seventeen full cycles of the moon ago. Both had aged more than the time they had been away, and Cacimar's former good humor was practically nonexistent.

When questioned about the lands to the east and its riches, they responded with an incredible story of death, destruction, captivity, and warfare contested at a level far beyond the means of the Aztecs. Only the reports of the huge warships, verified by Aztec eyes in the harbor at Chalchihueyecan, and the trustworthiness of the admiral, had allowed Ahuitzotl to remotely consider such tales as containing a grain of truth. Otherwise, he would have simply covered his ears and ordered Mextli and Cacimar away. The two explorers informed the emperor that they had brought friends, called the English, to help the Aztecs battle a great new enemy, an enemy more powerful than any before previously faced by the Empire. This enemy manifested itself in the form of men called Italians, and ironically, these men had arrived from the west with an invasion force because they had learned of the riches of the Aztec lands.

After recounting his travels in detail, Mextli tried to explain to the emperor how different the strange lands were that existed across the Eastern Sea, and the dangers this new world posed to the Aztec Empire. He also implored Ahuitzotl VI to meet with the English officers.

*****

While this was taking place, five English officers—General Andrew Jackson, Colonel Winfield Scott, and three other senior officers—were walking about the palace, a huge edifice that seemingly matched, or even possibly surpassed, the splendor of King Louis XVI's Versailles.

The building, better described as a collection of buildings, was spread over a vast area. The rooms were large and decorated with colorful draperies, depicting battle scenes or the hunting of wild animals, many of which the officers could not identify. The roofs were terraced and inlaid with rich and handsome woods. All about the buildings were spacious gardens filled with fragrant flowers. Fountains that jetted water high into the air were spread throughout these gardens.

In one corner of the palace, they discovered large marble tubs stocked with exotic fish and waterfowl. In another area, there was a huge aviary that enclosed hundreds of birds with multicolored plumage that had been assembled from throughout the Aztec Empire. There were tiny birds that darted from flower to flower, their wings a blur of motion. There were bright red birds and awkward-winged creatures with incredible golden tail feathers. There were hundreds of fowl sporting curved beaks who squawked like fisherwomen and whose feathers came in a rainbow of assorted colors. While Jackson and his officers watched, dozens of men fed these creatures or cleaned their habitations.

In another building were a number of huge fierce-looking birds also contained in latticework cages. Large black-winged creatures with redheads, evil yellow eyes, and sharp beaks and claws watched the men as if they were prey. Other enormous blackish-brown birds sat on large tree branches, their feet and beaks yellow in color while their heads, necks, and tails were white. One of these creatures, whose body was about three feet in length, spread its wings, and its wingspan measured an unbelievable seven feet.

In yet another building, there were a collection of snakes and reptiles. Some of the reptiles were five or six feet long. They appeared in a variety of shades of green, from a grayish green to a bright coloring. Each had large dark eyes, rough skin, and pointy scales running down their backs. They scampered about on long clawed fingers. There was little doubt that these were the distant relatives of the huge dragons that once wandered the earth.

When the Englishmen returned to their sleeping chambers, they were quiet and pensive.

*****

The next morning, General Jackson and his delegation, dressed in their finest attire, were presented to the Aztec emperor and his court. The five men wore stanch white trousers with precise creases and bloodred tunics buttoned up to cover their necks. Wide white bands crossed their chests and a broad belt held a scabbard that housed swords, extraordinary long knives similar to a maquahuitl, only brighter and thinner. Each officer also wore a tall red headdress called a hat, complete with a visor and plumes.

General Jackson, and the officer to his immediate right, also wore gold-colored braid, which Cacimar told the emperor was called swabs, on their shoulders. Jackson's long white hair covered his ears, and his face was narrow and stern. He did not smile as he bowed from the waist before Ahuitzotl VI.

With Cacimar acting as a translator, the English general took time to carefully explain the disposition and numbers of the Italian army under General Severoli. With forceful determination, he urged the emperor to begin fortifying the mountain passes leading to the capital and offered to train his army to fight European style. At this last offer, there was a laugh from one of the high-ranking Aztec officers standing to Ahuitzotl's right.

General Huetzin commanded the military units surrounding Tenochtitlan. At the emperor's bidding, he explained to the English that no force had ever bested an Aztec army and certainly no army of twenty-five thousand men would be of concern to an empire that, if necessary, could put half a million men on the battlefield. General Huetzin's troops were professional and well-trained. The military was an intricate component of the Aztec culture. Huetzin knew General Ocelopan, the commander of the eastern coastal region. He had served under the older man during the Inca campaigns. Ocelopan was capable of raising a hundred thousand men. If there was an Italian army, and if it did dare land on the Empire's soil, it would easily be crushed.

Jackson was aware of the looks of disbelief and disdain on all the faces of the Aztec gentry. He launched into an explanation of the role of the Italian fleet in support of their army and told them about cannon that could be used on land, muskets that could be reloaded and fired at three to four times the rate of a thunderstick, and cavalry that could encircle and cut down the slower infantry. The term cavalry was meaningless to General Huetzin and the emperor, and how could big blasters be moved on land so that they would be effective? Even with Admiral Mextli's urging to heed Jackson's words, the suggestion that twenty-five thousand foreigners could defeat one hundred thousand Aztecs was ludicrous.

"Unless they are gods, General Jackson," scoffed Huetzin, "they will not be able to best my warriors."

"And from the bones, we found on the islands of the Inland Sea," observed the emperor, "they certainly are not gods." His court erupted in laughter.

Andrew Jackson was not a patient man, nor one to be subjected to ridicule. The veins on his neck bulged and Cacimar noted the general's normally pale face was now dark red and would soon match the color of his uniform.

"I beg you, oh mighty one," Mextli began, only to pause when gasps and startled exclamations came from the Aztecs standing near the entrance of the great hall.

All heads turned in that direction; all except Andrew Jackson who remained staring straight ahead at the emperor and General Huetzin.

A single warrior pushed his way through the crowds of nobles and servants. He staggered across the great hall, past the strangers in their red clothing, and approached the emperor's throne. His uniform was in tatters, his body caked in sweat and dust, his feet bloodied from miles and miles of running.

Throwing himself at the feet of Ahuitzotl, the warrior spoke in a parched and cracked voice, yet a voice loud enough to be heard throughout the now totally silent hall.

"I come from the beaches of Xoco, O Great Emperor of the World," he began. "I have run for three and a half days, stopping only to drink water, eat a few handfuls of food, and sleep for an hour when my body could no longer respond to my will to run. General Ocelopan, with an army of more than a hundred thousand men, met the green men on the beaches of Xoco. The green men had powerful weapons, my lord, and they came from ships as big as buildings. Worse, they had beasts fighting for them, beasts three times larger than a man that could run as fast a deer."

When the runner stopped to catch his breath and organize his thoughts, General Huetzin blurted out, "And the army? What of the army? Did they drive these invaders into the sea?"

"No, my general," the messenger gasped, "they were destroyed. Half the army was killed, the others fled into the jungle in terror. General Ocelopan was also killed by the green men during the fighting."

The court erupted in frightened voices—men arguing as to whether or not this could be true. Without any change in his expression, Emperor Ahuitzotl looked directly at Jackson and calmly said, "Let us begin to make our plans, General."

Chapter 44

It was early in the morning, several hours before the sun would rise, when Cacimar returned to his sleeping room in the royal palace. Snuggling under the warm furs that made up his bedding, he reached out and found the warm body sound asleep under the covers. Drawing her close, he awoke his wife of one day.

"Did the emperor believe you and Mextli?" Coatlicue mumbled in a groggy but wonderfully sultry voice.

"He had to after the messenger arrived," Cacimar answered softly, nuzzling his chin into the back of her neck. "The eastern Aztec army has been soundly defeated. They are saying fifty thousand men died. We have been in a war council with the English General Jackson and his aide, Colonel Scott, since we received word."

Now awake, Coatlicue turned to face her husband, the warmth of her firm breasts pressing into his chest, her heart beating rapidly beneath.

"Does that mean you are going again?" Her voice was steady, not frightened. She was married to a warrior, and she was aware of the danger of the Italian threat.

By the great Huitzilopotchi, I truly love this woman, thought Cacimar. Out loud, he said, "We will train near the city from this half-moon until the next, then we will march southeast. We hope to catch the Italians on the coast, but we must be prepared if they advance toward the capital."

Coatlicue wrapped herself around the muscular body of her husband. It was true he was worn and thinner from his hardships in the lands to the east, but he was still all muscle. Her body fitted to his as she took in the scent of his manliness.

It was now Cacimar who was fully awake as his body responded to the warmth and touch of Coatlicue's flesh. Running his hand down the soft skin of his wife's back, he cupped one of her firm buttocks, sliding his hand between her legs. She was moist and parted her thighs to allow him to enter her.

"Not so fast, my love," Cacimar whispered as he kissed her neck and her ear lobes. "A serving wench I once met long ago taught me lovemaking as it is done in the civilized Empire. Now that serving girl is my wife and I want to demonstrate to her that I was a good student."

With that said, Cacimar continued to kiss Coatlicue, moving downward from her supple breasts, running his lips along her flat stomach, working his tongue downward, ever downward to that part of her body capable of sending waves of exploding passion through her loins and into every part of her body.

Chapter 45

The day after their exhilarating victory over the Aztecs above the beaches of Xoco, General Severoli dispatched a number of his cavalry units to search the surrounding area and bring back captured soldiers. He gathered together several hundred and then attempted to enlist their aid. He was looking for guides and translators. Promising both safety and riches to those individuals who would serve, the Italians were able to recruit a number of volunteers.

Over the course of the following weeks, three of the turncoat Aztecs had proved to have a gift for languages, picking up Italian to a point of proficiency that they could act as an intermediary between Severoli and the local population. Yaotl was the best of these individuals although it was apparent he was also greedy and untrustworthy. He was always kept under the watch of a guard but within summoning distance of the general.

Aware that a major harbor was not too far away, Severoli sent his fleet ahead to subdue the port and then marched his army south. Chalchihueyecan was the major coastal city on the eastern shore of the Aztec Empire's homeland, a large urban center inhabited by more than one hundred thousand citizens built around a well-protected harbor. The surrounding area boasted beautiful white beaches with large sand dunes that had been shaped by the prevailing north wind. The calm waters of the port were ideal for shipping. A wide level plain stretched out behind the city to the steamy tropical jungle and the mountains beyond.

This entire area had once been the home of the Olmecs, a flourishing civilization that existed two thousand years before the Aztec Empire. There were still many stone sculptures and temples remaining from these early people. The Olmec society had then declined and was replaced by that of the Totanacas. When the Aztecs had expanded east, they had conquered the Totonacas, who now lived on the lands bordering the eastern seaboard, and brought them into the beginnings of what would become a vast Empire.

Chalchihueyecan had then been nothing more than a fishing village with the capital of these newly subjugated people situated sixty-five miles north of this harbor. The Totonacas had been fully absorbed into the Empire's culture 250 years ago. As the Aztecs gradually developed into a sea power, the port grew to become a major center of commerce.

Work was first begun on the harbor thirty-two seasons after the fourth fire ceremony (or 1534 by the Christian calendar) at which time Chalchihueyecan was still just a small village surrounded by marshes. Over the next hundred years, these wetlands were drained and replaced by farmland, or converted into mangrove orchards. A number of small white coral islands lay several hundred yards to the immediate southwest of the port. On the closest of these was built a fair-sized stone fort to protect the entrance of the harbor. In later years, big blasters were added to the stronghold's defenses.

The Italian men of war had little trouble pounding this fort into submission. By the time Severoli arrived with his army, Garibaldi's naval forces had occupied the city and were in control of those citizens who had not yet fled into the jungle. The next several days were marked by wholesale rape and pillaging. The majority of the Italian soldiers remained drunk for almost a week. Finally, their officers were able to restore order and establish martial law, not only to govern the city but also to provide safety for its forty thousand remaining inhabitants.

Chalchihueyecan provided great spoils for the invaders. The Italians found warehouses filled with fruits and vegetables, as well as cotton goods and animal furs, apparently waiting to be shipped to distant ports or picked up from incoming merchant vessels. There were also plentiful amounts of gold and silver figurines, sculptures, and jewelry. It was now apparent that the stories of immense riches were true. Best yet, the natives spoke of even greater treasures deep in the heartland of the Aztec Empire, at its capital high in the mountains to the west.

Soon after the occupation of the seaport, the Italians were introduced to a new disease. Although fever and a deadly rash did not accompany it, the illness was certainly as frightening as the Colombo Plague. The soldiers called it the Fucking Disease. The symptoms manifested themselves several days after having sexual intercourse with certain Aztec females, usually those who seemed to welcome the Italians the most—the city's prostitutes. Although the disease proved not to be life-threatening and the pain was tolerable, those contracting the sickness reported open sores in their genital areas that were uncomfortable and irritating. Such a malady was unheard of in Europe.

General Severoli issued orders outlawing his men from having sex with the natives, but this command was generally ignored. As the disease continued to spread among his troops, he organized military brothels and required his doctors to perform weekly inspections of those females employed by these houses. The women rounded up to serve in the brothels received pay from the army and were required to examine their customers prior to transacting business. Guards were stationed in the brothels to throw out any soldiers who showed signs of the ailment. The cleanliness of these new bordellos, along with a growing reluctance on the part of the troops to engage in wanton sex because of their fear of the illness, began to reduce the number of reported cases of the new disease.

*****

After spending a month reorganizing and resupplying his army, Severoli left Captain Garibaldi in command of the harbor of Chalchihueyecan and, aided by his translators and additional Aztec guides who had been recruited from the port, began his march toward the riches of Tenochitilan, the Aztec capital.

The columns of the twenty-four-thousand-man Italian army filled the wide dirt road leading into the hot wet jungle to the west, sending clouds of dust into the still air that could be seen from miles away. Nearly one thousand infantries were left behind to garrison the port town, supported by the Italian fleet that watched over the city from outside the harbor. Thick green foliage, and strange trees yielding a dark-leaved fruit the Aztecs called bananas, grew to either side of this highway.

During their second day's march from the sea, the army began a gradual ascent into the mountains. The Italian force was led by a cavalry detachment, not only to keep careful watch for possible ambushes but also to instigate fear and awe amongst the villagers they encountered.

At the end of two full days, the army reached the large, and for the most part deserted, city of Xalapa. While there, General Severoli allowed his men a day of looting and foraging for food. There was little in the way of molestation of the population as few of the town's citizens remained in their homes with the vast majority of the populace hiding in the caves and rocks surrounding the city. Even had more women been located, rape had gained disfavor with the troops since the arrival of the fucking disease.

The following day Severoli's expeditionary force resumed its trek along the winding road that ran upward into the mountains. The march became more of a walk, with no attempt to maintain formations as the men tired. The Italian infantry grumbled to themselves about the moderate climb, unaware of what lay ahead. Five days out from the harbor, they arrived at a town called Coatepec, built high on a rocky cliff. Surprisingly, it had been totally abandoned, for its elevation would have made an excellent defensive position. Just beyond Coatepec, they entered a rugged pass, and the climate began to change. The gusty winds blowing down out of the mountains grew colder as they advanced, causing the men to put their tunics back on over their military blouses and, as it grew even more chilly, to wrap native blankets around their shoulders. As they climbed higher the Italians were forced to take constant breaks, their breathing becoming labored because of the altitude. This further slowed their progress. Still, despite these hardships, by marching morning to sunset, they had been averaging a little under twenty miles a day since leaving Xalapa.

"It is fortunate the Aztecs are not defending the passes," Colonel Paparelli observed during one stop in the march. "A few hundred warriors could defend these narrow passageways for quite some time."

"If they were armed properly," scoffed General Severoli, "our cannon would make short work of any resistance. I think the lesson we taught the heathens at Xoco has frightened them. I would not be surprised to find their so-called emperor on his knees and begging us for mercy when we reach their capital."

The Italians emerged from this first pass and then trekked through a landscape of absolute desolation; on either side of the road were acres upon acres of blackened land caused by prehistoric lava flow. Here and there, between the volcanic rocks, a few shrubs fought for life in the barren wasteland. Otherwise, there was nothing but rock.

Three days march from Coatepec, they passed through another gorge and entered an open plain that the guides referred to as table-land. The climate was more amiable even though they were now almost seven thousand feet above sea level. The plateau appeared to spread out for many miles. It was covered with fertile fields of crops, many with bright yellow clusters of flowers on their lofty stems. Hedges of cactus systematically divided these fields.

The guides explained that these yellow plants were called aloe. They were used to produce many different items, including both food and clothing. A paste from the dark leaves of the plant was made into paper. Its juice was fermented into pulque, an intoxicating beverage. The plant's leaves were also used as thatch for the roofs of the homes of the peasants who lived outside the cities, and its fibers were employed as a thread for sewing or twisted together to create strong rope. Thorns found at the extremities of the leaves, when properly picked, could be used for sewing needles and pins. When cooked, aloe was also a source of nourishing food.

As the army crossed the tableland, they came upon more fields that grew a hardy plant called maize. This was the mainstay diet of the locals and a plant for which the Italians had grown a taste. Maize grew on gigantic stalks, in patches so thick one could not see through or over the plants. Two-thirds of these fields had been harvested.

At the far end of the plain, just beyond the fields, was a broad and lush valley watered by a fair-sized stream. It was here that the walled city of Tlaxcala stood with its fifty thousand inhabitants. This city had not been totally abandoned.

The Italians were met in front of the city's walls by the cacique, or chief, of Tlaxcala. A proud man in his seventies, the cacique welcomed General Severoli and invited him and his staff to join him for dinner while his army established its camp in the harvested fields outside the municipality. He promised to provide the green soldiers with ample food and drink, as well as women. Genuinely impressed by the cacique, and convinced that these Aztecs did not want to fight, the general accepted. It appeared that rather than risk destruction, these people were willing to live peacefully under Italian rule. At the cacique's request, Severoli gladly agreed to spare the city and its populace from any plundering or damage, in return for its hospitality.

Severoli sent fifty cavalry troopers into the town to ensure that no enemy soldiers were hiding within its walls and to secure the center of the three wooden gates that provided entrance into the city. He also sent another fifty horsemen to reconnoiter the area surrounding the municipality. Once this was successfully accomplished, he left his army feasting on the plain before Tlaxcala, and accompanied by his staff and fifty infantry, he entered the city. Passing through the main gate, he noted that although the walls were thick, they were only six feet high. They could be easily breached by trained soldiers with ladders. Wooden platforms had recently been built alongside the interior of the walls to either side of the gates. They were about ten yards wide and twenty yards deep, capable of holding a great number of fighting men. When asked about these new structures, the cacique replied that, at first, he had not known whether or not to defend the city and he had constructed the platforms to help protect the gates. All the while, he had prayed for peace, and two days ago, his prayers had been answered. The Aztec emperor had sent word that he was to open his town to the men in green.

The city's dwellings were made of two-storied adobe buildings, plain but attractive in their simplicity, built side by side and stretching out for several miles. A wide street ran along the inside of the city's walls and hundreds of wooden stalls lined the sides of the closest buildings that faced these walls. This was the town's marketplace, but almost all the booths were empty. There were a few warriors here and there but no sizable force. The chief said many of his people had fled at the approach of the green men, despite his urging them to stay.

To the front of the three main gates entering Tlaxcala was flat open farmland. Behind its walls, three wide dirt streets ran into the urban center from each of these gates. The primary road, which began at the central gate, ran to the city's interior where there was a large plaza constructed of tiles and polished stone. In this plaza, there were numerous fountains that were fed from an aqueduct apparently coming from the mountains behind Tlaxcala. To either side of the city, narrow man-made canals fed the prosperous farmland.

*****

The general staff was seated with the city's chief magistrate and a number of other individuals who appeared to be of some importance, while a contingent of dismounted cavalry troopers roamed about the area, keeping their eyes peeled for possible foul play. The Italians were introduced to dishes made of maize and roasted meats, the smell of which brought water to their mouths. For dessert, they were served several different kinds of fruit, sprinkled with sugar from the maize plant.

During the course of the dinner, while enjoying the quiet night in Tlaxcala, General Severoli asked a lot of questions and learned more about the Aztec emperor and the capital city of Tenochtitlan. Through the interpreters, the cacique spoke of Ahuitzotl VI with great respect and reverence. He also mentioned that his emperor was capable of raising an army of half a million warriors. The city's chief must have noted the look of shocked concern on the faces of both the general and his officers at this pronouncement because he was quick to continue to explain to Severoli, "The emperor recognizes the great power of the men in green. He believes you are a god and that you and your green men have come to take their rightful place as the leaders of the Aztec Empire. It has been so ordained and foretold by our priests. My sovereign has sent you his greetings and asked me to inform you that he anxiously awaits your arrival in Tenochtitlan. Once there, he will obey your commands."

General Severoli settled back on his pillowed seat and smacked his lips. "That is more like it," he exclaimed with a happy smile. "A god! By Jesus, that is what I am to these people. I can't wait until Emperor Napoleone sees the first boatload of riches I send back to him from these lands. Perhaps he'll make me governor of the Aztecs. Perhaps even a king. Now that would be something, to become both a god and a king!"

Congratulated by Colonel Paparelli and his officers, Severoli and his entire staff ate, drank, and laughed the night away. No one noticed the fleeting smile that quickly passed from the cacique's lips.

*****

The next day, the Italians were again on the march. Once again, they left the gentle plains behind and advanced into rough mountain country. According to the cacique, their objective was now only four days distant.

On the morning of their second day out of Tlaxcala, they entered a rocky pass with steep cliff walls to either side. Several hundred yards into this notch, the Italians came upon an unexpected sight. An ancient wall of stone, nine feet in height and nearly two feet thick, ran from one cliff face to the other. A single opening, ten paces wide, stood in the center of this wall, and just above this opening was a parapet with small cannon pointing their way. All along the top of the wall stood Aztec warriors armed with their oversize blunderbusses or bows and arrows.

As General Severoli surveyed this obstacle, a lone warrior, bedecked in bright feathers, walked from the wall and approached the Italians. His face was stoic, and he looked at the green-clad soldiers without an inkling of fear. The general summoned his interpreter, Yaotl, who translated the words of the Aztec emissary.

"Hear this, leader of the green men," the warrior spoke, his voice loud and full of disdain. "It is here that your journey of conquest comes to an end. This is the great wall that protects the pass to Tenochtitlan. Twenty thousand warriors guard it, and more can be summoned if needed. Behind you, even now filling the plains before

Tlaxcala, is an army of two hundred thousand men led by Emperor Ahuitzotl's greatest generals. They have come from Apizaco in the north and have cut you off from the sea. Your small numbers will be overwhelmed. You have no choice but to surrender your army."

The feathered warrior glared derisively at Severoli as he waited for a reply.

"By god, we're not about to surrender to a bunch of ignorant natives, no matter how many of them there are," Severoli stammered, red-faced and angry. He could see that it would be fruitless to attack such a well-defended wall, and he did not have time to try to batter it down with his artillery, not if there were any truth to this proclamation that such a large force was at his rear.

"We will withdraw from this pass," the general said to his staff and translator, "and meet the Aztec forces on the plains behind us if this is not a bluff. There, our artillery and cavalry will prevail. I do not care how many natives we have to face. We still have the firepower to destroy them all. Then we will return here and blast this wall to rubble. Inform this wretched creature that we have no intention to surrender."

Before Yaotl could speak, however, Colonel Paparelli pulled out his pistol, aimed at the unflinching warrior, and shot him in the head. A roar of disbelief and fury came from the Aztecs on the wall as the warrior's crumpled body fell to the ground.

"I believe they all understood that message," Paparelli snarled as he turned his horse and began issuing orders for the army to march back to Tlaxcala.

Chapter 46

Alerted that Severoli's forces were wending their way through the mountains toward the Aztec capital, Andrew Jackson sent a messenger to the English fleet anchored, with the remnants of the Aztec navy, off the islands of Cozumel. He respectfully requested the naval units' commander to attack the Italian ships and either destroy or capture them. It was imperative, Jackson wrote, that the Italian army be cut off from the safety of its own ships.

Admiral Lord Horatio Nelson was not concerned with the size of the Italian armada. His Aztec spies in Chalchihueyecan had reported that the majority of the ships were nothing more than stripped-down brigs, devoid of armament. He also paid no heed to the fact that the Italians had three men of war to his two ships of the line. After all, his frigates outnumbered the enemy's fourteen to ten, and more importantly, the English navy was far superior in fighting ability to that of the Kingdom of Italy. What did concern Nelson was the monstrous man of war, *Emperor*. It carried 136 guns, far exceeding the 104 guns of his flagship *Victory* and the 96 guns of the *Intrepid*.

The three Italian warships were stationed just outside the harbor of Chalchihueyecan, as they were all too large to moor inside the port. The brigs were tied up side by side in a line about a mile or so up the coast, north of the harbor. The combat ships were anchored in a battle line even though there had been no indication of a formidable adversary within several thousand miles of their location. Captain Garibaldi had not exercised caution, just standard naval practice. The battle line was made up of five frigates, then two men of war in the center, followed by another five frigates. The Aztecs in the harbor reported that the Italians allowed half the ships' crews to take shore leave each night while the other half remained on board.

The *Emperor* was anchored alone, well off the coast of the coral islands situated just to the south of the harbor. The spies also reported that the Italians were using slave labor to rebuild the destroyed fort on the island closest to the port, but its walls were only partially completed, and no big blasters had, as of yet, been situated in these fortifications. Even at anchor, *Emperor* could easily outgun either of the two English ships of the line. With the support of the other two Italian men of war, both carrying over ninety guns, the English fleet was slightly overmatched.

Surprise was on the side of the English, however. There was no way that Garibaldi could know that Nelson's vessels were so close, and as the quiet weeks had passed by, the lookouts on the Italian ships had grown lax. The port was secure, the army was marching to subdue the Aztec Empire, and the locals offered nothing in the way of resistance.

*****

In the early morning of an exceptionally dark moonless night, five Aztec ships slid silently out of the south, using their shallow drafts to slip between the coral islands and the mainland so that they could position themselves just outside the port of Chalchihueyecan. These vessels had been converted into gunboats with their small big blasters having been replaced by English twelve-pound cannons mounted on the decking of their bows.

No Italian sentries had been stationed at the mouth of the harbor. The fleet protected these waters, or so it was thought. The few alert lookouts on the ships in the battle line a half mile beyond the port were facing out to sea. After all, the harbor was securely in the hands of the Italian infantry. With muffled oars, the Aztec craft turned away from the port and quietly approached the Italian fleet in the complete darkness, from their landward side.

The plan was to get in as close as possible to the two men of war and then fire the cannon simultaneously at these ships' waterline. This coordination was not easy to accomplish in pitch dark. The Aztec crews manning the boats had difficulty maintaining alignment in the night. As a result, two of the gunboats reached what they believed to be their targets ahead of the others. Immediately upon arrival, they both proceeded to fire their heavy guns directly into the hulls of two of the Italian ships, one a man of war and the other craft one of the frigates. The results were direct hits as a large gashing hole appeared just below the waterline of each vessel.

Alarm bells began to clang on board the remaining Italian ships as sailors rushed to their battle stations. A third gunboat unloaded its deadly shot below the waterline of yet another frigate, but the fourth Aztec ship panicked as the Italian gunports began to swing open, and its gun crew fired high into the upper decking of one of the men of war, causing little damage. This gunboat then turned directly into the approaching fifth Aztec craft, crunching into its side and driving the bow of this boat, and its cannon, away from the anchored fleet.

There was momentary chaos on both sides as three of the Italian ships began listing, water pouring into the gaping wounds in their hulls. Their crews hurried to man the ships' pumps, but they were too late to prevent tons of water from filling the holds of these vessels. On shore, the sailors and inhabitants of Chalchihueyecan, wakened by the sounds of battle and in a state of confusion, poured out of the houses lining the dark streets.

The gunports of all the remaining Italian ships had now clattered open, and their starboard guns run out to bear directly on the gunboats, two of which were reloading while the other three tried to turn in the water to flee. Huge black muzzles pointed down at the smaller boats. One of the Aztec craft got off another shot into the hull of the second man of war before the air erupted in a string of bright flashes immediately followed by the roar of ships' guns coming to life.

Within minutes, the five gunboats were literally blown to pieces, splinters of wood and body parts dotting the water along with the remnants of their sinking hulls. Cheers came from both the ships' crews and the Italian sailors on shore. This ovation only lasted for a few minutes. The hoots and applause came to an abrupt stop with the renewed clanging of one of the lookout's bells, a sound that was hurriedly taken up by the sentinels on the other ships further up the line. To the south, in the faint glow of the first morning light, the sailors could just make out the forms of fifteen large ships under full sail bearing down on the Italian fleet. These were not Aztec ships. From the cut of their sails, they appeared to be English.

The gun crews of the nine unscathed frigates, as well as those of the *Romulus*—the first man of war in the line—rushed to the port side of their vessels to man the cannon that faced away from the harbor. The second man of war, and one of the frigates, was already down forty-five degrees in the water, its port guns pointing straight into the air. The starboard gunports of these two lost ships had already begun taking in water, and their officers ordered the crews to abandon the sinking craft. *Romulus* was also taking in some water, but the members of her crew had manned the pumps and were winning the valiant fight to save the vessel.

Hugging the coral islands as close as they dared, fourteen English frigates sailed in a battle line straight at the anchored Italian fleet, while a single ship of the line veered off that formation and headed for the anchored *Emperor*. The monstrous Italian ship, alerted by the previous cannonade, was ready and waiting to greet this new adversary, her gunports open and inviting.

As if in slow motion, the English converged on the Italians until the two lines of warships made initial contact. As the English frigates sailed past the row of anchored Italian ships, the roar of rolling cannon fire from both fleets once again shattered the stillness. At the same time, the captain of the HMS *Intrepid* navigated his ship to the starboard side of the *Emperor*, and lowering her sails, she also dropped her anchor. This move caught the captain of the huge Italian man of war by total surprise.

"The Englishman must be crazy," Captain Garibaldi laughed nervously. "He cannot possibly think his ship can best mine in a straight-up confrontation."

The *Emperor*'s heavy guns exploded in a deep clap of smoke. A fusillade of cannonballs was unleashed into the outgunned English ship of the line, slamming into her with such force that she heeled violently in the water. Men were thrown across the deck, and several guns were destroyed by direct hits. Ignoring the shot thrown her way, *Intrepid* recovered and began to return fire.

Cannonballs pounded the hulls and deckhouses of each of the large ships, throwing showers of deadly splinters into their crews. Cannons flashed in seething clouds of smoke. The two ships pounded one another like massive prizefighters, neither giving an inch.

Shot fired from point-blank broadsides slashed through the rigging of both vessels and splintered their hulls. Shells landed with shattering detonations, maiming and killing the sailors unlucky enough to be in their path. The surviving gun crews on both ships ignored the growing numbers of the dead all about them and continued to load, ram, and fire their cannon. The force caused by the detonating guns caused them to buck back from the portholes where a breeching rope halted their backward momentum so that they could be reloaded and hauled forward to fire once more.

Some guns fired chain shot—two balls connected by a chain that expanded and tumbled in the air once they left the gun's muzzle—designed to destroy the enemy's rigging. The mainstay of the Italian man of war was parted by such a shot, leaving her mainmast a jagged stump under a tenting of ripped and torn sails. Two of the ship's three masts were down on the *Intrepid*, and her deck was littered with wreckage, torn rigging, blood, and the bodies of the dead and wounded.

Half of the guns of the *Emperor* had been knocked out in the fierce barrages, but almost all the English cannon were now silenced. Both ships were hull holed in a number of places, and those crew members who could be spared were working fanatically at the pumps.

Intrepid was a battered wreck. A bright yellow flag was raised on her one remaining mast as she pulled in her anchor and began to drift slowly to the north, away from *Emperor*. Captain Garibaldi had first thought it to be the white flag of surrender, but that was not so—it was definitely yellow. What else could it have meant? Was it a signal of some sort to the rest of the English fleet? As the heavily damaged enemy ship drifted further away, cheers burst from the crew on the Italian vessel. Backs were slapped, and sighs of relief were mingled with both the shouts of joy and the moans of pain of the wounded.

All was well for several minutes until the clanging of the alarm bell once again silenced the jubilation.

"What the hell?" gasped Garibaldi.

During the later stages of the fight, a second English ship of the line had rounded the southern islands. It was the *Victory* and its 104 guns, and she was sailing straight toward the battered Italian man of war. The piercing screech of boson's pipes filled the air. Those Italian sailors who were not too severely wounded tried to raise the ship's anchor and hoist her sails, so the *Emperor* could turn about and face this new challenge with her undamaged port guns. This effort was to no avail. The *Victory* was too close, and the *Emperor*'s hawsehole had been severely damaged so that her anchor chain was partially buried under the remains of a forward spar. The great weight could not be budged from the ocean floor. Within ten minutes, the English ship was mooring along the splintered starboard side the *Emperor*, in the same spot where *Intrepid* had anchored, and both vessels opened up on one another with everything they had. With so many of its guns damaged from its first fight, however, it was now the Italian man of war that was badly outgunned.

Victory had yet another surprise in store for the Italians. Small furnaces were mounted by a number of her gunports and twelve-pound cannonballs sat in these fires. The sailors called these balls hotshot. The red-hot metal was gripped with tongs and then loaded into the cannon along with wadding that had been soaked in water. Other than receiving a crippling round below the water line, hotshot was a captain's greatest fear. The wooden ships of war were heavily tarred making them extremely susceptible to fire.

Rounds of hotshot were fired into the *Emperor*. They struck the torn sails, deckhouse, and hull. Fires broke out in three different locations as men hurried to put them out with blankets or buckets of sand. The Italian man of war was taking in more of the sea than she could remove from her hold. Water was still being pumped over the gunnels, but many of the men who had been working the pump handles were now dead or wounded, or had been pulled from this duty to replace injured gun crews. *Emperor* was riding lower in the water, but she still fought on as, one by one, her guns were silenced.

Captain Garibaldi lay by the wheel of the great ship, dried blood caking a gash running from his knee to his groin. His deckhouse was shattered, and only two of his cannons were still returning fire. The others had been destroyed or lacked men to man them. With a hoarse cry from his parched throat, he barked his last order. The Italian flag came fluttering down to be replaced by the white flag of surrender. There were no cheers from the English victors. Instead, they quietly began going about the task of tending to their wounded and throwing their dead over the side of the ship. The sea all about the two vessels was littered with bodies and the wreckage of floating debris.

To the north, seven of the twelve Italian warships were out of action while four English vessels were badly damaged. The captain of *Romulus* was dead, as was his second-in-command. A lookout sent word to the third officer that *Emperor* was low in the water and had raised a white flag. It was inconceivable, but the pride of Napoleone's fleet had been defeated. The remaining ships of the Italian invasion armada ran up their flags of capitulation.

Chapter 47

A little less than two hundred miles inland from the sea battle, on that same early morning, General Severoli formed his twenty-two thousand men into ranks on the plains facing the walls of the city of Tlaxcala. As he had at Xoco, the Italian general positioned his cavalry to the rear of his infantry so they could later exploit the enemy in a flanking movement. Another two thousand troops had been left back in camp. They were out of action—incapacitated by some sort of fever that sapped their strength and left their bodies covered in sweat. Overworked doctors tended to their needs, mopping their brows with cool water. A few men had previously come down with what the natives termed "swamp fever" while on the coast, but never this many. Those on the coast had recovered after a week of dysentery, chills, and sweats. This new illness appeared much more serious. It was a damnable time to have so many men sick, the general fretted.

The three wooden gates to the city were closed, but outside Tlaxcala's walls were sixty thousand Aztec warriors who had been positioned in formidable masses. A number of captured natives claimed there were another one hundred thousand inside Tlaxcala's fortifications, but only a few dozen could be seen standing on the platforms that guarded the three entrances to the city. Even outnumbered eight to one, the Italians were confident in their superior firepower. The city's defenders could not match their huge tactical advantage in terms of both artillery and cavalry.

*****

Cacimar stood on one of the two platforms that had recently been built on either side of the main gate. Next to him was Winfield

Scott, Jackson's second-in-command. Colonel Scott was a young man and large in frame. The islander thought the hair on the colonel's head was quite unusual, as it grew well down past his ears and out onto his cheeks. This was not in the fashion that the English referred to as a beard. These were called mutton chops, and they did resemble the cuts of meat that came from European sheep.

Inside the walls of Tlaxcala, General Jackson walked the streets as he inspected the English infantry. They were standing on the broad street that ran just inside the city's walls in three formations of one thousand eight hundred men each, one such formation at each of the three gates that opened onto the plain beyond. Additional infantry was crouched out of sight along the walls on the parapets that had been completed barely a week before the Italians first arrived.

Based on the reports from Xoco, Jackson and Mextli agreed not to position the thundersticks in front of their capullis, as was the Aztec's traditional battle formation. Instead, spearmen formed the front ranks. Behind them were massive warriors armed with their war clubs. Bowmen were stationed behind both these groupings. The front ranks also carried round leather shields, and short obsidian knives were tucked in their belts. Aztec officers, dressed in metal plates tied to the front and back of their upper torsos, walked the lines talking to their men. The officers carried long wide knives, called maquahuitls, that were capable of chopping through quilted cotton vests or the wood and leather helmets that were worn by the ranks of the capullis.

The tens of thousands of Aztec warriors positioned to the city's front were restless and troubled. They had heard rumors about the green men's weapons; big blasters that could be rolled along with the infantry and thundersticks that could fire many times in a minute. They had also heard about the monstrous half men, half beasts. Each warrior battled with his own personal fear. In an effort to counteract these qualms, Mextli and Cacimar had spent the preceding week visiting the troops' encampments, explaining that the Italian muskets were nothing more than lighter thundersticks and were fired and reloaded in much the same way as the Aztecs' weapons. They also told the Empire's soldiers that there were no monsters, but men who sat on animals called horses. The warriors seemed to accept these explanations, but they had difficulty visualizing green men mounted on animals that were strong enough to bear their weight but still could run as fast as a deer. Despite being repeatedly told that thundersticks, arrows, and spears would bring down these horses, along with their riders, the same as any other animal, the troops were apprehensive. Only the fact that Admiral Mextli stood in their forward ranks, in the midst of the Aztec warriors, calmed their nerves.

It was hoped the Italians, unaware of the English presence in the new world, would fall into a number of well-laid traps prepared by General Jackson and Admiral Mextli. The greatest of these surprises were mounted on the six parapets built into the city's walls. Eighteen-pound cannons had been carried into the mountains from the English naval vessels, and now two were mounted on each of the platforms to either side of the main gate with single guns on each of the other four parapets. The cannons had been attached to newly assembled timber carriages at the rear of the parapets, out of sight of the enemy. They were, in turn, tied by restraining ropes to metal rods that had been driven into the front of the platforms. This was to prevent them from pitching back off the wooden parapets after they were fired. Each gun was loaded with grapeshot and an ample supply of powder, rocks, and musket balls filled containers positioned to either side of the cannon.

*****

Colonel Paparelli sat on a magnificent white stallion looking at the assembled Italian troops. He was resplendent in his green uniform with its polished gold buttons. The horse pranced lightly on the harvested maize field as if anticipating the upcoming battle.

"We are ready to begin the assault, sir," he reported to General Severoli who was mounted to his left on a black Arabian stallion.

"I do not remember that pole above the main gate, do you, Colonel?" responded the general as he gazed at the center of Tlaxcala's wall. A tall pole had been placed by one of the platforms next to the center gate into the city. A rope ran to its top. Instead of a flag at its summit, there were a number of bright feathers flapping in the light wind.

"I suppose it is some sort of superstitious omen to protect their army," observed Paparelli, "or the emblem of the city. I do not remember it being there a few days ago either."

"No matter," Severoli sighed. "A few feathers are not going to save this Aztec army. The men are prepared. Sound the advance."

*****

The Aztecs were startled when the reverberation of the shrill bugles of the green men shattered the tranquility of the early morning. At the front of his own battle lines, Mextli watched in fascination as the Italian infantry snapped to attention and, as a single entity, clamped bayonets onto their muskets.

A steady cadence of drums began behind the enemy's ranks and then the extended columns of foot soldiers, dressed identically in their green uniforms, stepped off smartly toward the city. Behind the infantry, the Italian artillery commenced fire; deep coughs of thunder sending deadly projectiles over their own troops and into the ranks of the warriors.

As they had prepared, the Aztecs spread away from one another so the cannonballs and exploding canisters would not take down great clusters of men. Jackson had been concerned the Italians would simply standoff at a distance and bombard the city, and his forces, into submission. Mextli argued that after their easy victory at Xoco, the Italians would be overconfident and advance on the Aztec forces in the open if there were an enticing objective outside Tlaxcala's walls. That is why he had placed half his force out on the plain before the gates. His men were too tempting a target with their clubs and spears. Mextli thought General Severoli would be anxious to defeat this force and then continue his march on the Aztec capital. He was counting on the Italian general, being confident that his infantry's muskets and cavalry units would make much shorter work of the enemy than a long term, big blaster barrage that might take days to destroy the enemy's resolve should they remain behind their walls.

The admiral reasoned that Severoli would go for a quick, decisive victory rather than take the chance the Aztecs would flood back through the city's gates under shellfire and then eventually melt away into the mountains through the rear gates of the city, perhaps to reappear again at the Italians' rear once they resumed their march. He had been correct in his assessment.

Aztecs fell, body parts torn off by careening cannonballs or struck down by the shrapnel of exploding shells. Despite the increasing bloodshed, they maintained their ranks.

The Italians marched steadily to within one hundred yards of their foe—cold, precise, all in step. Officers barked orders, and they came to a complete stop at this range, the front rank kneeling and then raising their weapons to point directly at the still motionless warriors.

*****

"What in blazes are they thinking?" General Severoli asked his aid. "I expected the heathens to launch a counterattack to try to overwhelm us with their numbers so that I could unleash our horse onto their flanks. No matter, we will take the battle to them and destroy their army where its stands if they fail to come away from their walls. Send word to the cavalry to split forces and advance around both of their flanks. They should be prepared to charge as soon as the Aztecs advance or break."

Colonel Paparelli nodded to a nearby lieutenant, and the young man dashed off to carry the general's order to the horsemen.

*****

The Italians advanced to within a hundred yards of their foe. As their front rank began kneeling to prepare to fire, three almost simultaneous movements took place in the Aztec ranks. On the plain before the city, the Aztec defenders began to draw back away from the men in green and in closer to the walls of Tlaxcala. By the time the men in green were ready to let loose a volley, the warriors had withdrawn to a position slightly more than 150 yards from the Italians, just out of the effective range of their muskets. This maneuver had also resulted in a clear field of fire over the Aztec masses from the parapets built on the inside of Tlaxcala's walls.

At the same time the withdrawal was made, the feathers were run down the makeshift flagpole by the center gate of the city and replaced by the English flag. It unfurled in the light breeze, displaying the red cross of St. George, trimmed in white and imposed over the two red and white crosses of St. Andrew and St. Patrick—all mounted on a field of blue. A cheer rose from thousands of voices within Tlaxcala's walls. Simultaneously, English artillerymen on the parapets strained to pull their large eighteen-pound guns to the edge of the city's wall, where their dark barrels faced the Italian lines.

Moments after the first Italian rank unleashed its initial volley, the English cannon exploded in a deafening roar, sending grapeshot into the lines of green. Men screamed in pain as jagged pieces of metal and rock ripped into their bodies. Scores fell, but their officers, immediately realizing that their only refuge from this bombardment was to close with the enemy, shouted orders and the front rank sprang to its feet. Seconds later, all the Italian columns broke into a charge toward the massed Aztecs.

*****

"By god, sir! That is the English flag!" gasped Colonel Paparelli.

"And those are English cannons!" snapped the general. "How in hell…? Colonel, have our cannon fire directed at the city's wall and take out those guns."

Colonel Paparelli rode forward toward his artillery positions to personally deliver this message.

*****

The Italians were coming at a full run, their faces grim, mouths drawn tight, and sweat streaming down their heads and into the necks of their uniforms. It was a fearsome sight, a wall of green holding bayonets before them like razor-sharp teeth.

Mextli shouted, whistles blew, and the Aztec front rank formed a wall of spears facing the onslaught. Behind them, the remaining Aztec hoards, armed with mascuahuitl and bow, moved further back until they were pressed against Tlaxcala's walls. Blocked from the Italians' view by the frontal ranks of the Aztecs, the gates to the city were opened, and English infantry began to slip out between the masses of warriors along the wall and the front ranks of spearmen.

Colonel Scott led these soldiers, and they rapidly formed in two lines, with a space between each man. As the forward ranks of the Italians violently slammed into the Aztec line, the English waited in place, with their loaded baker rifles and bayonets.

*****

The Italian artillery was now directing its fire at the English cannon on the platforms mounted on the walls of the city. Cannonballs screamed into the adobe brick, blasting serrated holes into its facade. These were professional gunners, trained by Napoleone's best, and as they found the range to their targets, the big naval guns were slowly being put out of commission.

There was an absolute melee on the plains to the immediate front of the city. Thousands of men dressed in green surged into thousands more in quilted cotton uniforms, cursing and screaming, stabbing and dying. Bayonets and spears slashed the bodies of the enemy, their former sparkle now obscured by the stains of dark crimson blood. The front edge of the battle degenerated into hand-to-hand combat, each man intent on preserving his own life by taking that of the man to his immediate front, while thousands more pressed on from their rear.

"Where the hell are my cavalry?" General Severoli screamed.

A breathless, flushed lieutenant ran up, his face pale and frightened, and snapped a salute. "Sir, oh my god, sir," he stuttered.

"Out with it, man!" shouted the general.

"Colonel Giovanni reports that a quarter of his horsemen are out of action, sir," the lieutenant gasped. "The men, oh sweet Jesus, the men have fever, and their bodies are covered with a rash. Many are dying. His remaining cavalry is in a state of fright and is scattered all over. He is trying to reassemble them. He says it is the Colombo Plague, sir."

Both General Severoli and Colonel Paparelli turned in their saddles, eyes wide with horror. This was something that both men feared when the emperor ordered the expedition, but that fear had subsided and then been forgotten as the days, then the weeks, passed following their landing.

"If this is true," Severoli said quietly, "may God have mercy on our souls."

*****

Up and down the line, the battle raged. A soldier in a green tunic, and sporting the beginnings of a grizzled beard, thrust his bayonet at Mextli, the cold blade just nicking his right side and drawing blood as the admiral spun away to his left. Coming around in a full three-hundred-and-sixty-degree turn, Mextli slashed his maquahuitl down across the soldier's neck before the man could regain his balance, spurting blood in all directions and nearly decapitating the man.

On either side of the admiral, men were dying, pierced by bayonet or spear, slashed by sword or maquahuitl. Short pops, and clouds of smoke, were intermixed with the other sounds of combat as the second rank of Italians forced their muskets between the bodies of their comrades, fired, and withdrew to reload. Slowly, but surely, the Aztecs were being driven back.

A surrealistic glow permeated the entire battlefield as the morning sun, reflecting off the smoke that now filled the air from the cannon and musket fire, turned that haze a dark red, as if mimicking the blood soaking the ground and discoloring the earth below the man-made clouds.

Immediately following the second blast of whistles, the well-trained Aztec spearmen made one final surge into the green men, momentarily stopping them in their tracks, before they turned and fled. The Italians paused to catch their breath for a few seconds, before letting go with a pent-up hurrah and charging forward after their retreating enemy. Those few intervening seconds were to prove critical. The withdrawing Aztecs slipped back between the rows of a new enemy, yet an old foe—an enemy dressed in a fashion similar to the Italians but with red jackets and high red hats.

As the last of the Aztecs disappeared through these ranks, with the Italians a scant ten yards behind, the English front rank unleashed a mortal volley, followed seconds later by another salvo by the men standing behind the kneeling front rank. There was no way to miss at such a close range. Hundreds upon hundreds of green-clad soldiers crashed to the ground and the troops behind them came to an abrupt standstill.

With a scream of both triumph and rage, the survivors of the sixty thousand Aztecs along Tlaxcala's walls now raced forward, through the English ranks, and into the stunned Italians. Behind them, through the city's open gates, came one hundred thousand more.

The forward ranks of green fought gallantly for a few minutes before they were swarmed under. Huge men waded into the terrified Italian ranks crushing skulls and breaking backs with their war clubs. The men further back in the columns had time to fire one round into the shrieking masses of charging Aztecs before they, too, were overwhelmed. Many Italians turned to run. Others raised their hands to surrender, only to be hacked down or speared in place. There would be no prisoners taken on this battlefield.

*****

General Severoli watched as the green of his men's uniforms was buried under the waves of Aztec warriors. His artillery had ceased firing at the walls of the city. Some of the guns were now lowering their sites and filling their muzzles with grapeshot and canister while the crews of others were running panic-stricken toward the general and his staff.

Behind the general waited the fifteen hundred cavalry troopers who were still healthy enough to ride. Colonel Paparelli had personally rallied these men. Behind the horsemen were the tents that held a dozen surgeons and the two thousand sick and dying men who had been left at this campsite.

Temporally frozen in place, Severoli watched as his artillery fired into a vast human wall of Aztecs who were chasing down his own routed infantry. Both warriors and Italians went down to the cannon fire, but the Aztecs did not waiver and engulfed the guns and the remaining crews.

"General," Colonel Paparelli pleaded. "General!"

Slowly, the shocked Italian general turned to look at his aid.

"General, we must withdraw," Paparelli cried. "We must get back to the safety of our ships."

Severoli nodded with mournful eyes. Then, without looking up again, he and his staff, along with the remaining cavalry, turned in place and galloped off toward the pass leading back to Chalchihueyecan. Behind him, the victorious Aztecs dashed crossed the plain.

*****

Angelo Conti lay in a pool of his own sweat, his body covered in the red rash that had infected him and hundreds of others. He was weak and exhausted. He had listened to the distant battle and then watched as the general and his cavalry turned east and withdrew. In their place, the plain was filled by a growing mass of enemy warriors, running toward the Italian camp and the hospital tents.

Conti was not afraid. He was a soldier and had always known that it was his fate to die in battle. That was far preferable to losing an arm or leg, or his eyesight, and returning to Pesaro for a life as a crippled beggar.

It took nearly five minutes for the Aztecs to reach him. Raising himself on his elbows, he shot the first one in the face before another drove his spear deep into his heart. Angelo died instantly, a fate far better than that befalling many of the stricken Italians who were butchered in their sleeping rolls or by their tents.

*****

The entire battle was over before noon. It was now dusk, and Colonel Scott stood on one of Tlaxcala's parapets overlooking the carnage strewn across plain below. Thousands and thousands of bodies, now being fed upon by birds, small animals, and flies, littered the field. The Italian dead had been picked over by the Aztecs and English alike—coins, clothing, food, and personal items retrieved from the corpses by the living victors. The Aztec dead had been stacked into neat piles. The bodies would lie there tonight, and then the gruesome task of burying the dead would begin at dawn.

Mextli and Cacimar stood to either side of the young colonel. General Jackson, infuriated by his inability to stop the Aztecs from killing the wounded, had withdrawn to his headquarters in the city.

"It was a good victory," Mextli said without emotion. For more than a year, he had been awakened by a singular nightmare. He could hear Tecocol calling for him as he watched his trusted friend struggling to stay afloat in the sea, clinging to a spar of wood. Laughing Italians were shooting at him, riddling his torso with countless mini balls. Tecocol's red blood spread out into the water all about him, but he still called for the admiral's help. Mextli would wake from these fitful visions with a start, bathed in sweat. Perhaps now some of this pain would leave him and the dreams stop. Perhaps now the Aztec Empire would be safe.

An English captain climbed up the ladder to the platform. A corporal accompanied him. The enlisted man was in his thirties with a cherub face and a tattered uniform. They both snapped to attention and saluted Scott.

"Colonel, I thought you might want to hear this," the captain began. "The men thought it was quite good, sir."

Pushing the corporal forward, the captain continued, "This here is Corporal Frank Key from Newcastle, Colonel. He was a poet before he was taken into the army. Read him what it is you wrote, Frankie."

Corporal Key looked scared to death, but Colonel Scott nodded his approval.

"We was inside the walls you see, sir, me and the boys in our company," the corporal started, unrolling a small piece of paper. "Well, we was scared, sir, and some of the lads were saying 'What are we doing thousands of miles from home defending a bunch of people we don't even know.' And then just before we went out on the plain, you raised our flag, sir, and just seeing it there on the walls of this city, it reminded us of home and reminded us of our families and how we were fighting to not only keep these Aztecs free but England free. I don't know how to put it correctly, sir, but just seeing our flag waiving there made it all right."

Without another word, the corporal looked down at the paper in his hands and read what he had written:

Oh, say can you see by the dawn's early light
What so proudly we hailed, in the sunlight's bright gleaming
Whose broad crosses on blue, through the perilous fight
O'er the city we watched, were so gallantly streaming
And the heaven's red glare, the bombs bursting in air
Gave hope to our troops, as our flag was still there
O say does the cross of St. George ever wave
O'er the land of the free and the home of the brave.

Cacimar looked at the colonel and there were tears in Scott's eyes. What strange people these English were.

Chapter 48

Six miles from the seaport of Chalchihueyecan, General Severoli and the fifteen hundred men still under his command came upon a camp of several hundred Italian seamen and nearly a thousand infantry. They had constructed a crude assortment of tents and thatched huts at the edge of the jungle after being driven out of the harbor city—living off the land by hunting or making raids to steal crops from the few local natives who still worked the surrounding farms.

Informed that the harbor was now occupied and under the guns of an English fleet and that English crews now manned those Italian ships that had survived the sea battle, the general lost all hope. Alone in an alien land with a dwindling force, his men stricken by the Colombo Plague and pursued by a huge army of vengeful hostiles, General Severoli chose to march into the city of Chalchihueyecan and surrender to the English naval commander. It was the only way he and his men would survive. He was sure the English would treat them as prisoners of war. Eventually, he and his officers would be sent back to Europe and exchanged for captured English officers. Better to surrender now than to be chopped down by savages who gave no quarter and took no prisoners.

Preceded by a lone rider bearing a white flag, the remnants of the once-proud Italian expeditionary army dejectedly headed for the coast.

*****

Emperor Ahuitzotl VI sat on his throne facing Admiral Mextli and his aid, the young man named Cacimar. They spoke in Nahuatl, the tongue of the Aztec.

"Can these English men be trusted?" the emperor asked the admiral. "They, too, have huge ships and improved thundersticks. You have said they have battled the green men and defeated them on their homelands. Will they not also experience greed and seek to take the riches of the Aztec for their own?"

Mextli had thought about this issue for some time now, and he answered quickly and honestly.

"I think not, Great One," he replied. "The English still fear this Napoleone and his empire. I think they want to ally with us and enlist our help in defeating the Italians. Their General Jackson has offered to teach us how to make 'muskets' and 'cannons.' With these weapons, our armies will soon be as strong as the English and the Italians."

"Ah," responded the emperor thoughtfully. "And we can merge the tactics used by the red and green men with our own to make our forces stronger still."

"We have many more people than these Europeans, O Wondrous One," Mextli continued. "Properly armed, we would be formidable. I think we should keep the captured Italians' horses to breed. Perhaps we can get Jackson to teach us how to ride these animals."

"Where are Jackson and the other English chiefs now?" Ahuitzotl asked.

"There is a sickness in their camp," Mextli explained. "Many of the English soldiers are ill with what appears to be jungle fever. A few have died. They are fearful and have withdrawn to their camps to be treated by their own doctors. They say that an Italian, sailing for a king of a country called Spain, came to our lands after three fire ceremonies and forty-two seasons of our reign, about the time Mocteuzuma II was starting to suppress the revolts springing up in the newly conquered territories around Tenochtitlan. These Italians also grew sick and carried the illness back to their lands where millions died. The English are afraid that by the time this disease runs its course, more than half of them will be dead and their survivors will not be able to return home for fear of carrying the sickness with them."

"That is bad for them," observed the emperor, "but excellent for us. If they stay, we will learn much. I will welcome these English as brothers and let them take wives and become citizens of the Empire. When next we cross paths with those from across the Eastern Sea, we will be as powerful as they are now, perhaps even more powerful. This is very good."

With those words, the emperor rose and left the room.

"Do you think the English General Jackson will stay?" Cacimar asked with a touch of doubt in his voice.

"I do not know," replied Mextli. "If he is forced to remain here because of the illness, I cannot believe that he would be content to disappear within our Empire. He is a leader and has ambition. I think he will want to take his men and carve out his own place in history, but whether that will be within the structure of our society or in one of our foreign territories, I cannot be sure."

"Perhaps he would want to lead our armies against the Inca," Cacimar mused.

"There is no telling what the future has in store for him or us," answered Mextli. "But what I do know is we are home again and no longer living on that accursed cold, damp island that spawned Jackson and his like. It has been a great adventure, but now I want to stay here and grow old while I enjoy the comforts of the Aztec Empire."

Chapter 49

It was the start of the summer six months after the Italians had been vanquished and surrendered to the English. The air was warm and the spring planting completed. By the European calendar, it was late in May in the year 1814.

Nearly a third of the English, and those Italians who survived, had come down with the fever and rash associated with the tales of the Colombo Plague, but most had survived. Fewer than 5 percent had perished from the illness. Most of the survivors carried pock-marks on their faces and arms.

True to his word, Andrew Jackson left Colonel Winfield Scott and a regiment of infantry in Tenochtotlan to teach the Aztecs how to make muskets and cannons. He had evaded the question, however, when the emperor had asked if the English might also teach them how to build great ships of war, replying that he would first have to consult with his first minister and Queen.

Two months ago, Jackson had marched the majority of his army to the coast where they had boarded Nelson's ships and, with the captured Italian warships, set sail for England. Prior to leaving, the English admiral had put the entire fleet of captured transport ships to the torch. Jackson promised to return to establish trade relations that would improve the quality of life for both the Aztecs and the English, and he took samples of the strange plant and animal life found in the Aztec Empire back to his own nation. He also invited one hundred young Aztec nobles to sail with him to see England, to learn English, and to teach the English Nahuatl. Properly indoctrinated, these young men would become the first ambassadors and tradesmen between the two great powers.

Before leaving, the general had also obtained Emperor Ahuitzotl's promise not to kill the Italian soldiers who had surrendered at Chalchihueyecan. Most of the green men were sold off as slaves after being informed they would never be able to buy their freedom, as was the custom extended to all other captives held in bondage in the Aztec Empire. Slavery was not the fate in store for General Severoli and Colonel Paparelli, however.

*****

Standing on the summit of the twin pyramids in the center of Tenochtitlan, General Severoli gazed stoically at the huge sprawling city that spread out below his feet. It was alive with the hustle and bustle of busy, excited people. The streets and canals of the Aztec capital stretched into the distance to all four corners of the compass. Canoes and small boats filled the waterways. Men and women in bright exotic clothing were crossing over the causeways and merging into the crowds on the plaza before the pyramids.

The streets leading away from these bridges were jammed with the capital's population, as well as citizens from all over the Empire, their numbers filling the streets of the symmetrical metropolis. In the far distance, beyond Tenochtitlan, Severoli could see wide fields of crops, and beyond them was an unbroken circular range of mountains, their snowcapped peaks distinct against the clear blue sky. Beside the general, Colonel Paparelli stood white-faced and trembling. Behind the two men were six burly guards and two priests, Tizoc and Itzcoatl, who were busy mixing some sort of drinking concoction.

All dressed in their finery, thousands of nobles who served as government and military officials jammed the plaza between the temple pyramids and the palace. Musicians had started to play all around the plaza. Everyone had come to observe and celebrate the tenth fire ceremony.

The entire Aztec capital seemed to be in a festive mood, alive with people dancing and laughing and holding up their children to see the temple pyramids of the Teocalli. The dual pyramid was a solid structure made of earth and rock, coated by hewn stone. Severoli and Paparelli had been guided up the long flight of steps to the platform at its peak earlier in the day before they truly understood the significance of their role in this ceremony.

At the summit, there was a broad terrace paved with flat stones and at its center, toward the front and closest to the plaza below, was a large block of jasper with a convex surface. At the far end of the terrace, a three-story tower had been built of stone and stucco. Within the tower was the carved image of Huitzilopotchi, the god of war. A second identical platform and tower stood nearby within which was an image of Tlaloc, the god of rain and fertility. Immediately to the front of each of the towers were altars upon which were stacked piles of wood in preparation for a fire. Two great drums, that when struck could be heard throughout the city, sat next to the altars.

For the past several months, the two Italian officers had been attended to and fussed over, their every wants satisfied. Unlike the fate meted out to their men, Ahuitzotl VI insisted these two officers wear their full uniforms wherever they went and be treated with the utmost respect. The nobility of the Empire came to meet with them and to ask questions about Europe and its people. They were given lavish quarters, incredible meals, and gorgeous, exotic brown-skinned women visited their chambers each night. The colonel actually grew to enjoy his captivity and this unique life as a foreign celebrity.

This afternoon, their new world had changed. The emperor summoned them to meet him at the top of the Teocalli, the tallest point in the capital city. On the flat terrace that overlooked Tenochtitlan and its entire population, a translator had informed the two men of the honor being thrust upon them and, as a result, just what the Aztecs had in store for them later that evening.

"Oh my god, sir," Paparelli stammered. "Oh my god!"

"Relax, Colonel," Severoli replied with a half smile, still staring down at the great city. "The emperor said only the greatest and most worthy of their adversaries are treated in such a manner. We should feel exalted. Besides, I understand we will be heavily sedated. We should scarcely feel our hearts being cut from our still-living bodies."

Epilogue

When Christopher Columbus discovered the New World in 1492, he brought much more than just three ships and their crews to the new lands. He brought disease—European diseases for which the native peoples inhabiting the Americas had no resistance.

Over the next century the Spanish conquerors and settlers, and then those of the other European nations, spread typhus, influenza, measles, scarlet fever, diphtheria, and (perhaps the deadliest of them all) smallpox into every corner of the two continents. These illnesses were far more accountable than war, genocide, and/or colonial rule in bringing about the downfall of the Aztecs, the Incas, and the hundreds of North American tribes.

There is some contention over the size of America's native population in 1492, but an unassuming approximation is that seventy-five million people lived in Central, South, and North America when Columbus made landfall. This would have accounted for 15 percent of the world's population at the end of the fifteenth century. It is also estimated that upwards to 80 percent of these people died from European diseases.

Smallpox broke out in Hispanola in 1518. Annals written in the Mayan language indicate native traders brought the disease to the Yucatan Peninsula by canoe even before the Spanish invaders arrived in 1520. There were an estimated fifty million people living in Mesoamerica (i.e., present-day Mexico and the northern regions of Belize and Guatemala) in 1492. There were four million remaining 150 years later.

The spreading diseases also ravaged the Incas. Huayna-Capac, the ruler of the Inca Empire, and his designated successor, both died from smallpox before the Spanish arrived.

Francisco Pizarro found a nation embroiled in a civil war and depleted by more than half of its pre-infection population. By the time the Spanish began settling in present-day Peru, the population of the Incas had been reduced from an estimated nine million people to a mere six hundred thousand.

Illness and death spread northward from both the former Aztec Empire and Florida and then inland from the two coasts. Estimates put the North American native population at four to seven million people in 1500. Diseases, spreading well before the first permanent settlers arrived, reduced these populations to the point that there were only four hundred thousand Native Americans remaining in North America at the start of the twentieth century.

Alternative history speculates as to what would have happened should a historical event have experienced some significant change. What if Robert E. Lee had won at Gettysburg? What would the world be like if Jesus or Muhammad had never been born? What if Alexander the Great had not died at such a young age? How would history have been altered as a result of these changes?

This novel postulated, "What if instead of bringing disease to the New World, Columbus and his crew had instead contracted a deadly illness on the Caribbean islands and taken it back to Spain?" How would the history of Europe and North America unfolded had the tables been reversed and it was the Mesoamerica natives who had become immune to a devastating disease for which Europeans had no resistance? The infectious disease chosen for this alternative history is variola major smallpox, but in this novel (set in the early nineteenth century more than three hundred years after Columbus's initial voyage), it is seldom mentioned. When it is, trembling lips refer to it as the Colombo Plague.

About the Author

Hugh Auchincloss Brown is a history buff who has a BA in English from the University of Vermont, as well as an MS in educational psychology and a doctorate in education administration from the University of Utah. He lives in Ivins, Utah.

CPSIA information can be obtained
at www.ICGtesting.com
Printed in the USA
LVHW091352230222
711833LV00009B/73/J